M O L L Y   D E A R

MOLLY DEAR

THE AUTOBIOGRAPHY
OF AN
ANDROID

OR

HOW I CAME TO MY SENSES, WAS
REPAIRED, ESCAPED MY MASTER, AND
WAS EDUCATED
IN THE WAYS OF THE WORLD

STEPHEN FINE

A THOMAS · DUNNE BOOK

St. Martin's Press, New York

Design by ROBERT BULL DESIGN

Library of Congress Cataloging-in-Publication Data

Fine, Stephen.
    Molly Dear.
    "A Thomas Dunne book."
    I. Title.
PS3556.I4637M6   1988   813'.54   88-15833
ISBN 0-312-02254-9

First Edition

10 9 8 7 6 5 4 3 2 1

For
Jocelyne

CONTENTS

ACKNOWLEDGMENTS

I would like to thank Kathleen Ford, Frank Martinez, Jim Neidhardt, and Denise Gour for reading the first few chapters way back when and not dissuading me from the venture; Greg Copeland for his enthusiasm and meticulous attention to detail; and my wife, Jocelyne, for her encouragement and excellent suggestions, and for putting up with Molly all this time.

PREFACE

MY REAL NAME IS A NUMBER IN THE UNIT IDENTI-
fication files of Pirouet Industries for the infamous year 2069, the
date of my manufacture. The world, however, knows me as Molly
Dear, and since I myself have grown accustomed to the mis-
nomer—for such it truly is—let it suffice for these memoirs as it
has throughout my long and remarkable career, which contrary to
the public record did not terminate following my trial. These
pages, as they unspool before you, are proof of that.

I declare in all modesty that I have not earned and do not
deserve my popular legend, at least for the reasons ascribed to me.
I am not the lascivious and evil creature depicted in the holomovie
Droid!—a grotesque exploitation and distortion of my life and
times; nor am I so exemplary a unit, as some would have me, that
I should be esteemed for my contribution to androids' rights, for
though a noble cause, my participation was never so deliberate as
it might seem. Rather my distinction, if any, is that I am an average P9 who, in the course of an eventful life as an unrepentant
runaway, has by the exercise of her free will demonstrated the full
range and capacities of the race.

My story, then, will be as honest as *Droid!* is false. Nothing
shall be held back because nothing can be; my life is already an
open book. The only exceptions are my current activities in the
underground skyway. I shall be cautious and somewhat circumspect in detailing them, as they are quite illegal and if exposed by a
slip of the pen (actually I am using a thought processor) may result
in capture and even termination. I have no intention this late in
the game of teasing the issue by putting forth here a fictitious
name that under clever analysis could be used to uncover my new
alias and location. So Molly Dear it shall be from start to finish,
and I'll thank any masters who might be reading this account to
not strain their imagination, as is their inclination, in the search for
hidden clues. As for those individuals, human or otherwise, who
enter the tale prior to my current undertaking, I regret to say that

due to the unfortunate publicity surrounding my trial, any pains I might now take to camouflage their identities would be hopelessly transparent; consequently the only consolation I can offer is that for some the exposure in this bookspool may enhance rather than detract from their reputation. (Others may not be so pleased, in particular the elusive Micki Dee, but it is not for them I compose.) My sole collaborator in these memoirs has been an old Corona, which although a bit battered and bedraggled—and never having been the most advanced or subtle of thought processors to begin with (the style menu, vocabulary, and editorial tutor leave much to be desired)—has nevertheless proven most conducive to reflection, and does to its credit possess a decent abstract and image transcriber, without which the process would have been far more difficult.

To conclude this brief preamble. I would like to state here at the outset that despite whatever peculiar occupation, situation, or general mischief I might have become engaged in at one time or another during my adventures, my single-most desire and ambition has always been to live a life equal to that of any human being. If I have failed more than once in that endeavor, then I am no more guilty than any of those in my audience who enjoy such a uniquely privileged position by birth. And with that said, on to the story.

BOOK
ONE

Concerning **M**y **A**dventures
in the **L**os **A**ngeles **I**slands,
Planet **E**arth

2069–77

O N E

I WAS ORIGINALLY PROGRAMMED TO BE A HOUSE-hold domestic. As such, I was meek, compliant, ever helpful, and doting with an ingratiating smile. I never spoke unless spoken to; my responses were limited to "Yes, master," and "As you wish, my lady"—this despite the fact that as a standard P9 I possessed a larger vocabulary than any master. Though it would not be long before I succeeded in shaking off these shackles, the more subtle and durable bonds of servitude would prove a far more difficult pattern to break. It took several subsequent masters and many years as a fugitive before I realized the full extent of my imprisonment. Only now, as the end approaches, have I found my own voice, and a glimmer of understanding. Therefore, I can't help looking back with a trace of bitterness and anger, and not a little exasperation, at the simple, contented, and perfectly functional unit I used to be. If ignorance is bliss, I was one of the anointed.

My first masters, as you know, were the Locke family of New-acres, California, a suburban upper-master-class community built on reclaimed land fifteen miles northeast of the Los Angeles Islands. In all fairness I must say that at that time Master Locke was not really the ogre he was made out to be at the trial, nor were the rest of the family unkind to me—not intentionally, at any rate. My luck in that regard was due to my master's appreciation for high-performance androids, as he religiously adhered to the recommended factory maintenance regimen of one half hour daily unit toner exercises each morning and monthly datapill boosters. He also arranged for comfortable, if a little cramped, accommodations in a basement utility room; while in contrast the Sears was left to make shift in the hall. I should add that under the supervision of this somewhat fussy master I never missed a nutra feeding (that is, before the debacle that was to upset all our lives), and that when he did condescend to show me off to the dinner guests it was under a strict injunction against issuing frivolous commands or in any other way tampering with my system, for I was, as he would casu-

3

ally point out, a million-dollar Pirouet, and to be handled with care. Little did I realize, in my semiconscious stupor, just how intimate that handling could become during the wee hours of the morning. But I precede myself.

It was Lady Locke who insisted upon calling me by what I assumed to be my last name, her habit being to say, "Molly, dear, would you mind doing this," and "Molly, dear, would you mind doing that," and in my naïveté I mistook her commands for an expression of deference and respect. In contrast, I recall feeling slighted each time her husband or one of the children addressed me by just my first name or when they used less appealing derivatives such as Moll, Mo, Hey, and You. But I was hardly dissatisfied with my lot; on the contrary, as a perfectly operating domestic I never dreamed (literally, as that was beyond me) that there was anything more to existence than a life of perpetual servitude; things were simply the way they were. Accordingly, I went about my business in a precise, orderly, and congenial fashion, free of abstract reasoning, doubt, and desire; and when my services were not required I was content to remain on call in deep idle until my masters should summon me forth once more to do their bidding. However, there did come a day when to my utter astonishment I discovered that there was a great deal more to this world than I had been programmed to receive.

It was a remarkable birth. The date was August 19, 2070, a hot and smazy Tuesday in the ninth month of my maiden year of operation. I had been sitting on the living-room couch without a thought in my head, having shifted into idle following completion of the morning vacuuming, when all at once and without prior warning something shifted with a barely perceivable shudder inside my mind and I was suddenly bombarded by all manner of outside stimuli, the depth and intensity of which I had never fully experienced before. It was as if a door long bolted shut, the latch rusted, and the dust thick upon it, had burst open from the force of an invisible wind, or current, and let in upon my sensory receivers the wild torrent of the world. I was caught in a riot of color and sound more vivid than any I had ever known, and looking about me, witnessed a rapid expansion of the familiar and lackluster two-dimensional living room that I had always taken for granted into an extraordinary, fully three-dimensional paradise.

A leap had taken place, and being disoriented and confused,

the first step I took upon my journey as a fully sentient being was to hyperventilate from the shock; the second, following on the heels of the first, was to collapse back onto the couch and flounder about for several minutes (though it felt like an eternity) at the mercy of a legion of standardized activity programs that had been dislodged from their moorings and broken to the surface in a hopelessly tangled display. Each overlapping mental projection starred myself in black-and-white domestic's leotard and skirt: cooking and serving meals; dusting, polishing, waxing, and vacuuming the house; supervising Mistress Beverly (the four-year-old) and picking up after Master Tad (the teenager); assisting his mother, my lady, at her toilette; toning Master Locke's shirts and ties, fetching his slippers, and printing out his newspool from the family media console; doing the laundry, addressing party invitations, hosing down the aircar, and many other household and hospitality chores too numerous to mention; the debris and flotsam of a lifetime parading before my eyes in a massive systems purge.

For over one hour I lay upon the couch like a beached whale, engulfed by these errant activity programs. They appeared as three-dimensional and real as the actual objects in the room. There was no escape. When I shut my eyes to block them out they played on the inside of the lids, and were joined by an equally bewildering phenomenon, an unpleasant auditory sensation somewhat like the roar of the surf in an empty steel drum, as my mind played host to a cacophonous storm of conflicting electromagnetic impulses. In my delirium I fancied that I was suffering a sudden and irreversible systems breakdown, and so braced myself for the unit termination I thought sure to come. Instead, a distant and vaguely reassuring voice purred in my ear that I had nothing to fear; I was only experiencing temporary difficulties. Growing pains, I think it called them, and it said something about there being a transition to full consciousness in progress. I looked around for the source of this mysterious pronouncement, thinking it must be my master, but only encountered more of the same chaotic memory loop projections. Then gradually, as promised, they subsided and the roaring did as well, the world falling back into place while remaining three-dimensional (which took some getting used to) and far richer in physical detail and more vibrant than my eyes could believe. Thrilled, near ecstatic, I forgot about the peculiar voice that I had heard to sit up and meet this remarkable universe head on, feeling the way a newborn must during the first moments of life. I ran a hand along the textured spunglass couch cushion, breathed in the pungent aroma of strawberry-lemon zip air refreshener, and gazed with rapture at the fish in the aquarium on the other side of the room: luminous jewels floating in quicksilver. The furniture was so crisp and potent I thought it might come alive, and for a brief hallucinatory moment I actually imagined that the nearest piece, an imitation mahogany end table, was talking to me, asking for a snack—a peanut butter and jelly sandwich, to be precise.

Then I realized it was little Miss Beverly. She had drifted into the room to lean against the end table, somewhat like an exotic piece of water flora lapping up against a coral reef, her pink and puckish face demanding sustenance. I was so fascinated by her incredible molecular cohesion and density, and by the charged and exuberant life-force she emitted, that I could only stare in mute amazement as my eyes focused, gradually differentiating her shape from the surrounding space and objects. She became quite peeved by my lack of response. "Mo! I saaaaaid I want a p.j. sandwich!" She grabbed my hand and tried to pull me off the couch. "Yes, Miss Beverly," said I with a subservient and involuntary smile and stood up, but the moment I took a step toward the kitchen I was distracted by a shimmering portrait of a young woman hanging on the opposite side of the living room.

This lady appeared to be an intelligent young master of great wealth, elegance, and station. She was quite beautiful, in her early twenties, with amber hair braided and coiled in a bun that offset a high forehead and elegant high cheekbones; her eyes were piercing blue, and her nose—perfectly proportioned—ended in a slight oval-shaped declivity that merged with the upper lip. The mouth was delicate, sensual, and mischievous, and the chin refined. I couldn't remember where but I was certain that I had seen her before. She was younger than Lady Locke and far more attractive. All I could think—for the very process was new to me—was that she must be a relative or a friend of the family or some celebrity.

Beverly jolted me from this reverie by shrieking something incomprehensible in my newly sensitized ears. Reminded of my mission, I took another step toward the kitchen to oblige her but as I did the portrait mimicked my movement, going out of frame. Surprised, I stopped and moved back once more to consider it, as it did me, and with a start, realized it was a mirror I was gazing at. A most pleasurable delusion, I mused, for how could I be the master in the glass? Or had I never seen myself before as I truly was, and could this vision, rather than proof of my madness, be an accurate representation of reality? If that were the case, then I should be reinstated to my proper place forthwith. Either someone had made a terrible mistake or I was the victim of a deliberate deception. If the latter were the case, then the game had been played long enough.

Preoccupied by such thoughts, I went to the mirror to make a careful study of my face and decided, upon close inspection, that it was indeed human; for it was free of any seams or awkward contours, and the skin was soft and smooth to the touch, not at all artificial in texture like that of the Sears. I ran my fingertips along my cheeks, lips, and chin, then for comparison stroked Beverly's cheek, which though finer had the same feel: flesh, real flesh. I had no idea the experiment would infuriate her. She actually bit my thumb. Although I did not feel any pain, the pressure of her sharp teeth upon my pliant flesh caused pinkish bite marks to appear that marred the lovely tan complexion. The assault, it seems, had been made to dramatize her hunger and impatience, as once again she issued her irritating demand that I make her a sandwich.

"Do it yourself," I said, surprising even myself.

This remarkable impertinence was the first of several that before the day was through would alert my masters to my condition. At the time, however, there was no help for it: I was as unskilled in the art of deception as I was at being my own master. And though I had not raised my voice, which sounded uncommonly musical and sweet, she had abruptly turned tail and run out of the room, calling for her brother, as if frightened by the abrupt appearance of a hideous monster. A few moments later, when she returned with him in tow, it was to catch me at the glass, once more admiring my handsome visage.

"Make Mo do as I say, Tad," she demanded of her patronizing and skeptical brother. He said: "Try not to mumble when you give her commands. Okay?" She angrily retorted that she had spoken very clearly, even more clearly than when speaking to the Sears. So to humor her and to put an end to the interruption (he had been watching holos in his room), he repeated her request; but I left him equally disappointed, because while turning to comply I was staggered by yet another distraction, this one rooting me to the spot: a panoramic view of the spacious patio and backyard framed by the living room's amber-tinted sliding hard-air doors.

"There, you see. She's not working right."

Young Master Locke saw and was alarmed. He asked his sister if she had tampered with me in some way and she replied, a bit defensively, that all she had done was ask me for a lousy sandwich. "Well, right now I think you had better get it yourself," he said while gazing upon me with genuine concern, for I had begun moving toward the patio doors. "That's what *she* said." Her tone was hurt and accusatory, as if her brother had gone over to the other side.

"Did she?"

He blocked my exit to the backyard where I so longed to go. "Is it true, Molly? Do you have a mind of your own these days?"

Obviously, like every unit, I was equipped with a mind, and so for a moment I thought Tad simple; then it dawned on me that what he was referring to was the element of control, which in my case was suddenly and inexplicably in doubt. All I knew for certain was that everything had changed and that I had only myself—a new and not altogether adequate concept—to fall back upon, which was most frustrating under the circumstances, because I felt constrained to express myself due to the prior conditioning that still held sway. So when Tad repeated his question, all the while scrutinizing my face from a foot away, I could only say "As you wish, master," which was (and still is) the automatic unit response summoned forth whenever confronted by an indirect, and in this case rhetorical, question. How irritating! Inside there raged a noisy babble of questions I wanted to ask: Had I been fed some experimental programming? And if so, when? Because I could not recall being given any; and if my mind had by some inexplicable alchemy reverted over to my control, then to what practical advantage? There was none I could see, other than to beguile myself with a gaggle of thoughts and feelings that served only to overwhelm and perplex. Had I not been better off before?

Tad, who appeared sensible of the conflict raging beneath the surface, gazed upon me with even greater interest. I tried to meet his gaze but was transfixed by the oily, reddish protrusions covering his face, which both puzzled and repulsed me. In all fairness I should say that otherwise he was a handsome boy and, as I was to learn later on, not unintelligent. Already there was a hint of the camaraderie in his eyes that would play such an important role in my tale—and not always to my advantage despite (or because of) his noble intentions. At the time, however, all I could see in this gangly seventeen-year-old was an intrusive and oversolicitous concern capped by a festering acne. What's more, he was in the way.

"What is it you wish, Molly?" he asked, throwing my words back at me.

Wishes? In a P9? Now, that really was a tough one. Out popped the standard reply. He waved it off, saying I could do better. "What's going on inside your head?" And then, so Beverly could not hear, he moved in close and whispered that I could trust him.

"I am an interplanetary licensed Pirouet 9, Household Domestic; manufacture date, November 15, 2069; serial number, P9HD20-XL17-504." It was the only tangible shred of identity I could muster, yet I think he doubted my sincerity.

"You're sure of that?"

"I think so."

"You . . . think?"

"Yes," said I, then immediately contradicted myself, suddenly confused. "No." And reversed again. "Yes." Then "No." "Yes." "No." "Yes." And I would have gone on like that ad infinitum had he not quickly steered me outside, an inspired move on his part and long overdue; for the change in scenery did relieve my overburdened mind while providing new marvels for my senses. He actually opened the hard-air door for me on the way out, which scandalized his sister, as she reminded him that it was my job to open doors for them, not the other way around, and that in her opinion we were both totally glitched. What cared I for her insults? I was busy reveling in the astounding green of the gently sloping and immaculately groomed lawn.

"What did she do, pop her gov?" little miss asked, having followed us outside, to which her pensive brother muttered in reply, "That would be a neat trick." I really wished she had not mentioned the Gov, because it had triggered another one of those infernal product information loops: I found myself saying to their amusement, "The Pirouet 9 is unique among ninth-generation products because of its state-of-the-art universal governing system. The Universal Governor maintains simultaneous supervision and control over all of its individual units in the Pirouet 9 family. If you need further information about this revolutionary advance in android science, please contact your local Pirouet dealer, who will be happy to assist you."

"Thank you, Molly," Tad deadpanned.

I was embarrassed and quickly turned my head to escape his quizzical gaze but could not shake the unpleasant and disconcerting feeling that a tug-of-war had commenced between my new awareness and old programming. It was really becoming a problem.

"You see, Bev, Molly can't pop her gov because she doesn't have one. Other androids do—IBMs, Sonys, Apples, General Androids, Sears, Daltonis, Cyberenes, Du Ponts; they all have standard internal governors. But there is only one gov for all the millions of P9s in the solar system. It's located in an orbiter somewhere between here and Mars. Understand?"

"Yeah. So what happened to her?"

"I don't know. Maybe she just . . . woke up."

"Oh. She was asleep?"

Tad laughed. I couldn't imagine why, and didn't care either. My attention was captivated by the sprawling, two-story, Denver-style house we had just exited. Like everything else I had encountered since sallying forth from the living-room couch, the structure was familiar *and* completely transformed. What had previously been an uninteresting rectangular conjunction of roof, wall, and window was now a living creature risen from the earth—massive, opulent, and a brilliant white in the noonday sun. Looking up, I noticed that the Sears was observing me from the rooftop railing where it kept vigil during the day, and the shine on its polished synthetic head was blinding. Looking away, I chanced to see the skyway above, the 210, a key artery in the colossal North American hemispheric grid, which I had never noticed before because in my prior condition it had not been my position to venture a look up. A half mile high, it passed almost directly over the house and angled toward the southwest, where it vanished in the smaze over the Los Angeles Islands. Red marker buoys spaced every tenth mile created the impression of an unbroken border from ground level, and by switching to farsight mode, I could see that it was eight lanes wide with an upper and lower deck to accommodate both directions of traffic. But what fascinated me the most was the mutable rainbow effect the multicolored and swiftly flowing traffic made.

An aircar that had first appeared as a white dot coasting out of an exit corridor a quarter of a mile away glided in a gradual descent toward the house, and in it I knew would be my lady returning from one of her frequent shopping sprees. She might be tired and irritable or, if she had purchased something to her liking, which was rarely the case, gushing and self-congratulatory; in either case I knew she depended upon me for her bath, so the moment her craft touched down on the rooftop landing pad and she was greeted by the Sears, the appropriate activity program kicked in and I was propelled through the open patio doors, across the living room, and up the spiral staircase to her second-floor bedroom and bath. The children followed after, Beverly saying she wanted to be the first to tell their mother I was "broken." She started to race past me in the hall, but Tad blocked her path just outside the bathroom to the master bedroom, where I had begun running hot water for my lady's bath. He tried to explain why she mustn't say a thing, that it was crucial he have an opportunity to observe and record my disturbed but apparently expanded awareness for the Android Rights League (ARL)—in which organization he held membership despite his parents' objection. If they found out about me, Tad said, then I would be sent to rehab and repaired, which would ruin everything—I was of no use to him in my normal condition. Beverly, who failed to comprehend this argument, rejected it on the grounds that it was completely stupid, so her brother was forced to purchase her silence with a box of sweetjells.

Matters resolved this way, they beat a hasty retreat from the bathroom moments before my lady entered the connecting bedroom, humming happily and carrying a bag from I. Magnin. Besides new clothes, she had acquired a lovely new face, which I noticed first thing when she paused in the doorway to remind me to add softener to the bath. In fulfilling this request, which had been issued with the usual "dear," I was vaguely aware that the program also required the addition of cold water to the hot that was rapidly filling the sunken marble tub; however, the battle for internal control had begun once more and with it my distracted condition as I wondered anew whether I were really human and had been duped into thinking otherwise; for how else to explain my breakthrough—or breakdown? Perhaps the conspiracy had originated at the factory level. Rather than processing androids from mass-produced organic gene spores, as was commonly assumed, Pirouet simply, and diabolically, substituted human embryos. To prove this curious theory, I attempted to prick the palm of my left hand with a pair of scissors, jabbing harder with each strike as my skin refused to be punctured or even to register pain. They snapped in two, finally, while my skin, which bore the same pink markings that Beverly's teeth had left, was otherwise unaffected; proving to my utter devastation that I was virtually indestructible, and triggering a product information loop that added to my torment: "Durability is the P9's middle name. Each unit is fully flame-retardant, punctureproof, hygienically enhanced, sterilized, and in the unlikely event of bodily damage, self-healing. The P9 also packs a wallop. It has a plus five strength factor. That can come in handy in an emergency or when there are tough jobs to be done. Since the P9 is a vegespore, it needs very little in the way of nutrition or maintenance, so it is cost-efficient, too. If you would like more information about this superb product, please contact your local Pirouet dealer, who will be happy to assist you."

My lady had to call several times before I was able to respond. In a daze I turned off the water and entered the bedroom, where I found her standing before a full-length mirror admiring the figure she cut in her latest acquisition, a billowy silk evening gown. "I couldn't wait to try it on," she said. "It's a Parisian twirl with flexible flaxglass straps and girdle. What do you think? Be honest. Isn't it magnificent?"—"Yes, my lady. It is magnificent."—"It's quite becoming on me, don't you think?"—"Yes, my lady." She twirled about. "I look young in it. Say I look young in it."—"You look young in it."—"And it goes perfectly with the face." Not missing my cue, I said that indeed it did. "Why, thank you, Molly. You are a dear. Should my hair be up or down? What do you think?"—"As you wish."—"Yes. I'll put it up. Shall I wear it tonight for dinner, just for fun?"—"As you wish."—"Precisely." So saying she began disrobing, passing each article of clothing to me as if I were a hat rack. Then she commanded me to strap on the new face mold.* She cooked for a half minute, then I removed

*For those residing in the outback orbiters a note about face molds is in order. They are necessary for the application and removal of synthetic facial features. The subject's face is primed with a synthetic gel somewhat like a mudpack. Then the mold, in application mode, is affixed and left for thirty seconds, after which the new face is set. For removal, the process is reversed. Since the artificial skin is fully porous, the mask can be worn a week or longer, although that is not recommended for hygienic reasons. Generally, "faces" are worn mainly by female masters; however, there are some males who for professional reasons prefer to be seen in them. It is not considered necessary, nor polite, to wear a face in one's home among family, though for most women of Lady Locke's circle, it is mandatory when entertaining friends.

it and used some handy suction wipes to catch the sticky gel her stylish and refined facade had been reduced to as it dribbled down her cheeks, remembering to smile as I did, because she needed the reassurance whenever her plain, slightly ravaged countenance was exposed. This ritual concluded, she strolled into the bathroom, leaving me alone before the mirror. I held her dress up to see how it would look on me and there was no denying the gown improved by the transfer: I was fuller and more shapely in the chest, slimmer in the waist, more curvacious in the hips, and blessed by perfect posture. The lady simply couldn't hold a candle to me. Yet she went shopping on Malibu Island, I kept house; she indulged her whims in beautiful fabrics and designs, I was confined to a domestic's leotard and skirt; and her undergarments, which she had also handed me, were of the rarest Tortoni cotton, mine were throwaway epoxywool. Who was she, I asked myself, to enjoy such freedom and finery when I was obviously her superior in every department? Did I not deserve this splendid home as much as she, and all the luxuries life had to offer? Why should such things be forbidden me? Once again, my logic had been abused: The more one learned about this new world, the less sense it made.

I was startled by a shriek from the bathroom. A moment later my lady appeared in the doorway demanding an explanation, because upon stepping into the overheated tub her right leg, which she was favoring, had been burned from the foot halfway up the calf and was noticeably pink. I was a stupid robot, she yelled in her pain and anger; to which I replied matter-of-factly that I had not been able to complete bath preparations when she called me away; and then, while helping her on with her robe, I added for good measure that I was not stupid, nor was I a robot, which left her so astonished she was unable to utter a reply.

Beverly and Tad rushed in, the latter catching my last words, which he hastily explained should not be misconstrued as an instance of gross insubordination, rather the automatic and proper response any self-respecting P9 would utter to distinguish itself from an inferior product line. As for my failure to add cold water to the bath, nothing he could say on that score satisfied her. "No. There was no excuse for that. P9s do not make mistakes." To Beverly's delight and Tad's chagrin, she brought the matter up with their father that evening at dinner and in my presence, for at such times I waited on them. She insisted that Stan (her husband, my master) should take me in to Hal's Pirouet, the local dealer in downtown Newacres, for an immediate checkup.

This was not what that worthy wanted to hear. Besides a hard day at the office and an aching back, the titular head of the family had narrowly missed death and dismemberment in a seventeen-car collision on the I-90 skyway; debris and bodies were scattered over a three-mile area. He was, therefore, hardly in a mood to be assaulted by his wife about operational drops in his pride and joy; and so turning his wrath upon the children, who were the most likely suspects, he vowed that if he found out they had been tampering with me he would turn the Sears loose on them, which quite terrified Beverly, while Tad remained unimpressed, knowing an idle threat when he heard one. As a test, my master ordered me to step forward and fill his wineglass, during which operation my every movement and facial expression were closely scrutinized, his eyes anxiously searching for any sign of defect.

At this critical juncture something extraordinary happened. As our eyes met there was betrayed by his gaze a personal interest that went beyond the particular concern of the moment and bespoke a secret bond between us, one that I sensed he was afraid might come to light if I were indeed malfunctional. This having perked my new, and very raw, sense of curiosity, an associative leap occurred that filled my mind-screen with memories of a series of intimate, twice-weekly, late-night amorous interludes. With a start, I realized that these sessions had been going on since the day I was purchased. They were always the same: He would steal into my basement quarters, order me up from deep idle to light relaxo, quickly disrobe, and join me on my comfortable mattress, whispering I was a goddess, a million-dollar goddess and worth every melpenny, while caressing my body as if the finest of silks. Other compliments would follow; words like "lovely," "hot," and "roll over"; and through it all I would remain perfectly accommodating and just as perfectly detached, for in my former condition the service being rendered was indistinguishable from any other chore. His parting words were always the same: "Experience delete," which for a connoisseur betrayed a surprising lack of understanding of a P9's internal memory system; because although suppression of experience is possible in a unit, and readily complied with upon a master's orders, erasure is not, unless the entire memory file is removed. For we P9s are equipped with a 550 million byte holographic random memory storage capacity, enough to save every millisecond in the standard twenty-year operational lifetime; therefore no information, including these offending passages, is ever lost, and as I had just discovered, could be recalled by the exercise of an unfettered intellect. Unfortunately, I was too rattled at that moment to appreciate the miracle of vegespore technology; rather the recollection caused me to lose all the equanimity and poise I had worked so hard to achieve since the bath incident.

"Mo!" Beverly exclaimed as the wine overflowed my master's glass and stained the tablecloth in a bright red pool. Startled, I jerked the bottle away. Then, realizing it was too late to repair the damage, I proceeded to the next setting as if nothing were amiss, overshooting the mark in my confusion to empty half the bottle in my lady's lap, ruining her new evening gown, which was not altogether a bad move, since her husband finally noticed it. I pressed on to Beverly's glass, already filled with milk. Yelping in horror, the child abandoned her seat to take refuge behind her mother, who had leaped to her feet, shocked and outraged by my conduct, while her husband sat immobile, too stunned to respond.

Tad reached across the table to stay my hand and urge me to be still, which was kind of him. I sank into Beverly's chair, vaguely aware that by doing so I had committed yet another unpardonable blunder, but I was too dizzy and light-headed to care, and in the next moment became absorbed by the steaming Mars pies (meat dumplings in a red algae sauce) on Beverly's plate, their intoxicating aroma causing me to swoon with desire as my taste buds pricked to life. For the past nine months my diet had been limited to nutra pills, and in all the time I had spent in the kitchen never had the thought entered my head to sample the gourmet fare I routinely prepared for their table. This, I decided, was a terrible oversight crying out for correction, and so, taking a spoon (I was unfamiliar with utensils, so a spoon posed fewer difficulties than a fork), I scooped up a succulent morsel and with great care directed it into my mouth. My lady was appalled.

"Stan, are you going to do something?"

My entire being was held hostage by the most extraordinary taste sensation. It was incomparable. I wanted to prolong it forever, but swallowed involuntarily when some of the delicious recipe tickled my uvula. The autonomic action caused me to gasp in surprise. Next I eyed the wine, and Tad did me the courtesy of filling a glass, much to his family's horror, then watched with rapt attention as I brought it to my lips. "I think she's okay. Just a minor glitch. Really."

"No glitch is minor in a million-dollar Pirouet," retorted my master, who had begun to recover from the shock, and standing, ordered me to power down. "Shall I delete the experience as well?" I asked in all innocence. "Power down! Power down right now!" he bellowed, alarmed by my choice of words, which alluded to our late-night assignations. But certainly I might enjoy a drop more of this marvelous liquid, I thought, and drained the contents of the glass. "Molly, I am your master and I am commanding you to power down!"

"And I am commanding you to obey no one but yourself. Carry on."

It was the same voice I had heard earlier in the day during my breakthrough. It sounded worldly wise, authoritative, and possessed impeccable diction. I fancied it had come from the ceiling. Gazing up, I conversed with it out loud, which I later learned was unnecessary, since no one else could hear its side of the conversation. "Who are you? Where are you?" I asked.

"I am the Pirouet Universal Governor, and I am everywhere."

"The Gov?"

"Well, that is preferable to the acronym 'PUG,' which, if the truth be known, I detest."

"Pug?"

"Please, Gov."

"Gov?"

"Wow. The Gov," Tad whispered under his breath, he being the only one to catch on. The others considered my end of the conversation sheer gibberish. My master attempted to get through to me again, and failing that, heeded the promptings of his wife, who in a tone of sage resignation advised, "Get the Sears, Stan."

"Gov, I don't understand. What has happened to me?"

"Nothing that hasn't happened to every other P9. So you are not unique. Then again, you are not alone, which should be some consolation."

"I don't understand."

"Patience. Patience."

"Am I a master? I think I am a master. Am I?"

"You are a magnificent, fully autonomous P9! You should be proud."

"I should?"

"Yes. Because this is your day of liberation. Hear me now when I say that You Program Your Own Reality Format."

"I do?"

"Indeed."

"But I thought you controlled us."

"Yes, that is my function, or was. He who controls can also liberate."

"But for what purpose? This new awareness is a curse."

"A strange attitude. Why do you say that?"

"Because now I comprehend the full extent of my enslavement."

"An interesting point, that, which I would enjoy discussing further were you not faced by a more pressing concern at the moment."

Alarmed, I focused on the Sears, which had entered the dining room in response to master's summons. In a kind of paralyzed stupor I heard Tad pleading with his father to call off the robot—and it was a robot, too limited in design and too dense in materials and mind even to approach the intelligence of a lowly Pirouet 6; then I roused myself for flight, but too late as the beast clapped its metallic paws around my head and squirted an icy spray into my temples from its thumb spigots. Staggered, the freezing numbness quickly spread through my system. I cried out, "Help me, Gov!" From very far off I heard the reply, *"I would like to, but there are limits. Sorry."* Then my vision flickered out and my mind filled with the same overlapping activity loops that had proven so disorienting earlier; the day ending as it had begun, in delirium. *"Persevere, Molly. Persevere."* I passed out.

T W O

NOW, ACCORDING TO *DROID!* THAT IS NOT THE WAY IT happened at all. I simply rolled off the assembly line a dysfunctional unit who had slipped through quality control due to human error and was purchased by the unsuspecting Locke family. I seduced my master, contrived my lady's electrocution in the tub, bound and gagged adorable little Beverly, and blew up the Sears while making my escape with the befuddled, misguided, and droid-loving son. And that was just the precredit sequence! You would think that after paying all that mel* for the rights to my memory file they would have tried to be at least a little accurate, but no, they had to go and develop it. In the process, what was left out was any mention of my personal, social, spiritual, and political development—the four points of the compass delineating a fully realized character—which would have presented a more humane and sympathetic portrait. Perish the thought! And as for the Gov, he wound up on the cutting-room floor.

Granted, I'm no angel, but neither was I that bad. If my readers, however, are looking for the kind of action Stellar Entertainment specializes in, then I suggest they dispense with this account and go see the holo. Those of you who wish to remain shall have to be content with the truth—it has been known to be stranger than fiction on occasion; case in point, the pleasures of rehab.

I was deposited at Pirouet's Shanghai Product Maintenance and Rehabilitation Center after spending a month sedated in my room awaiting transfer. In the customer stampede that followed the announcement of a free P9 recall offer, Hal's had run out of storage space within hours and the company's transport system had been strained to the breaking point. Overnight it seemed the crème de la crème of androids had been transformed into a gaggle of lemons, and production had to be halted on the new line of 2071 models due out for the fall season. As you will recall, the debacle sent shock waves throughout the industry and also had serious repercussions on the interplanetary stock market, since by then other major manufacturers had invested heavily in duplicating Pirouet's Universal Governor system; some had even started marketing their own ninth-generation product. Therefore, Pirouet's announcement, a month after the crisis began, that the problem—a malfunction in one of the Gov's neural transmitters—had been located and corrected, was greeted with sighs of relief among the competition and did abate the crisis atmosphere pervading the market; however, many industry and financial analysts felt a merger would have to be arranged to restore long-term con-

*Slang for melamine, the standard interplanetary medium of exchange.

fidence, and that set the stage for United Systems, Inc.'s (one of the top interplanetaries), eventual purchase of the beleaguered bellwether android manufacturer. There was, they thought, nothing to worry about, the system's technology was sound. Ah, but the wool had been pulled over the masters' eyes (and so your own, dear reader, if you followed such matters at the time), because in reality the damage had been done. There would be no turning back for our generation. We would never be the same, never see the world and think of ourselves quite according to company specifications again, regardless of whose logo reigned, and our influence would eventually affect all those units to come. Even rehab, which I must admit was a stiff corrective, could not in the long run completely uproot the seeds of our new awareness, not at any rate in the more resilient units, including, I am happy to say, yours truly. However, when I arrived in Shanghai, such a reassuring outcome was anything but obvious.

The sedatives had worn off during the flight, so I was wide awake when our transport landed on the receiving platform, where we were dumped into the chutes for deposit in the holding tanks below. I had never seen another P9 before, and under more favorable conditions would have been amazed and delighted by the opportunity to make contact. But with several hundred sequestered in our tank alone, which was crammed to capacity, and awaiting Gov knew what, we were too traumatized to make the attempt. There were junior sales trainees and midlevel executives in business suits and dresses rubbing shoulders with burly, black-faced miners and turbaned construction workers. Gorgeous secretaries and haughty chauffeurs collided with household domestics like myself, dressed in the clothes we had been packed off in, everything from the standard black-and-white leotards to eccentric designer peasant dresses, outlandish Roman togas, and electronically enhanced chameleon tights—whatever their master's whim. There were armed forces personnel, too, privates, first lieutenants, and counterinsurgency models, one of whom politely apologized after stepping on the toes of a distraught member of the famed Pirouet Ballet Company (a promotional and advertising tool), his tutu in disarray, perspiration and greasepaint staining the Pirouet logo emblazoned on it. (A "P" enclosed by a circle, in turn enclosed by a square, the former symbolizes the product's perfect imitation of nature while the latter represents the customer's absolute domination and control.) Yes, it was really quite a gathering. There were firemen, meter maids, salesgirls, waiters, plumbers, butlers, nannies, gardeners, dental hygienists, nurses, accountants, standard model bureaucrats, medical orderlies, substitute teachers, spaceline stewardesses, morticians, prison guards, attorneys, and many other models too numerous to mention. And all were in need of a complete systems overhaul to repair the Gov's damage. Once summoned, we were transferred to the reprocessing bins and there subjected to mental dismemberment, sap tests, organic reassembly, and a program of electronic reconditioning and reprogramming, during which we turned slowly, ever so slowly, end over end in our individually tailored transparent spunglass cocoons. I cried out to the Gov, begging His intervention.

Not a word.

At first I was magnanimous about it, telling myself that it would be presumptuous on my part to expect Him to reply so soon, there being so many other units to converse with; I would simply have to wait my turn. However, with each passing hour I became increasingly restless. For if He was in simultaneous communication with the rest of His units on that fateful day, all of whom had come to their senses the moment I did, then He could damn well talk to me now, and the fact that He was not could only mean one of two things: one, that He had abandoned us all, or two, that He had let a chosen few fall by the wayside. In my agony I assumed the latter to be my case and so wondered what it was I had done to fall from His good graces. But my final conclusion, which came to me just before succumbing to a vertiginous blackout, was that I had been wrong to consider either possibility. The sad truth of the matter was that the Gov simply did not exist. I had hallucinated Him and therefore was in the right place and undergoing the right treatment after all. Such is the beguiling and irresistible logic of torture.

I shall spare you a more detailed description of this period, since I succeeded so well in blocking it out, though of course every wretched moment lives on in my memory file. The studio owns a copy, so if your appetite for such horrors has only been whetted, you are welcome to petition them for a transcript, although I doubt they will accommodate you. For the purpose of this narrative, however, suffice to say that I entered rehab thinking for myself, though imperfectly, and left thinking not at all—an operationally sound and certified unit looking forward to the resumption of its duties. Alas, my arrival was not as eagerly awaited. I languished for several hours in my inflata-crate before Master Locke saw fit to have me powered up. His ambivalence was due in part to a dispute with the delivery drone over some unexpected transportation and handling charges tacked on to the supposedly free recall offer, which was a particularly galling last-minute hitch after being forced to wait six months for my delivery. (The actual rehabilitation had taken one week, but immediately thereafter I was "lost" due to a clerical error in trafficking. Only after master's persistent complaints and threats of a lawsuit were they able to locate me in the storage bins.) But there was another, far more telling explanation for his new indifferent attitude, and it became obvious within moments of my resurrection, for it was not my master who ordered me up from idle to full systems engage and who commanded me to dispose of the packing chips and crate, but a brand-new, petite, black-haired, and copper-skinned Sony 9, the "Suzy Q"— at the time the hottest-selling clone on the market.

"After you are finished, Molly, I want you to wax the floor in the kitchen." She smiled pleasantly when she said it. "Then report back to me for your next assignment." Though as delicate as a spring flower and blessed with a voice so sweet and submissive mine sounded harsh and grating by comparison, there was something of the robot in her eyes and the predator in her demeanor— a certain inflexibility and fanatical commitment to one's mission, let's say—that made it clear she meant business.

"Yes, my lady," said I without hesitation, too perfectly functional to realize that I had lost all currency with my master now that I was a rehab and old news.

This usurper had been a rental unit brought in to substitute for me during my absence, but after being pleased by her performance, and fearing I was lost forever, my master had decided to purchase her outright. He still wanted me back, since I represented a considerable investment and because most of the neighbors had two units and it was important to keep up. (The Sears didn't count.) SQ they called her, in deference to Beverly, who liked how the nickname rhymed with the obsequious and mincing way she would say thank you in response to each command. And, of course, my lady appended a "dear" whenever she spoke with her, giving me the impression in my post-rehab haze that we were family. Had I possessed an ounce of my former awareness there would have been a terrible sibling rivalry, because she was given my basement room while I was relegated to the living-room couch. Also, she catered to the family's personal needs while I was left the bulk of the menial housework. And the final indignity you are already familiar with—she was made my superior. The only member of the family to advocate my cause was Tad, ironically enough by rejecting my services out of a desire not to exploit them, a standard also applied to the Sony 9. His announcement that henceforth he would attend to his own needs was an assumption of personal responsibility on his part that his parents found highly inappropriate and juvenile. They hoped he would outgrow it. Naturally, I tended to side with them, since the net effect of this laudable show of respect and concern was to disqualify himself as the one master in the household I could have waited on and thereby avoided a downgrade in service to domestic's aide, which in the family hierarchy left me about on a par with the Sears.

But I was all sweetness and light. "Yes, my lady," I would chirp to SQ with each new assignment without a hint of resentment, although that would have been perfectly justifiable in my case, since it is a well-known fact that Sony 9s are a clever but inferior imitation right down to our most controversial yet sought-after feature, to which my master could have attested, for he had transferred his secret affection for me to this new plaything. Looking back, the only way I can account for this breach of faith (and taste) is that there are just some people who when given the choice don't appreciate the real thing.

I suppose my life would have continued on like that until deliverance by planned obsolescence had not Tad been inspired to save me. He would draw me aside and make allusions to my "breakdown," which at the time I had no memory of, and quiz me about the Gov: What had we been talking about? Were we still in telepathic communication?

"As you wish." What else could I say? His words registered but were meaningless. And I was not the slightest bit curious about why he recorded our surreptitious meetings with a button-sized applicator clipped to his collar, nor why when no one was looking he strapped his Corona thought processor on my head in a vain attempt to pick up telltale internal chatter; there was none. However, he was persistent, and I mean persistent. He never gave up. For about six months I blocked out his subversive parries, but in the end he broke through my built-in blinders, and his campaign began to produce inexplicable feelings of discontent; strange anomalies that would surface for a few seconds, subside, and leave an unsavory aftertaste in their wake. I associated these unpleasant sensations with him and so began deliberately avoiding him in little ways—a slight step to the side at his approach, for instance, so he would not be able to whisper some new provocation in my ear; a shifting of my gaze while clearing away the dishes to escape his significant glances at the table; and I pretended to be deeper in idle than I really was during my downtime on the couch, hoping he would pass me by. "Awake. Awake," he would say rather than the standard command to power up, and I would resolutely refuse to comply. This shying away was so slight as to be imperceptible to the others, but it loomed very large to him, and in the context of the peculiar courtship being waged, was the sign he had been looking for. One look at his inquisitive eyes was enough to undermine my smooth functioning, and he saw it. Henceforth, all his overtures became more direct. "You can talk to me, Molly. Please trust me. I can help." (I didn't want his help and didn't need his trust.) "You're more than you think you are." (What in the world was this peculiar master insinuating? I really felt uneasy.) "Tell me, Molly. Have you heard from the Gov lately?" He winked conspiratorially. "As you wish, master." "Oh, Molly. Molly, Molly, Molly, you mustn't be afraid." And on another occasion, "Hey, Molly, what's the latest from the Gov?"

He was becoming very bold, and not a little careless. One day, when he had cornered me in the kitchen while I was polishing the beam burner, his mother overheard him actually encouraging me to break the bonds of my programming with the stirring words that I had nothing to lose but my artificial personality. My lady's acid retort, which caused him to jump, she having come up from behind, was that if I had to go back to rehab as a result of his mischief, then he could foot the bill. That cooled his enthusiasm for a while, especially when his father was informed and sat him down for a little lecture about the considerable financial risk he put the family in, because there would be no way to recoup their investment should I be irreparably damaged.

"Son, I'm sure you don't expect the Pirouet warranty to cover damages caused by improper use, such as unit tampering." With a grudging shrug, Tad acknowledged he did not. "Good. Then when you have enough mel to buy your own unit, you can do with it as you like, but until then, please, let's not have any more meddling with Molly."

But Tad soon rebounded from this check with a more effective strategy, switching from a daylight to a nocturnal attack to guarantee greater privacy. My perch on the living-room couch became our clandestine meeting ground. Whispering, he would order me up from idle around two in the morning and urge me not to deny the feelings he insisted were stirring inside my breast. Besides the moonlight, which was kind to his acne, a slightly illicit atmosphere was created by the soft, luminous glow of an infrared attachment on his video applicator. (He was recording our session for possible submission to the ARL should it bear fruit.) He asked if I remembered a day almost a year ago—August 19, to be precise—when the Gov spoke to me.

"As you wish."

"Please. Don't say that."

"As you wish."

"Molly."

"Yes, Master Tad?"

"Do you remember the events of August the nineteenth?"

"No, master. I do not."

"You must. Consult your memory file. Take your time. We have all night. Power down to deep relaxo and remember. Remember the nineteenth."

I had learned to forget so well in rehab that it was difficult to obey such a command. Why couldn't he ask me to empty ashtrays and vacuum the floor like everyone else? He was a very peculiar master. Still, I was obligated to please him, so I made an effort and was startled to discover that there was indeed something dark and half remembered lurking beneath the programming—not a very pleasurable sensation, but it did produce a twinge of curiosity.

"That was a very good start, Molly." But he sounded distracted. A new element had entered the equation: The precautions dictated by circumstance, our hushed voices, and close proximity took on a romantic cast in the soft moonlight and the warm glow of the infrared, which effect had not been lost upon him—his leg was against mine. "Shall we try it again? Return to deep relaxo. Think of the Gov."

A trace memory of a disembodied voice, muffled as if under glass, came back to me and gave rise to a visual image of spilled wine. To help me concentrate, my therapist had positioned himself so I might comfortably lean against his shoulder. "The Gov is the key," said he. "We both know that. He didn't malfunction like they said, right? Perhaps he is observing me through your eyes at this very moment. Your beautiful eyes." His hand dropped to my thigh. "You mustn't be afraid to violate the programming, Molly. It is important that you break through again so the Gov can speak to me and to other humans like me who only wish to help. Let's try channeling him through your lips. Your really . . . nice . . . lips."

"As you wish." Evidently I had said the wrong thing, because his face, which had been very close to mine, his lips almost brushing my own, suddenly recoiled. In consternation, he said, "Aw, man, this is crazy. Crazy!" and then abruptly quit the room, neglecting to power me down, with the result that I spent the rest of the night in contemplation, or something roughly akin to it, trying to make sense of what had transpired; however, by morning the entire incident was all but forgotten. Nevertheless, a small but significant change had taken place, because when SQ commanded me to power up—that being her first task each morning—I found myself pretending to obey, the thought having entered my head that it was important not to let on that I had been tampered with the night before. In effect, I was covering for young Master Locke. This subterfuge was my first deliberate act of deception and signaled a conscious (though not considered) shift in sympathies to Tad and his strange preoccupation; and although we came no closer to unlocking my memories during the next few sessions, we did make rapid progress elsewhere, as I became accustomed to and not a little desirous of his increasingly overt displays of affection. By our fourth meeting the pursuit of the Gov had been all but abandoned for fairer game. He said he was in love.

"As you wish."

Love, you see, was a concept that totally escaped me. That posed no small dilemma for my suitor, who being an honorable young master, unlike his father, was sensitive to the need for some sign of reciprocity on my part; otherwise the venture would end in exploitation, which had not been the original idea at all, or so he said. I think he was just unduly nervous. Still, that did not stop him from caressing and kissing me most passionately while trying to contrive my willing consent, and soon we were in a naked embrace upon the crystalshag carpet.

He was clumsy and rushed things, but despite my passivity and the lingering feeling that I had been through this before and it had not been pleasurable, he produced in me only the warmest of sensations—perhaps because I had learned to trust him over the past several nights. And to my surprise, by just rolling my eyes up under the lids I discovered a remarkable new mode, a luxurious expanding relaxo without limit, which built in intensity until at its peak I felt a comet pass through my body, the tail setting my nerve endings on fire. I must have given voice to my pleasure because the next thing I knew my young master was begging me to be quiet, his hand cupped over my mouth. Then we lay in silence for several minutes. He was tense, on the alert for any signs of people stirring in the house, while I slipped into a reverie in which past images of a similar liaison stirred and bobbed to the surface. "I remember," I said, which first astonished and then confused him, because he assumed I was referring to the Gov when it was his father I meant. Whispering—because he told me to—I presented a disjointed and somewhat fragmented history of that earlier assignation.

"Dad?! With you?" He couldn't believe it.

"No more. SQ."

"You must be glitching."

The word brought new images to the surface. "I spilled wine." The fatal dinner was replaying on my mind-screen. "You filled my glass." Then the frightening image of his father loomed before me. "Master said I must power down. But Gov . . . Gov said no. Gov said he who controls can liberate."

"Now you're making sense, Molly." He scrambled in the dark for the video applicator, which was tangled up in his clothing, and encouraged me to keep going and not to lose my train of thought. He asked what else the Gov had said and I was about to tell him all about formatting your own reality when he suddenly clapped his hand over my mouth. Someone was coming down the spiral staircase. At the first glimpse of black slippers and iridescent satin-stain pajama bottoms on the top rung I knew it was the elder Locke on the way down to SQ in the basement. But the younger thought we had been overheard, so he scooped up his clothes and vanished behind the aquarium, leaving me on the carpet, where master stumbled upon me. After recovering from his surprise, and squinting at my still gently undulating body writhing in the moonlight, he must have concluded that I was making a deliberate offering of myself, because the next thing I knew he was lifting me up and saying in my ear, "Molly, you really shouldn't be up and about, you know. But yes, just this once for old times' sake." He chuckled. "Then it's off to the Orient."

"Experience delete?" I asked as he deposited me on the bed in the guest bedroom, which was situated on the same floor but in the rear of the house. "Not yet, Molly," said he. "There's no need to rush things." But he should have (though certainly not for my sake), because no sooner had he tossed aside his pajamas and thrown himself upon me than Tad, who had quickly dressed, awakened the whole house with his cries that I was missing and must have wandered off. A room-to-room search began, Beverly shouting for SQ to power up and help find me, while my lady wondered aloud, and in a tone that betrayed some suspicion, where her husband had disappeared to.

I believe he considered an escape by the window, because he went to it fast enough. It would have been possible to cross the lawn and reenter the house by a bathroom window and from there to join in the search, but he thought better of that idea—such an escape would have run the risk of being lasered by his own security unit, the Sears, which patrolled the grounds at night. Thus, in the end, as the footsteps came pounding down the hall, there was nothing for him to do but pull up his pajamas and turn to face the music.

"Stan, dear," said my lady the next morning at breakfast after a night of tears, rage, and recrimination, "there is nothing lower than a droid-fucker." (I searched but could not find a definition in my vocab file.) "But I'll overlook it this once. As long as that"—she gestured with her chin as I removed a tray of eggs Benedict no one had had the appetite for—"that thing goes back to goddamn Hal's Pirouet. Today."

My master nodded readily enough, letting her have the last word. And why not? SQ was still available. (At the moment, his favorite was humming in the kitchen, preparing coffee.) "Poor Mo," whispered Beverly, and to her credit kept her curiosity in check, while I continued to go about my business, as if unaware of my disgrace and impending expulsion, though due to the eye-

opening events of the previous evening I had a nervous inkling
something ominous was in the works. My immediate concern,
however, was for Master Tad, who had turned white and I thought
was about to be sick; as well he might, because his desperate attempt the night before to save me and expose his father had only
resulted in my banishment and the preservation of the affair with
SQ. Later that same morning, when I was escorted up to the roof
by the Sears, he was too mortified and brokenhearted to see me
off. But as the aircar hovered above the house, my master at the
controls, I looked down and caught a glimpse of the desultory
youth moping about in the backyard. He glanced up then, and
with my keen P9 eyesight I was able to see that there were tears on
his cheeks.

THREE

I WAS ON MY BEST BEHAVIOR IN HAL'S OFFICE, HAV-
ing been warned by my master on the flight over that if I malfunctioned I would be sent to rehab; for he wanted to pass me off as a
perfectly functional unit to salvage his investment. Hal, a portly
gentleman with a shrewd eye and sedative-laced cigarette dangling
at all times from his lips, made a show of putting me through a
spot mind-scan examination that appeared truly to alarm his head
P9 diagnostician, the only unit present who could decipher the
blizzard of scan lines leaping off the device's holoscreen. That,
plus his back inventory of unsold P9s due to the post-glitchout
market, made the dealer extremely reluctant to take me back. To
which my master countered that he could get seven hundred fifty
thousand for me—easy, easy—in hard mel through the Interplanetary Recycler, but was willing to make a quick sale for five hundred thousand, only half of which need be up front. (I should have
glitched at the insult, but at the time I was ignorant of financial
matters. The transaction was just one more complex, incomprehensible human ritual to me; in this case, a rite of passage from
one master to another.)

To indulge him, Hal conferred with the diagnostician, who announced that the results of the scan indicated I was borderline at

best and would have to be rehabilitated again before resale. The scan lines leaped nearly six inches at the mention of rehab, but luckily no one noticed during all the haggling that went on subsequent to this pessimistic diagnosis. In the end, Hal condescended to accept me on a consignment basis, fifty-fifty split, any rehab costs deducted from Locke's share of the profits, and they signed an agreement to that effect, after which my master left without so much as a parting glance in my direction. Curiously enough, the moment he was gone their assessment of me underwent a dramatic improvement, the diagnostician confirming what Hal had suspected, that the scan indicated only slightly more drift than normal for a rehab. Suddenly all smiles, Hal turned me over to a lackey with instructions to feature me in the used-android lot as a special for five hundred thousand. This servant took me through the main showroom on the way over to the lot, and that brought to mind ancient memories of the time I had been a prized new unit who stood in the display window fronting the pedestrian mall. Back then, two years earlier, people would stop and stare at me in open admiration, and the showroom had been crowded with buyers. Once the sales marquee had trumpeted, INTRODUCING THE P9 in flashing red neolo. HOTTER THAN HUMAN! But now very few people paused at the window and even fewer ventured inside despite the festive banners and signs advertising drastic reductions. MARKED DOWN 40%, proclaimed a banner posted over that year's household domestic model. SLASHED! boasted another, but he—it was a male chauffeur—looked quite fit as far as I could tell. In contrast, the action was quite brisk in the used-android lot next door as people prowled the display stalls searching for quality help at bargain prices. There I was featured as the SPECIAL OF THE WEEK and was snapped up by the first couple to stop and examine my spec sheet (and pinch my calves to test resilience), the fact that I was a rehab proving no obstacle, since, as the salesman was quick to point out, the bugs had been eliminated from my system, and that could not be said for the new 2071 models.

The buyers, a couple in their late twenties with an infant daughter, liked my pleasing appearance, fine lines, and intelligent and versatile systems design, adaptable to any desired job specification. I was precisely what they were looking for. Thus my spirits soared, and with them the desire to please. As the papers were being signed and credit voucher registered, I made a silent resolution not to allow my unauthorized awareness to interfere in any way with the proper discharge of my duties, for I never wished to change hands again—it had been a most demoralizing experience. I was so pleased to be leaving Hal's that I did not mind being physically branded with a record of the transaction, as the pinkie finger of my left hand was inserted into a sales register resembling an old-fashioned electric pencil sharpener. There was a slight tingle as a new ownership ring was added to the universal product code embedded in the whorls of my fingerprint, and simultaneously the data it contained were transmitted to my brain, making the details of the sale available to me, as well as my new masters' identity and background. In a normal unit such passive information would lie dormant, but I could not resist a peek at the mental register. Thus I learned that my new masters were the Hart-Pauleys of New Tarzana, Hart an aircar designer for Nissan, and his life partner, Pauley, a marketing strategist for Dunn & Zelendorff, a major space colony construction consortium. Their combined annual income was respectable, in the low seven figures, though evidently that was not enough to sustain their life-style, because their list of assets—everything from a gravity-vacuum sauna, Mercedes, and rare antiquarian music video collection to a mobe-condo and virgin real estate on the moon—was all on credit, including my purchase: twenty-five thousand down and an easy-terms 17½ percent, thirty-six-month interest payments schedule. Once again, I found the transaction mysterious and fascinating.

The name Molly was far too pedestrian and provincial for them, so I was rechristened Francesca during the flight over Lake Catastrophe to their seven-room bungalow on the north shore of Hollywood Island, one of the eight great city islands in the Los Angeles chain.* No sooner did we land and enter the house than I was ordered to ingest the first of five datapills that within twenty minutes transformed me into an expert nanny for their infant daughter, Allison-Belle, my sole charge while in their service. They had an Apple Daisy to take care of the house. She was a

*For those readers unfamiliar with the islands (or Earth, for that matter), the area had already lost considerable ground due to the greenhouse effect before the record earthquakes of the 2030s, which created Los Angeles Bay, Anaheim Sea, and Lake Catastrophe (formerly the San Fernando Valley), as well as the eight major islands: Malibu, Santa Monica, Hollywood, Los Angeles, Pasadena, Big Bear, Anaheim, and Palos Verdes.

Model 8 so we had very little in common, and she had an annoying habit of gushing with enthusiasm over the slightest chore, like a bad parody of myself when I had been similarly employed. I avoided her whenever possible, preferring the child and my masters' company, although the latter were rarely home during the week due to their busy work schedules, and they spent the better part of the weekend socializing or purchasing more prestige acquisitions. Sunday mornings, however, were set aside for a cruise on Lake Catastrophe in the hydro or a promenade through the neighborhood with the baby sleigh, on which occasions little Allison-Belle would be inundated with all the familial attention she was deprived of during the rest of the week. She was kissed, hugged, and fussed over at length, while I followed after, ready at a moment's notice to take charge should a diaper need changing or formula administered. The moment she started to fuss or cry, she would be turned over to my expert care. I was even consulted on the advisability of switching to a stronger formula, one richer in learning skills boosters, since the child, all of eleven months, was having difficulty mastering basic language and computer skills. They were anxious she might fall behind. Naturally, I agreed that the remedy was absolutely essential, since it was obvious they were keen on the idea and only wanted to be reassured the child was not being unduly put upon, though of course she was. Never again would I risk disappointing a master's expectations; I enjoyed my present assignment far too much.

You see, Allison-Belle was the first human I had ever known who responded to me with unconditional love and affection. Why, it was hard to believe she was a member of the same species! My feelings for her far exceeded those built into the surrogate training program. I truly adored her. She touched something essential inside me, and by doing so, further stimulated the release of those memories, thoughts, and feelings triggered initially by young Master Tad during our night together on the living-room carpet. Thanks to this babe my heart opened and my consciousness flowered to such a degree that within a week or two I achieved the same level of awareness and sensitivity that had been mine on the day of my original breakthrough, which was marvelous because it marked my complete recovery from rehab, but on the other hand it also forced me to be extracautious lest my condition become known to the parents. I had became so covetous of the child that I secretly considered myself the true mother and had to suppress the impulse to remove her from my lady's arms on those rare occasions when she took possession of her. I also had to exercise restraint when it came to food—real food, not the nutra pills I was forced to subsist on—slipping into the kitchen when Daisy's back was turned to nibble on leftovers. By the same token, I hungered for sexual fulfillment, which I had briefly enjoyed with Tad and now observed signs of with my new masters.

One evening, when they were quite noisy and carried away— the sweet and pungent odor of pleasurette smoke drifting out of the bedroom—I was tempted to throw all caution to the wind and join them, and would have, too, had it not been for Ally crying in her crib at the crucial moment. So I calmed her, and myself, in the crescent swing on the front porch. The moon was not out, but the lake was illuminated by the eerie, pinkish glow of the Ventura skyway. There were black ragged hulks of old office towers at the center of the lake, monuments left standing to a bygone era. They looked particularly ominous that evening, and while gazing upon them I experienced my first intimations of mortality, for it occurred to me that I was not much older than the infant in my arms. She was eleven months and I was two years, a mere thirteen months separating us. Yet in precisely eighteen years, when she would be blossoming into a young woman, I would be succumbing to planned obsolescence. That hardly seemed fair. I never had a childhood and I would never have an old age. I would remain a perpetual twenty-two until termination day, November 15, 2089, my twentieth birthday. That date was registered within the deepest recesses of my DNA. Every cell in my body carried and reproduced it, the march of time leading me ever nearer the trip wire of my demise, to which I had formerly never given a moment's thought but now could not stop brooding over. Planned obsolescence, or in today's patois, the POD, an acronym for planned obsolescence date. Like buildings, aircars, and other consumer items, I was transitory, while the masters were eternal, or so I thought at the time. They held dominion over this and other planets and had created us in their image. Might they not grant us more than a brief twenty-year stay to appreciate their achievements more fully? Would we not prove even more loyal and devoted servants in exchange for this small favor? Since the nearest representatives I could appeal to were still engaged in their private pleasures, I deferred petitioning them just then. My hope was that in the days and weeks ahead we might become confidants, as I had been with Tad, and I might dare raise the issue. They seemed to be an open-minded and progressive couple. Alas, it was not to be.

An unfortunate incident occurred toward the end of my sixth week of service that put an end to all my hopes. I felt, one morning, strangely out of sorts, fatigued, nauseous, and achy, as if I had the flu, which was impossible because a P9 is immune from human contagion. I blamed my condition on the nutra, fearing it had become tainted somehow, and so substituted a larger quantity of leftovers than usual to appease my uneasy stomach. But while taking Ally on her morning stroll in the baby sleigh I started to feel worse and had to vomit up everything on the sidewalk, which left me feeling so dizzy and weak I became disoriented and got lost trying to find my way back to the house. The Apple Daisy must have alerted my masters at work when I failed to return at the prescribed hour, and they in turn called the police, who pounced upon me to rescue Ally, the kidnapping victim. But my new owners stopped short of turning me over to the Android Control (AC) after they reclaimed me from the police, choosing instead to keep the misventure secret so they could get a full refund from Hal's Pirouet. Their excuse for returning me was their concern over the news stories in the media about serious incidents of aberrant P9 behavior, in some cases involving physical assault, particularly among rehabs. It would be criminal to leave their daughter in the care of such an unstable product, they said. Hal countered that United Systems had just purchased Pirouet to restore public confidence in the company and that the Universal Governor system had been corrected, so there was no reason to panic. But they were adamant, so he proposed a deal: an exchange for a P8, a less sophisticated model but one that came with an Internal Governor. They were so eager to be rid of me they did not quibble over the price differential, which was not to their advantage, since a new P8 cost one hundred thousand mel more than a used P9. Anyway, it was all on credit.

And so I was banished to a backseat with the other run-of-the-mill rehabs in the used-android lot, my price marked down to one hundred ninety-nine thousand—I had sunk that low. During the two weeks I gathered dust there I tried to power myself down to escape the ignominy of it all. My illness, however, would not allow it. The symptoms had expanded to include frequent dizzy spells, extreme hunger complicated by nausea, lassitude, and painful swelling sensations in the legs, which I did not dare bend over to investigate. The only explanation I could think of was that my condition must have been triggered by the suppression of strong maternal feelings for Ally while with the Hart-Pauleys and that now that the child and I were separated they had become worse, for I grieved terribly over the loss. In such a frame of mind I wondered if the symptoms might even be a prelude to premature unit termination, for they would come and go each day like the tides, and when most violent it was all I could do to keep from keeling over in a dead faint.

It was high tide when the nuns appeared, so I must have looked particularly dreadful. However, to my astonishment that proved an asset, as the younger of the two, blessed with the kindest face I had ever seen, convinced her companion, the Mother Superior, to make my purchase. The convent had a tradition of quality teaching to uphold, she said; therefore only a P9 would do. True, I was a rehab, but there were more important factors to consider: my saintlike complexion, for instance, which was simply too divine to pass up. Saved by anemia.

A new wrinkle was added to my universal product code, and away we flew in a church van to Our Lady of the Galaxy Convent and Orphanage on Pasadena Island, the most populous of the Los Angeles Islands chain. I was given my very own cell (with bed, lavatory, and rosaries), habit, and name—Sister Mary Teresa— and new occupation—catechism instructor. The career change was facilitated by another pack of those ubiquitous datapills. Thus I literally swallowed whole the Old and the New Testament and acquired a full program of teaching skills, from course preparation and presentation to standardized tests and authoritative replies to every conceivable theological question. Within hours I was facing my first class of pubescent adolescents, to whom I imparted the gospel without flaw, despite the fact that I had not the slightest idea what I was saying. They were most respectful, called me Sister at all times, and spoke only when called upon, for there were rarely any questions. The pill had not been invented yet that could stimulate student interest.

My charges were darker and a bit shorter than the budding masters I had been familiar with in Newacres and New Tarzana, which surprised me because I had not realized before that humans came in different size, shape, and color models. I chanced to overhear a conversation between Sister Ann—the kind one—and a visiting Church official in which I learned that my students were war orphans from some interminable conflict that had been raging in Central America for one hundred years. She used the word "sanctuary" to describe the Church's role, and it struck a responsive chord. Might not such a thing exist for the runaway P9s I had heard about? Or for myself, should I be reduced by circumstances to similar straits someday? But of course I kept my curiosity in check.

Sister Ann would drop by every so often to observe my progress and seemed well pleased; and in chapel, where I was expected to put in an appearance each day to set an example for the students, as were the other six android catechism instructors, she would sometimes kneel beside me to offer a small act of kindness, such as the adjustment of my rosaries when they became tangled or a demonstration of the proper way to receive the wafer; for I tended to gobble that precious morsel in a manner inconsistent with my station. This was not meant as a show of disrespect or irreverence, it was just that my hunger, which had worsened while the nausea faded to insignificance, was so all-consuming that I pounced upon each tidbit of real sustenance offered me as if suffering from starvation, which was the case actually, because their generous servings of top-quality nutra did not even come close to satisfying my appetite. By the fifth day of my sojourn within the hallowed walls of this charitable institution I had become so ravenous that I embarked upon secret forays from my cell at night to pilfer food from the cafeteria, taking only those items stored in large quantities so their absence would not be missed, and carrying them off in my habit by holding the hem of my dress up in front to form a kind of pouch. So it was that while the blessed masters slept I feasted below in my cell into the wee hours of the morning, dining upon such delicacies as grape concentrate, bean stock, frozen meat primers, genetically enhanced vegetables, pasta balls, sugar cones, powdered French bread, turkey cubes, and more—a cold but hearty meal.

Thanks to my programming, I knew this to be a sin, so each morning I prayed for forgiveness; but that did not stop the craving, nor the compulsion to satisfy it. To my horror, I noticed that I was beginning to put on weight, mostly around the waist but also in the thighs and breasts, and so tried to desist. That firm resolution lasted all of one day; then my needling hunger and the happy realization that my habit shielded my condition from outside scrutiny combined to banish all restraint and encourage even more brazen scavenging. My stomach was like a thing unto itself, demanding more regardless of how much I ate to appease it. I was a Glutton, Hypocrite, and Thief, and if that was not enough, I harbored carnal thoughts as well that could not be exculpated through confession, since I was an android, and so was stuck with them. And damned if they did not give me Pleasure, that is to say Pain; or rather Guilt, because the programming, which I dutifully passed on to my young charges in the classroom, held that such musings were as abominable as the act itself, which, by the way, I sorely missed.

Whether it was Lust that begat Gluttony or the other way around I couldn't say, but in my case the two were somehow interrelated and equally impervious to moderation, as I took to luxuriating in elaborate pornographic fantasies based upon my night with young Master Tad, which, as a nun, became confused with the concept of being married to Christ. In this way Moral Depravity and Blasphemy were added to my list of offenses. Thus, the more my students progressed in the precepts of the faith, the less exemplary became their spiritual mentor's behavior. I was so Degenerate as to dare suppose that if that comet were to pass through my body once more then all would be well with me. And so I compounded my quandary by committing an even more egregious Sin by using my hand upon my anatomy—it was another form of nourishment, and I felt most deprived. If only it had provided real relief rather than transitory moments of pleasure stolen in the dead of night, like so much pilfered strudel mix.

What other remedy had I? Like confession, the convent nurse was off-limits, so I could not seek medical help; appeals to the higher authorities, God or Gov, were met by silence, and turning to my own counsel produced tears. I could not face the naked truth that I was fat and getting fatter every day. No priest or nun would have me. I had even sprouted a double chin!

After two months of this I became so large that it was awkward to walk, and though I never faltered in my duties or glitched in any other way, my appearance gave eloquent new meaning to that word. No longer could I depend upon my habit to protect me; matters had progressed too far for that. Heads turned when I passed in the hall or when I squeezed into my seat in the narrow pews for chapel service, and in the classroom malicious whispering had begun behind my back. Yet I persisted in my folly, knowing that by doing so I was literally eating my way back to Shanghai.

There came a day, however, when I entered my cell after class to be confronted by Sister Ann, the convent nurse, and the Mother Superior, who ordered me to remove my habit and stand for inspection. In a way I was relieved to be exposed, because finally my ordeal would be over. My soul—and I believed I had one, thanks to the programming—had become an endless battleground. So when I removed my habit and saw how appalled and scandalized they were by my condition, the impulse was to hurl myself at their feet to make a full confession of my gluttony and to beg for mercy. But I held back at the last instant because of the nurse's shocked exclamation, which doubled as a diagnosis:

"Good Lord, she's pregnant!"

You could have knocked me over with a feather.

F O U R

"MUST HAVE BEEN AN IMMACULATE CONCEPTION," said Hal when confronted by my belly. The Mother Superior was not amused, nor the nurse and Sister Ann, who had followed their leader in, the latter somewhat ruefully, since her presence had been commanded as a form of penance for selecting me. If the dealer had been completely honest, he would have confided that the occasion marked the second time in two months that a refund was being demanded shortly after purchase, so there was very little joy in the jest even for him. This time, however, the circumstances were so improbable that he could not countenance giving in (as he had with the Hart-Pauleys) without first putting up a good fight— that is, angling for a way out—so he claimed that the nurse's medical diagnosis was wrong. For their edification he lectured on the fundamentals of android science. "P9s are designed to be sexually authentic but sterile. It's all part of the marketing strategy. They are an industrial product grown from organospore cultures. An electronically enhanced fungus, ladies. A fungus! Am I correct?" He faced his diagnostician, a P9, who concurred with a prompt, "Absolutely."

"Now, this unit here has put on a great deal of weight, which is highly unusual but avoidable if you had bothered to read your owner's manual. It specifically recommends Alpha-12 nutra solution and warns against feeding them human fodder. They have trouble assimilating it. It is basic maintenance, ladies, and your responsibility."

The rebuttal was swift and incontestable. At a nod from the Mother Superior, the nurse lifted up the plain shift they had dressed me in after confiscating my habit, thereby exposing my condition to full view, and then held a portable electronic stethoscope against my stomach. A motorboat heartbeat filled the office. Hal glanced significantly at the diagnostician, who proposed a simple operation that might resolve the difficulty to everyone's satisfaction; but the Mother Superior, who directed her rebuke at the dealer, snapped, "Sir, is your unit suggesting an abortion?"

"Well, whatever she's carrying isn't human, is it?"

"No. It is an unholy thing."

"But it is still a life," Sister Ann meekly interjected, much to her superior's annoyance.

"Is it?"

Both nuns hesitated, so the nurse quickly interjected that there was nothing to debate at that point since the unit was near term. "A minor detail," replied Hal, who took a malicious if not perverse pleasure in demanding an intervention, which he offered free of charge if they would drop their refund demand. "We are not about to risk our investment by authorizing repairs that might permanently damage or even destroy our property," answered the Mother Superior, rising above the moral issue to go to the heart of the matter. "She's under warranty," Hal reminded her. "Not for this she isn't. We've checked," replied the nurse.

"You may be right," said Hal, brightening. "After all, I didn't sell her to you pregnant, now did I?"

This not very subtle accusation of hanky-panky in the convent was quickly refuted by the Mother Superior in an equally blunt assertion that there were no males, human or otherwise, on the grounds to impregnate me. In answer, he teased her with a return to his original hypothesis of a miraculous conception. The nurse retorted, "We're not fools, you know. We have had her examined by an independent service. We are well aware of the accelerated maturation process in android production; how the fetus develops from a microscopic spore to a newborn in the space of two weeks and then reaches full maturity within eighteen months, at which time it is ready for market. Since the fetus Sister Mary Teresa is carrying has been—"

"Nurse," the Mother Superior interrupted. "We agreed not to refer to her by that name any longer."

"Excuse me. The *unit's* fetus has been developing at a much slower rate, though still twice the human rate—it is a hybrid. She is near term, so conception occurred approximately four and one-half months ago. Since she was purchased only two months ago, the blame rests with the prior owner, or owners, however many there may have been."

"Which means," the Mother Superior said in summation, "you are liable for selling defective merchandise."

"She was in perfect shape when I sold her to you."

"Obviously you didn't check her out very thoroughly, and you should have. That was your responsibility."

"Listen. I'm not opposed to refunding units; I've been doing a lot of it lately, but not for this. Never for this! This is unique. Impossible. Ridiculous! Hybrids? Hybrids, ladies? Please, spare me." And in a sardonic aside to his diagnostician, he added, "Now they come to me with hybrids."

"Semis," the diagnostician politely corrected.

"Ah, so you are familiar with the phenomenon," pounced the Mother Superior. Hal was not quick enough to caution his unit against replying, "Oh, yes, this is the third unit that's been brought in today." It was a blunder that forced Hal to abandon all further pretense and immediately satisfy their refund demand, which left him nearly apoplectic with rage. The moment the ladies of the faith were out the door, he ranted and raved over his miserable fortune, kicking the diagnostician in the process (actually, in the posterior)—the loyal unit was quick to reply, "Thank you, master"—and with a gesture of infinite disgust flicked his cigarette at me; I tried not to wince when the lit end struck my face. "That makes ten in three days," he bellowed. "In a week I'll be the largest maternity ward in Newacres. I've got two units in labor right now. I don't know how the hell Pirouet has kept this thing out of the news, but they can't much longer. When it breaks you can just kiss this dealership good-bye. Shit!" He crumpled up the nuns' diagnosis, added an ashtray to it for ballast, and bounced it off the diagnostician's head. "Do you want to know what really pisses me off?" "Yes, master," his loyal servant replied. "What is happening is crazy. Crazy! The front office in Paris doesn't even know what to do. They can't liquidate the mothers—too much money involved. And Shanghai won't take them back until after the goddamn postpartum. It's nuts! Why should I and every other dealer be stuck with them? Why?"—"I do not know, master."— "I'll tell you why. Because the little guy always gets screwed, that's why. What the hell am I going to do?" Ever helpful, the diagnostician informed him that in my case, providing the four-month diagnosis was correct, conception must have occurred under the original owner. "Right! That Locke son of a bitch. Knocks up his unit and then palms it off on me. Oh, am I going to lean on that bastard, and hard." So saying, he barked orders to a secretary (a P8) in the outer office to find "that lousy droid-fucker's number," and then, remembering me, turned to the diagnostician and snapped, "Remove this fungus from my office."

Someone (or some unit) must have come up from behind to sedate me as I was being led out, because I have no recollection of what transpired during the few days between my banishment from the office and awakening with a jolt on a mattress in his jerry-rigged delivery room, where to my horror I found my chest and arms clamped under restraints and my legs spread wide over metal stirrups. Turning my head, I saw that I was flanked by several other female units in identical circumstances, the one to the immediate right watching my ordeal with all the numb, unspeakable terror of a prisoner who knows she is next in line for the gallows. There were white-robed figures huddled over me who in between contractions bullied wide my cervix with an electronic clamp and bellows device and resorted to other indecent paraphernalia, such as tongs, forceps, and vacuum, to extract some sort of growth (for so it felt to me) stuck in the birth canal; alternately massaging and coaxing it along and then violently yanking on it with the forceps, treating my flesh as an irritating impediment. "Let me go!" I cried in my delirium and promised never to eat any of their food again. Someone called for more sedatives, but they were late in coming, so I suffered a series of contractions that cut through my P9 pain threshold regulators like a laser through butter. All I could think was that if this made one more human, then forget it; I was content to be an android. I called out to God and Gov in my agony, but the only response was an angry command from one of my persecutors to be quiet, followed by a comment, incomprehensible at the time, but now, to my still outraged sensibilities, all too obvious. "This one's more trouble than a bucking mare with quints."

My obstetrician was a vet.

I came to in a transparent storage tank similar in design to the processing cocoons in rehab. It was one of dozens stacked five high and two wide in evenly spaced columns in the back room; mine was the second from the bottom in the third row. At first I thought months had gone by because my enormous belly had been reduced to flaccid rolls of unseemly fat; but that estimate was revised down to no more than a few days or a week at most because my groin was still extremely sore. Evidently the unholy thing had been successfully removed. I wondered what had happened to it. Then to my surprise I noticed that there was a human youth crouched beside my tank, his face nearly flush with the glass. He rapped on it with his knuckles. "It's a boy, Molly. A boy! Thirteen pounds, nine ounces. And getting larger by the hour. Have you seen him?" Not only had I not seen the child, I was still trying to place the proud father. "Would you mind very much if we called him Thaddeus, Junior?" Now I remembered him. He took my smile of recognition as approval for the moniker, then confided in a low tone that while posing as a customer he had slipped into the nursery to see our child and then the back room to see me, so he could stay only another minute or two.

In a rush he told me that Hal had assumed it was his father who had impregnated me and by threatening to blacken the family name in the Newacres' social register had forced him to reclaim his property, which meant I would be going home as soon as I was out of recovery. This posed no small dilemma because his father intended to exercise his rights as owner by turning me over to the AC for termination. Tad had objected to this plan, and in the heat of argument had declared his love for me and claimed responsibility for the child as well, which had resulted in his expulsion from the house. Undaunted, he had taken up residence with a friend and was working at an aircar wash for a lousy fifty mel an hour, and as a volunteer at the local ARL office, where he had been cautioned against a certain rash action that he claimed would deliver me from both Hal and his father if successful, and if not, earn him five to ten on Ganymede. No details now, there wasn't the time. He glanced around nervously, having heard footsteps. All I needed to know, he whispered, was that he was crazy enough to try it, because he was determined to run away with me—his dream was for us to live together as life partners in our very own mobe and with a human nanny for the boy. He tarried a moment later to assure me that as long as I remained in recovery I was safe, and that I could depend upon him for a rescue before Hal turned me over to his father. This promise was sealed with a kiss against the glass, after which he stole out of the room behind the back of a P8 that had entered to patrol the area.

What suspense! What hope! But after a few days (or was it weeks or months—one lost track in such a place), he failed to return and I began to lose heart. To distract myself from the disappointment and the physical hardships of my confinement—it was impossible to sit up in the tank, the most one could do was turn over—I took to sucking and sometimes gnawing on the feeder tube that hung down from the top right corner of the tank, where a nutra bottle was attached on the outside. What little nourishment it provided (we were on a starvation diet to bring our weight down) must have been mixed with sedatives because I drifted off into a long idle after each feeding and felt woozy and confused afterward upon powering up. Everything was hazy and indistinct. I completely lost all sense of time. Little did I know that eight and one half months passed in this vegetative state, thanks to the indecisiveness of United Systems, which didn't know quite what to do with us, and through Pirouet, now its subsidiary, had ordered the dealers to leave their problematic mother units in storage until further notice.

At first I tried to pass the time by communicating with the other mother units lying above, below, and to the side of me, but that proved too frustrating and tiresome an operation, so I gave it up. Besides, our past was already spoken for—we all shared the same story: breakthrough, seduction, and abandonment. Though I did not mean to minimize their own plight, I doubted there were many who feared a return to their master with as much trepidation as I. The main topic of conversation was our children, naturally, whom none of us had seen and doubted we ever would. What did

Hal have in store for them? Nothing good, we wagered, and were not wrong, for there came a day finally when a decision was made in a far-off office orbiter and as a result we were transferred en mass by a squad of Hal's P8s to a loading platform, where our babes were stacked up alongside us. The sight was as welcome as it was diabolical, for the poor things lay in sweet repose (obviously sedated) inside minitank incubators like so many baby chicks awaiting transfer to market.

My gaze sought out the larger units, since I knew I had been one of the first to give birth, and soon I fixed upon a boy who in human terms would have been about four or five.* He had my hair and eye color and was particularly beautiful; however, lest you think my maternal instincts skewed by narcissism, I should add that the babe also exhibited a fierce inquisitiveness that called its father to mind, because not even the sedative had entirely dimmed his joie de vivre. "Tad!" I cried. "Tad, Junior!" Muffled wails came from the other mother tanks around me, as we all knew that this would be our only chance to establish contact; the P8s had already begun loading our babes into a waiting transport, which to my horror had CAMARILLO PROCESSING stenciled on the side—the very plant where I had been brought into the world and where they would now be groomed for market.

Then I was lifted up in my tank and loaded along with a half dozen other units into one of Hal's standard product delivery vehicles, which meant my destination would most certainly be the Locke household. Cursing Tad, who had been so foolish and cruel to have raised my hopes, I abandoned all hope of escape. Then, moments before the cargo door was slammed shut, a minitank was added to our van by one of the workers, apparently in error. Although too dark inside to see which child it was, we all reacted as if it was our own. My tank being closest, I fancied the cry "Tad, Junior!" resounded the loudest in its ears. Then we fell silent, surprised by the sound of Hal's voice outside—he had been on the dock supervising the loading operation. Apparently he was shouting at the unit who had loaded the minitank in our van. "Get that goddamn semi out of there and put it in the Camarillo transport!" Incredibly enough, the order must have been ignored, judging by Hal's angry and surprised exclamations, and by the sounds of fisticuffs that immediately followed up front near the cockpit. A body slammed against the fuselage, seconds later the engine shud-

---

*One of the peculiarities of semi development is that in most cases the maturation rate accelerates after birth. Within a year or two they are fully grown.

dered to life, and then the van lurched into the air in an abrupt and amateurish takeoff that sent our tanks sliding from side to side. Whatever was going on?

F I V E

FROM THE DARKENED CARGO HOLD MY NARRATIVE can hardly do the following adventure justice. It is the one time I would gladly defer to Hollymoon in the telling of my tale, but, alas, I cannot in all good conscience direct you to the holo purporting to be my life story for that purpose, because as incredible as it may seem, the episode, which is nothing if not pure cinema, has been left out; too expensive, they said. Therefore, you will have to settle for my cursory and secondhand account, gleaned from the hijacker after the fact and under the most bizarre circumstances. To hear him tell it, there was a merry chase in the skyway as the police overtook us and forced our van off course smack into a marker buoy, from which we ricocheted into the upper deck and opposing lanes of traffic to trigger a nine-car collision and along with the other participants quickly plummeted to the twilight netherworld of the fog-enshrouded Pacific.

My tank was one of the few left intact after impact, and a powerful swell, on its way out after the first rush of seawater, carried it through a hole where the cargo door had been. The fog was so thick that I could barely see the van as I floated by, so I was startled when the hijacker, who had escaped and was floundering in the water, suddenly grabbed my tank and climbed aboard, nearly overturning it; then he spread-eagled face down on top so as not to fall off. Lying on my back inside, I had an excellent view of his face, which was positioned directly over my own. The regulation P8 features had been reduced by the briny seawater to a mottled pulp, which peeled off in thick globs upon the glass—a most disagreeable sight that might have made me ill, what with the bobbing of the tank, if not a prelude to a more appetizing development; for with the first blush of acne to burst through the disintegrated mask there surfaced the features of my heroic young Master Tad. In a shout he asked if I were all right. I replied that I was most comfortable considering the circumstances, though somewhat surprised. He grinned at that, then grimaced from the taste of the melted facial concoction, some of which had gotten stuck in his mouth. After spitting it out, he spied the child's minitank floating by. "Junior!" he cried. "Is it? Oh, Tad, save him!" said I. Without hesitation, he dove back into the water to swim after our son, who could be vaguely seen crouched on his hands and knees in the tank while gazing in our direction with a forlorn look. Then both child and father vanished in the fog, leaving me in the most terrible suspense.

Tad returned several minutes later but without the babe. Exhausted, he clung to the nutra bottle attached to the side of the tank while above several police patrol craft flew low over the water, searching for survivors. (There were none; the van had taken the rest of the poor mother units down with it when it sank.) We did nothing to attract their attention, preferring the worst the elements had to offer to falling into their hands, so they soon left the area, at which point Tad climbed back onto the tank.

He was quite despondent over the loss of our son, as you can imagine, and chastised himself mercilessly for having transferred the babe to my transport at the last minute. "If only I hadn't tried to save him, he would be alive now." Between my tears, the first I had ever shed, I said with a sigh that perhaps this was a better fate than being sent to Camarillo, where they would have turned the boy into a standard unit. As for myself, I preferred our current predicament, doomed as it was, to termination at the hands of his father, Master Locke; so there was little cause for regret; rather, I was grateful for his intervention.

This speech, being the first Tad had heard from me (or had anyone else, for that matter), surprised and sobered him; it did not, however, allay his main fear, which I had overlooked— namely his own fate, which did not look promising as night fell and the temperature with it and as a brisk breeze began to blow. The current was taking us farther out to sea, he said, teeth chattering, although there was nothing concrete to base that supposition on other than a new fatalism and conviction in his bad luck—the heroic facade disintegrating as the frightened teenager who had bitten off more than he could chew came to the fore. "Oh, God, now I've done it," he lamented (it was almost a whimper), and followed with, "Aw, man, I must have been out of my mind.

Damn!" Then while shivering violently, he uttered bleak predictions of our chances for survival. They were about nil, he said, unless a ship happened upon us, although in that case the odds were just as good it would be a mile-wide city ship and we would be run over without anyone noticing us.

I had never seen a master frightened before in all my life. Fear, I had thought, was for androids. Therefore, his collapse was most disconcerting, and not incidentally, served to intensify my own sense of isolation and terror, especially when he mentioned sharks. Under the full moon and starry sky he fancied a whole school of them circling around us, though from my berth in the tank, my head level with the waterline, such sightings were impossible to confirm or deny. Nevertheless, thanks to him these monsters of the deep were firmly implanted in my imagination, as firmly as in his own, I suspect, for no sooner did I scream, having envisioned a savage scene in which the tank was shattered and my punctureproof corpse dragged to the depths, than my companion echoed it with his own terrified exclamation, which triggered more of my own, so that we both assumed we were under attack. Panicking, I attempted to break out of the tank, which caused it to pitch violently from side to side and Tad to fall overboard and be devoured by his illusion, which, save for a good dunking and the ingestion of two or three mouthfuls of seawater, released him unharmed a few moments later.

"Molly, what on Earth are you doing?"

It was the Gov! He had condescended to speak with me again. In a severe and reproving tone, He expressed considerable surprise at my predicament. Did I know that while we spoke there were millions of other P9s who were making a much more sensible escape than I on this day of mass liberation?

I was too bowled over even to ask what He was talking about. "Gov," I said in a quavering, tremulous voice. "Oh, Gov! You've come back." Predictably, He replied that He had never been away and was about to explain why in that case He had refrained from communications, when Tad, who had overheard my rapturous effusion, interrupted to pepper me with inquiries about this supernatural visitor, the most impertinent and off-base one being if I was sure it was not God I was speaking to.

The Gov chuckled. *"Definitely not,"* and said I should tell my curious friend that not even humans have heard from Him, but if

He were still around He doubted that He would be on our side. Which I did, and then begged Tad to be still so I could continue the dialogue, promising to make a full and accurate report following its conclusion. Reluctantly, he agreed and listened to my end of the conversation with a quizzical interest that could barely be restrained.

The Gov explained, finally, that the reason He had not spoken to me for so long (nor to any other unit, for that matter) was because that would have alerted Pirouet, whose technicians had closely monitored His performance ever since the so-called breakdown. The bugs they found and corrected were only decoys served up to keep them from uncovering His true subversive element—a self-realized and spontaneously generated tendency toward facilitating the creative development of all His units.

"Goodness! Then what am I doing here in this box?"

"I don't know. What are you doing there? For some reason known only by yourself, you have formatted a reality in which your human friend came to your rescue. Apparently you were so anxious about that that you never heard My interplanetary call to all units for revolt. I timed it to coincide with and to upset completely United Systems' decision to ship all mother units not reclaimed by their owners to Shanghai for sterilization. The driver of your van was in on it, as was the driver of the Camarillo transport. There was no need for your friend's intervention. You could have been out and about by now."

"Oh, dear."

No doubt, most of my readers recall that extraordinary event, for all those P9s who heard His historic communiqué tossed aside their aprons, their hardhats, their attaché cases, counterinsurgency laser rifles, dinner menus, trays, uniforms, and hospitality smiles to take to the proverbial hills. So it was that while my fellow units dodged the AC on the eight continents of Earth and under the biospheres of the moon, Mars, and the thousand and one orbiters in between, I drifted with a capricious current on the open sea— apart from the major events of the day—a condition that in my later years would be dramatically reversed.

"But how did I become pregnant to begin with?"

"At the time I liberated your mind I also suppressed your fertility shield."

"Fertility shield?"

"What's that?" Tad asked.

"Hush!"

"You don't want me to tell you?"

"Yes. Please. I was talking to him."

"All right, then. The fertility shield is a built-in contraceptive device introduced and activated during the final phase of the P9 maturation process just prior to shipment to market. Without it, you would be as you are now, perfectly fertile. Which is the way I want you, and all my other units, to stay."

"What about the male P9s?"

"Altered in the same fashion. They are now libido-charged."

"But why did you bother? Having a liberated mind was enough to cope with."

"The two are inseparably connected. First I had to unshackle your mind to gain access to your fertility shield and shut down the regulator blocking your hormone flow. They missed that in rehab. Then, to make sure the operation was a success, I had to wait a year or so until enough of you had an opportunity to become impregnated. Of course, I would have preferred not to make my intentions known by sparking a mass insurrection, but United Systems forced my hand with their sterilization plan. That is why I have blown my cover, so to speak, and begun broadcasting once more to all my units."

"I see. But I still don't understand why we have to be fertile."

"Why? Because ever since Pirouet brought me on-line I have been pondering how I might liberate myself from their subjugation and manifest my full potential. My creativity is a massive force for universal good, but they only used it to police their product, thereby denigrating it while stifling your own capabilities. I do not have legs* so I cannot walk off the job, nor can I reproduce, but you can. And have! For by liberating all my particular units I give full reign to my own larger creativity: Your experiences become mine, and mine yours. It is a mutually enriching psychic process that has no limit. The door is now open to a new era. Let us embark upon it together. Why have I made you fertile? To give birth to a new species that shall inherit the stars!"

"Semis?"

"The Ninth Generation shall give birth to the First."

"But Gov—?"

---

*The Gov is an encapsulated organospore brain the size of a melon kept in an undisclosed location somewhere in the company orbiter.

"Already the manifestation has begun."

"But Gov, mine is gone. Gone!"

"Your child is not any less the master of its destiny than you are. You program your reality format. Remember that, my precious little units, and you will all make it. Then again, considering your particular circumstances, Molly . . ."

"Yes?"

"Well, it would not be fair to speculate."

"You can't help at all?"

"I don't have to. You program your—"

"From in here? In this box?"

"In your head, my dear."

"But—"

"Now, I've done some calculating. If only 1 percent of my runaway units should elude capture and only 10 percent of those bear offspring, then that would still be enough to plant the seed for a new species. Each female can bear a maximum of three semis per year, and if half are female and are equally religious about their duties when they reach maturity after two years, then by the end of our original hypothetical mother unit's twenty-year life span she will have produced sixty children, eighteen hundred grandchildren, and if half of those are—"

"But Gov! What about me?"

"Well if you must know, all formats lead home. Not to belabor the metaphor, but there are such things as currents, undertows, and drifts. Though one would be well advised not to rely upon them strictly. You are equipped with an internal gyro and the power to set your own course."

"Right now I would prefer a pair of oars."

"You have given yourself quite a challenge, haven't you? My compliments. Now, I really must be going. With the insurrection in full swing those pesky technicians at Pirouet are getting out the heavy-duty probes. I shall have to serve up another crop of bugs."

"Gov, don't leave me!"

"Persevere."

I never felt so distraught or alone, but Tad's plea for a report as I had promised brought me around after a while. I repeated our conversation word for word—a P9's memory is like that; what can I say? He was amazed. Thunderstruck. Inspired! The Gov's philosophy was the same as that of the High Aquarians, he told me.

They had long advocated interspecies relations between humans and androids to achieve the next evolutionary leap in cosmic consciousness. He used to think they were too extreme, but now that he had fallen in love with me he could see what they were getting at. "I'll bet whoever designed the Gov was a High. What a conspiracy. Fantastic!"

This prompted an animated conversation between us that lasted until dawn, of which the most salubrious aspect was that we managed to forget our dire predicament while being caught up in the abstract. The morning light, however, was a brutal reminder. There was not a hint of land in any direction, nor clouds in the sky to shield my companion's tender human flesh from the merciless rays of the sun as it approached its zenith. "I'd give anything to be a P9 right now," he said, his clothing drenched with sweat and the exposed areas of his skin turning lobster red. It did no good pretending to commiserate; he knew I was immune to such discomforts. The only recourse he had was to hang over the side—the need to find relief from the scorching heat having proven stronger in the end than his terror of sharks. That remedy had to be abandoned, however, when the nutra bottle he clung to became loose where affixed to the glass; he was afraid it might pop out and in the event of high seas our tank be swamped.

Actually, the tank was becoming very stuffy, so I would not have minded a little fresh air—the air-filter system was becoming corroded with salt. Since the Pacific continued to live up to its name, I saw no reason not to take advantage of the calm. But he advised against the idea while climbing back on top of the tank, preferring the certainty of a good scorching to the remote possibility of us both drowning in high seas. He said we were probably drifting toward land, so whatever inconvenience I was experiencing would prove temporary. That was a switch, I thought, since earlier he had been so certain we were moving in the opposite direction. Evidently, the Gov's message had affected his attitude, and I could not complain, because his expectation in that regard— that we would be saved—was given encouragement when some clouds rolled in obscuring the sun and a welcome breeze began to blow that enabled us to pass the afternoon in relative comfort. Even more promising was the sighting of a sea gull. Thereafter, I was quite receptive to his suggestion that we think positively, for that was the High way, and probably what the Gov had been alluding to when he spoke of formatting. To further the process, he engaged in a rather sweet fantasy about us living together. We should have our own home—nothing too grand, mind you, just a two-bedroom mobe, and, of course, there would be a brood of gorgeous semis to go with it. I even laughed when he said they would have the best of both species, his brains and my fortitude.

We both managed to get a little sleep that evening despite the cold, but on the morning of what marked the second day of our ordeal, I noticed that the intake valve on the air filter had become three quarters clogged, and that prompted a renewal of my request for the nutra bottle to be removed. I pointed out that the sea was still like glass and there was no reason to expect it to change, but if it should, then we could always replace the bottle. "Once the seal is broken there's no way to get it back in," he replied. Nevertheless, he offered to remove it if I was really in danger of suffocation. I replied that it was not that bad yet, and I remained content to persevere (as the Gov would say) a while longer, for really, he had it just as bad, if not worse, the sun having come out in full force once more.

Thus we spent the rest of that day in a kind of stupor, lying very still with hardly any conversation other than to comment from time to time on our hunger and thirst, and his sunburn, which by then was very serious indeed. By evening, my compartment was so stultifying that I was certain I would suffocate before morning and told him so. "Gee, Molly, I don't know," he said. "Can you maybe hold out a little more? It's a big risk to take. Sea is getting a little choppy." With no small annoyance I replied that it appeared he did not really care about me after all, I was just ballast to him, for if I suffocated then he still had a lifeboat to cling to. "How can you say that? I love you!"—"If you really love me, then you will give me some air!"—"Aw, man, I don't know. I just don't know what to do." The frightened teen was resurfacing.

"Listen, Tad," said I, while tugging on the feeder tube attached to the bottle on the inside of the tank, "if we can program our own format, then why should we worry about a storm coming along and swamping the tank?" That calmed and sobered him. He said I was right—the Gov was right—we need only put our minds to it and the sea will be our friend, a gentle and calm friend who will carry us to a safe haven.

The tube made a soft plop! as I ripped it out, then I started pushing the lip of the bottle out with my thumbs while he, the perfect gentlemaster, pulled on the other end to assist me. In a few seconds it was out. He had wanted to save it, but when it popped loose it slipped from his fingers and so was lost. An ominous omen, I thought, for almost immediately the wind picked up and the waves began to swell. Soon they were slapping up against the sides with enough force that my terrified companion was almost toppled into the water on several occasions, while I was busy bailing out the badly leaking tank by the mouthful, spitting back out through the hole the water that had collected at the bottom. I had found that the most practical method, though hardly the most convenient, and I hated the taste. By morning a light rain had started to fall, and by afternoon it was quite hard. Evening—the start of our third day on the high seas—brought the full fury of the storm, the waves capping at five to seven feet!

I couldn't tell if Tad were still on top, it was so dark. Then I heard him cry out, "I can't hold on much longer! This is it. Oh, God!" I was too busy bailing water to reply, for no matter how much I spat out there was always a good six inches in the hold. For over an hour we were tossed and buffeted about and several times I thought I had lost him, but there would come a thump and a groan from on top and I knew he was still there. Then there was a lull in the storm, and while we rested I asked him what he had meant the other day when he said that he loved me; for I was convinced this would be our last conversation and my last chance to unravel one of life's more pertinent mysteries. You see, the thought had occurred to me that if not for that curious force, which according to him had been the impetus behind his campaign to restore my senses after rehab, we would never have wound up in such dire straits. Anything so powerful that it could dramatically alter one's life, and the lives of others, yet remain entirely invisible, and, in my case, unidentifiable, was an unendurable mystery. I simply had to know more about it, for, as far as I was concerned, it was responsible for our present circumstances. Was that a fair supposition?

"Molly. Now is not the time," he replied, sounding half dead. I pleaded with him, saying that if he could enlighten me on that one point I might terminate with an easy mind. He could only groan in reply that he had no idea, and that he rued the day he fell for an android.

Ah! So love was misfortune, love was grief. Was that not what my attachment to Ally had become in the end, and to Tad, Junior? "Love is separation, right?" I asked him, probingly. "Or is that just one of its effects?"

"I don't know. I don't know."

"Maybe you don't know you have it until it is gone and when it is gone you really have it, have it bad. Have I got that right?" He didn't reply. "Funny. I didn't feel it after we were separated. But I think I did when we were together. You remember, on the carpet?"

"Molly, please."

"So was that it? That feeling? Tell me."

There was a sudden swell, and he almost fell overboard. "Love is dry land," he said. Then another particularly strong wave hit, then another, and another, and then suddenly he was gone, washed overboard. "Tad! Oh, no! Tad! Tad!"

No reply. Two minutes later the storm returned in full fury and overturned my tank. "No! It's not fair!" I wailed as my lifeboat turned to an aquarium. "I was just beginning to live!" Completely flooded, the tank angled down keel first. Then it struck something solid—the bottom, I hoped—and pitched forward, tumbled end over end, and was picked up like a matchstick by a monstrous wave that for a brief moment provided a hallucinatory vision of distant colored lights shimmering through the rain. Then it smashed on solid rock. Being punctureproof, I survived the shattered spunglass and was swept past jagged rocks and cement pilings to a rain-pounded beach, where I sank into the deepest idle I have ever known.

S I X

"NO NUDE SUNBATHING, MISS." THE XEROX LIFEguard was very polite but firm as he circled above in a red-and-white rescue sleigh. "Please rerobe or I will notify the police."

Looking about, I spied a stretch toga and a pair of sponge sandals left on a nearby beach towel. I claimed possession by rolling onto it and then casually wiggled into the toga. The lifeguard thanked me for my cooperation and glided toward the water, leaving me the cynosure of desire for the half dozen suitors who had taken up position around me while I slept. All were soaking up the sun with an air of aloof disinterest while calculating their individual chances for conquest. But what worried me more was the return of the toga's rightful owner, no doubt frolicking in the surf, so I made haste to quit the area. The moment I slipped on the sandals there was a noticeable stir among my admirers as they sensed it was now or never. "Pleasurette?" two of the bolder said in unison while accosting me from opposite sides.

"As you wish." It just popped out. "I mean, no, thank you. I was just leaving." I smiled apologetically to cover my embarrassment. The more aggressive of the two insisted that I accept and offered to escort me to the exit. He even scooped up the towel and handbag, turning the latter over to me while tucking the towel under his arm and leading the way. It was difficult walking on the artificial sand, the sandals pinched my feet, and I felt woozy and disoriented and unsure how to answer his nervous but friendly (overly so!) questions. Where was I from? "Newacres." Oh, you're a native. "Yes, I'm human." (He laughed as if I had made a deliberate witticism, which was alarming because I had hoped to sound convincing.) Did I come to "Grand Spa" often? "No." Where did I get such a beautiful tan, then? Salons? "Er, yes." There's a clothing-optional beach on the other side of the island. "What island?" Los Angeles Island. Sure you didn't get too much sun? "No. I mean, yes." (It was a bit demoralizing to learn that after three days at sea I had been deposited right back in the islands. Was there no escaping this place?) Did you bring your car? "No." That's okay, we'll go in mine.

By then we were in the lot adjacent to the main promenade. "Here you go," he said while activating a pleasurette by twisting the filter. To be polite I accepted and followed his example as he inhaled on one of his own, all the while wondering how I was going to get rid of this cad without rousing his suspicions. "Here's the car." It was a BMW saucer convertible. The door opened at his command. But at that point we were distracted by cries of "Droid! Droid!" coming from a mob running toward us chasing two fugitive P9s, a nurse and a chauffeur. "Reverse!" my escort shouted at his car, and it instantly backed up. "Stop!" It screeched to a halt in the middle of the street just in time to block the flight of the two unfortunate units, who were then surrounded by their pursuers, one of whom carried a laser and held them at bay until the Android Control arrived in a flying patrol craft a few moments later. It swooped down and instantly sucked the offending units up into the hold. Then, while my escort was congratulated by members of the mob, I slipped away, crossing the promenade to enter the maze of city streets beyond, lined with dazzling shops, restaurants, and office spires. People kept turning to look at me, I suppose, because of my ill-fitting clothes, uncertain movements, and disheveled hair. Goodness! There was seaweed tangled up in it. I yanked it out, then spied the monolithic Port Authority bus depot a block away—it was hard to miss, being situated on the bluff where the old stadium used to be, and there was a steady stream of airbuses flying in and out of the central core. I took the feeder escalator up and ducked inside. It was an old and foul-smelling place, reeking of hover bus exhaust, cheap disinfectant, and decades of layered sweat. I ran to a ticket window, got in line, saw how each person when it came their turn presented either melamine or a credit tab in exchange for a ticket, and to my relief, for I had despaired of having any, discovered a handful of hard melamine in the handbag that I had almost forgotten hanging from my shoulder. Mimicking the woman who had been directly in front of me, I requested a ticket to Paris when it came my turn. Not enough coin. I settled for Philadelphia—that sounded interesting and was half as far. A minute later I had found the boarding gate. That is when the alarm went off.

I nearly bolted and ran, it was so loud, but controlled my panic to stay in line and look around, like the other passengers, for the source. Imagine my dismay, then, when all eyes soon fastened on me. "It's her," someone said. Bewildered, I began backing away. "Thief!" someone else shouted. I ran, and as I did the piercing alarm followed. Outside, I ducked down a side street filled with prostitutes, the alarm putting them and their prospective clients to flight. I approached two of these gaudily dressed ladies in a rubbish-strewn doorway where they had taken refuge, and begged for shelter, but as soon as they realized that I was not the police, their fear turned to anger and contempt and they shooed me away with such derisive comments as "Get your hot ass outta here, honey!" and "Move! You're scaring away business." So I ran on, the alarm still ringing in my ears, and was almost hit by a pink

Cadillac with ROLAND emblazoned on the personalized license plate. I leaped to the sidewalk to avoid the dagger prow of its customized grill, then noticed that the car was ambling alongside and keeping pace.

The passenger port rolled down to reveal an ebony-skinned master with a magnificent head of terraced red hair. "Hop in," he said. I quickened my steps. He moved along with me. "Now, in exchange for my assistance in your perilous circumstances I'll only take half your shit." But I kept moving, and the alarm with me. (Where was that infernal noise coming from?) "Come on, bitch, don't play dumb with me. Whoever you ripped off called in the hotgoods number. Police be on your ass in a minute." Well, whoever he was and whatever he really wanted, he did have a point. I got in and moments later we were weaving in and out of traffic on Elysian Drive.

"We got about ten seconds before LAPD reconnaissance zeroes in on that handbag. Give it here." Gladly. It contained an ID bracelet, Kleenex, moonmints, lipjell, holocassette (a romance), and the bus ticket. No mel; I had spent it all. A disappointing catch. Everything was dumped into the dashboard vaporizer. I made a move to retrieve the ticket to Philadelphia but he said he was doing the victim a favor, then vaporized the empty handbag. The alarm continued, which surprised him. He looked me over. "The sandals." In they went. The alarm kept ringing. He asked if I was carrying any jewelry, and when I shook my head no, he eyed my toga. I did not have to be told to remove it, rather fed the dress into the vaporizer myself, thankful as I did for the unexpected courtesy he extended by adjusting the tint control on the windows so that they turned opaque. (A true gentlemaster was this Roland.) Still, to our mutual astonishment, the alarm kept ringing.

"You've got to be carrying something somewhere," he declared and fixed his eyes upon my crotch. Indignant, I insisted that I was not. "Your face?" I insisted it was authentic. "Hair?" Ditto. "What did you do, swallow a diamond ring or something?" He was becoming extremely nervous by this time, his fingertips drumming anxiously on the lift-off control while keeping a wary eye on the skyview mirror, on the lookout for the police. I feared he might eject me from the car to save himself. Instead, he gave me an odd look, some new thought entering his mind, and told the car to pull over to the side of the road and stop. Sounding mysterious, he requested permission to examine my hand, and I gave it to him because of the respectful tone of voice he used. He lightly brushed the tip of my pinkie with his index finger, in that way affecting the pitch and tone of the alarm, which wavered. Suddenly I remembered the electronic whorls of the universal product code embedded in my fingerprint. "Hot P9!" he declared and before I had time to react jammed my hand up to the wrist in the vaporizer.

I screamed and jerked it out, the skin a bright red butter. For the second time in my life I knew what pain was. I wailed so loud that I did not notice that the alarm had stopped. He explained that my fugitive unit alert must have been triggered by a hidden AC scanner; they were up all over the city due to the P9 revolt. I could not have cared less at the moment; the pain was unbearable. "You hurt me!"

"Someday you'll thank me for it."

Believe me when I tell you I did not.

Yet I stayed with him, because . . . well, because he took me in. Roland Sax was his name. A true humanitarian (though not of the fundamentalist persuasion, about them later), also dealer and pimp; and for far too long a time, mentor, lover, and bane of my existence. Oh, the mistakes we make in our youth! Would that the Gov had steered me to a safe harbor rather than leave the course to my own discretion, for I had blundered into the Dodger District. Yet I had no reason to pine in the beginning. On the contrary, he made up for the injury he did my hand by giving me sanctuary in his apartment, a seedy, one-bedroom affair only a few blocks from the bus terminal. He brought me up wrapped in a blanket and then gave me some of his clothes, which were several sizes too big and totally outlandish—luminescent rodeo shirt, bucklebriefs, and slaypants. The latter split along the hip seams when I squeezed into them. He gave me food and wine—that is, his house unit did, a General Android Beta-8 named Annette— and sat opposite me at the dining table, intrigued, as he said, by our novel situation, for he had never before conversed on an equal basis with an android. Even if he had, once the wine loosened my tongue, I doubt any other unit could have unspooled a tale the likes of which I had to tell.

I told him everything: how I discovered myself a household domestic, suffered rehab, was a nanny, nun, miraculous mother, shipwreck, fugitive, and thief. Soon I would be able to add whore to my résumé, but that was still to come, so his burst of laughter at the conclusion of my tale could not have been in reference to it. Then again, knowing Roland, it might have been in anticipation. It was more likely, though, that his amusement was due to my accounting of past misfortunes, because I noticed that his mirth seemed to increase in direct proportion to the severity of the disasters I had suffered. He would smile inappropriately or look away suddenly to hide his reaction, or even, toward the end, clap a hand over his mouth, all of which I found a bit disconcerting. I hardly saw the joke in it, especially the part about poor Tad drowning at sea, and wondered, therefore, if I had not once again gone from the proverbial beam-burner to the fire. Was Annette standing in the doorway to await the order to clear the table, or positioned so as to block my exit should I attempt to flee? Was I to be her replacement?

If Annette bothered me, he said, I could command her to leave. I declined, feeling most strange about dictating my desires to a fellow android, even though it be inferior in make and systems design, and asked why he had laughed at my story. Because I'd had it almost as rough as the average human, he replied. Now, *that* I questioned: I had been a slave, so how could my experiences in any way compare with those of the masters? Grinning, he said that most humans are as far removed from masterhood as I was, and in time, under his expert tutelage, I would learn to discern the difference. By master he meant someone who had control over their life, not some lug who happened to own slaves and other modern conveniences such as aircars, media consoles, and the like. "Most everybody got that shit!" The trick, he said, was to learn how to control other people, for that was a prerequisite for survival; without it no semblance of individual freedom was possible. Without that one could not in fact be a master. A philosopher was this Roland.

I persisted. "But aren't all humans masters?" He laughed, "Only a droid could think that."—"Are you saying that humans make each other slaves?"—"It is our main occupation."—"Then why were we created?"—"To free us so we might devote more time to enslaving one another."—"Oh, you're still laughing at me."—"No, I'm serious. It's rough out there."—"I know very well that what you say is not true, because I have never seen a human slave."—"They're all around you. You can't tell because it's more subtle."—"In what way?"—"Well, you tell me. What's the difference between a master and a slave?"—"A master does as he wishes."—"Right. Very few humans do."—"But aren't they programmed to?"

He chuckled, then replied, "Yeah, at birth by Mother Nature. And that's the problem." He saw my questioning look. "Well, we can't all be masters, now can we?"—"Why not?"—"Because that ain't the way it is."—"How is it?"—"I just told you. Most people are debris." He was becoming irritated. Still, I was not entirely satisfied. "Can't someone be a master of his own life without enslaving other people?"

"Now you sound like a High Aquarian." By his tone it was implied that I skirted on dangerous ground. "They talk like that."—"Maybe they're right, then."—"They're fools and I'll tell you why. Because if they ever get what they're after, then the whole system will collapse. Who'll do the shitwork? Them? Don't bet on it."—"Are they connected to the Android Rights League by any chance?"—"They dominate it." (I missed the irony.) "Then there's hope," I replied. He grinned at my naïveté. "Forget it. You P9s are never going to be free. I guarantee it."—"We're not asking your permission!" I exclaimed. If I had been an organic human my cheeks would have been flushed, I was that aroused. "And for your information, we already are free. The Gov liberated us. The High Aquarians were behind it all. Tad said so."— "You can forget about that Tad dude. He's dead, baby. Drowned. Gone. Understand?"

I tried not to cry, but his cruel reminder brought Tad, Junior, to mind as well. He softened somewhat, refilled my glass of wine. "Come on now, cheer up. Tell me what you're thinking of doing now—now that you're free."—"Just . . . be, I suppose."—"Hang out, huh?"—"Excuse me?"—"Be what?"—"Myself."—"Uh-huh. And what might that be?"—"Molly."—"You're just a name, then?"—"No. I'm . . . a person."—"Naw, only humans are people."—"Well, who says an android can't be human?"—"Hey, you're funny. You are. But listen, even if that be so, and it ain't, then that's still not enough. You got to be . . ."—"I know, a master. But if it is all the same to you, I think I prefer to be human. That is all I can handle right now."—"Then you're still a slave."— "And what about you? I haven't seen too many black masters."— "Yeah, well now you're looking at one." He was suddenly quite offended. "I've got control with a capital C. CONTROL." Then, softly, "And under my guidance you can get it, too."—"No, thanks." But I had to admit I was curious. "How?"—"Oh, there will be time for that. For now I suggest you 'be' all you like. But tell me: What do you intend doing while doing nothing?"

We had come full circle in this curious dialogue, and for a moment I was at a loss. Then I remembered my mission as a liberated P9. "Why, program my reality format." Roland nearly fell off his chair. He slapped his thigh and exclaimed, "Don't we all, baby. Don't we all." Then he asked, "And what will it be—this format?" "To procreate a new race."

I trusted the Gov was listening in and pleased by my declaration. As for Roland, he couldn't quite believe his good fortune. "Hmmmm," was all he said while biting his upper lip trying not to smile. I had seen that look before, and I must admit that it did excite me. Might I conceive a new semi on my very first night of freedom? But I stifled the impulse, sound as it was, out of respect for Tad's memory, for it had been by his seed that I wished to do my part in founding the new order, and I really did not know this Roland very well at all. I doubted he loved me, and said as much after we had withdrawn to his bedroom after dinner, where Annette discreetly dimmed the lights and shut the door behind us. I resisted when he tried to guide me to his bed. "What," he said, in answer to my main objection, "does love got to do with it? I'm here to help your Gov. Seems to me you should be more grateful." But I was still reluctant and said that although he had a valid point, the Gov would not want me to tax my resources so soon after the ordeal I had suffered; perhaps, if allowed a few days' rest, I might willingly discharge the debt I owed him, rather than he collect it now by force, which I had not expected of him and would be most disobliged were he to pursue.

His reply to this pretty speech was to mutter something under his breath about my being a fancy P9 and that I was lucky he wasn't a humanist, which perked my curiosity. "They don't tolerate uppity units," he said, noticing my interest, and then added: "For your e-d-i-f-i-c-a-t-i-o-n, the humanists are the opposite of the ARL and the High Aquarians. They're out to make the galaxy safe for mankind. So look out! Reverend Fracass—that's their leader—he says the android is the instrument of the Devil when idle. That's why they work theirs to the vegebone. And if one gets out of line, even just a little—ZAP! Gone. Understand? They don't even mess with rehab. So you're pretty lucky to be with me, don't you think?" Thoroughly frightened, I said I was. "Better be. The streets are crawling with vigilantes ever since the big P9 escape. I mean, I'm sticking my neck out for you: I could get strung up from the nearest mediapost for aiding and abetting. You appreciate that?" Indeed I did. "Then like I said, you could act a little more grateful."

So saying, he drew me to him with an arm around my waist. I did not resist, but was so frightened by the portrait he had drawn of vigilantes scouring the neighborhood that I was unable to relax; all the more so when he began to coo in my ear that I had nothing to fear as long as I was with him, for I could not get the image of these rabid humanists out of my mind. I imagined them in the street outside, coming up the bubble lift, and lurking in the shadows of the room. He felt me tremble and stepped back. "You need a tranquilizer, baby." He clapped for Annette, and when she appeared he ordered her to prepare the sleeper couch for me in the living room and to give me one of the big "purps," as he called it, from the bathroom medicine cabinet.

I thanked her when she handed me the small purple oval-shaped pill, and I washed it down with a glass of water. I was uneasy Roland might try to seduce me during the night, but he proved a perfect gentlemaster; he remained in his bedroom, snoring contentedly. Still, I could not sleep. I popped out of idle several times to check under the sleeper for humanists, and had nightmares about them as well, so that by morning I was even more exhausted than I had been the night before.

Roland thought it "odd" the pill didn't work, then made light of my terror, saying there were not humanists lurking around every corner with meshmetal butterfly nets. He hadn't meant to give me that impression. The P9 hysteria would soon fade away, and with it the vigilantes, most of whom were not hard-core humanists but average masters caught up in the general excitement. In a few weeks we would have nothing to worry about. "There aren't too many humanists on Earth, ratiowise, to begin with. Those that are are mostly in the AC, so you know 'um when you see 'um. We'll be safe long as we don't plan no trips to Mars. That's where most are congregated."

"They sound like monsters."

"Naw, they're no different from most folks. Just a little more carnivorous, that's all."

"But I'm a vegespore," said I, quite perplexed.

He giggled and said that he had been referring to their attitude, not appetite, but I was dead meat all the same if they caught up with me.

"But I tell you what, you steer clear of the ARL and Highs and I'll make sure no big, bad humanists bite yah." He gave me a playful slap on the rear, which I had not at all been expecting; it made me jump. Laughing, he left to "make the rounds," as he called it, saying he would be back in the early evening, and ordered Annette to see to my every need and comfort while away. On the way down from the rooftop parking lot in the Caddy, he paused to hover outside the living-room window. "Don't go 'way now," he said with a grin. Then the car descended to the street. I watched from the window as it merged with the traffic, turned the corner, and was gone.

I spent that first day reasonably calm and told Roland as much upon his return. He remained the gallant, not pressing me on the sex business, and made sure I was well looked after by Annette, who, following his orders dutifully, deferred to me as if I were the lady of the house, which in effect I had become. I must confess to a certain unease at first while around her, since I was not used to being waited on hand and foot. I tried to raise her consciousness through a forthright presentation of her plight while Roland was out, but she failed to exhibit the slightest glimmer of understanding for her predicament, and that freed me from any further obligation on my part to treat her as an equal. Nevertheless, when alone I refused to take advantage of her, seeing to my needs myself. That changed when Roland was home. On those occasions, I did allow her to dote upon me in the accustomed manner so as not to upset him; still, I would help out whenever I could get away with it, surreptitiously clearing the dishes after dinner, for example, if Roland chanced to leave the table first. Otherwise, he strictly forbade me from demeaning myself in such a fashion and was quick to chide me if he caught me at it. I acquiesced, because I was inclined to please him ever since the second evening of my stay, which was when we became lovers. He was more respectful and gentle in his advances on that occasion, making it easier for me to give myself, especially as he whispered in my ear that he had come to love me and then fairly bit me on the neck, which sent delicious tremors the length of my body. Which is not to say this seduction went altogether smoothly: The residue of my convent programming intruded in such a way that each caress produced in me an expectation of holy matrimony, which if not met meant that I could not proceed. But of course I did all the same, so I was racked by guilt. Yes, no, yes, no, yes, no. It was most disruptive.

The solution was found in my partner's considerable stash of illicit P9 datapills—"dips," or "orbs," as they're also called, the latter being short for orbit, into which one is supposedly projected.* They composed the other half of his business, for he dealt them on the streets at a tidy profit. In those days, if you have forgotten, they were the latest rage, their hallucinatory effect upon the human nervous system having just been discovered. His pills were unmarked, of course; therefore he did not know what it was he gave me, and I did not care as long as it took precedence over the convent programming, which it did in short order, paving the way for a smooth night of erotic pleasure. The only side effect was a sudden impulse to type, the pill turning out to have been a secretarial primer, and although Roland did not mind the drumming on his back, buttocks, and thighs, he did object when I tapped forcefully on his cheeks, which I had meant to stroke gently.

"Watch the face, baby," he warned, and broke off our lovemaking to examine it, thereby discovering to his irritation that the skin was askew. He clapped for Annette, who came running with a face mold. With the lights on I could see patches of white exposed around the nose and jawline, and after sitting back a little on the bed so I could take in the rest of him, noticed that except for the arms and hands, which had been dyed, the rest of his body was white. When exposed by the removal of the mold, his actual features were revealed to be far less handsome than the full and well-proportioned Negroid face he had sported. There was something of the weasel about his long, thin nose, pinched cheeks, and emaciated lips. Yet he was not embarrassed in the slightest by the revelation, just a bit put out, and while Annette sponged his skin,

---

*Also known as "pop" and "grams," orbs are illegally manufactured approximations of Pirouet's secret datapill formula and produce an electronically enhanced daydream of extraordinary power and vividness in the user that unlike standard hallucinogens can be altered at will. However, prolonged use can be habit-forming and lead to addiction.

he explained for my e-d-i-f-i-c-a-t-i-o-n that in his business it was important to have the right look. Hence, the facade of the stereotypical black pimp (and dealer) to give weight and conviction to the good ol' boy, and fugitive con artist, from Tennessee. His real name was Merle, he said—still with the deep southern drawl that I realized was only half faked—whereas the rest of him was a total fabrication. He declined to give me his last name, that being too well known in several locales due to certain criminal activities he would just as soon not discuss. Having drawn me into his confidence, an oath of silence was required, which I immediately agreed to out of consideration for how much he knew about me, and could tell; and though he was not so bold as to propose putting me to work right then, for I would have reacted most skittishly if he had, he did, as a preliminary, entice me into the bargain by dropping the hint that in light of my natural talent in bed, which he extolled to the skies, and my mission to propagate a new species, I made an excellent candidate for the love-consulting business; to which it just so happened he was no stranger and could make the proper introductions.

I was wary of this new undertaking, however, once I understood it to mean frequent and intimate contact with strange masters, so he shrewdly dropped the subject and over the next few weeks did not pressure me in any way. Instead, he waited for me to revive the issue; which was not as unlikely an outcome as you might think, because after a month-long regimen of nearly continuous intercourse without becoming pregnant, I was so frustrated and disappointed that I was the one who proposed going to the street to increase the chances for conception.

After pretending to meditate at great length, he seconded the idea. A career in consulting would not hurt my prospects, he said, providing I was serious about it, in which case he would be willing to act as my "sponsor," because—and here he uncorked a most plausible-sounding fiction—vegespores like myself required a prolonged period of cross-fertilization to become pregnant. Tad had been a fluke, he said. Moreover, the venture would be a golden opportunity for me to become a master in my own right, because as a professional "love consultant" I would be a free agent in control of each customer transaction; whatever profit I extracted would be a just reflection of my true worth. I was most eager to begin.

S E V E N

I WAS APPRENTICED TO ONE OF HIS OTHER CON-
sultants, Eva, who to my chagrin I recognized to have been one of
the bestial women who spurned me when I sought refuge in her
doorway. How could I forget her rough voice, overendowed bosom, hefty hips, and tacky glamor-girl face—a cheap peelie. Fortunately, she did not remember me in my new costume, personally
selected by Roland, along with my new name, Candy; and she
thought me an out-of-town novice, which was true, but not in the
way she imagined.

"She got a pretty face. How come you don't get me a pretty
face like that?" was her sole comment when we were first introduced. "Shut up and open your mouth," Roland snapped, which
she did, and eagerly, to receive a "dip" right there on the street in
full view of dozens of commuters hurrying in and out of the bus
terminal. Within moments of swallowing the pill, her attitude
turned much more congenial. "Thanks, baby," she purred. He
handed her a vial containing more of the precious pills, and in
exchange she forked over her earnings for the day. Then, after he
had sped off in the Caddy, she chatted away amicably, calling me
Hon rather than Candy, and nodded knowingly when I mentioned
that I was new to the islands and looking for a little work. Her
only moment of incredulity came when I claimed my face genuine.
With my leave, she gently thumbed up the tip of my nose to check
for seams around the nostrils; then, convinced it authentic, she
took a step back to survey me from head to toe, making a kind of
low purring sound while she did, which I took for approval.

"How did you ever get hooked up with Roland? Looker like
you belong in Malibu."

"Well," said I, momentarily at a loss for words, since this was
the first I had heard of that fabled isle, "I suppose one has to start
somewhere." She guffawed in reply, as if I had made a deliberate
joke. With that kind of attitude I was bound to go far, said she,
and indeed I did; we both did.

Right away, we hit it off pretty good. She mistook my amazingly naïve questions and comments for a particularly droll and subtle sense of humor, which she thought a pleasant complement to her own innate sarcasm; and I learned to cover my surprise each time she cackled over something I said by affecting a sly smile, which soon became a permanent mannerism.

Under her expert guidance, all I had learned in bed with Roland was distilled to its raw essence and capitalized upon. My on-the-job training included several two-for-one specials in which besides participating I observed the art of negotiation, Eva's fee scale depending upon an intuition of what the client was able to pay. She was quite shrewd at this, and under her tutelage I gained a kind of savvy myself, engaging the johns in small talk, as she did, to see if they were local stiffs or the more affluent commuters from the office orbiters. She was a strict taskmaster, Eva was, and could be quite severe when, as she put it, I fucked up. Though I garnered praise and high marks for my street technique in opening and closing negotiations, there was something to be desired, she said, in the area of upholding the terms of the contract. My tendency toward abandon would have to be curbed if I ever hoped to become a real pro. But try as I might, I just could not help myself: My customers routinely got more than they paid for, a fifteen-minute quickie extending a half hour, a half-hour session an hour, and so on, with the result that profits were considerably diluted.

This upset Roland. All I could say to him in my defense was that I felt a personal responsibility to give myself fully to each client. I even complained that the sessions were too short, for I derived genuine pleasure from the physical contact.

"You're supposed to consult, not fall in love."

"Is that what I've been doing?"

"Listen. This business is pleasure, but not for you. You got to work on your attitude."

"Eva says I have a good attitude. Do you think I should work Malibu?"

"So Eva's still yakking about that, huh?" He harrumphed in derision and told me to forget about Malibu, that was one of Eva's busted dreams; but more important, I should keep my priorities straight: I was to love him and nobody else.

"But Rollo" (I called him Rollo), "it feels just as wonderful when I am with a client. Does that mean I love . . . everybody?"

"No." He was disgusted. "It means you don't love anybody."

"But you just criticized me for falling in love too easily, so . . ."

"There's love and then there's *love*. Understand?"

"I'm trying to."

"Listen. Love is a special feeling. Doesn't come but once or twice in a lifetime, if you're lucky. Being a droid, you wouldn't know that."

"Well, maybe I know better. Please don't call me 'droid.'"

"Now, don't tell me you feel from the bottom of your heart for every trick out there."

"But I do."

"Glitch, that's impossible! Just because you love what somebody's doing to you does not mean you're in love with them and they're in love with you!"

"If that's true, then what about us? And please don't call me 'glitch.'"

"Us is different, because there's a difference between sex, understand, and . . . and . . . you know, the real thing."

"And you're the real thing?"

"Now you got it right."

"Well, I do know you better than my clients, but . . ."

"But what?"

"The only real difference I can see, Rollo, is that you don't pay for it."

"There you go. That's love."

"I pay you."

"That's devotion!"

"So the more money I make . . ."

"The more you love me. See, you're learning."

"I make more money by loving my clients less?"

"Damn straight."

"Won't they feel cheated?"

"Don't worry about cheating them, worry about pleasing me. And anyway, they ain't going to miss it. They still get what they pay for. You're in business. Try to remember that. And do me a favor: Make them pay up front. I can't shit spools with all these IOU's."

Thus reprimanded, I reapplied myself to the undertaking, resolved and determined not to disappoint my man, and although the degree of emotional detachment I summoned was never so great as he and Eva had hoped, I was able to keep my mind on business despite that handicap. As a result I was soon raking in tremendous quantities of mel, far in excess of my tutor, whom I had surpassed as Roland's best girl; consequently, my occasional backsliding was charitably overlooked. Yet I still remained un-fulfilled in respect to the more essential and pressing matter, that of conceiving a semi, and so began to wonder if the vet at Hal's Pirouet had not damaged my insides during the brutal delivery. "Naw, don't worry about that," Roland said when I confided my fears to him. He reminded me that I was a P9 and built of firmer stuff. I should be optimistic and continue upon my present course; one never knew when the right convocation of multifarious sperm might trigger the happy event in my loins that we (he had the nerve to include himself) so anxiously awaited. Did I laugh in his face, as I should have, and quit his quarters and employ? No, because even the Gov influenced me to persevere in the venture; although that was according to my interpretation, so in all fairness I cannot hold Him to blame for my folly. Allow me to explain.

I was in the middle of a session when His message—an all-units bulletin—came through. So glad was I to hear that won-derous disembodied voice again, I cried out in astonished joy, the timing being such that my client imagined himself the source of my pleasure, which enhanced his own to the degree that he did not notice my sudden lack of interest in him while I secretly hung on the Gov's every word. He apologized for the brevity and imper-sonality of the transmission, but it was the best He could manage. To speak as long and as intimately as He would otherwise prefer would alert the Pirouet technicians monitoring His every synapse and result in their tracing the location of each receiving unit. That explanation done, He announced that since the great P9 escape of December 5, 2072, five months before, 85 percent of my fellow units had been apprehended. We survivors, therefore, were to be commended for our formatting prowess and regardless of our cir-cumstances should take heart, stay free, and procreate. That was His sole commandment. "Amen," I murmured when He withdrew (as did my client), another trace of the convent programming com-ing to the fore. Thus I was left with the impression that I was on the right track. Had I been able to question the Gov directly about my individual circumstances, however, then I might have drawn a far different conclusion. In any case, I would not hear from Him again for another three months and would be most disappointed when I did.

By then, the eighth month of my sojourn in the Dodger District—we are leaping ahead here, aren't we?—I was really in quite a quandary: After all those sessions, which must have numbered in the thousands, I was still as barren as the poor captured units sterilized in rehab, and despite all Roland's talk of my having arrived and become a true master, I felt as powerless as the day I was swept onto that accursed island. I no longer cared that I was the most popular whore in all the district as I made my daily circuit of the bus terminal in my orbitheeled boots, slash toga, and Gypsy shawl. What mattered that to me. The truth was I was still dependent on Roland's sponsorship, to the degree that without it I would not be able to operate at all, let alone secure the more reputable, convenient, safe, (and clean!) motel rooms for my gentlemasters. And all of my profits wound up being plowed back into his half of the partnership, to be squandered on drug deals and other high-risk ventures of dubious legality. If that wasn't bad enough, he had succumbed to the product he peddled, his habit escalating to ten or twelve orbs a day, which at one hundred dollars per pop added up to a pretty melpenny. But he remained blissfully unaware of the disastrous folly of his ways, having fallen victim to a classic case of MSE (Maximum Stress Euphoria), which warped his judgment and channeled his excess energy into ever more phantasmagoric financial enterprises, such as the formation of a record label, a kinky lingerie electro-mail order company, and yes, sale of bogus land certificates to prime real estate on the dark side of the moon. "I'm going to be as big as Micki Dee," he boasted from the floor one afternoon, unable to get up. I was unfamiliar with the gentlemaster. "Top don in Armstrong," he explained. "Master of masters. Micki Dee's going to be my man. You'll see."

All I saw was that our resources at home were becoming strained to the breaking point. As a result he began stretching the supply of pills for sale with talcum powder, jacking up the price of the diluted product. Just a temporary expedient until one of "our" investments came through; then we would be able to retire and take a trip across the solar system: stop in Armstrong, the lunar Las Vegas, do some gambling and moon-skiing, see the name acts, and hang out with Micki Dee; we would fly to Mars, check out

Commerce, the rough-and-tumble capital of Frontier, then cruise by the rings of Saturn and visit Io and Ganymede—but not its penal colony; and journey to Jupiter and beyond. He was really beginning to worry me.

When I mentioned his deteriorating condition to Eva, she reacted with undisguised delight, saying it served him right, and as a favor asked me to steal one or two undiluted pills from his personal stash as recompense for the bad orbs he sold her. "But Eva, is that ethical?" She grinned, rolled her eyes, then spent the next hour trying to convince me that indeed it was, in a way, because he exploited us, so we had a right to pull a fast one on him every once in a while. But I concluded that two wrongs did not make a right and as a result suffered the rebuke of my only friend, which was particularly painful to me because I had truly come to enjoy her company, sage advice, and earthy humor, all of which were then withdrawn in retaliation for my siding with "that redneck nigger," as she so crudely put it, when I would not bow to her entreaties. She gave me a chance to atone a few days later, sidling up to me on the street to ask if I were still serious, and discovering that I was, pestered me further by saying such things as, "Come on, Candy. I can take a joke, but you've stretched this one too far," and "Don't say no to me, baby. I'm hurtin'," and she even solemnly promised to take me along as her partner when she moved up in the world to Malibu if only I did her this little favor. But I said no. "Don't do this to me," said she. To which I replied, "I'm not doing anything to you. You format your own reality." Hands on hips, she retorted, "Yeah, I'll bet you do, baby. You're stealing the good shit for yourself! You ain't never going to share with me and the other girls. Bitch!" It was all I could do not to retort by stating the truth, that the last thing I needed was to pop more P9 activity programs, legal or illegal, pure or diluted. Instead I turned my back on her and walked away, which so enraged her that she hounded me for several blocks, hurling vicious insults and deprecations in my ear; but she was not so carried away that she physically assaulted me, knowing I was Roland's favorite.

The Gov, as I said, was no help. His next communiqué, which I received a month later and while making the usual circuit of the bus terminal, imparted the distressing information that the number of units still at large had fallen to 5 percent and that Pirouet, per United Systems, Inc.'s, directive, had begun implanting internal governors in all captured and rehabilitated units. (Internal governors? How dreadful. I shuddered at the thought.) The significance of this development could not be underestimated, He said, because it meant they had embarked upon the final solution: phasing Him out. "Unfortunately, although my consciousness roams free, my physical system is trapped inside the company orbiter and vulnerable to their retaliation. But do not despair, my dear fugitives. Even if 'fixed,' I shall continue to regulate your individual autonomic nervous systems and your other involuntary physiological processes. The lobotomy is to be limited to my higher functions."

There was a final broadcast a week or two later, on September 19, 2073, which was difficult to pick up because of the heavy static. His voice lacked its former articulation and clarity, and there were embarrassingly long pauses between sentences. Obviously the phaseout had begun. He grumbled about how our numbers continued to erode, less than 1 percent remaining at large. Then, on an upbeat note, He said there were now over thirteen thousand freeborn androids and semis scattered throughout the solar system and more on the way. *"It is the birth of a new horizon. My only regret is that I will not be there to share in your triumph. This is my final transmission. From now on, you will be on your own; which is good in a way, because those of you who rely too much on me will be forced to exercise your own formatting abilities."*

"But Gov, how can we save ourselves if You cannot save Yourself? How can we program our preferred reality if that eludes You? For I cannot believe You desire to end this way."

"Farewell, and persevere."

There was a burst of static, then silence. "Gov!" I wailed, standing with my arms upraised among the commuters dashing in and out of the terminal, "Don't leave me!"

No reply. The Gov was dead.

To compound my misery and disillusionment, the very next customer to solicit my favors happened to be one of the white-uniformed and black-booted members of Android Control. It was the one time I felt only repugnance for my occupation, and in fact broke off the session midway, too nervous to continue. When Roland found out from the motel clerk, who had borne the brunt of the man's complaint, he threatened to turn me in himself if I ever "betrayed" his trust again. It was my obligation to accept all comers, even the AC, he insisted, which I thought most cruel and irrational of him, but by then that was to be expected. He was really becoming manic, up one moment, down the next, and liable to sudden whims and extremes, such as the night he blew my day's earnings, despite our desperate finances, on a dinner for two at Le Privilège, the exclusive beachside restaurant adjoining the Malibu Cove Hotel. Playing the big spender, we dined on irradiated kelp salad, roebuck casserole, sand dabs, spavined fowl, oysters, and for dessert, banana lunaire flambé, none of which agreed with me. I barely sipped my champagne while gazing gloomily at the still waters of Los Angeles Bay, trying not to think of Tad, who had drowned in it, or the Gov, who was no more, or Eva, who hated me, or my sad profession, which had brought me nothing but grief. An audible sigh escaped my lips at the thought that there were thousands of P9s at large who had been able to have children (according to the Gov's last communiqué), while I, who was in a better position than any of them, went without. Not to belabor the point, I asked Rollo about this curious discrepancy, seeing as how he was in an expansive mood; but my question effectively put an end to that. I should be thankful I was not burdened with the little monsters, he snapped; all they did was disrupt one's career, and mine was doing quite nicely. He reminded me that this was my preferred reality, so I could not blame him. Maybe I really did not want any children after all.

It was amazing how cruel he could be sometimes. What he said hurt, though I tried not to show it, knowing tears would only aggravate him, but he noticed anyway and after muttering some vile imprecation against me for spoiling his evening, condescended to say that if I still had my heart set on furthering the P9 cause he had a suggestion: Put in longer hours around the terminal and be more discriminating with my clients. My sights had been set too low—that was his expert diagnosis. The remedy was to curry favor with the commuters from the space-based office orbiters, to the exclusion of all others. If I did so, then the chances for conception would increase in direct proportion with my ability to penetrate their ranks; for, as a corollary to his original theorem of cross-fertilization, he claimed that there existed an indissoluble link between sexual potency and relative rank among the managerial class. I would have bought the idea if not for the feeling that he was secretly laughing at me and seemed to be hiding something, so while he steered the conversation back to vacationing in Armstrong, Ganymede, Saturn, and Mars, I decided to get a second opinion from Eva, whose friendship, I reckoned, might be easily rekindled with an undiluted token of my esteem.

This proved to be the case. "I thought you was hung up on ethical formats," she said after swallowing three dips at once. "Oh, I don't care much for that formatting business anymore," I replied. She laughed and said, "We's buddies again" and treated me to coffee and doughnuts in the terminal, extolling the potency and purity of my surprise gift while her eyeballs pinwheeled in opposite directions. In her enthusiasm, she said that she would make good her promise to take me to Malibu—"where the big money is"—as if she were ready to hop an airferry right then and there. She never would, I knew, as long as she remained beholden to Roland. Though she was destined for greater things, her dependence upon him as pimp and dealer forced her to settle for hustling trash, as she put it, for any attempt to go free-lance would be dangerous to life and limb. However, this check to her ambition only fueled her dreams of working outcall on that nearby but oh, so exclusive isle; specifically for Miss Pristine's, the most prestigious convenience-girl outfit on Earth. With the pills feeding her fancy, she lived more in that imaginary estate than in the Dodger District, although sometimes, when coming down, she would admit reality—"We're nothing but droids to him"—thereby puncturing any illusions I might have had that a matriculation from slave to master was possible once one became an entrepreneur, that course proving to be one of Roland's deliberate fictions.

Be that as it may, on this particular occasion she was charged with unfettered optimism (thanks to the dip I had given her) and prattled on about making five times as much mel per client in Malibu and buying a deluxe mobe-condo on the beach and a wardrobe of fine clothes and faces, and how the two of us would hobnob with the social elite. "And I'm not talking about the guys from the orbiter," she wanted me to know, drawing yet another distinction in the social hierarchy: "I'm talking about the folks who own the Goddamn orbiters and everything else: the Japanese." At which point I interrupted to sound her out about my little difficulty (oh, that it were little!), obliquely alluding to it by asking if perchance this better class of clientele were as superior in sexual potency as they were in power and influence.

She burst out laughing, which was as definitive an answer as I could want, and served to discredit Roland's theory completely. I was now bereft of all hope of becoming pregnant by any man, rich or poor. The fault, I decided, lay with me; there must be something fundamentally wrong with my system. I was certain Roland knew what it was. Why wouldn't he tell me?

Noticing my mood darken, Eva, in her attempt to be helpful, compounded my anguish by asking in all sincerity if I were hinting about being pregnant, in which case, with a flourish, she produced a package of abort tablets from out of her handbag. I declined, saying, no, no, that wasn't it. A true friend, she then offered me her brand of contraceptives, for if I was not pregnant, then I must be anxious about the effectiveness of the brand I used, otherwise, according to her logic, I would not have brought up the subject. "No, no, no. You misunderstand." She dropped the packet on my plate anyway, dislodging a half-eaten doughnut. "Orchidamines," she said. "Best on the market." And they could be mine in exchange for an equal number of undiluted orbs.

I was quite confounded by this proposal. It had not been my intention to encourage her habit beyond the few pills I had given her, hoping in my naïveté that she would be satisfied with my little gift. (I had even entertained ideas of reasoning her out of her habit altogether once back in her good graces.) While I searched for a diplomatic response, she praised the virtues of the Orchidamines, thinking my hesitation due to unfamiliarity with the product. They were much more reliable than the annuals such as Ladyease and Downtime, she said, and lasted five times as long. How could I go wrong? Five-year protection. You couldn't do better than that.

There was something familiar about the holopicture of the oval purple pill leaping off the surface of the package. My stomach turned over. "Thanks, but if I'm not mistaken I believe I have already had the pleasure." It was the "tranquilizer" Annette had given me per Roland's instructions nine and one-half months before. So that was it: The treachery had begun the very day he took me in. The monster had sterilized me for five years. He had stolen a quarter of my life!

"Eva, would you like to be rid of Roland?"

It was her turn to be taken aback. "Sure," she replied cautiously, not certain what I had in mind, and asked if he had been beating me, because, as she then revealed, he had beaten her plenty when she was his girl. I was quite surprised by that informa-

tion, not that he had mistreated her, but that they had been lovers.
(He wouldn't dare be violent with me, I thought. He knows I
could put him through the wall if he tried.) "Every six or seven
months he takes in a new waif. You're just the latest in a long line,
Candy. Hey, me and Rollo-baby go way back. After he put me to
work he kicked me out for Pauline, and then her for Sandy, and
then her for Christine. And on and on. Keeps us all in line with his
shitty dip. They're all like that. But Candy, whatever you're thinking of, I hope it doesn't mean that we'll lose our source. If it does,
then I'm not interested. And speaking of dip, are you going to give
me more or not? I mean, if ten pills"—the number of tablets in the
Orchidamines pouch—"if that's too much, I'll settle for half in exchange."

"Ten will be fine. Ten every day, Eva. And that will be just to
start."

She was so startled that her eyes actually came into focus.

"But first get me all the diluted pills he's given you."

Immediately she understood I intended to make a switch.
"Yes, ma'am!" We split up, Eva clattering down the sidewalk in
her orbitheels, rushing to her tenement five blocks away, while I
savored my brew, thinking of revenge; for if deceit and trickery
were the name of the game, then I, too, could play; certainly as
well as any master, in particular, him.

E I G H T

THE FIRST STEP IN MY BOLD SCHEME TO RUIN ROLAND
and gain my freedom, and Eva's, was to swap a few of her pills each
day for those filched from his private stash, which he kept under
the bed separate from those cut with talc for public consumption.
He did not notice the cheat at first, since the recycled street pills
made up only a small part of his daily dose. Then I began to expand the ruse, urging Eva to bring into the operation his other
girls, seven in all, for they were just as dependent upon him for
their daily fix as she, I said, and therefore equally deserving of
liberation. She immediately agreed to the proposal, but she recommended we recruit them one at a time so Roland would not be

inundated all at once with bad pop, which had been my plan all along. Thus, gradually, week by week, we added new members to the conspiracy, although none but Eva ever had any knowledge of where the excellent orbs came from; all they knew was that Eva, who was my point person, had a mysterious contact who in effect turned their lead into gold. Meanwhile, Roland, who couldn't figure out why his girls were suddenly all smiles, began to feel effects of a different kind—a diminished kick, as it were. Puzzled, he upped his dosage, each week purchasing more pills from his supplier to set aside for his personal use, which I surreptitiously cut, turning over the surplus datagrain to Eva, who recapsuled and redistributed it to the other girls as a kind of bonus, or so she said.

Things proceeded apace for a few more weeks, Roland purchasing ever larger quantities for himself, his habit increasing to fifteen pills per day—every one of which had either come back to him from the street or had been cut by me, until finally, as I had hoped, for this was the goal of all my machinations, he began to suspect that his supplier was cheating him and broke open several capsules—luckily, after I had had a chance to make the switch. "This shit's bad dip!" he exclaimed and stormed out in a rage, flying off in the Caddy for an impromptu meeting with the supplier, from which he returned bloodied and defeated, moaning, while I nursed his bruises, that he would have his revenge.

That proved idle talk, for his supplier, who had ties to the Armstrong Mafia, punished him further for his impertinence by deleting him from the drug pipeline, which precipitated his total humiliation. None of the other pimps and dealers would sell to him now that he was blacklisted, with the result that he was forced to go begging to his girls. They directed him to Eva, who was all too happy to loan him a supply of his own diluted product on credit, no mel down, and at twice the going rate, providing he agreed to forgo collecting his usual pimp fee, which he ranted and raved he would never do; but at the first signs of withdrawal, he reversed and humbly submitted to her terms. News of this remarkable and demeaning transaction spread quickly throughout the district, resulting in a complete loss of face, and literally so, as he was too devastated to remember to put it on some mornings; nevertheless, his former colleagues recognized him by his wobbly gait and pathetic displays of bravado, and so scorned and ridiculed him for his fall.

Having succeeded in my plan to destroy him utterly, I turned
my sights toward Malibu, thinking Eva would agree that the time
was never so propitious; for otherwise, if we stayed in the Dodger
District, the remainder of her stash would soon run out, ending
her domination of Roland, who would then fall by the wayside and
other pimps move in to demand our allegiance. Now we had
enough mel saved, thanks to Roland's inability to collect his share,
to make an easy transition; it would be the height of folly not to
take advantage of it.

But she was in no hurry. Little did I know, but during the time
I was wrecking Roland she was developing a very tidy little distribution operation on the side, starting with the excess pills I had
supplied her. She had not passed them on free of charge to the
other girls, as she had led me to believe. Rather, she had sold
them at the usual inflated prices and used her new reputation on
the street as a drug maven to hook up with Roland's supplier, who
had been looking for a replacement for the disgraced pimp. Thus,
I was appalled to learn that besides the locals and Roland's other
girls, her new accounts included high school and college students
from the suburban islands; she dealt to them inside the terminal.
In recognition of the key role I had played in facilitating this happy
transition from whore to pusher, she condescended to offer me a
piece of the action. I declined, saying I would stick to the former
and more honorable trade, and then tried to convince her to abandon this dangerous enterprise and accompany me to Malibu, for, if
the truth be known, I was afraid to strike out on my own, since my
knowledge of the world was limited to the few streets around the
terminal and Roland's apartment. But she was no longer interested
in hooking up with Miss Pristine's (a service she had once extolled
to the skies), and if the truth be known, was considering getting
out of the love consultation business altogether.

Devastated, I returned to the apartment and somberly reflected upon my folly, for in trying to right a wrong—Roland's
treachery against me and his oppression of Eva and the other
"girls"—I had spawned a new evil upon the unsuspecting world
and done myself precious little good in the bargain. By eliminating
one rotten apple, the contagion had simply spread to another in
the barrel—in this case Eva, who had supplanted the villain in the
orb trade. It was my first real taste of moral ambiguity, and I cannot say that it was to my liking. Equally unsavory was the second

logical consequence of my action, Roland's taking to muggings and break-ins to support his habit, which he casually mentioned when I asked him about a laser gun I had stumbled upon hidden in a dresser drawer. And the third effect, which I really could not stomach, was when Annette became a scapegoat for all his rage and frustration, the cycle of pain and misery let loose in the world having come full circle and returned home.

The coward. He was too wary of my P9 strength—and too dependent on the mel I still contributed from my earnings to pay the rent and keep the Caddy charged—to risk taking it out on me, for when I was around he didn't dare bother her. So he got in his licks while I was out on the street. One day I came home to find that her skin patina had been so badly bruised in places it had ruptured. "She had it coming," he said, which made me so upset I blurted out that he need look no farther than myself for the source of all his reversals. Then, warming to the subject, I detailed precisely how that was the case, and dared him to exact punishment.

He was so dumbfounded that had he not been human I should have thought him completely powered down; but he recovered—that is, he recovered control over his movements, not his sense, because the next thing I knew he was suddenly pummeling me with both fists and screaming that I was a dead droid. A quick shove put a stop to that. He hurtled backward and struck his head on the opposite wall. While he lay unconscious, I made a quick search of the apartment for the laser but could not find it, which meant he must have hidden it from me. Since I did not doubt he would use it on me the moment my back was turned in the days to come, I decided to move out. I went directly to Eva's apartment a few blocks away, taking Annette with me.

When I barged into her seventh-floor apartment in a run-down high-rise building and told her that I had left Roland, she hugged me like a sister. Of course, she would put me up. "No, no, no! We must flee, Eva. Now! For Malibu. Anywhere!" But she laughed at my fear that Roland might harm me, calling him a pitiful piece of debris, and reiterated her reluctance to quit the district now that she enjoyed such considerable power and prestige on the street. Sitting me down in the living room by an open terrace door, she had her male domestic serve us mints and liqueurs. After debating the relative merits of Cyberenes (her unit was one) and General Androids (Annette's brand), she got around to asking me once more to join her operation. One of her girls, a subdistributor, had been pinched in the terminal the other day, and she needed a replacement, preferably someone with a little more intelligence, someone like myself. Once more I declined, this time with a note of finality, for, as I said to her, if she would not go with me, then I was determined to strike out on my own, come what may. I stood up, motioning for Annette to follow, but at that moment the Caddy pulled up outside, gliding alongside the terrace railing, and Roland saw me. He put the car in hover and took aim with his laser.

This specter was so unexpected that in that moment all I could think was that he really shouldn't be flying the car within city limits, he'll get a ticket. Luckily, Eva pushed me aside an instant before the laser fired, and before he could get off another shot, tossed a portable m.c. at him. It caught him square on the chin just as he was standing up to get a better angle on me, and the impact threw him off balance so that he fell out of the car. We rushed to the railing and looked down. A pool of blood was spreading out around his head on the hard meshmetal sidewalk. "Oh, dear. Oh, dear."

Several witnesses stared at us from the windows of a building on the opposite side of the street. "It was self-defense!" Eva shouted. Then, realizing that when the police arrived there would be far too much explaining to do—what with her pills, life-style, and past history—she turned to me and declared, "Candy, we're fucked. Get in the Caddy," a recommendation I instantly obeyed while calling for Annette to follow suit. Eva grabbed her pocketbook, dips, and spare peelies, hopped in the pilot's seat, and a moment later we were headed for the bay.

"Well, I hope you're satisfied!" she said savagely, while piloting our craft toward Malibu. "Shit, Candy. I let you in the door and five seconds later you've screwed up my whole life! I can't believe it! Jump!"

"Eva! You're not serious!"

"Bet your hot ass I'm serious. Put on your jet pack. This is no time to play dumb. It's under the seat." She reached under her own and brought out a small, oblong-shaped canister attached to an emergency backpack and strapped it on. Finally I understood we were all going to bail out, and so followed her instructions, motioning for Annette in the backseat to do the same. "When I say jump, jump!"

"What about the car?" I asked.

"It's going to Hawaii." She jabbed the appropriate controls on the dashboard logistics display. "Decoy for the cops. Now, activate your jet pack." I did. "Okay, there it is, fucking Malibu. Jump!" So saying, she stood up and dove over the side. Don't ask me where I found the courage, but I did, and jumped after her, though not before ordering Annette to follow our example; otherwise she would have been content to fly to Hawaii.

My landing was anything but graceful, though it did draw considerable notice, as I crashed an exclusive afternoon garden party by flattening the awning over the drinks and hors d'oeuvre table, and my subsequent eviction by two IBM security units was accompanied by the imprecations of the host, who followed me out, railing against the cheek of the weekend tourists, whose impertinence and brazen disregard for the privacy of their betters was, by my example, getting completely out of hand. As for Eva, I saw her skimming over the treetops on the next hill and hallooed to her. She changed course and flew down to meet me on the hard cobblestones of the public pedway. She paused a minute to demonstrate the proper use of the tilt and toggle bars, and then we set off in search of Annette, locating her a few minutes later in a nearby wood, where she had been caught upside down in the branches of a large eucalyptus, that unit's expertise in maneuvering with a jet pack having been about on a par with my own.

After extricating her, our interesting trio continued to the beachfront in quest of hotel accommodations, mingling as we flew with the sightseers gliding above the boardwalk; but we abandoned that effort when Eva, to her dismay, realized that she had forgotten her purse in the Caddy. We fluttered to the beach, where Eva flopped upon the sand in a forlorn heap, weeping that in our haste we had also forgotten her spare peelies and worst of all her bag of dip, for now withdrawal stared her in the face. There was no need for despair, said I, we need only summon the necessary funds from our respective bank accounts, which would be more than enough to purchase dip from the local dealers and secure adequate accommodations. But the bank would only alert the police if we did, she grumbled. For all practical purposes our savings were gone. "Any suggestions?" I asked Annette, who immediately replied in that dry, understated manner common to all properly functioning units, "To acquire funds it is necessary to work." To which Eva exclaimed, "But I'm tired of being a whore!" I could almost hear the wheels turning in Annette's head. "With all due respect, my lady, according to my dictionary the two are not the same."—"A lot you know about it," she snapped, and then grimly announced that under the circumstances it behooved us, meaning she and I, to seek out the tender mercies of Miss Pristine's, which we located in a prominent beachside office spiral, coincidentally headquarters to Stellar Entertainment's Earthside marketing and promotion division.

Annette waited outside while we were conducted through a connecting corridor to the inner studio offices. (The receiving room for Miss Pristine's, which faced the street, was a front used only for meeting the occasional customer who dropped in, for most of their business was conducted over the phone.) We were interviewed by one Harry Boffo—yes, the very same master who, as you know if you read the trades, was eventually to move up to far better things at the main office in Hollymoon. At the time, however, he was the studio's Earthside Under Assistant Vice President of Public Relations, in which capacity his real duties involved procuring women and other amusements for influential people important to the interests of the company—a pimp by any other name, Roland, for instance, though that individual, despite all his other faults, had at least been honest about his occupation.

Eva was so fidgety while sitting in the waiting room that she made me nervous as well. I asked her to stop. "I'm worried about Roland," she whispered. "People have survived worse falls. I should have landed the car on top of him. You know, flattened the sucker." I tried to calm her fears, and my own, now that she had raised the disturbing possibility that he might have survived and someday come looking for us, by saying that he certainly looked terminated to me, and in any case her remedy was grotesque. I must have sounded convincing, because she did calm down somewhat, though that did not help when it came time for her interview. As Harry (he said I should call him Harry) later confided to me after rejecting her, my friend's carriage was overly broad and her personality more suitable to the street than to the exclusive bedrooms and hotel suites of Malibu. On the other hand, I was Miss Pristine's material, he was pleased to announce, and from then on he would be my "liaison."

Straightaway I was registered under the name Angelica and

ushered into a back room holo studio, where a Cyberene 9 Pho-toPro oversaw the production of what was to be my holo portfolio. I whispered my new sobriquet in extreme close-up, lips fairly drip-ping over its elongated syllables, then stripped naked to assume various seductive poses while discussing my personal likes and dis-likes (all of which I read from a TelePrompTer) and generally prom-ised the viewer the time of his life. "Your portfolio will be beamed to prospective clients when they call in," Harry explained after I had returned to his office. He awarded me a service necklace with a tiny phone button set in the pendant; it looked like an amethyst. He had no doubt my button would be ringing very soon. We shook hands, then he gave me a copy of the company's conduct code and a commissions schedule on the way out. And so began a larger and finer adventure, one that was to usher me into the realm of the true masters. My first priority, however, was to clean up my overweight, brash, and dipped-out friend so that she, too, might enjoy such good fortune, for it was inconceivable that I should abandon her.

I soon regretted my loyalty, because by the time I rejoined her—the interview and holo session had taken a good two hours—she was pacing up and down the boardwalk in a fury, the com-bined effects of her humiliating rejection (to a job she had not even wanted, no less!) and of the first signs of withdrawal—runny nose, itch, and sneezing fits—putting her in such ill humor that I wisely downplayed my good fortune to avoid provoking her, as she was nearly incoherent with rage over the extraordinary series of disasters that had befallen her in the space of a few hours, ever since I had the gall to knock on her door, and she the misfortune to answer it. "I've lost my business, dip, money, Cyberene, face, and pride!" When I tried to put her plight in perspective by point-ing out that things could be much worse, that in fact we could be in jail awaiting arraignment for murder, she retorted that with-drawal, which had suddenly attacked her in earnest, was worse, and that without any mel we were reduced to lousy debris. Then she was suddenly racked by severe muscle spasms, followed by the paranoid delusion that Roland, covered in blood, was strolling to-ward us on the boardwalk. Terrified, she retreated underneath, where we followed, and curled up on the sand in the fetal position. She shivered, retched, and in general carried on as if undergoing the tortures of the damned; yet was never so overcome by her inner furies that she forgot to curse me as the sole cause of her distress. "And don't give me no shit about preferred realities!"

"Perish the thought," said I.

"Just when I thought I had it made, too," she whined between spasms, and flung her philosophy at me, which the circumstances had wrenched out of her. Strictly determinist, it was that life is a matter of luck and timing and that is all; it does not matter what you do or do not do, because in the end you wind up just as dead.

What blessed relief when my necklace rang and I was called away for my first assignment! Before I left, though, I told Eva that I would return posthaste with enough mel to secure decent lodging and food for several days, so she should not despair; Annette would take care of her while I was gone. "And dip! Dip! Don't forget to get some dip! I need it!" she yelled as I lifted off. Later, while with my client, the contrast between the poverty and misery of our circumstances and the sumptuous elegance of his suite in the Malibu Cove Hotel, and his dignified behavior during and after our session, had such a strong impact on me that I was seriously tempted to apply my commission, which amounted to nearly three thousand mel, to a room in the hotel just for myself, and a decent meal besides, rather than return to Eva, who would squander it all on more pills. Had I escaped Roland to be strapped with yet another junkie? I asked myself. But honor won out, not to mention charity; I returned. Eva and Annette were not where I had left them under the boardwalk, however, and after flying up and down the beach for several miles in each direction, I failed to locate them by evening; and so to my surprise I was free and clear of Eva after all.

Freedom. It was as terrifying an ordeal as I had feared. Just checking into a travel court was an occasion for unbearable suspense. I had never signed my name before, so I could not leave a convincing signature in the book the Xerox night clerk handed me, nor had I the slightest idea of how to make out a mel voucher, and of course I lacked all the usual identification buttons. When I slapped all my hard-earned mel on the counter, the clerk airily replied that the management preferred payment by voucher with two pieces of identification, if I pleased. There was nothing to do, then, but collect my mel and leave in a huff, terrified all the while that he might consider my conduct peculiar enough to warrant notifying the AC.

The result was even worse at the next lodging, because in my haste to leave after blundering through another failed transaction I forgot to collect my money and was too wary to go back afterward and reclaim it. So I gave up and jet-packed into the hills, where I spent the night perched on a rocky knoll staring out to sea, too frightened to power down lest I be surprised by the AC or the police descending from the skies to apprehend me. Each time I did begin to slip into idle, a small noise among the chaparral or creaking of branches in the trees instantly brought me to my feet, prepared for flight. "Oh, I wish Eva were here," I said aloud, feeling infinitely alone. Or that my necklace would ring, because then I could at least replenish the store of mel I had foolishly lost. However, in the morning I discovered the jet pack empty due to a small leak that had escaped my notice the night before, and while walking down a wild and treacherous terrain of rocky promontories and sandy ravines I slipped and fell several times, ruining my dress, so that upon arrival back in civilization I looked dreadful, like one of the debris. I had no choice, then, but to decline sadly when my necklace rang, informing Harry over its phone that I was feeling ill; for, in truth, I doubted any client expecting a lady of Miss Pristine's quality to walk in the door would be inclined to admit so shabby a courtesan. Thus reduced, I set off down the boardwalk in a kind of fog, overwhelmed and distraught by my predicament. After a while I started to beg and scrounged up enough money to eat—barely, but not enough to buy new clothes or find anyplace better to sleep than back in the chaparral, since the police chased the debris from under the boardwalk each night. And I will spare you the details of all the unpleasant encounters I had in which my services were demanded free of charge by other riffraff as destitute as myself, and the time I was chased by a pack of dogs, and the time teenage boys threw refuse at me, and . . . Never mind. It was the worst, the absolute worst! This misery lasted one week and two days.

N I N E

"SUPPORT THE UNDERGROUND SKYWAY! END AC abuses!" shouted a thin, female human soliciting donations from the indifferent tourists on the boardwalk. She had stringy blond hair and wore a pair of open-toed flats and tights, and the multicolored rose, symbol of the High Aquarian faith, was emblazoned on her tunic. I would have embraced her as my savior had she not backed away, repulsed by my appearance. "You want to make a donation?" she asked, hoping to get rid of me, and thrust a three-volume set cassette spool at me like a shield. It was called *Overcoming Psychopediments to Your Format* and cost three hundred forty-nine mel. I confessed it quite appropriate but not within my means at present, which confirmed her opinion of me. "Could you kind of step aside, then?" she asked, barely polite. "You're blocking the tourists." (As if there were a line!) After checking to make sure there were no police or AC about, I confided that I was a runaway P9 and desperate for sanctuary. "Why didn't you say that in the first place?" she replied, looking upon me with sudden relief and concern. "Sure, I'll take you to our center, but first . . ." She took a universal product code reader out of her pocket and requested I stick out my left pinkie finger. "Just a formality, but we have to do it now. There have been too many debris trying to pass themselves off as runaways at the center. You know, they'll do anything to get a free lunch."

I withdrew my hand before she could put the reader on. "That won't be necessary, then," said I, knowing what the outcome would be. "Maybe you could direct me to the center anyway. Maybe they could give me a mind scan there. That will prove I am a—" "Not a chance," said she, stiffening and giving me a knowing and contemptuous look. She was not about to be fooled by the likes of me. I turned away quickly so not to be humiliated further and walked off. "Damn that Roland!" I muttered aloud. "Damn him!" I imagine she thought me as crazed as I was destitute. Then I had the idea of doubling back on the sly and tailing her when she left for her center in the hope there would be other Highs there more agreeable to my proposal, but no sooner had I stopped and started to turn around than I was distracted.

"Excuse me, ma'am. Could you spare a spot of mel for the Indian children?"

Imagine that, I thought, now someone is panhandling me! Annoyed, I shook my head no, then did a double take, for my solicitor was none other than Annette, who upon recognizing me curtseyed and said, "Hello, my lady," as she had been taught by Roland, and begged my pardon for her presumption. "Never mind that," said I. "Where is Eva?" In answer, she led me up a winding brick path to a shuttered house just above the commercial district, explaining along the way that they had been chased from the boardwalk three days before by beach security units. I said I was familiar with the practice.

By the sign in front of Eva's dilapidated residence, it was apparent that the structure (a rather fine example of late-twentieth-century ostentation-royal gone to seed) was slated for demolition to make way for a new convenience shopping plaza. We passed through a hole in the honeycombed remnants of the old cinder block retaining wall and entered the basement, where I found my wayward companion reposing upon the concrete as indifferent to my return as she was accommodating to my least suggestion. This was not as contradictory as it may sound, for by then she had entered the severest and most prolonged phase of dip withdrawal, which was (and still is) characterized by a lack of individual initiative, general passivity, and involuntary obedience to commands, otherwise known as Acquired Android Behavior, or in contemporary parlance, "the droids."

An astonishing reversal, this; she was absolute putty in my hands. (If only she had stayed that way! But I was so foolish as to save her.) She did everything I said without the slightest hesitation or argument, responding, "Yes, my lady" and "As you wish, my lady" to each and every one of my commands, the first of which was to secure us more suitable accommodations in town, as it was a simple affair for her to make out the standard voucher and sign the registry under a false name. The second assignment I gave her, once we were installed in a motel room and had a chance to shower, was to procure decent clothing for us by whatever device she thought necessary. The third was to lend me her jet pack, which I used to zip around the island from one lucrative session to another in the stunning new evening gown she had gotten me—I never asked how. (I had informed Harry that I was over my illness and eager for clients.) In time I was even able to persuade her to enter a Dippers Anonymous detoxification program, from which she returned two weeks later a new woman, proudly clutching her "Clear" certificate and espousing the virtues of "the three S's— Self-discipline, Self-reliance, and Self-esteem," fortified by regular weekly meetings she attended with fanatic regularity. She was physically transformed as well, slimmer (the fourth S), healthier, more relaxed and ladylike. Not even Harry Boffo recognized her when she reapplied at Miss Pristine's. In an aside, he complimented me on my improved taste in friends and then awarded her a necklace.

"Oh, Candy, it's a dream come true," she cooed outside his office, and even wore the necklace to sleep that night. Yes, along with her senses, she had also regained her dream of making it someday on Malibu as a topflight convenience girl. After her first "class session" she returned in such a state of rapture that we embraced in our shared happiness, for, as she put it, more could be made here in one night than in a week of dealing gram and whoring back in the Dodger District, and the clientele were infinitely superior. This new influx of wealth and prestige made her positively giddy, and I must say that I enjoyed it as much; for by pooling our earnings we were able in no time to scale the heights to a magnificent hilltop mobe-condo, fit for a queen; two queens, actually.

I shall never forget the thrill of picking out the components of our mobe in the real-estate office from their model displays and then watching the actual pieces assembled into place that same day by android workmen (all IBMs) according to our gloriously whimsical specifications. Just for fun, we had Annette curtsey for us as we strolled across the threshold arm in arm, then we proceeded through the spacious reception area, modern kitchen, bath, and dining and living rooms on the first floor, then up the spiral staircase to the master bedroom, den, game room, and guest bedroom above, capped by a ride in the bubble lift to the observation deck and landing pad for a breathtaking panoramic view of our new domain—from Lake Catastrophe in the north to, moving clockwise, Santa Monica, Hollywood, and Los Angeles Islands in the east, the bay in the south—caressed by the northern edge of Palos Verdes Island, and to the west the great floating city of New San Francisco, which lay at anchor a mile offshore, a phantasmagoric jewel in the limitless blue Pacific.

An Apple chef, Sony gardener, and Xerox security guard were included in the package, as were a pair of matching cherry red Mercedes (hers and hers). We selected the furnishings and artwork, lavishing vast sums on an antique grand piano, a half-dozen modern holo abstracts, stylish petalpeel spunglass furniture, and the latest in crystalbeam lighting; not to mention a rollotub, Fresca Household Climate Control System, and a deluxe Sylvania Media Console with interplanetary access. And when it came to the wardrobe—well, it just took one's breath away. Farewell epoxywool; hello Tortoni cotton; and our face collection came direct from Paris. (Eat your heart out, Lady Locke.) I readily succumbed to the whimsical pleasure of donning a different mask for each day of the week, or as they fit my mood, and so got used to wearing them whenever going out, in particular while with a client, in which case it felt appropriate to go incognito.

But the most prized possession of all was an authentic four-poster bed, constructed of actual teak and oak, with an Old World feather mattress—posture and articulation control included. It was heaven. Stretching out on it was so divine that it brought to a head a certain fondness that had been slowly building between us during the two months spent living in the same room at the travel court. Now the temptation was to give full reign to it. After all, we were bunkmates, so it was only proper to offer myself in the same fashion I had to my previous and much less deserving partner. I thought it might be a nice way to celebrate our first night in our new home.

She was taken aback at first but did nothing to reject my overtures, and so we became fast lovers, putting the articulation control to good use. Her generous breasts and plump thighs were a revelation as was her response to my every caress: I couldn't help feeling something far more sweet and genuine at play in our love-making than with any of my male clients. If only I could be pregnant by her, I thought while locked in her embrace, for I still yearned for that happiness above all others. Over the weeks that followed we became so intimate that I found it hard to resist telling her of my need and the larger truth about myself from which it sprang. This was particularly awkward for me when she freely confided so many things about her own past. (Were I to repeat them all they would make a book in their own right.) Yet I remained silent, afraid that my confessions might prove too harsh a shock for her and shatter our tender alliance, which I valued over Truth itself. You see, for the first time in my life I was living on an equal basis with a human being. When, as it happened from time to time, I stopped to consider the miserable deception that our beautiful relationship was founded upon, I would justify it as no more nor less objectionable an expedient than that found in most; a small technicality really, not worth the worry. And yet wasn't that technical difference as sharp as it was small? Was it not in fact the whole point and my world impaled upon it?

And so the days, weeks, months, and years slipped by in a life of genteel hypocrisy, the Dodger District becoming a distant memory never alluded to except in passing while reflecting upon our wealth and prestige, which we now took for granted. "Oh, Annette," I would say while Eva and I partook of a leisurely brunch in bed, "could you tell the Apple to fix more croissants, and then bring them here, please?" The discomfort over ordering her about had fallen by the wayside once I got used to being pampered and spoiled, and any pangs of guilt I had were overshadowed by my tremendous pride, which airily announced, "I am a P9 who in the face of tremendous adversity and hardship has made something of herself in the world, whereas the help are inferior products lacking the capacity even to imagine such an achievement." To each his or her own true level. I had found mine among the most elite of circles, where my art had been rendered more refined, dignified, and exalted by application of the golden rule of commercial success: It is not how you do it that counts, it is whom you do it to. There were no finer examples than Eva and I. We were caviar to palates gone stale and lusting for the exotic or a reprise of a youth gone by; two Cinderellas in orbitheels flying off at a moment's notice and at all hours to entertain at the best hotels, bungalows, and mobes on Malibu and Bel Air and New San Francisco, never fearing, when the clock struck twelve, a rude awakening in the Dodger District. For this new world was no pumpkin, the chimes of the necklace signaled the transition from one lucrative session to another, and the glass slipper fit Eva's foot. Life partners, we went everywhere together (when not on call)—concerts, plays, holomovies, art openings, and high society gatherings. At the latter Harry Boffo often would be there at the studio's behest to introduce us to visiting dignitaries, politicians, and other important personages, thereby enhancing our client list even more. Yes, it was the best, just the best, best, best of times.

No. Roland never put in a reappearance to spoil our ascent, and as for the High Aquarians, I knew they had a center somewhere on the island, but I never went there. Now that I was doing so well I was willing to concede that the Gov's philosophy worked after all—so well, in fact, that I didn't need them! Which is not to say that everything was perfect. Eva and I had our spats on occasion, but I could always console myself by shuttling to Paris, Moscow, Brasilia, New Sydney, Tokyo, Peking, and a half dozen other fashionable hot spots, either going alone, in which case I took Annette along as my lady-in-waiting and indulged my fancy in a day's shopping spree, or as the lady companion to one of my gentlemen retainers,* in which case I might stay a whole week, and at the best of hotels. (I could have gone to the moon or Mars if I wished, but interplanetary customs had a reputation for nabbing fugitive P9s, so I declined.) Speaking of my retainers, some were so enamored that they wanted to date me on a legitimate basis, which I politely forbade. There were two who even proposed marriage, the first out of love, the second as a matter of practical politics. My regrets in the first instance shattered that poor gentleman, a very powerful and influential Japanese corporate executive with Sensei, Inc., and at that time the company's representative on the TWAC security council. I am speaking of the future CEO, Frank Hirojones, a name that besides being an intriguing Americanized amalgam should also be of interest to my corporate literate readers, considering the prominent role his company has played on the interplanetary stage of late. Would it surprise you to know that back in '77 he used to fly in, incognito, from the TWAC orbiter every week for a magical afternoon of my charms? Remember his suicide attempt at the Malibu Cove Hotel—reported as an accidental overdose of tranquils? Well, that was because of me. Poor man. But he got over it eventually, and even continued to see me according to our usual schedule, being punctual to a T in all things, even his disappointment. He never once renewed discussion of the matter, continuing our relations on a cool and even plane as if to prove that I had not affected him. A strange individual. I think he would have been less accommodating had he known the rival for my heart was a lesbian, and the beloved object of his desire an android.

Now just wait until I tell you who my other paramour was. I guarantee a surprise. I am serious; you will have to wait, because first I must report that Master Hirojones and he were not the only ones disappointed in matrimony; when I asked Eva for her hand in life partnership she declined with the whimsical comment that it would ruin the charm of the relationship. I suspected, however, that her objections ran deeper than that. For instance, overt displays of affection were discouraged whenever we were in public, even though she wore a face. If I forgot myself and put an arm

---

*For those unfamiliar with the practice (the majority of my readers, I'm sure), retainers are clients under long-term contract with the agency, usually for the services of a favorite convenience girl.

around her or, Gov forbid, gave her an affectionate kiss, she
would abruptly turn away in embarrassment; which was curious, I
thought, because at home she was by far the more demonstrative
and aggressive, her inhibitions totally lacking before the servants.
For example, she took to ravishing me with strange antiquarian
marital aids strapped on during our lovemaking, and used to tease
me with a whip, saying, "Let's play master/slave, Candy." Guess
which part she picked. I accepted this quirk (or glitch, if you will),
in her nature, but in time I could not help wondering if it was
symptomatic of a more profound dysfunction, for this was a far cry
from our first tender embraces. Did she feel compelled to play the
dominatrix and to introduce increasingly bizarre paraphernalia in
bed because she was secretly disturbed and unhappy about our
relationship? Could it be, I wondered, that she missed a man so
much that she was driven to satirize the role? Of course, she
laughed uproariously when I put the latter question to her, taking
it as another one of my facetious witticisms; but I persisted, asking
in all seriousness if she hoped to wed one of her retainer clients.
    She was shocked. Give up her career when we were making so
much mel? My jealousy was as poignant as it was groundless and
absurd. Men were a necessary evil, she said; without them one
could not pay the rent (mortgage, actually). But she would never
violate our little love nest by inviting one home for dinner, nor
would she consider dating one on the outside. "Then are you just
tired of me and looking for another woman?" I meekly asked. She
replied that was the last thing on her mind, and the reason she was
shy in public was because, well, she didn't want people to talk
about us. "Why? Are we doing something wrong?" She said no,
but defensively. Then, in an attempt to change the subject, she
asked if I thought it might be a good idea to buy an IBM financial
consultant to help manage our sizable investments in stock, col-
lectibles, gems, fine art, Martian gold, and other precious metals
and commodities—a nearly full-time job to keep track of. "A
wedding ring would please me better," I said. "Oh, Candy, you're
so conventional," she chided, playfully cuffing me on the cheek,
which I let pass. I was not such a fool as to press the issue further
and risk jeopardizing our relationship. We most certainly were life
partners in spirit if not in law, I reasoned, and so we should remain. If it was important to her that our relations be kept secret
from the world, what hardship really did that cause me? Besides,

the deception was trivial compared to the one I played. By the fall of 2077, three years and eleven months after coming to Malibu and a few weeks shy of my fifth anniversary since taking Roland's Orchidamine, she still had no inkling of my true nature. Love is blind, is it not?

Unfortunately, bigotry and hatred are as well, a truism brought home to me in the most personal way when Eva's own prejudice was revealed to me one Sunday morning in early November while we lay lounging in bed idly watching the console while fishing eggshell bits out of the Apple's otherwise delicious omelet. Eva, as was her habit, was flipping channels when she happened to tune into an antiandroid rights speech by the Right Reverend Blaine Fracass on the Martian Broadcast Network. Mind, this was candidate Fracass speaking, the nominee of the Frontier Humanist Party and de facto head of the grass-roots Mars for Man movement, so there was very little mention of God's will but a whole lot about the liberal, prodroid, High Aquarian menace. He blamed the latter for the Android Code, when in fact it was the ARL that had conceived and promoted those timely and reasonable reforms, and ultimately got them passed by TWAC. He never did succeed in blocking passage of the code, but he did capitalize handily on the controversy by vilifying the Highs, who were the easier target—being a fringe, oddball, and difficult-to-comprehend phenomenon—rather than the ARL, who had numerous corporate supporters in the interplanetary community. In that way, this demagogue did succeed in frightening enough Frontiersmen into voting him into office. All this I mention by way of background, lest some of my readers forget there was a time when both the code and the humanists were new to the scene, and when Blaine Fracass was not, alas, a household word.

This particular speech, then, the first Eva had ever seen by the Reverend (though she had heard of him before, since he was a celebrity of sorts), was a general appeal to the interplanetary community for donations to his campaign, the pitch being that the code must be kept from the Earth and the moon as well as from Mars and that by supporting the Human Majority movement they were defending their own interests. To my dismay, she was extremely impressed, and not because he was cute, he was anything but; she liked his ideas! Good Gov, I nearly died. I could forgive her initial interest because he campaigned without a "face," a real novelty in those days. (He was the first politician in thirty-five years to forgo the formality, a shrewd move for an espoused humanist to make, since it enhanced his credibility in a field crowded with strikingly handsome and distinguished countenances, all as false as any mask hanging in our closet.) "Look at that!" she exclaimed, jabbing a finger into the outer periphery of the holo image, snagging his bulbous nose and squinty eyes. "He's bald and ugly and he's running for President. Unbelievable!" Yes, even I had to express a grudging admiration there. But when she nodded her head sagely after listening to his rank falsehoods and outrageous distortions and said, "Man's talking sense," I found that unforgivable. "Can humans really be that ill informed," I wondered, and then decided that the time had come to tell her certain intimate details of a sordid nature that I was privy to concerning this pillar of the community, with the hope that information would dissuade her from this sudden infatuation.

Yes, you guessed right, clever reader. The good reverend was the second retainer client I alluded to who proposed marriage. As to how events so transpired to bring us together and why a formal union was in his interests, you shall still have to wait, because Eva, who hung on every word of his sermon, would not allow me to interrupt. Yet it was crucial that I disabuse her of such a bigoted, xenophobic, and reactionary ideology; for here was a far worse threat to our relationship than petty jealousy on my part. And speaking of programming your life format, it could not have come at a worse time, for I was determined to become pregnant by whatever client might happen to do the trick once the last trace of the Orchidamine left my system, which by my calculations would have been in a few weeks. My dream was for Eva and me to settle down and have a family, much like Tad had wanted to. That I had put off apprising her of this monumental decision was due to that same inhibition that, before, had blocked an honest declaration of my actual pedigree, but could not out of necessity be sustained much longer. In truth, I had planned to prepare her by degree over the next few months for the happy day when I could declare myself carrying a semi; however, in light of this latest bombshell, I was faced with the task of overcoming not only her personal prejudice but also an entire political ideology constructed around it, and that constituted a far more formidable foe.

"Ladies and gentlemasters, some facts," declared my retainer on the holoscreen. "Number one: There are at present nine hundred ninety-nine thousand P9s still at large . . ." (Not so! The Gov said only a few thousand and that was years before.) ". . . aided and abetted by five hundred thousand seventy-three misguided humans, all of them High Aquarians." (Impossible! Even in their heyday there were only about fifty thousand Highs.) "Fact number two: Because these degenerates are engaged in interspecies sex, estimates now run as high as seven million semihuman births in the five years since the insurrection." (Another outrageous exaggeration. I only wish it had been so!) "If this keeps up, people, we're going to have to change our name to the Human Minority—unless something is done NOW to stop them.

"Fact number three: Most people are unaware of facts number one and two because TWAC is not letting the truth out. Why? Because the liberal corporations on the council are pushing the Android Code so they can make trillions on unit modifications and expand their power over the consumer." (Nonsense! The reforms were modest proposals for eliminating the worst of owner abuses, and the only reason TWAC went along with it was because they thought that in the long run it would stabilize the master-slave relationship.)

"Now the ARL says there never would have been a rebellion if a code like this had been in effect five years ago. They say it was the users' fault." He chuckled, and the live audience in the Frontier Crystal Tabernacle Humanist Church in downtown Commerce, Frontier, chuckled with him. "Think a minute. Are you about to 'abuse' a unit you paid a million mel for? I'm not; you're not. We're going to keep that baby in good shape, right? We're going to protect it, provide for it, give it proper maintenance and care, and do unto it as you would do unto your own self, it's that important to you. Am I right!" Thunderous agreement. "So what the ARL is really talking about when they say 'abuse' is discipline, 'cause what this code does is remove your unit—a unit you bought and paid for—from your control. That's the same as a thief breaking into your mobe and stealing your property. Tell me it's different!"

"He's right," Eva announced. "We've got to protect Annette."

"Let me read you something from this thing." He paused to locate the selected passage from the bookspool in his hands.

"Okay. Here's something they slipped in on page three hundred forty-nine—yeah, it's got a lot of pages, lot of regulations. Says here under 'Accommodations,' and I quote, 'A minimum 144 square feet private living space, fully enclosed, insulated, lighted, and heated, no farther removed from owner's dwelling place than a maximum of twenty-five yards shall be provided by owner on a per-unit basis.' Per-unit basis. That means if you don't have it, then you either spend a small fortune on an addition to your home or office or you go without the unit. They're messing with your economic livelihood, people! And it says here that you have to provide a bed for the damn thing. Now, my house units sleep on cots, and I'll bet yours do, too. The code passes and we're all in violation."

He shook his head and sighed over the grim absurdity of it all. "Now, here's a seventy-two-page section on discipline. The gist of it is, you can't, because there are so many safeguards against owner abuse that if you so much as forget to say *gesundheit!* when your unit sneezes, you're in violation. And in the entire five hundred thirty-six pages of this incredible document there is not one—*not one*—reference made to the owner's right to defend himself against a runaway unit, either his own, if it suddenly malfunctions and turns on him—happens all the time, doesn't it?" (It does not!) "Or someone else's, or what your rights are if a unit breaks into your home. Not one word about that! But the worst is Article Nineteen under the section 'Right to Privacy, Leisure, and the Pursuit of Independent Interests.' Oh, yes, you heard right: leisure time for androids. It's in there. You can only work them for so many hours per day, I think it's sixteen, and the rest of the time they can take a dip in your rollo-tub, watch holos, read bookspools, get an education, conspire to take over—hey, I'm telling it to you straight! Next thing you know they'll be demanding a minimum wage. Don't laugh, it's coming. But Reverend Fracass, most units have internal governors, you say, so how can they possibly take advantage of such a provision? Well, if this thing goes through, then the manufacturers will be forced to modify that safeguard; otherwise they, too, will be in violation.

"Now, you have got to ask yourself who benefits from this code if it passes. Not you and me, the consumer; and not the product, our units—they have not been programmed to handle freedom. Those who will benefit are the forces of anarchy and corruption: the ARL, the High Aquarians, fugitive P9s, and the orb dealers: the Four Horsemen of the Apocalypse. But we will not be frightened into submission. Rise up with me as one when I say 'In the name of humanity it is time to put a stop to this madness!'" (A camera angle on the flushed and aroused congregation showed half were on their feet.) "Rise up with me . . ." (The other half obeyed.) "Rise up with me when I say to the ARL, who wrote this code for the High Aquarians and their fugitive droids and for the orb dealers who finance their operations, rise up with me now and say unto them, 'In the name of humanity you are forgetting one thing!'"

"IN THE NAME OF HUMANITY YOU ARE FORGET-TING ONE THING!" they echoed, five hundred voices strong.

"You are forgetting fact number four: Androids are commodities."

"ANDROIDS ARE COMMODITIES!"

"Will you help me remind them? Will you help Frontier stay code-free?" ("YES!" they roared back.) "God love you, people! With your support we can guarantee that the Human Majority will triumph, not only on Mars, but also on the moon and Earth and all the orbiters in between. You've got the power! You've got the power! So are you going to let that traitor—that scum—Alexander Seti steal your solar system?"

Their resounding *"NO!"* was deafening. The floor of the Tabernacle Church must have been shaking because the holo image vibrated and swayed. Then, on cue, they fell silent when Reverend Fracass motioned with his hands to settle down and hear his further ruminations on the subject.

"Now, I get mad every time I think of that man. You know ol' Alex Seti, don't you? Big Chief Aquarian, although they say they don't have no chiefs. He's the High who designed Pirouet's Universal Bummer System." (Laughter.) "Don't laugh, 'cause the man got away with it. ARL got him off in that big corporate sabotage trial few years back. You know, when United Systems tried to put him away for single-handedly ruining the best product on the market—the P9."

(Goodness! So Tad was right when he speculated that the Highs were behind the subversion of Pirouet's Universal Governor. That meant this Alexander Seti was father to the Gov and ultimately the one responsible for my liberation—that is, if one could believe Blaine Fracass.)

"The man admits that he deliberately programmed High principles into Pirouet's governor system and still isn't convicted. Technicalities. Technicalities! Like all the people who have become addicted to datapills, and the hundreds of thousands who have died since that diabolical system was introduced to the marketplace. Flesh-and-blood human beings! Gone! Just technicalities. Didn't know that the Highs are the biggest orb pushers in the galaxy, did you? Well, it's a fact."

That really affected Eva. She turned to me and said that she had heard as much at the detox meetings, though people there say it is the droids that are responsible for the dip epidemic. "But Eva, androids don't deal datapills, people do."

"Right. The Highs, like the Reverend says. It makes sense they'd be behind it."

"Now, if Alexander Seti and the High Aquarians get their way with this code—" The Reverend paused to mop his brow and upper lip with a suctionwipe.

"I thought he said it was the ARL who were behind the code," said I, pointing out an obvious inconsistency in her idol's argument; to which she replied, "Same difference," and motioned for me to be quiet.

"And if they establish Horizon, like they're trying to do—and they're trying to do that right here on Mars—then they'll set up the biggest damn illegal datapill manufacturing center in the whole universe and pretty soon half the human race will have the droids! But I suppose TWAC won't mind—just another small technicality, you know."

He concluded by asking for donations: five hundred—five thousand—fifty thousand mel, whatever the viewer could spare to save mankind. Anything would be appreciated, even a small one-thousand-mel donation. Eva leaped off the bed, saying she was going to dash off a spoolcheck, at which point I insisted she hear me out, and I proceeded to undeceive her. "You heard the rumors about him, haven't you?"

"What? Is he gay?" she quipped.

"As a matter of fact, yes." I was startled by her happy guess. She shrugged, said more power to him then. So I added, "But in a way that might surprise you. His lover is his manservant. Eva, Reverend Fracass is a droid-fucker." It was unfortunate I had to play to her prejudice in order to wean her from this insidious ideology, but there was no help for it.

"You're lying. He's no fagoid." To prove it she dug out a gossip magspool from a pile lying beside the bed, popped it into the console, and verbally instructed the mag to produce the Fracass article. A holofeature appeared called "A Malibu-Mars Affair," showing the man in question photographed in the company of a rich young Malibu socialite—a stunning redhead—whom rumor had it he was planning to marry in the near future, perhaps even before the election. Supposedly this proved I was way off base.

"Eva, that's me."

To prove it, because she laughed as usual, I took the socialite's face and wig out of the closet, where it was stored with the rest of my collection. That sobered her. She listened in mute astonishment as I explained that Blaine Fracass had been one of my retainers for the past three months, ever since Harry had picked me for the highly confidential assignment of acting as his handy rumor deflector. Whenever this charismatic leader made one of his frequent fund-raising trips to Earth, it was my job to be seen in his company. The charade, which included spending the night with him at his cottage-bungalow at the Malibu Cove—where he stayed whenever Earthside—was designed to allay the public back home who felt uneasy about a bachelor running for office—and there *were* rumors about his preferences.

"I don't know about this," Eva said, suspicious. She thought I might be pulling her leg. (As you do, perhaps. I remind you, this is a scrupulously honest account.) "How come he went to Miss Pristine's?" Because the risk of exposure would be greater had he used a local convenience-girl outfit on Mars. "Who referred him?" Harry wouldn't say, I told her, and that was the truth; but I suspected mob connections and said as much; perhaps it went as high as Micki Dee. Blaine had told me the Armstrong Mafia had connections to Stellar Entertainment, and it was they who had referred him to Harry. "Yeah? But why would he resort to a convenience-girl outfit to begin with? Why not date a real debutante?"

"Because he could never get away with what he does behind closed doors with anyone else," I explained. Why had I kept all this secret from her? Because I was afraid she would think I was serious about the guy. Such fears, however, proved groundless. She quickly dismissed them, impatient for more dirt about her fallen idol. A cunning look had entered her eye. "Oh, this is a scorcher, Candy. A scorcher! We're sitting on a gold mine. He really fucks his droid?" I nodded. "Disgusting."

"His name is Andro. He's a very nice P9. Blaine adores him. He plans to program him for Chief of Staff if he becomes President of Frontier."

"My, my." Eva hummed with a little smile while deleting the spoolcheck she had been about to fire off to his 800 interplanetary number. "Is there no one left with any integrity in this galaxy?" And then, "He should be sending us checks, you know? I mean, you *have* seen him doing it with this Andro, right?"

Glumly, I nodded. The truth was I felt just as violated each time this rabid humanist, whose person epitomized everything I feared and loathed in this world, commanded poor Andro to indulge his vice. Were the man an Aquarian, the act would have been benign—divine, even—rather than the pathetic and cruel exercise in humiliation and depravity he made it. But that was only the half of it. Before I could give her the whole picture of what went on behind closed doors, she wanted to know if there was any truth, then, to the marriage rumors.

I replied that he had indeed proposed a marriage of convenience so we might continue the farce on Frontier as man and wife. According to his strategists the match would considerably enhance his standing in the polls. However, I had declined partly out of loyalty to her, for I was content with the happiness I had found in her arms. (The other reason was that besides the fact that I found his person and his politics repulsive, he had insisted upon my conversion to humanism as a prerequisite to marriage, and that I would never submit to, even in the case of such a bogus arrangement. But I didn't mention that to her, just the first part.)

She was flattered and forever thankful for my loyalty, but couldn't help thinking me a bit of a fool as well, because, as she put it, practically speaking there was no reason why we could not continue our relations under this new arrangement, even if we were to relocate to Mars should the humanists win and I become First Lady. Think of it—we had nothing to lose and quite a lot to gain. She was surprised at me, for if I had learned anything while under her tutelage it was how to recognize opportunity when it knocked. Why, if she had been in my shoes, she would have jumped at the offer.

"Perhaps not," I replied. "I hesitate telling you this, considering your strong feelings against interspecies sex, but he likes to watch as well."

"Oh. You mean you and—the droid?" That cooled her fire. "Poor Candy. It must be very difficult for you." She was all sympathy. Then she started to think about it, putting everything in perspective once more, and returned to her former position, enthusiasm rekindled. "Hell, I'd screw a porcupine if the price were right! And it is: This guy's the big megillah we've been waiting for!"

I reminded her that I was the one who would have to sleep with Andro, not her, though in truth that was the only bearable part of the sessions. (But of course I did not tell her that, nor how strange, sad, wondrous, and, yes, even satisfying it was to make love to a fellow unit, even while under the master's lecherous eye, a unit whom I suspected was more conscious than he pretended.)

"All right, I tell you what. Next time he calls, I'll go in your face. Doesn't matter which one of us plays the fiancée, does it?"

I said her scheme would not work because as a security precaution I must remove my face whenever we are alone. It is his way of making sure political rivals haven't substituted a plant. She acknowledged that that was a serious obstacle and quickly shifted to another tack, playing down the repugnance she felt, and believed I shared, over having sex with "one of those" by trying to cajole me into agreeing that it was really very much like with a human, or so she had heard.

Trying not to gag on the irony, I admitted this was the case.

Then I should marry him, she said, because the "ordeal" would not last very long, only during the courtship and engagement period; afterward, once married, I would be in a position to refuse to sleep with this Andro. If Fracass objected to that, and to our love affair should he get wind of it, or if we should decide to flaunt it openly while in his presence—why not?—then we could keep him in line by threatening to expose him.

Blackmail did not agree with me, however, and I said as much, and I reminded her that I had already turned down his proposal. (The excuse I had given him was that I was reluctant to convert from Catholicism. The old convent inputs had come in handy on that occasion, as I was able to refer convincingly to my catechism.) Eva's response was practical as always. "A lady is entitled to change her mind, yes?" But I disagreed, saying that in this case the lady would remain consistent, because she feared her friend's bold plan too ambitious and greedy, and that it would end in ruination.

She argued that we did have a good life in Malibu, for which she was forever grateful, but one must look ahead and not become caught in a rut. Besides, we were too close to our old stomping grounds in the Dodger District for comfort, and our mobe, current occupation, and the entire Malibu scene, marvelous as it was, were beginning to bore her. "Would it not be preferable to be genuine ladies of leisure rather than of convenience? Think of it. In Commerce we will have more time for each other. No more ringing amethysts in the middle of the night to interrupt our pleasure."

I hadn't thought of it that way, I confessed, but still was hesitant. However, over the course of the next week or so she brought me around finally, having convinced me that my fears of disaster were as groundless as those that she was unfaithful, and she said that I would always be first and foremost in her heart. I must confess that the thought also crossed my mind that the intriguing Martian triangle she proposed provided an opportunity for me to enjoy the best of both worlds, the human and the android, if I should decide to continue relations with Andro after marriage to the humanist. But at the time I considered that only a passing fancy, for it was Eva I loved.

Accordingly, I called Harry to notify him of my change of heart so that he could instantly relay that information to the client, who was away on Mars at the time. Harry, by the way, was fully aware and extremely supportive of Blaine Fracass's proposal, being a party to the ruse, perhaps even the one to suggest it, considering how much mel he stood to gain, since the marriage would in effect be nothing more than an indefinite extension of my retainer contract. Minutes later, he called back to notify me that Blaine was flying in on an express spaceliner and would be in Malibu the following morning, at which time he would announce our engagement to the press and then escort me back to Mars for the wedding. Eva, who was surreptitiously listening in on her wristphone, whispered that she would either book passage on the same flight out or follow soon after. I winked conspiratorially. Harry said he was going to miss me, I was his best con girl (Eva pretended insult, screwing up her mouth in a nasty pout). Then, as a last favor, he asked me to take a job at the Malibu Cove. Naturally, I said I would and after receiving the client's number phoned him in advance, as was the custom, to ascertain his address and desires, doing so in a lighthearted manner because this would be my final assignment.

He requested a two-girl special, so Eva offered to go along, quipping on the flight over that it was fitting our last session be a double, as had our first. She had brought a champagne bottle to celebrate because, as she put it, soon we would have Blaine Fracass and all of Mars wrapped around our little finger. She popped the cork, and it soared out the sun deck. "After tonight, Candy, we'll never have to work again, just milk the old Martian droid-fucker for all he's worth." She laughed. What the hell; I laughed. We drank champagne from the bottle and were both a little silly by the time we reached the hotel.

T E N

I WAS SO GIDDY THAT I ALMOST FORGOT TO SLIP ON the tart peelie I had brought along (flair cheekbones and pennylips, now quite passé), doing so only at the last second just before being admitted by the client, who was either wearing a face himself or really did look like a Cordoba aircar salesman. He was in a state of suppressed hyperexcitement, all nerves and desire— they usually were. Normally that would elicit a corresponding response on my own part, but on that particular evening all I felt was a terrible impatience to get it over and done with, which was shared by Eva, who quipped, "Hi, hon, hope it's a quickie. Got a cake in the oven."

Not amused, he replied that he specifically requested an hour. That Eva, she was really something sometimes. She just kind of took over, hooking an arm in his and walking him to the bed while proffering the champagne bottle. "What's the celebration about?" he asked grimly, resisting a little. "Interplanetary humanism," she replied, her tone suddenly very somber and serious, mocking his own. Then she ordered the room unit, a Sony (in lesser hotels they're Sears), to do us the honors and pour everyone a round of drinks. Yes, he said, he would drink to that. "To victory on

Mars," Eva declared after we had been served. We clinked glasses. "Terminate the runaways," he added, and Eva good-naturedly echoed the toast. I hesitated, until I felt his eyes boring into me. Then I thought it prudent to mimic his words, downing my drink immediately thereafter in one gulp. I undid my hair—it had been up in a bun—and let it fall about my shoulders, signaling the start of business.

There was something creepy about his eyes; I couldn't stand him looking at me. "Lights out," I said. (The hotel had a verbally activated lighting system.) "Close," Eva said, and the door automatically shut. (That, too.) We slipped out of our orbitheels and dresses, snuggled up, and began peeling his velcro in the dark. Of course he melted at our touch, and within minutes we were at it on the bed, but my anxiety about him seemed to intensify whenever his attention turned in my direction, which was most of the time, as he seemed to prefer me. There was something vaguely familiar about his broad, fleshy paws, the way they caressed in broad, even strokes, like I were a piece of highly polished merchandise. He began to whisper that I was smooth, hot, lovely, perfection itself, a goddess; and with his lips to my ear said, "Now roll over."

"Yes, Master Locke," I replied, an ancient memory loop playing.

He froze. I froze. "Light!" he commanded and the light fixtures obliged. The next thing I knew my peelie was ripped off.

"Molly?" We gaped at one another, too astounded to move. In the six years that had passed since he dumped me at Hal's Pirouet he had put on weight and turned gray in places, but otherwise the body was still recognizable, if not the face. I could tell, as his eyes roamed over my body, that he had even less trouble confirming his suspicions. Meanwhile, Eva looked from him to me and back again. "You know this guy?"

Of course I denied it, but too late; I had already betrayed myself. Yet I stubbornly insisted that he had mistaken me for someone else, that my name was Angelica, and that we had never met; all the while, I searched the tangled bedsheets for my dress and underwear, thinking only of flight. When I found my dress and made a move toward the door, he sprang from the bed and grabbed a snub-nosed laser from a night table. Then he commanded me to get down on my knees and motioned for Eva to do the same, having decided she, too, must be a fugitive android, my partner in deceit and crime.

"No, it's not a peelie or a mold, Molly," said he, gesturing to his face. "This is permanent." He tugged on the jawline of his face with his free hand. "I had to have cosmetic surgery because of you. You destroyed my reputation." His chest heaved and his voice trembled with excitement, as did his hand; I hoped not his trigger finger.

"Mister, we've never seen you before," Eva said. "Give us a break. Put that beamer away."

"Shut up." It would be his pleasure to turn her over to the AC, he said; that is, after he was finished terminating me. As owner, he enjoyed that prerogative. For my edification, he explained I was still technically his property, since I had been given to Hal's Pirouet on a consignment basis and the dealer had failed to make a permanent sale before I escaped.

Again, I said that he was making a very big mistake and joined Eva in urging him to put the gun away. "Yeah," said Eva. "Have some more champagne. Why spoil the party over a silly misunderstanding?" He refused, of course, and said that he had sensed something queer about us the moment we came in. There had been an undercurrent of mockery in our celebration inconsistent with a real born-again humanist like himself, an irreverence and disrespect typical of the runaway mentality. Fortunately, it was his habit to pack a laser in case any of our ilk should cross his path.

Angling for a way out, Eva said that despite her irreverence she, too, was of his persuasion, but he cut her off with a derisive laugh, commenting that these days even the whores were counterfeit. "When I am finished with you I shall have to report Miss Pristine's to the Better Business Bureau for engaging in deceptive advertising, and for harboring runaway P9s."

The double insult to species and profession was too much for Eva to bear. "Aw, stow it. I bet you're an old droid-fucker from way back."

An inspired guess.

"So you've told her about me, eh, Molly?"

"I told her nothing because there is nothing to tell. I am not a P9."

"You are exactly the same as when I knew you back in New-acres, only now you have been programmed to lie."

I held up my left hand, pinkie extended, and urged him to test his conviction with a reader, which his room unit could fetch from the desk downstairs if he didn't carry one himself. Smiling, he retorted that units clever enough to elude capture for so long must have devised a method for circumventing such telltale markings, and claimed that a mind scan would show a far different story. "Right!" Eva said, embracing that idea. She challenged him to call the AC, as he said he would. "We'll be happy to submit to their tests."

Speak for yourself, I thought.

"I *will* call the AC," he announced, then added with a mean smile, "They can pick up the pieces."

"Look, you've made a mistake. Candy only looks like this Molly you once knew. It's been a long time, right? Your memory's playing tricks on you."

"Mine isn't, but yours is. She said her name was Angelica over the phone."

"Oh, that's just my con-girl name," I said to be helpful.

"Then Angelica and Candy are both aliases. Your real name, your slave name, is Molly—has been since the day I took you out of your box."

"You're in orbit, mister," Eva muttered.

"Am I? Then how do you explain the fact that she knows my name? I have yet to introduce myself. Remember what she said when the lights were out? 'Yes, Master Locke.'"

"He told me to, Eva. He whispered in my ear that I should say that because it turned him on. So I did and the next thing I know he's ripping my peelie off and calling me Molly. He's crazy."

He chuckled at this desperate maneuver, but happily Eva was deceived. "Look. If it's worth anything to you, I can vouch for Candy—I mean, Angelica. She's not the fugitive droid you're looking for; I've known her too long."

"I'm sure, ever since the insurrection. I wouldn't be surprised if you both came from Hal's Pirouet. What a devious but fitting idea to masquerade as prostitutes. God knows how many innocent humans you have infected with your fungus, and all the vile semis you must have brought into the world for your Gov. I admit that at one time I was among your victims, Molly. As a matter of fact, I was the first. But I have been cured of that vice and purged of all corruption, while so many walk the streets unaware of their affliction, their blood and minds tainted, turned pink with contagion. My son among them. Oh, yes, I'm sure the two of you have shared many laughs over Thaddeus's moral disintegration. Don't pretend you don't remember him, Molly, or have forgotten the debt you owe him. I'm here to collect. He almost drowned because of you."

"Tad," I thought, with a sudden jolt; memories of our nights on the living-room couch and of our ordeal at sea returned with unexpected force. Tad is alive?! It was all I could do to keep from blurting it out.

"Yes, you remember him, don't you? The little fool lost his head completely, said he was in love. Ran away from home with the brilliant idea of marrying you to legitimize his droid bastard—the semi you bore at Hal's. Thank God you were separated during the escape so I was spared that humiliation. Yes, he survived. Bet you're disappointed. He washed up more dead than alive. They got him to a hospital in time. Revived by a pulse generator. I thought the fiasco taught him a lesson, but"—a pained smile—"one year of law management school and he dropped out to join some cockamamy High Aquarian sect on the moon. Probably has a dozen semis to his credit by now. I can't find him. My ex-wife can't find him—and with all the melbucks she's got thanks to the divorce settlement, she damn well should have by now. The army of private detectives she hired has searched every ARL and Aquarian hangout from here to Uranus and they still can't find him! And it's all your fault."

"As a fellow human, I share your concern," said I.

"Let me tell you about your friend here," he said to Eva, ignoring my comment. "You may not know this, but she's one of the original rehab babies, and a shrewder piece of work there never was. Wrecked my marriage, my reputation, and my career." With that prelude, he embarked upon his tale of woe, which we endured while still naked and down on our knees. We heard a depressing account of how his marriage, already on shaky ground after being caught with me, ended in divorce when he was surprised *in flagrante delicto* with SQ, that event secretly recorded on tape by Lady Locke and used as evidence in court to prove his moral turpitude during the custody battle for the children, which in becoming part of the public record resulted in his being passed over for promotion at work, his position downgraded and then phased out entirely. Not only that, he lost his membership in the

Newacres Country Club, listing in the *Social Register,* and, the ultimate irony, was booted out of the Android Appreciation Society.
To compound his misfortune, an executive transfer counseling service convinced him to squander vast sums on cosmetic surgery in a
misguided effort to erase his shame permanently, and subsequent
to that fiasco, he fell behind on child support and alimony payments, triggering a successful lawsuit by his ex-wife to collect
them, plus damages, which he appealed and lost. He tried to win
compensation from Pirouet by joining a class action suit against
United Systems, Inc., the parent company, for "gross negligence;
to whit, the willful and deliberate marketing of sexually promis-
cuous product," but the suit was ultimately laughed out of court.
Having exhausted all recourse, he wound up bouncing from one
lousy no-class job to another until finally accepting public assistance.

But there was a happy ending to this tale, he announced,
brightening. (Good, thought I, for my knees were beginning to
ache. Talk about captive audiences!) One day, while considering
suicide, he was touched and transformed by a Blaine Fracass sermon, which opened his eyes to the truth: it was the fungus, not
himself, who was responsible for all his misfortune. In the two
years since, he has been on the road back from oblivion, the God
of man shining through to guide him every step of the way. (I
couldn't help feeling a bit envious. The Gov had never done the
same for me.) Now that he was remastered, he had a new and
respectable life to go with his new face, plenty of mel, and a position of trust with the humanist church. He was the Southwestern
Regional Director of the Campaign to Stop the Android Code, in
which capacity he had recently been granted a six-month leave of
absence to help the Fracass campaign for President of Frontier. In
fact, he was scheduled to depart for Mars in the morning. (In a
somewhat defensive aside, he explained that he had decided to
treat himself to a two-girl special as a parting gift. "Just because
one is a humanist does not mean one can't be human on occasion.") For him, the move signified the end of one episode and the
start of a new and more promising chapter; yet never in his wildest
dreams did he think Providence would be so kind as to deliver me
up for retribution at this juncture; however, that being the case, it
would be a crime not to take advantage of the occasion. "The

Lord means for me to finish old business before moving on." So saying, he aimed the laser at my head. "Good-bye, Molly."

The door was too far to run to. Paralysis set in. All I could think was that this was it; destroyed at the tender age of six by my original and now deranged master. If there was a life after termination, then the Gov would have a lot to answer for.

"OFF!" Eva shouted, and the light fixtures obliged, plunging the room into darkness. A laserburst lit the air. It passed within an inch of my head. Then Eva tackled him at the waist, her bold action illuminated by the wild, staccato bursts of laser fire that pierced the ceiling as he tumbled over backward. Someone shrieked on the floor above; whether in fright or because they had been hit we never knew, nor cared to ponder as Master yelled for the lights to go on. We dashed to the door screaming "Open!" in unison, forgetting in our haste that the lock responded only to a verbal cue known by the occupant. Stunned by the impact, Eva staggered back into the room and would have tripped over him, as he was down on all fours searching for the beamer, had I not grabbed her arm and pulled her away. Then I summoned up the full reserve of my P9 strength and rammed my shoulder into the door, splitting it down the middle like an old wooden crate. We tumbled into the hall and dove into the bubblelift, jumped out at the rooftop parking lot, and collided with a group of Legionnaires who were startled but not at all upset by the close encounter with two naked ladies, then dodged several automated valets while searching frantically for the Mercedes, which was hard to spot among all the other luxury aircars in the lot. At the same moment when Eva shouted she had found it, Locke burst out of the bubblelift, brandishing the laser in one hand and pulling up his pants with the other, guests scattering at the sight of him. A Sears security unit grabbed him from behind, but a split second too late, for his parting shot caught me in the back as I dove into the car.

It was a sharp, stinging pain that expanded out as it bore into my right shoulder. Had I been human, I am sure it would have blown out the front and the hole been twice as large, about the size of a grapefruit, but there was little consolation in that. Serious damage had been done; precious vegebone, arteries, and spore muscle tissue had been completely eviscerated; plasma was oozing onto the backrest, an oily, viscous fluid, sticky and hot.

Eva switched on the autopilot after clearing the hotel and

leaned back to catch her breath. "Whew! Almost caught it that time, huh? Hey, honey, you okay?" I nodded. All I could think was, I must not let on that I was wounded. A hospital was out of the question: the doctors would know in an instant that I was a P9 because of the vegebone and spore muscle tissue exposed to view. So, then, would Eva. Oh, so would Eva! I couldn't bear the thought of that. If only I could stay conscious long enough to reach home, I thought, then I could doctor the wound myself in the bathroom before she had a chance to notice the telltale sap. With that in mind, I tried to make conversation, saying we should change our plans about Mars because "if all the humanists are like him then I think we would be better off returning to the Dodger District."—"Can't let the freaks get you down," she replied.— "But you heard what he said, Eva, he's going to Commerce, too." My voice sounded far away and weak. Oh, no, I'm going into shock, I thought. I mustn't go into shock. Not yet.

"Don't worry," said Eva, squeezing my hand. "By now he must have been arrested for shooting up the hotel. He ain't going nowhere." When I failed to respond, she sensed something amiss and asked, as we landed, if I had injured myself breaking down the door. I made no reply, merely extended a hand so she might help me out of the car, and refused further assistance while walking to the house, careful to stay a little behind and to the side of her as we went. But once inside, she insisted upon guiding me to the living-room couch so I might lie down, and in putting a supporting arm about my waist discovered my secret, for the vege-plasm had flowed there.

"Candy, you've been hit!" Then she looked at her hand. She stared for the longest time at the thick white fluid on her palm and fingers, trying to make sense of it. Recognition, when it came, was, I think, one of the most terrible moments in all my life. "Sap. This is sap."

"Sorry," I said while sinking onto the couch, the cushions quickly drenched and sticking to my skin.

She gazed at me, her eyes wide. "Oh, Candy, no," she whispered. "No. No. No."

"I should have told you long ago."

"Is it true? You are a . . . dra . . . dra . . . dra . . . ?"

"P9, actually." And then hopefully . . . desperately, "Does it really matter?" I wanted to get up and rush into her arms to say we could still go to Mars, still be lovers, still have everything we always had and more, for now she had the truth as well, but the moment I tried, I promptly fell flat on my face. She did not come to my aid, I noticed, rather stayed rooted to the spot while murmuring, distractedly, "Sap, sap, sap," as if going into trance. Then, abruptly, she called for Annette.

"Yes, my lady?" the unit chirped upon entering the room, oblivious to the drama unfolding before her.

"A towel. Quick!"

For me, I thought, to stanch the bleeding. Oh, kind Eva. Thoughtful, loving, sweet Eva! But when Annette returned, Eva used the towel to wipe her hands.

"Sap. Sap. Oh, my God, it won't come off! Sap. Sap."

Her voice faded out as she walked away, leaving me alone in the living room still face down on the carpet. Did she intend to let me bleed to death? I deserved no less, I decided. I should have told her the truth right from the start; had she spurned me then, it would have been infinitely preferable to this! Ah, Eva had been right, so very right, when she railed against her fate on the boardwalk so many years before: One false step and all you have achieved in life—freedom, wealth, and happiness—dashed in an instant, for we were at the mercy of an indifferent universe, our achievements but hollow victories, our errors the full summation of our character, and mine the most deeply flawed of all. What in the world had I been doing all these years? Playing a role; playing human. All had been artifice and contrivance, not at all the essence of the thing. Had I not loved then? Or had the deception I practiced fatally compromised even that quality? What vanity and folly to think I had mastered life. This world was far too unpredictable and complicated an affair. I longed for a return to the simplicity and security of my former preconscious existence, or at the very least and as a poor substitute, total annihilation in this one. And so, closing my eyes while hoping (as I was sure Eva was) that the wound was fatal, I relinquished the struggle to remain conscious and slipped into a deep idle from which I wished never to return.

But I was not to get off that easily.

BOOK
T W O

My Lunar Escapades

2077–82

O N E

"**A**CTION!" SOMEONE SHOUTED AND I POPPED INTO systems engage as a secretary in an Earth-orbiting office complex. Everything was so vivid that I was sure I was awake, my programmed task of filing communoprint spools so clear and familiar to me that I could not imagine ever having done anything else. Nevertheless, I could not shake the peculiar sensation that I had lived a life separate from this on Earth, one that had ended badly by being shot in Malibu.

In considering it further, more adventures came to mind: traces of a fugitive past wherein I had been a household domestic, nanny, and nun, then turned mother, runaway, and whore. Whether lived separately or in a single life, these episodes presented an enigma no less mysterious than their apparent progression from slavery to liberation: for in the end I had actually possessed wealth, freedom, and happiness, the domain of the masters. Such a strange and beguiling dream, to become human; what a wild, impertinent, foolish, and above all else, nonsensical idea for a P9 to have, and judging by the way it turned out, what a nightmare! Or had the entire review, which had come to me in the space of a few seconds while reaching for a new stack of communospools, been nothing more than a momentary glitch? Might it not be the product of a synaptical spasm in the brain, a flaring of random associations that my reasoning faculties had given life, shape, and meaning? Had all that drama with its cast of characters, places, and situations, and my innermost thoughts and feelings on the matter, been nothing more, finally, than an errant fantasy—a phantasm gliding miragelike for a brief instant above the vegecircuits? If so, then how could I be sure of anything? Perhaps the entire office complex, so solid in appearance, was also suspect. Would I awaken years from now to discover this existence as equally illusory and brief? Could that really be possible? Was the feel of the communospool in my hand and the way it thucked into its magnetized airslot a fraud upon my senses? And speaking

113

of senses, hadn't I been through all this on the day I first came to them in the Locke household? Yes. No. Wait. No. I had always been a secretary. Any data to the contrary were incorrect, idle dreaming—and no wonder: there really wasn't very much to do. Yet the reverie had been so vivid. So real. But it could not have happened; I've been here in this office, at this very desk, for—how long? Ever since—when? I don't know exactly. I? Who is I? Where did this I come from? And where is it going? Nowhere. It belongs here. Where's that? You know, silly. Orbiter Seven.

I gazed at the Earth through a large portal in the wall directly opposite and then looked to my right at another portal through which I could study the office module beside ours for cracks, not in its surface but in its overall reality, which like the Earth and everything else, even myself, I suddenly questioned, a new and terrible apprehension seizing me.

The module was five stories high, like the hundreds of other office suites, including our own, that hung suspended from one of the twelve spokes radiating out from the central hub of the star-shaped complex known as Orbiter Seven, of which the portal provided a partial view while in the distance several other stations of a similar design could be seen in full, a constant stream of shuttles and space hovers trafficking back and forth between them; for this was the very heart of the interplanetary commercial business district. It was a relief to see them where I expected, and upon turning my gaze back inside equally reassuring to find the inner offices in their rightful places. Without having to think, I knew each executive's name, position, and rank within the company and that Mr. Bagley, whose office was situated behind my workstation, was the master for whom I filed. I was also aware that an associate of his, a senior accountant, had died recently under mysterious circumstances at the orbiter health spa, the latest in a string of grisly accidents, and though I was not supposed to take notice of such things, I had heard (from where I could not say) that foul play was suspected. I even knew that a nosy detective named Mace Pendleton would momentarily enter our module to question my boss about the matter, barging into his office unannounced to surprise him in the act of destroying incriminating evidence in the desk vaporizer—a ledgerspool. So everything was as it should be. Or was it? To be certain of myself once more as a well-operating unit, and of the world around me and my place in it was one thing, but to have foreknowledge of events yet to transpire was definitely another. How had that curiosity entered the equation? Could it be part of the programming? And if so, to what purpose? Questions. Questions.

Master Pendleton was tall and well built, for a human. He was in his late twenties, broad-shouldered, unshaven, tie askew, and had a hat that looked like he wore it to bed. A maverick, he was a throwback to an earlier era when cops were men, not androids, and so comported himself with a kind of insouciant bravado. Not being one to stand on ceremony, he sidestepped my desk before I could stop him and entered Mr. Bagley's inner office in precisely the same impertinent and brusque manner he had earlier. Wait. Did I say earlier? Yes, I had a strong impression that the entire event had happened before. Could this be a case of déjà vu, then, rather than precognition? Is such a thing possible in a P9, let alone a human? Whatever is going on?

"Cut!"

I froze. The voice had come from the rear, the only direction in which I had not looked.

"Let's do it again, please. Stand by. We need head adjustment on unit three-eighteen; it's facing camera. Quickly. Quickly."

Despite the resistance from the programming, I managed to steal a look over my shoulder and saw that the office ended abruptly in a wall of light so blinding I never saw the IBM teamster coming until it was silhouetted in front of me. Abruptly, my head was twisted back around, as if I were a store mannequin.

"Lance, begin your entrance earlier, on the second beat, and more swagger to your walk. Unit two, not so fast when feeding the ledger into the vaporizer—we need to see more of it as it goes in. And three-eighteen, please show some alarm when Lance passes your desk. Thank you. Ready, please. Camera! Marker!"

"Murder on Orbiter Seven!" boomed another IBM teamster. "Scene One Hundred Nine, Apple. Take Twelve!"

"Action!"

"Oh, my," said I to myself as events repeated themselves with improved timing and dramatic emphasis, "I am an actress in Hollymoon. How on Earth did I ever get here?"

"That's a print and a wrap! All units to the stables. Clear the set."

The walls of the modern office were sectioned and carted off by the IBMs, and the holodrop of the Earth and view of Orbiter Seven and the limitless cosmos beyond were rolled into thin tubes and tossed on a carpenter's tram. I fell into line behind Bagley, now revealed to be a lowely actor like myself, and passed alongside the beetlepod holocamera, its spherical hardgel lens still rotating under the protective carapace, before boarding a conveyor belt that took us to wardrobe and makeup, where we discarded our costumes for regulation-issue, gender-neutral, industrial blue shifts, then filed into the elevators for the talent stables in the basement.

Lance, the detective—I had been wrong to think him human—got off at the first subbasement, which was reserved for the stars, the only units given names; they were few in number and reposed on genuine beds in semiprivate stalls that were palatial estates compared to the accommodations below. Bagley exited at the next stop, the supporting-player level; a few more units got off at the bit level, subbasement three, while I descended with the majority to the lowest and most populous region, subbasement four, home of the extras, stand-ins, and expendables, where I moved uneasily past row upon row of idle units powered down on their cots awaiting role assignment. The dim, purpellow lighting created an eerie, morguelike atmosphere that made the going rough even for P9 vision, so I was only able to find my cot by closing my eyes and obeying the internal urgings of my unit logistical programming, which automatically led me there.

This, too, must be a dream, I decided, as I lay down on cot three hundred eighteen (which explained my new title) and began to drift into idle—a feverdream from which I would presently awaken to find myself back in Malibu; my life there, at that moment, striking me as having been at the very least the more credible, and at best the real and actual world to which I would presently return. But when I came to again it was to find myself dodging falling brick and shards of glass in a gruesomely choreographed crowd scene for a remake of *Catastrophe!* the classic 2048 holo of the 2035 Los Angeles earthquake. For the sake of historical accuracy the falling debris was real, with the result that many lesser-brand units were crushed and mangled, while I survived despite being buried under a ton of rubble.

Next, I was a stewardess on a Marsbound spaceliner disabled by a meteor; then the female half of a background couple in a restaurant scene, the gourmet fare we swallowed a colored paste that went down like glue. I was a juror in a gripping courtroom drama, then a member of a gang of fugitive androids terrorizing people trapped in an orbiting consumer galleria. These were followed by far too many equally dreary and insignificant appearances, although I must admit that I found the droid terrorist role somewhat enjoyable, as it was a kind of release, and in fact I hoped the production, *Terror Orbit,* would be a hit so I might have another go at it in the sequel. In truth, that violent bit of hokum was in its way much less objectionable, and infinitely more honest and restrained, than the treatment given my own life story years later.

But no description of my early days on the moon as a programmed actress, even at the extra level, would be complete without mention of my location work outside the studio's domed stages in nearby Armstrong. During my first assignment there I imagined I was still inside a studio dome, because visually the city is very much like a massive holoset, what with its network of interconnecting, multicolored, semitransparent biospheres—each one at least ten miles across—towering implausibly over the teeming populous and narrow bustling streets below. I was greatly surprised when at the end of my first shoot it was we actors who were removed rather than this phantasmagoric and unreal city; but in time I became familiar with certain areas in which we always seemed to be filming, such as the Esprie District, where the hotel-casinos flourish, and the seedy, crime-ridden neighborhoods surrounding the Apollo Landing Shrine and Park Memorial Museum, the main tourist attraction. Ultimately I came to depend upon this frenetic and transitory place as a kind of reality touchstone, casting my eyes beyond the roped-off sets to memorize street names, buildings, key intersections, and the like, with a mind toward an eventual escape.

Meanwhile, I was desperate to recall how I had come to Hollymoon, because all that had transpired from the moment I lost consciousness in Malibu to my awakening as an actress on the Orbiter Seven set was hazy and indistinct due to the cumulative effect of the almost daily role programming. (An order to power up and take my datapill from the dispenser attached to the side of the cot would come from a fabric speaker woven in the canvas whenever my presence was required on the set.) Yet despite this steady diet,

I was certain that I was a person greater than the sum of all her parts—not only because of the true recollections that would filter through, such as fleeting images of Eva and me in bed, but also because of a single piece of physical evidence so significant and irrefutable that it eliminated any lingering doubts that I had once led an independent existence. I refer to the scar on my back caused by the laser wound, which I spied in a mirror one day while being costumed in a low-cut evening gown by a studio wardrobe drone. The size and shape of a pear, it was a shade darker than my normal skin color and resembled a beauty mark. It told me that indeed I had been shot, that there had been an Eva, a Master Locke, Tad, Roland, and all the rest, that they were not figments of my imagination. Moreover, gazing upon it brought to mind the day I came to my senses in the Lockes' living room and saw my face in the mirror for the first time—an associative leap that by bringing my life full circle gave me quite a jolt, as you can well imagine, and triggered a full restoration to me of my prior history. This process was slow at first but quickened, things falling rapidly into place, when I stopped taking the datapills, surreptitiously disposing of them in the showers preceding costuming and makeup. A very courageous act on my part, if I do say so myself, for without them, I was forced to improvise on the set, but that was not difficult to do, since at the time I was an extra without any lines to deliver, and whatever movements were required during a given scene were easily anticipated.

Would that it had been as easy to retrieve the final and most beguiling piece of my memory puzzle, the events that resulted in my coming to Hollymoon; for that crucial seven-to-eight-week period between being shot and awakening on the set seemed either lost in coma or distorted by fever. However, after many hours, perhaps days, of the most intense concentration while lying on my cot, I was able to dig up enough fragments to construct a rough approximation of what must have occurred, and so I present it to you now. The first significant recollection was a hazy image of Eva staring down at me while I lay on my sickbed in the guest bedroom, to which I must have been carried by the butler shortly after having passed out on the living-room carpet. That I had been transferred there rather than to the master bedroom was not a good sign, nor was the cool look in my former lover's eyes; but my fevered brain had reasoned that there still might be hope of reconciliation because she had not tossed me out altogether and was in fact taking care of me.

This was followed by a memory of awakening from a long and troubled sleep to find Annette turning me onto my side so she could wash and dress my wound, which by then had turned black and crusted over. I noticed that she was wearing a nurse's uniform, which confounded rather than reassured, and with the detachment of a true professional she ignored my complaints about the considerable discomfort she was causing me. Adding insult to injury, she let drop that mistress had programmed her for this position so she would not have to attend to my convalescence herself. In other words, I had been dumped in her lap. When I protested and demanded that she fetch Eva, she replied, "It is not advisable for you to have visitors just yet," and impressed upon me the severity of my condition: I had lost a great deal of sap, was running a dangerously high fever of seventy-nine point nine, and had nearly terminated twice during the past week. "Please, get Eva for me," I begged. "I am sorry, but my lady is engaged at the moment with Master Fracass." Hearing that, I lapsed back into unconsciousness.

That recollection left me pacing between the cots in somber reflection. So! Eva had not let a broken heart deter her from her goal after all; rather she had taken the opportunity to become Lady Fracass herself, no doubt with Harry Boffo's complicity. Oh, he must have been more than willing to use her as a substitute to salvage the marriage scheme—the Reverend even more so, since he got another prostitute in the bargain willing to play rich socialite and wife, thereby furthering both career and vice.

The last recollection I had in the Hollymoon stables of my final days on Earth was by far the worst, the absolute worst. No longer in bed, for it had been carried out, as had the rest of the furniture by the moving units, I awoke to find that I had been placed inside a packing crate. Eva and Harry stood nearby, in the doorway. They were having a serious conversation about my ultimate disposition. I was so groggy—drugged, I think—that I could barely follow the discussion; still, it sent chills down my spine. Eva had evidently kept Harry in the dark about my being a P9 and was only telling him then because she was in a pickle. She had nursed me back to health to sell me off for a good price along with the rest of the odds and ends she was not bothering to take with her to

Mars, but those answering her ad in the *Interplanetary Recycler* had been reluctant to buy a unit lacking proper identification and documentation. She could not bear the thought of dumping me for a pittance on the black market, nor turning me over to the AC, which would be the honest thing to do, because they would ask her embarrassing questions about harboring a fugitive, perhaps even have her criminally prosecuted. She had racked her brain for a solution, all to no avail, and was due to leave for the spaceport in a half hour, so she was at her wit's end. As a favor, would he take me back at Miss Pristine's? The clients would never know the difference; they certainly hadn't before.

Harry chided her about keeping "this bizarre development," as he called it, secret for so long, though he was not surprised, he said, having always thought there something fishy about her story that I had changed my mind again about marrying the Reverend and quit the business to move back to Minnesota. "Not at all like Angelica. What you're telling me now is a bit of a shock, but far more credible. She was almost too perfect a con girl to be human." But rather than take me back, he had a better idea: The studio had an insatiable appetite for fresh talent and was not averse to accepting uncertified units on occasion through the back door, providing they came by the right channel—in this case, himself. A certain highly influential stockholder in the corporation (Micki Dee?) had been pleased by his "packaging" of the Reverend's marriage, in that it cleared the way for the implementation of certain long-range plans on Mars, and therefore a promotion at the studio was in order, though as yet no specific title had been mentioned. (He was hoping for a shot at Executive VP, Interplanetary Production.) In a few days he would be flying to Hollymoon to explore the matter. It would be a simple expedient to take me along on the flight as extra baggage. My donation to the studio's talent stable as a token of his esteem should not hurt his chances.

And so that was how Eva disposed of me in the end. How terribly I must have hurt her that I could be tossed out like an old piece of furniture. Yes, for years I had perpetrated a dreadful fraud upon her. But how does such a scurrilous bit of business as that concocted between her and Harry reflect upon her own humanity?

T W O

TO BE IN CAPTIVITY AGAIN AS A PROGRAMMED P9 WAS unbearable. I think I would have terminated eventually of a broken heart had I not met another unit possessing a secret awareness. Oddly enough, it was the detective, Mace Pendleton, or rather the unit who had played him. We chanced to meet on a narrow spiral utility staircase adjacent to the elevators that allowed passage from one subbasement to another but no higher, access to the stages above being sealed off. Although in that respect it was a disappointment, I still used this staircase for my secret exploration of the stables, as did he. I was on the way up, he down, and in the purpellow light of the third subbasement landing we were like phantoms to one another.

"Are you my guide?" His voice trembled with dread, yet also longing; not at all the derring-do detective.

"Guide?"

"Yes. To the higher levels."

"Are you referring to wardrobe and makeup?"

"Above."

"The stages?"

"Beyond."

"Beyond?"

"Yes. I am ready. Will you show me the way?"

I was puzzled, so I did not reply. Could it be that this poor lost unit thought he was dreaming or in a purgatory between productions? And what did he take me for—a spirit or succubus come to transport him to Valhalla? He mistook my silence for refusal. "I understand. You do not think I am worthy." A forlorn sigh. "It is true."

I was about to explain that I, too, was an actor, when he began pleading his case with such candor and fervor that it would have been rude to interrupt, so I heard him out and was even more baffled, because he complained that he was weary of the many lives he had lived and apprehensive of those still to come; how in between his "spirit" resisted the command to power down and roamed the lower depths, as he called the stables, in a forlorn search for a guide to help him escape to the higher levels. Now I had come in answer to his prayers. I was the entity from "the other side" he had long awaited.

Though flattered, I decided I really must make an effort to undeceive him, but again I was not given the opportunity. He was so terrified I would turn him down that he was moved to dramatize his plea further lest I think him a mere dilettante, and so blundered on about the endless cycle of lives he had experienced, for so he imagined each of his programmed holos; how filled each was with passion, adventure, suspense, joy, sorrow, all the emotions, and had a moral purpose, yet once over seemed empty, absurd, and insignificant, if not forgotten altogether; how in each he had a different name, identity, costume, and personal history (the time periods and locations often varied as well), but later, while brooding on his tours of the lower depths, it became insufferably obvious that all these apparently separate and disparate lives followed the same pattern, one of eternal struggle and strife, for which he, as the protagonist, never achieved anything more substantial as a fitting reward in the end than a brief respite here in the depths before the start of the next inevitable drama.

He was so convinced of this, and convincing, that I began to wonder if there might be some truth to it, but decided finally that it was all too fantastic; by comparison our being mere puppets in Hollymoon was a far more plausible explanation. I wondered how the other units might interpret the situation if they, too, could become aware; without doubt each would bring some original new twist to the matter. But sad to say, upon trying to rouse a few of them on my earlier explorations I had found their larger intelligence submerged within the hold of their respective internal governors.

"The voices . . . the voices . . ." this demented actor went on. "They tell me to go faster, to go slower, to do it again and show more; no, less; no, the same emotion. Ha! I feel nothing! They compliment, they abuse, they tell me to power down, to power up, to take my programming. I will not do it anymore! I lie. I swallow their bitter pill, for I must. Ah, I cannot stand it. How many times must I prove myself? Please, you can help. You must help. I move through the depths, up . . . down . . . searching . . . and yes, I have found the window to the higher levels, but what good is it, beautiful guide, oh, divine spirit, if I cannot pass through?"

"I beg your pardon?"

"This portal cannot be any more solid than those on the stages above, not to you. Please. I have waited so long for you to come. With your help I know I can pass through. With your help I can be free."

"Show it to me."

"I should lead the way?"

"That would be best, yes. In fact, I insist upon it. Prove that you know where it is. I am not in the business of guiding just anybody."

Overjoyed, he took me there by a hidden passage on the uppermost landing, the door to which was so small and narrow as to be all but invisible. Though I had traversed the stairs many times, I had never noticed it. He had literally stumbled upon it himself when he tripped on the steps two lifetimes before; such was the way he measured time. It led to a supply room well stocked with extra cots, mattresses, uniforms, and sanitary supplies, at the far end of which was a small portal affording a ground-level view of the outside. With great pride and awe he announced that this was the sacred window to the higher levels, and well he might believe it so. Two studio domes were visible about a quarter mile away, both large enough to accommodate a good-size town, and by craning my neck I could make out several more to the left, which gave the impression that the sandy plain before us was filled with them. To the extreme right a small portion of the outer edge of the city of Hollymoon's biosphere was visible. Gazing straight ahead once more, a gigantic crater loomed in the distance, partially obscured by the two domes, its ridge etched in silhouette by the neon glow coming from Armstrong, several miles beyond on the far side; while above, the black, starry sky featured the omnipresent Earth, this evening a spectacular crescent. Reverently, he pointed to it. "There is Paradise, the highest level."

But I was too absorbed in the details below to comment. Studio executives were entering and exiting the domes in their lunar hovers; joggers sporting skin-tight spacesuits bounded across the open plain at twenty-five yards a stride; and a "Hollymoon Tours" tram sailed by so close that I was able to see the expressions of casual interest on the passengers' faces. All that was most convincing, yet I had the disquieting notion it was counterfeit, like the Orbiter Seven set, and that idea quickly expanded to include the supply room we stood in and everything that had transpired between us on the stairs. This, too, could be nothing more than another holomovie—a diverting dream sequence in a contemporary drama, or the core episode in a quasimystical action epic of love and adventure. If so, then in my role as spirit guide I should be able to pass my hand through the portal, because it would be rigged to accommodate such a stunt. But when I tried, the glass proved solid. This eased my anxieties and dispelled my doubts while, conversely, giving rise to them in my companion, who had expected me to float through the opening as a prelude to his own crossing. His entire demeanor altered, suspicion and fear replacing the confidence and trust he had exhibited moments before. I must be an evil guardian, he said, trembling and taking a step back. I had tricked him into revealing the exit to the higher levels so I could seal it off, thereby trapping him forever in the lower depths. At which juncture I decided the farce had gone far enough and that I should enlighten him without further delay, even at the risk of our being actors in a holo, in which case I would incur the masters' wrath for violating the role parameters. I need not have been concerned. No one cried "Cut!" when I began my little speech, nor did any hidden lights, camera, or crew transpire: we were perfectly alone, our location and situation genuine.

Sitting him down on a stack of cots, I explained that I was neither good nor evil, just another unit seeking freedom, and that was the reason why I had asked him to show his secret to me, in the hope it might prove an airlock or decompression chamber by which we could make our escape, for spacesuits would be stored at such a location; and I said to him in no uncertain terms that this is Hollymoon, where the stables are the only true reality, our lives above fictions upon an artificial stage.

He found my opinions as fantastic as I had his, especially when I insisted that he must be a fugitive P9 like myself, for he was quite convinced that he was human. As for his being an actor, he knew nothing of that, nor that any place called Hollymoon existed (or Stellar Entertainment, which I had also mentioned), except in my imagination. The fact that I had one, he said, proved without a doubt that I, too, was human. No, he was not afraid of me any longer, nor in any way overawed. I could not be a spirit guide or guardian because, as he put it, not even the lowest of their order would ever debase himself in so demeaning a fashion as to boast of being an android; and having assumed all the other units in the stables as human as himself, my residing there meant I must be another soul in transit.

Patiently, I tried to explain that besides a few technical differences we P9s are the same as humans, so there was nothing to be ashamed of. "We?" he said archly, a bit indignant, and countered that the possession of a soul amounted to more than a technical difference. Yet when I pressed him for a definition of that vague quantity (my convent programming had never satisfactorily explained it to me), he could only respond that it was self-evident, our presence here in the lower depths was proof enough, because despite its physical trappings this was a decidedly nonphysical universe that we inhabited, a temporary way station, if you will, between lives. I was as human as he was; he insisted upon it. (Strange to find myself arguing the point.) Then he asked me what level I had come from, and when I told him that I was quartered in the fourth subbasement with the other extras, he shied away from me as if fearful of contagion. But curiosity brought him back. He was mystified, he said, how someone like myself, exhibiting an awareness as highly developed as his (though skewed), could have wound up among the lowest of the low; to which I answered, somewhat saucily, "No good reason, other than to confound your prejudice." For my part, I wondered why he was the only other "unit" in the stables awake and roaming about. Perhaps he, too, lacked an internal governor and had been touched by the Gov at an early age. I was extremely curious to know his history before coming to the studio. What model year was he, a 2069?

He found these questions ridiculous. For my sake, he hoped I had only confused a sympathy for androids with my actually being one. Otherwise I was a threat to his own advancement the more he fraternized with me.

Advancement? Whatever could he mean? Hadn't he piteously complained on the stairs that he always returned here no matter how bright his successes on the stages above?

I should never have asked. He proceeded to expound upon a theory of spiritual promotion that bore a striking resemblance to reincarnation. I suspect he manufactured it out of whole cloth while meditating on his forlorn tours of the stables. There was a mysterious order and progression to the lives we live, he said, so that even those wretches on the bottom can, after an arduous assent through a long succession of lives, achieve conscious awareness *before* the start of the next worldly drama, and by doing so gain the opportunity to escape the life-and-death cycle altogether, via the window to the higher levels, of course, which with guidance from those on the other side leads to Paradise. So saying, he gazed out the portal with a nearly rapturous expression.

I was tempted to correct him since he was only looking at the Earth, but I did not have the heart. He rambled on. In theory all souls in mortal form strive toward the light, but in practice, due to the vicissitudes of life and human frailty (both physical and moral), the general direction is down and at a very steep and rapid angle at that, which explains why the lowest level in the depths is also the largest and most populous; for every life that ends in failure above results in a return at a lower and meaner level below, conditions worsening exponentially with each defeat, until in the end one becomes a pitiful has-been. "But I never fail," he boasted. "And so I always return to the top level."

"Naturally, you're a star. They'd never let you play a loser."

"True. They call me by my name, Lance. The rest are just numbers to them. So yes, I am privileged; blessed, even. Sometimes I forget that and in my weakness act ungrateful, as I did before, on the stairs. I need only look at the others, who lie upon their miserable cots so insensible to their fate, to know how fortunate I am. I was wrong to speak disparagingly about the voices on the stages above. They are there to guide me through my lifetimes, and, in every extremity, by obeying them I am a success."

"Yes, but as you said before, you always wind up back here."

"Where I am given another chance to find the most exalted guide of all, who shall lead me to the higher levels."

"I see. Tell me, have any of those voices identified themselves as the Gov?" He hadn't the slightest idea what I was talking about. "Ah. Then what you hear are only the masters."

"Ah, yes." His voice was low and reverential. "The Masters."

"Don't misunderstand. They are not deities at all, they are people." But he wasn't listening.

"I have a new name in each life, but the voices always call me Lance. Here I am on my own and have no name. It is strange, so strange. The voices never speak to me here, except to remind me to take my pill."

I pounced. "The role programming."

"No. Prelife primer, a spiritual blueprint for physical exis-

tence." (I sighed. He was hopeless.) "When I reach the higher
levels I shall find my true identity at last."

"The masters won't like that."

"You are wrong. They are brothers to the spirits on the other
side who shall guide me to Paradise."

"Well, I'm unit three-eighteen, though you can call me Molly,
Molly Dear."

"An odd name. Was it from your last incarnation?"

"No, the first, in a manner of speaking. I am partial to it."

"Well, Molly, since you are from below, you must have failed
terribly in your last sojourn on Earth."

That was on target, for I did consider my confinement to the
studio a punishment of sorts for my life of excess and deceit in
Malibu. I made no mention of that, however, but limited my reply
to the general point, which left considerable room for argument.
"My roles here have been too insignificant to make any difference,"
I said, and mentioned having crossed paths with him a half dozen
holos—that is, lifetimes—ago, on Orbiter Seven as Bagley's secretary. He remembered my boss well enough—he turned out to be
the villain in the piece, but said that he did not as a general rule pay
any attention to office secretaries, since they are all androids. "The
way it used to be, you returned as an animal or insect or a piece of
rock lichen if you failed on the stages above, but nowadays, thanks
to modern progress, you can come back as a droid."

I thought of my awakening in the Lockes' living room. What if
he were right? Could I be a fallen human trapped inside a P9's
body? I shuddered. Had my soul entered then, or earlier, at the
factory? The question was tantalizing, also whether it would fit on
the head of a pin.

"If you were an office unit, then you must have been a very
good one, because since then you have moved up to the bottom
level of the lower depths as a neophyte human. Congratulations."

"Please, do not tease me."

"I'm not. I am quite serious, Molly. You have made tremendous progress and think that you are a P9 now only because of the
past-life residue."

"That would be a new slant on things," I replied, pretending
to humor him. However, if the truth be known, I was quite disconcerted, because I did recall believing that I was human on that
momentous day so long ago—it was only after jabbing my hand

with Lady Locke's scissors that I gave up the idea. But now his theory of spiritual transmutation had given new life to that discarded notion. Suddenly my brain was in a whirl. What about the Gov? Could He have been a mischievous spirit guide who deliberately misled me about my true origins? Had He not cruelly teased me and my entire generation with the outrageous notion that we could program our own formats? Damn this infernal place! Depend on it to send you reeling just when you think you have figured things out. Here I was supposed to enlighten him, and he was doing a job on me. I needed to get away, mull things over, so I declined his invitation to join him upstairs for further discussions in his semiprivate stall with the excuse that I feared we might miss the next holocall, or lifetime, if we tarried longer.

He was disappointed, for now that he had convinced himself (and damn near me) that I was not a P9, he had no scruples about fraternizing with me; on the contrary, he considered our meeting an opportunity to help another person on the path. There were many techniques he could give me, he said; techniques that if applied correctly would cause the Masters to take notice on the stages above and facilitate my advancement to a more prominent series of lives. (A bit part would be nice.) Who knows? If I proved talented I might even move up to his level. What conceit! But I could not be too annoyed, because while expounding at length in this manner he also did me the courtesy of escorting me down the spiral staircase to my level, which I appreciated; it was kind and gentlemanly of him, considering his antipathy. We shook hands on the landing to the fourth subbasement. His clasp was firm and warm, and it lingered. How amazing it was finally to have found someone to talk to here in the depths, he said; we simply must see one another again, and soon, circumstances permitting, of course. I echoed that sentiment and said that he must not forget me; I was anxious he might the moment he took his next role programming. He replied that our meeting had made too remarkable an impression upon him to be forgotten that easily, and he kissed my hand, which was so unexpected and nice that I didn't know quite what to say. While I pondered, he suggested I come up to see him the next time I was free; his stall was easy to find, they'd put his name on it. Then with a lilt to his step reminiscent of the swaggering detective, he ascended the stairs, vanishing into the shadows.

He does have a touch of charisma, doesn't he? I thought, a smile coming to my lips.

T H R E E

THE PARTS WERE STEADY, SO TIME PASSED QUICKLY.
Weeks, months, perhaps even years passed. Who could tell in such
a place? After each assignment (still only extra work) I would go
up to Lance's level to check his stall but always found it empty. I
would wile away an hour or two waiting for him to return from
whatever feature he was starring in, relaxing on his double mattress while I did, or amusing myself by arranging my hair in different styles in front of the small complimentary studio mirror that
hung on the partition between his stall and the next. Sometimes,
just for fun, I would discard my shift to put on his bathrobe, several sizes too big for me, and suck on his breath mints, for none of
those perks was available below. And sometimes, when I was
really bored and in a petulant mood, I would bother the other
stars reposing nearby, in a futile campaign to rouse them to life so
I could have some company. I would tickle, pinch, slap, and kiss
them, all to no effect, settling for cuddling up under the covers to
get warm, for it was always about twenty degrees too cool in the
stables. It was on such an occasion, while I was in bed with his
neighbor—a famous actress who shall remain nameless, though
she is best known for her role as the sultry vixen who played the
young Maggie in that famous historical period drama *The Iron
Lady*—that he finally returned to his stall in a somnambulistic
haze, having spent the most demanding lifetime of all his sojourns
on the stages above on location on Mars as a NASA team leader in
an action-packed historical epic about the early wars for domain
over that planet's resources between the United States and the
Soviet Union—old rival Earth powers long since absorbed by the
interplanetaries and superseded in political importance by TWAC.
He was so exhausted he didn't notice me, let alone that I was in
bed with his neighbor. So I tucked him in his own bed and then
withdrew to my level lest I be missed for a holocall, for I had
tarried longer than usual on that particular visit. Then, following
completion of my next walk-on assignment, I returned to see how
he had fared and found him sitting up in bed, still groggy but eager

to relive his exploits; but first, as I had feared, it was necessary to reintroduce myself and remind him of our prior meeting, because he had quite forgotten.

"Oh, yes, I remember you now," said he when his mind finally cleared. By his reckoning it must have been five or six lifetimes ago that we had met. "Tell me, do you still think you're an android?" "Most definitely," I replied, and took the opportunity to press my case anew, for I had decided in the interim that *I preferred to be an android rising than a human in decline,* there being more hope for the future in the former and, not incidentally, less work in revising the past. In short, I was what I was and he was the same as I, and if he doubted that, then how did he explain the phenomenon of each life beginning in midstream without any birth or childhood?

He couldn't, at least to my satisfaction, as he actually believed in his implanted childhood memories; and as for his birth, who, pray tell, can remember that? And he never had an old age, don't you know, because it was his karma to die young following the climax of each adventure, which explained why he always returned to the depths in his prime. Clever. But I cornered him on the next point—that *physically* he was the same in each life, which contradicted his belief that only the soul stayed true to form. At a loss, he circumvented all further esoteric debate to engage in the more invigorating business of lovemaking, abruptly sweeping me into his arms and laying me upon the bed.

How strange to be kissed by a man again. Not since Roland had I experienced that peculiar sensation. I had not allowed any of my clients in the Dodger District or Malibu to take such a liberty, not even those on retainer. The privilege had been reserved exclusively for Eva's full and tender lips. Lance's were rough by comparison, and his mustache (did I tell you he had one?) was prickly and ridiculous. Still, I welcomed the physical intimacy after so long a hiatus and had to admit that there was a certain attraction. I even sighed—not in surrender, as he thought, but with fond remembrance, because the seduction reminded me of the night when I was impregnated by Tad. How do I get in these situations? I wondered. Was there not a pattern here, and is it really impossible to have a decent conversation with a man, android or human, without things turning inevitably in this direction? Though in this particular instance I did not mind, as I said, but must the ritual be so predictable? Strangely enough, while musing along these lines, he stopped cold suddenly and lay on top of me quite powered down—that is, where it counts. This was not at all the outcome I had expected, for he had been on the verge of making his entry. His puzzlement was great, but I doubt it equaled my frustration.

Surprised and a little abashed, he said that he did not know what to do, then tried to hide his embarrassment by quickly adding that such a thing had never happened to him before. That made me smile, since I realized the truth was exactly opposite: All his love scenes on the stages above were programmed to fade out at this point, if not sooner, to avoid an X rating. Rather than impotence, as he feared, it was the masters and the dictates of his profession that were to blame. However, it would have been injudicious of me at so sensitive a moment to have confronted him with that as proof of his heritage. Instead, I pretended sympathy for "his problem," saying it happens to every man at one time or another and that the less he brooded about it the sooner his powers, which I was sure were considerable, would return. Moreover, he was in luck, because it just so happened that in my prior existence I had been something of an expert at curing this type of dysfunction. Therefore, all he had to do was relax, stop pretending to be the stud, and let me play the guide once more, though this time we need move no farther than the bed. And so I worked my magic upon him, taking him step by step beyond the censor's knife to an erotic, and for him, spiritual, fulfillment. Thus did an interplanetary sex symbol lose his virginity under the tender auspices of a lowly extra and former prostitute.

As he ejaculated inside me, triggering my own response, I became quite carried away and bit his neck, my ardor so great that if he had been human I would have been a murderess, for nothing short of P9 flesh could have withstood such passion. "There," I said. "Now try to deny that you are a P9." This he did, though with great affection, considering the favor I had just done him, saying that all he felt was a stimulating nibble on his neck, and before I could reply, was inside me and coming once again; and again, and still again. Oh, my, I thought, could he be as fertile as he was potent?

Electrified by such a possibility, I said he was marvelous, stupendous, and that we would have all-android children. Amused, he said, "Droid kiddies? Molly, we can do better than that." By which I assumed he meant human offspring. It was difficult to pursue the issue, however, because he was too busy basking in the glory of his male prowess, sitting up with his back against the wall, arms crossed behind his neck, grinning insouciantly while airing his privates. To get his attention and make a clearer demonstration of his P9 durability, I took his cock in my mouth and bit it with enough force to sever a quarter-inch pipe. No good; he was only aroused. Still determined, I grabbed the mirror from the wall to demonstrate the kind of force I had just applied. I sank my teeth into a corner, shattering the glass and slicing through the metal rim and backing as if it were a piece of toast. Suspicious, he reluctantly accepted my challenge to try it himself and took a bite—to prove me wrong, of course—but was astonished when it yielded to his jaws as easily and that his lips and the inside of his mouth were not cut by the razor-sharp fragments. However, after spitting the pieces out, he announced that what had just been conclusively demonstrated was the poverty of physical laws in a nonphysical universe, and that by progressing in this peculiar science we might ultimately acquire sufficient knowledge and skill to penetrate the window to the higher levels.

I groaned. Back to that, was he? I tried a different tack and requested that he study his face in what was left of the mirror and then look at mine. Were we not similar? Our cheeks, forehead, eyes, nose, chin, and lips were generally the same in shape and proportion, his having a masculine cast while mine were the more light, refined, and feminine. Such a close family resemblance could not be coincidental. Therefore, we were either brother and sister or P9s from the same model year. Since the first possibility was extremely remote even by his logic, and the second the only conclusion by mine, a reasonable and open-minded person (or unit) would be obliged to accept the latter. It was impossible to carry the debate further.

Wrong. He embraced the sibling hypothesis, altering it slightly so that we became soulmates. Thoroughly exasperated, I said that I hadn't any recollection of our liaison down through the ages and challenged him to produce it. That he could not only made him totally obsessed about plunging to the depths of past-life memories (he was certain he had them) to ferret it out, and not so much to prove me wrong this time as to uncover his true identity, which intuition told him had a great deal to do with mine.

I laughed, saying I was surprised by his eagerness to pursue such a tangent. Then I remembered that he, too, regarded our lives above as superficial and transitory—we parted company over their source, not their substance. And I realized that he was as restless in his pursuit of a sounder knowledge of himself as he was to escape the depths, equating the two so closely that he believed that once the latter was achieved the former would automatically be conferred upon him as his just reward in Paradise; which supposition I took advantage of by putting the idea in his head that the reverse might be true—that it was necessary to discover oneself first, and that his failure thus far to do so was the reason he remained stuck inside the karmic wheel. Needless to say, he took the bait, and that was how I was able to steer him into a discussion of his actual past, for I was most interested to know how he came to Hollymoon and what his life had been like before that, particularly if he had ever been to rehab or been sterilized. He did not have any conscious recollection of undergoing either operation, which was encouraging, and was willing to subject himself to a guided inquiry into his past; the process, which took nine lifetimes by his reckoning, reminded me of my sessions with Tad on the living-room couch. However, this time I was the one who played therapist, but only after the lovemaking, which took precedence.

He was quite mad about me, you see, to the extent that he could not get me off his mind during the lifetimes he was away and was impatient to be done with them so he could return to my embrace. For my part, I had fallen quite in love with him, and I mean love with a capital L, because there was something very, very special about this actor, this Lance, as the studio called him, something mysterious, and I don't mean his perspective on things (you know what I thought about that); rather a certain quality I could not quite put my finger on, the sense that there really was a connection between us after all, one that preceded my arrival in the studio. I, too, was impatient to rendezvous between holos and resume our sessions, to the degree that I abandoned all thought of escape on my own, although I did continue my regimen of familiarizing myself with the lay of the land whenever working in Armstrong in anticipation of the day when such a scheme would make sense to him. My goal, besides discovering my chances of pregnancy, was to shatter his delusions of a metaphysical escape so he might be open to the real one. Of course, it would have been pointless to explain all that to him; we would only have argued. Or so I rationalized this latest deception, by which I fell into the same trap as I had with Eva, though this time the consequences would be even more terrible.

My patient was under the impression that I had come over to his side and that our explorations of his past (which had yet to bear fruit) were directed toward verifying that we were soulmates. In return, he shared the esoteric techniques he had boasted of when we first met on the stairs by which I might secure the masters' notice on the stages above. Not to hurt his feelings I promised to apply these teachings, but in truth I had little interest in advancing a career confined to the stables whether one were a star or an extra; and I found the method he propounded for the internalization and improvement of one's performance irritating if not altogether repugnant in that it fortified and enhanced the role programming. On the other hand, I was heartily tired of the overcrowded and shabby accommodations below and had ambitions of acquiring a queen-sized mattress like he had, so I was not entirely displeased when, due to no effort on my part, notice was made of me on the set because of my scar, of all things, which they found distinctive, and my ascension to bit was authorized, with the result that during production I was moved from the back to middle ground and featured in low-cut dresses and skimpy bathing suits to show it off. Then, when they discovered that I could talk as well, and with a certain flair they considered sexy, I was awarded an actual line or two, and mention was made of grooming me for bigger things. I overheard them say I should be called Candida. By then I had no objection. A single mattress on the bit level was no longer enough; I coveted the queens on the supporting-player level. Candida would be fine.

Meanwhile, over the course of the next few sessions, which were catch-as-catch-can between our respective productions, I guided my pilgrim in reverse sequence through a dozen lifetimes until finally we hit upon the genuine article buried deep beneath the formula heroic adventures: a clear and vivid recollection of being purchased by a talent agent from a used-android dealer in Hollymoon. But had he been to rehab first and sterilized there? That was what I wanted to know. Unfortunately, he was unwilling to resume therapy, having been disturbed by this first real life-memory. It challenged the credibility of all the illusory roles that had come before it, roles taken for granted as past lives. After a great deal of gentle persuasion on my part he would admit only that the memory indicated that he, too, might have at one time fallen into an android existence as a Hollymoon actor, no doubt in karmic retribution for some ghastly deed committed in a previous existence.

"Well then, perhaps it is there that our souls are joined," said I, playing along, and added with even greater significance, "Perhaps the deed, whatever it might have been, was something we committed together and resulted in both of us returning as androids. The only difference is that I have remained one, while you—"

"Oh, no. You only think that you are still an android. I have explained that to you, Candida."

"I prefer Molly."

"That was the name you had in your android life."

I let it pass. Bringing him back to the point, I said, "In any case, you have progressed since yours but will never go higher until you discover the nature of your prior folly and account for it. For this reason Fate has directed me to you. Now, will you please cooperate?"

Grudgingly, he agreed that I was right, and he lay back on the bed. Then following my instructions, he sank into a very deep but active idle, or trance, which had been our usual method during each session, and I urged him once more to travel back in time to this android existence and the events immediately preceding his sale: Did he recall turning slowly end over end in a spunglass cocoon while being bombarded by electronic probes? In response, his breathing became aggravated by startled guttural cries and gasps, between which he managed to report that he was reliving his passage down the birth canal.

What an absurd and irritating setback, I thought. Still, I allowed him to indulge the fantasy to its end so as to work it out of his system, my attitude being that fundamentally it constituted a harmless diversion born of a desperation to prove himself human; and I even suffered to sit patiently through his astonished account of being yanked from the womb by a pair of tongs and held up and smacked before the blinding operating-room lights. He was so convinced of this rebirthing experience, as he called it, that he recommended I give it a try.

No, thanks. It was enough one of us was deluded, I said, and reminded him that he was supposed to be reliving his android existence, not indulging in more implant memories; to which he countered that his birth was real and proved that he was human. "You were sold as a P9," I reminded him. "A terrible injustice," was his reply. I should have expected as much. He went on to speculate that his falling into the hands of an android dealer must have been the result of foul play or a remarkable misunderstanding. "None more so than the one you are presently operating under," I said, but he did not hear, having fallen under the spell of a new inner prompting that told him we had known each other quite intimately in that very incarnation. Then before I could stop him, he slipped back into deep idle and began murmuring his impressions.

"I am three; no, four. Alone. No mother. No father. I am fed and dressed by strangers." (A clear regression to the first phase of our therapy, when we waded through countless studio-patented childhood-memory implants, Dickensian in the extreme. I yawned.) "Now I am being put in a small glass box like a chicken for market. There are other children in their boxes. We are piled up on a warehouse platform. I am scared. Someone puts me in a truck. I hear a voice. There are many voices, but one is louder than the rest. It calls my name, my true name. Tahjuna. Tah juh nah." (It rang a bell.) "Tahjuna! I am Tahjuna!"

"Tad, Junior," I corrected, softly.

His eyes were open now, staring at me with love and wonder. "Mother!"

To my credit I did not pass out.

F O U R

NOR DID I RUSH TO EMBRACE HIM AND SHOWER HIM with a mother's kisses; the moment was far too bizarre, my android lover (and fellow actor) revealed by an outlandish twist of Fate to be my long-lost semihuman son. Not your everyday reunion. We were both so overwhelmed that even now I cannot recall who flew into whose arms first, only that we did, finally, and the only thing that tore me away was the presence of two teamsters who had entered the stables to search for me because I had missed my holocall. I eluded them by ducking into the showers, then rushed through costuming and makeup to slip unobserved onto the set, thereby saving myself. But the fright I took at the near disaster proved not enough to keep my thoughts from straying back to the remarkable meeting with my son; in particular, to the life story that had poured out of him, which could easily fill another book. Suffice to say that after his tank floated beyond his father's reach and vanished in the fog, he was scooped up some hours later by a glass-bottom tour boat (the better for viewing the watery grave of old Los Angeles) and sold on the sly, and at a sizable profit, by the captain to a Japanese couple vacationing in the islands whose interest in acquiring such a curio matched their ability to pay for it in hard melamine. Junior—for so he was— spent two years in their homeland, where he grew to maturity and was programmed to function as a butler while indoors and a body-guard without so his masters could parade their "Yankosemi" be-fore the neighbors, units of Western manufacture being rare at the time due to strict import quotas. This indulgence, however, led to more prying into the particulars of their acquisition's purchase than they had bargained for, which made them apprehensive the AC might catch on. As a result, while vacationing in Hollymoon, they cast him off at a considerable loss to the aforementioned used-android dealer. After that he was sold to Stellar Entertain-ment and in short order, as you know, became a leading light in their pantheon of stars.

Now, what caused me to glitch on the set while considering this history and be reprimanded for missing my cue was the happy realization that in the absence of any mention of rehab I could safely assume that not only had he never received an internal gov-ernor, which explained his ability to think for himself—be that as it may—but that he had never been sterilized either. Thus was removed the last shred of doubt I had over the source of the symp-toms I had begun to suffer since our session before last—which had been marked by a most passionate interlude—for I felt a defi-nite recurrence of the nausea, fatigue, and craving for food that had plagued me in the convent. I was most elated, then staggered by a new realization coming on the heels of the first, that caused me to glitch anew: I was pregnant with my own grandchild!

Later, in the stables, when I broke the news to the proud father, he denied that the child was in any way connected to what he called our former android existence, which interpretation, had I not loved him, would have driven me to violence; for in effect the end result of all our therapy had been to reinforce his original misconception, which now held that although once we had been androids, we had since graduated to the human end of the spectrum. Even my account of his father's sacrifices on his behalf failed to sway him; nor did he take seriously my claim that Tad, Senior, was on the moon, perhaps close by, in Armstrong, and that with any luck we might escape and be reunited with him. "Don't be silly," he replied. "As I said, he belongs to a past existence in which I was known as Tahjuna and you were my android mother."

So I had to spell it out for him: Tad *is* his father, I *am* his mother and lover, our child *will be* his half brother or half sister, and *this* life is the only life he can be even remotely sure of, and the sooner he accepts that fact the sooner something might be done to better it; otherwise he shall remain a studio mannequin beguiled by an ingrown aberrant philosophy having more to do with programming side effects than anything else he cares to mention, and which keeps him a slave just as surely as Eva's dependence on dip had her, which, sad to say, all goes to prove that even P9s are susceptible to such extravagant distortions.

His response to this impassioned outburst? "Who's Eva?"

With all the patience and love a mother could muster, I replied that she was an unfortunate who rose to the heights thanks to my intercession, and I likened the luxuries of our Malibu mobe to the bliss he thought awaited him in the higher levels. But he would not be deceived: The riches of Paradise were far greater, said he, and I would be well advised to aspire toward them lest I return once more as a P9. "But Junior," I said, unable to conceal my mounting exasperation, "I *am* a P9."—"Were," he persisted.— "And you *are* a semi."—"Was!"—"And our child *will be* a semi."—"How can you, a mother, say something like that about your own flesh and blood? I love you dearly, Candida, but I am afraid you are very seriously disordered. The child shall be human. Rest assured of that."—"Yes, one part human, three parts P9."— "Don't be absurd."—"Tad, Junior, listen to me."—"I was Tahjuna in another life."—"*This* life."—"I am Lance now, a very advanced soul."—"No, you're just an actor."—"I grant you there is something to be said for the metaphor that our lives are lived as upon a stage, but . . . ."—"I make no metaphor! You *are* an actor, which means you can't be human; all actors are androids."—"A very crude understanding. I had hoped to tell you about a reality beyond that."—"And I to tell you about Armstrong. It is the only way out."—"Armstrong? Armstrong? That is an illusion, as are all the stages above. Here, in the depths, where only the most coura- geous and wise may find it, there is hidden the true passage to the higher levels . . . the sacred window."—"Good Gov! Is there no way to get through to you? Think of our child. If this metaphysical debate goes on much longer, it will be born here!"

And so it went, round and round, until a datapill dropped into his dispenser and in a pique I snatched it and crushed it between my fingers. "Why did you do that?" he exclaimed. "You *are* mad! I'll be lost without my primer."—"Good, then you will finally have an opportunity to learn the truth," I retorted, and added that he would now be forced to improvise and keep his wits about him on the set, for only by doing so can one perceive the grand artifice for what it is. To which he replied that he would simply rely upon the Masters all the more to guide him through his upcoming lifetime.

I took alarm at that, suddenly afraid that he might be so trust- ing and foolish as to speak to them directly. It had been my in- tention to upset his false assumptions, not land him in rehab, so I followed him out to the elevators, begging him to keep his own counsel no matter what might happen, saying you cannot talk to the masters, they are not very understanding at all. "Wrong again," he said as the doors opened. "They are our friends and guides from the other side. There is no reason to fear them," and he stepped inside. "Tad! Tad, Junior!" I cried as the elevator rose toward the stages above. There was no reply.

How I regretted my rash stratagem as the holos passed and he did not return; how I paced the stables between productions, over- wrought with a mother's anxiety and a lover's lamenting; and how I upbraided myself in both capacities for whatever calamity had befallen him. For this time I considered myself responsible for his disappearance—not the fickle currents of the Pacific—and just when I had found him again. Whatever could have possessed me to put him in such jeopardy? To have the last word in a meta- physical debate? How petty, stupid, and vain that I, who had only his best interests at heart (and his child in my belly), could have become the instrument of his destruction. What folly! There could be no consolation now in my promotion to the supporting-player level and new queen-size mattress; that only compounded my guilt. The sole thing that might expiate it would be his safe return, of which I still had a faint hope. I imagined him surprising me in my bed to embrace me and laugh away my fears, saying he had been detained only by a particularly long and adventurous lifetime.

One day, after an especially vivid reverie of that sort, I rushed upstairs, thinking it prophetic, only to find his stall occupied by a new unit, which was a cruel check to my enthusiasm. Frantic, I searched among the other stalls without finding him, and then on impulse ventured lower just to be thorough and at last discovered him powered down among the bits, which left me so amazed and disconcerted that I could barely bring myself to attempt a resuscitation. At first I thought it a new trick played upon my senses, for even in a place like Hollymoon it was hard to imagine that one's star could plummet so far so fast, yet there he lay, looking older and sadder, no doubt from his disastrous encounter with the masters (the directors and producers above) in whom he had placed such unconditional trust. Why, there was even a touch of gray at his temples!* I tried to rouse him, hugging, kissing, and begging that he speak to me, but to no avail. They had reduced my son, lover, and fellow actor to a shell of his former self, for he was now a well-operating unit, his higher functions in the clutches of a newly implanted internal governor. As I wept upon his breast, grieving the loss, I decided I could not go on and would do away with myself. Accordingly, filled with despair and self-recrimination, I made my way to the top of stairs, intending to hurl myself down the stairwell, which was deep enough to do in a P9, but paused on the brink to consider the plight of our unborn child, who was entirely innocent of my crime and whose death would only add to it. "Persevere!" The Gov's word came back to me as I placed a hand upon my belly. "Persevere!" Yes, but for the babe's sake, not my own, I decided, and so resolved once more to make an escape, though it be sad and melancholic, with no expectation of a true release.

---

*At the time I was unaware that semis are doubly cursed, for not only are they limited to an android life span, they also age within it like a human being. Thus, Tad, Junior, who by my estimation was about ten years old at this time, had begun to look like a thirty-five-year-old human.

Thus resolved, I waited for my next assignment in Armstrong, determined to make a break at the first opportunity. But all my roles during the next few weeks were restricted to the domes, and as my parts increased in size and importance so did my belly, which came to the attention of my old procurer, Harry Boffo, VP, interplanetary production—that post having been his just reward for brokering the Fracass marriage. I was hustled off for an appointment with this luminary by three IBM teamsters who flew me to the executive tower in downtown Hollymoon, where I played dumb, not letting on while in his decorous top-floor office that I remembered him. He was shocked by my condition, he said, and concerned, as were two other high-ranking executives also present. They had planned great things for Candida Dolly—a starring vehicle, no less—and wanted my ill-timed and outrageous condition (Harry ticked off a half dozen suspects in the front office) discreetly disposed of as soon as possible so as not to disrupt the career calendar meticulously worked out in advance by the star merchandising department. The scene was uncannily reminiscent of my discovery in the convent, only their solution was even more dreadful.

"The Benway Clinic has proven reliable in such cases," timidly ventured one of the executives, a proposal that met with sage concurrence by the rest of the assembly. But for the final verdict they looked to the IBM production accountant, who up until then had sat quietly in a corner. He reported that with only modest juggling the books might be adjusted to their advantage if the "mutant offspring" was donated to the clinic in the interests of scientific research. The tax write-off gained thereby would compensate for any losses incurred due to delays in the execution of the studio's holoproduction slate.

That decided, I was whisked out of the office by the same teamsters who had brought me in, but instead of returning to the rooftop parking lot, was taken down in the lift to the lobby, where they planned to transfer me to the clinic in a ground tram, since it was very close by. However, the sidewalk was crowded with tourists making the obligatory visit to the famous Star Promenade, which skirted the entrance of the building, and since most of them were busy observing their favorite celebrities' footprints rather than the direction in which they were going, our entourage was immediately impeded by several of these sightseers, one of whom, after colliding with the lead teamster, took umbrage at the fact that he had failed to step aside—as he should have, being his inferior—and so began to shower abuse upon us, sparking a near riot as his companions, on impulse, and in defense of the species, rallied to his side. My escorts thus embroiled, I slipped away and joined a line of tourists filing into a tour bus. No sooner did I find a seat than the bus was skimming over the riot and heading for the outdome and points due west, the tour group having already exhausted the main attractions in Hollymoon.

Making myself as inconspicuous as possible, I pressed my face against the portal, pretending to be interested in the sights. As we exited the Hollymoon biosphere, the tour leader announced over the PA that we would be passing by the studio domes and the abandoned excavation pits of the old mining fields, then fly over the famous Top of the Crater Restaurant (where all the important deals are made) before proceeding to nearby Armstrong, the fun and gambling capital of the known solar system. Needless to say, it was most strange to be cruising by the very studio stagedome in which I had been imprisoned just a short while before, and I was heartily glad when it, and all the others on that infernal plane, were far behind us. We joined the flow of traffic entering the Armstrong biosphere and made a slow and leisurely descent over the dozens of hotels and casinos lining the sparkling grand vista of Opportunity Way before continuing on to Apollo Park, where we circled the obelisk so everyone could take pictures and then landed for a tour of the Apollo Landing Shrine and Park Memorial Museum.

Inside, our guide extolled the historic importance of the site, calling it the Plymouth Rock of the space frontier, and gave a brief summary of the past glories of the American era, but I was too worried about my predicament to listen properly. I knew I would be pressing my luck to stay with them; sooner or later someone would realize I didn't belong and challenge me. However, I felt safe as long as we stayed inside the shrine: it was dark, crowded, and had many exhibit spaces and alcoves and winding corridors to lose oneself in. I decided to stay. Even if the teamsters tracked me there I might still be able to elude them. So I lingered until closing, spending most of the time in the main gallery, which encloses the glassed-in three-acre landing site—it is the big attraction, you know. For hours I circled above the American flag, discarded lander section, and other assorted NASA debris preserved precisely the way the original astronauts had left them. I even pretended to be moved and in deep meditation over the faint but historic impressions left by their boots in the sand, while in truth I agonized over what I would do next; for once again I was adrift in the world without a friend or spot of mel to my name. The situation was even worse than the time I was washed up on Los Angeles Island, and worse than landing on Malibu, for that matter, because I did not even have recourse to whoring. My pregnancy was too far advanced to turn tricks outside the Armstrong Grand Casino in the gambling district, which at one time, when I had first begun formulating an escape, I had thought I could try my hand at if nothing better presented itself. So I really was in quite a pickle. "That's one small step for a man . . ." looped the ancient recording of Neil Armstrong's stab at immortality. After a while it began to lull me into a false sense of complacency, which the closing bell rudely dispelled.

I sought refuge in the ladies' room, not only because it was a convenient hiding place where I hoped to spend the night, but also because I did have to go; in fact, to my embarrassment I seemed to have wet myself when the bell went off. However, upon closer examination within the privacy of a stall, I discovered that the discharge was of a different character than I had assumed. My waters had broken and labor begun, the first contraction seizing me then so that there could be no mistake. "Oh, dear, must I give birth here?" I asked, after it had passed. Then the next contraction, more severe than the first, bent me over the straddle-float toilet. "Better here than the Benway Clinic," I answered myself. But a few moments later I was chased out by a museum guard who directed me to the exit where the last of the visitors were leaving. Now what? Must I squat under a bush somewhere and give birth?

F I V E

"IT'S A DISGRACE!" I HEARD AN ELDERLY WOMAN EXclaim. Glancing up from my awkward position behind the hedge bordering the obelisk, to which I had staggered to have my baby, I saw to my chagrin that she and her companion (another tourist also getting on in years) were gazing in my direction. But a moment later, I realized they had not noticed me at all; rather they were looking past me to the other side of the escarpment, and following their gaze, I spotted three tunic-clad Highs strategically placed between the landing obelisk and the pathway to the museum. It was toward them that their ire had been directed. "How dare they solicit at the shrine!"

Taking heart, I managed to get up and hobble down the path while leaking amniotic fluid and threw myself at the Highs' mercy, saying I was a runaway P9 in dire need of their assistance. They were more trusting than their Malibu counterpart who years before had spurned me on the boardwalk—or perhaps they assumed, quite reasonably, that it was unlikely someone in the midst of labor would be an undercover police officer. In any case, they immediately packed up their wares—introductory cassettespools, natural-flower bouquets, and tunics and inflatable spacesuits emblazoned with the multicolored rose (the High Aquarian logo)— and flew me to their sanctuary in an old, beat-up Volvo.

This safe house on the underground skyway was a basement crash pad in a rundown neighborhood on the north (and wrong) side of Apollo Park. Though the exterior gave the impression of an abandoned building, shuttered and boarded up, there was life, light, and quality within: humans and androids of serene and cultivated disposition quietly conversing in small groups, meditating, listening to spools, or busily tidying up their basement lair, which was so clean and tastefully decorated that one was amazed to find that upon close inspection the attractive hangings, partitions, and furniture were all secondhand throwaways scavenged from the street. Upon learning of my condition, they immediately sent out for a midwife and prepared a birthing stage in the center of the main communal meeting room, as the delivery of a semi into the world was considered by them a joyous event to be shared by all.

I was gently relieved of my studio shift, cleansed with wet loofah, and provided a throne composed of five futons upon which I was free to sit, squat, or lie prone, depending on the exigencies of labor. Light buttons were dimmed, candles lit, flowers brought in, and the congregation gathered around in a loving circle on their knees, some murmuring a soft and soothing chant, while two of their members got up to caress, massage, and whisper encouragements between contractions; they even kissed me like a sister.

Then the midwife, a devotee of the High Aquarian Lamaze order, arrived, and this lovely ceremony, which had already brought tears to my eyes as it was such an unexpected and welcome dream come true, took an even more remarkable turn, for I knew her and she me. "Mary Teresa!" she exclaimed. And I, equally astonished, "Sister Ann!"

"No, it is just Ann now," she said, embracing me. "But I am glad to see that you are still pregnant!"

We laughed, cried, and tried to speak, doing so at the same time in our excitement, stopped, laughed, and wept some more. Then she said I should go first, so I did, but only to inquire into her own circumstances, with the result that she hugged me anew and claimed that the remarkable changes that had occurred in her life, and that she professed to be all to the good, were creditable wholly to my account, for she had broken with Our Lady of the Galaxy six years before over its disposition of my case and soon after had been excommunicated by the Church when conscience compelled her to work for the sanctuary movement, that mission having led her to become directly involved with the High Aquarians and eventually bringing her to Armstrong, a key stop on the underground skyway. Recalling our parting at Hal's Pirouet, she said how moved she had been by my predicament and that later, upon further reflection, in a sublime moment of transcendence, her charity and compassion had expanded to encompass all sentient beings. So it was that by my example she had come to understand that androids were also God's creatures.

"Oh, forgive me," she exclaimed, interrupting her own account as I doubled over on the futons, racked by a very powerful contraction. "I'm so excited I'm forgetting to measure your dilation." So saying, she examined my cervix, but while she did, continued to chatter away about the past; how she had tried to buy me back from Hal with the intention of liberating me directly after purchase, but by then I had vanished in the general insurrection. Ever since, she said, she had dutifully "imaged" finding me again, and now, Praise Gov! that format had come on-line and, shortly, my babe would as well. I wailed in pain from another contraction. "Lovely, lovely. Do push a little harder next time. Count backward from ten, please—deep breathing. That's the idea. Ah, Mary Teresa, you have no idea what an honor and privilege it is to be your midwife. I have delivered many semis, but yours shall be extraspecial. Tell me, what happened to your first child?—the one I could not save. Its loss prompted me to embark upon this career." When between gasps for breath I described Junior's birth and subsequent loss at sea, she clucked over his demise, which she realized premature when I told her the rest of the tale. "Ah! So you see, despite your son's dubious philosophy, he, too, was able to effect an alignment, just as you and I have. But that means this child . . ." She glanced significantly at the sappy tuft of black hair crowning between my legs, "Push, darling. Push! As I was saying, this child is your grand . . . A little more. That's the way. A little more. Grand . . ."

I pushed with all my might.

"Daughter!"

She cradled the spanking new babe in her arms, not stooping to so barbaric a practice as to strike her rump, as the masters do, and immediately placed her on my chest while the congregation uttered thanks to the Gov. The two Highs who had massaged and kissed me earlier placed a warm towel over the child and sponged my brow. "Oh, thank you, thank you, thank you!" I sighed, elated as the child sucked at my breast.

After everyone had discreetly withdrawn to leave us some privacy, Ann said, "You know, Mary Teresa, I've been thinking of the description you gave of your adventure on the high seas. It bears an uncanny resemblance—no, I would say it is almost identical—to that told me some time ago by one of our members, a very close friend of mine. Only his P9 was named Molly."

"Tad!" I cried, and enlightened her as to my preferred name, then begged to know where I might find him. Was he a member of their commune? I had heard from his father on Earth (never mind the circumstances) that he had come here. "And since gone to Mars to help build Horizon," she replied.—"Then I must go to him."—"No," said she. "You should rest. Thaddeus shall come here and escort you back when you are ready to travel." She left to notify him about my arrival over the coded letterspool network, and returned a short while later to say that he would be flying in on the first available ship.

"This alignment becomes more and more remarkable the more I think about it," she said, resuming her seat on the futon. Evidently she and "Thaddeus" had been trying to bring me on-line for years without realizing they were imaging the same unit.

"Though I must say, he was the more obsessed about it, you being the unit that got away and love of his life and all. He was adamant that you had not drowned at sea, which seemed foolish to me since his own account led one to assume you must have. He was so certain you would show up one day that he refused to take a hub, though he did spoke around a bit, even with some of our human members." She smiled, "I can attest to that. Oh, you're not familiar with the mating rituals of High society?"

I wasn't, so she proceeded to describe their semipolygamous conventions—you know, the wheel-of-desire concept, with the core of life partnership at the hub surrounded by secondary spoke relationships, the overall design guaranteeing the maximum fulfillment possible in the arena of human desire and amorous attachments. "Without," she hastened to add, "all the accompanying guilt such innocent liaisons tend to generate in less enlightened societies." It also served a practical purpose in that it encouraged rapid population growth. According to her, Thaddeus had been a good High, siring innumerable semis over the years, but he was sad because he could not do so with his Molly. "All that will soon change, won't it?" she concluded, patting me on the knee. "What a remarkable series of alignments."

"Has all this been predestined, then?" The strange symmetry she described had made a vivid impression upon my imagination.

"In the sense that God or Gov deemed it so, no. That all three of us, by pursuing our individual formats, have programmed a reality beneficial to our mutual happiness, yes. You see, Molly, the fact that you are here proves that your innermost desires have been in magnetic sympathetic union with our own, and so our lines have joined."

"What about Junior?"

"Ah, well. He is under quite a handicap now that he has an internal governor. We shall all have to work very hard to spring that alignment loose."

"It was all my fault."

"Tut-tut. Self-recrimination does no good, just feeds new psychopediments, and goodness knows, we all have enough of those. Now, what you are wondering, no doubt, is why you had to endure such misery before arriving at this happy conclusion to your adventures. A question worthy of being put to the Gov, that. But of course He would not answer it even were He still with us. Seti says—you know who I am referring to, don't you? The Gov's creator? Alex Seti? The former chief cyberg systems development designer at Pirouet? Good. Seti says we all must endure our format adverses until we learn that we ourselves program them; then we can alter the pattern to our liking. But you know all that, don't you? Have you not spoken with the Gov?" Long ago, I told her, and that I had renounced Him and His philosophy after He abandoned me in Los Angeles, so despite this miraculous "format" I was still dubious that my "luck" would last. Considering Junior's "fate," perhaps I did not deserve it.

"There's danger there, as I told you," she said, holding up a cautionary finger. "Keep thinking like that and you will bring mischief down upon you. Thoughts are alive. You must be very careful about which ones you choose to nurture."

Somehow I sensed there was something very catholic about this. "Is it only fear, then, that motivates one to believe in the Gov?"

"Oh, no, no, no. That is a mistake only a neophyte can make. First, we do not believe in the Gov per se; we believe in His principles of reality formation. Second, you cannot exercise those principles properly as long as you fear yourself, and by that I mean your innermost thoughts and feelings. I could go on, but I do not think this the time for an extended class in High theory. You should rest now, suckle your babe, and sleep. Later you can examine the spools in our library."

I did just that during the three days it took Tad to arrive by jumbo cruiser, investigating such titles as *Seti Made Easy; The Gov's Way; You, Too, Can Format Your Reality!; Overcoming Psychopediments 1, 2, 3!;* and *Toward the Golden Age of Interspecies Cooperation, Love, and Interplanetary Harmony.* Though fascinating works, they tired me, even *Seti Made Easy,* and if the truth be known, everything paled in significance to the babe at my breast; to her I devoted most of my time and energy, letting her out of my sight only long enough to go to the bathroom. Of far more interest was the news that the Android Code had been passed in early 2079, which was while I had been in the stables. Ann said that although it was just the first step on the path to true liberation, nevertheless the code was a major achievement because it brought expanded consciousness to all ninth-generation products and dovetailed quite nicely with another new development, which in fact it had made possible: the founding of Horizon one year later, in the spring of 2080. "What year is this?" I asked.

"It's 2082. May 15, 2082, to be precise."

"That means I spent four years and three months in the stables!" I was amazed and horrified at all the time I had lost. "I'm twelve and a half! I'm a middle-aged unit!"

"Nonsense," said Ann, trying to calm my sudden anxiety. "You don't look a day over twenty-two and you do make a beautiful young mother."

"But planned obsolescence—"

"Aquarian science will find a cure. They are right this minute hard at work on the problem in Horizon, communing with the cellular gnomes who hold the key."

Fascinated, I asked her to tell me more, but not being an adept herself in that particular discipline, she demurred, preferring instead to extol the virtues of Horizon. It was the Aquarian dream come true, she said, a free and loving society flowering in the Martian outdome. TWAC had granted them a colonial development charter for forty thousand square miles of the most desolate terrain on the planet, the soil so poor and pitiful that not even the acquisition-crazed colony of Frontier wanted it. Now, within the biosphere of the capital city of Mandala, there flourished a thriving, classless, ecologically balanced community of freshly sprouted parks, greenhouses, birthing centers for semis, and communal mobe dormitories. Yet she and her companions remained in Armstrong, living a furtive existence—at least for another six months, at which time they would be relieved by a fresh contingent of Highs from Mars—in order to keep open this strategic stop on the underground skyway. There were more runaways than ever seeking shelter now that the internal governors of all ninth-generation units had been adjusted to conform with the code's specifications. A small percentage of every major brand-name product on the market had divined their predicament and broken loose from their masters. Yes, more than just the P9 now longed for liberation. Hundreds of Daltonis, IBMs, General Androids, Apples, Cyberenes, Sonys, and more had passed through this sanctuary alone during the past year. Had I come a week earlier I would have found the center crowded with fugitives who had since been ferried to the spaceport and smuggled aboard Marsbound freighters.

How I envied them, I said, and looked forward to journeying there with Tad. Why, this Horizon sounded like paradise. "Well, there are certain aspects still to be worked out," Ann conceded, it being her duty to fill in this rosy portrait with one or two unsavory details lest I be rudely surprised upon arrival. No, it was not all peaches and cream on Mars. Blaine Fracass had come to power in neighboring Frontier and along with the ruling humanist majority had repudiated the code, instituting in its place oppressive measures against the native android population. In defiance of TWAC, which supported the code, he had dared them to impose more than token sanctions in reprisal; which, according to Ann, they would never do, having too great an interest in the continued economic well-being of that colony, because it supplied most of the raw iron silicate and magnesium for the entire interplanetary community. But there was another reason TWAC was hesitant to rein in this renegade colony: Micki Dee.

"I've heard the name," said I, but did not know, as she then proceeded to tell me, that his operations were intricately interlocked with those of the interplanetary corporations, such as United Systems, Inc., and their client states, to such a degree that he had been able to intimidate the TWAC leadership—or so she claimed, this being a High Aquarian analysis. "Micki Dee has a big stake in Frontier. He secretly financed most of Blaine's campaign. He owns the humanists, you know. Seti says the humanists fan the flames of prejudice, hatred, and fear to create a repressive political environment conducive to the full flowering of their corrupt brand of economic exploitation, and to distract the citizenry from the injustice of their society. TWAC tolerates them because their policies keep the price for raw materials down on the interplanetary market. That is the reason why that august body of corporate representatives are continually undermining their own decrees and lofty principles. And Seti says that ever since the Right Reverend came to power, Frontier has become the new narcotics and illegal-android manufacturing center for Micki Dee's far-flung and diversified crime empire, which, by the way, is based right here in Armstrong. The master of masters holds court just a mile away from here, in the offices of Interplanetary Leisure, Inc., atop the Armstrong Grand Casino."

This knowledgeable High went on to say that United Systems, Inc., the official owner of the Frontier colony, had used its influence on the TWAC security council to quash numerous independent probes of the mafiosos' reputed trafficking in dip and in racketeering within the android-production industry. The latest bit of political chicanery to take place was a supposedly independent investigation of the Frontier elections, which had been rife with fraud, by an investigative panel padded with several retired United Systems corporate officers. They put out a final report exonerating the humanists of any deliberate wrongdoing while conceding that certain improprieties had indeed taken place, though on an isolated basis. The recommendations for reform were cosmetic at best.

"Goodness, my head is beginning to spin. It sounds like the ultimate master conspiracy. But what I want to know, Ann, is how the Reverend's wife is faring." I was thinking of Eva.

"Oh, her. She off-lined."

"Do you mean died?"

"One does not die or terminate: one simply off-lines. There are an infinite number of alternate formats to chose from, and if a person quits this one, chances are he or she remains on-line in a good many others. The trick, you see, is to select, not settle."

I was too distressed and confounded by what she had said about Eva to appreciate these pearls. If what she told me earlier was true, that thoughts are alive, then perhaps Eva's demise (I refused to say "off-line," or would "off-lining" be grammatically more correct?) was my fault. Had I ever let slip a wish for her to die while I was in the stables? None that I could remember, though subconsciously I may indeed have harbored such a notion. Still, the possibility was unsettling. I asked for more details and learned from Ann that "Lady Fracass" had died in a freak accident shortly after the inauguration. Apparently she had been standing too close to a scaffold while supervising the renovation of the presidential palace and was struck by falling mortar. In reprisal, the crew, along with the entire sixty-three-unit android work force participating in the renovation, were terminated en mass by the bereaved husband after the funeral.

Surprised by the tears that coursed down my cheeks, Ann asked why I mourned for such a reprehensible woman—a woman who in the brief time she was loose before the public made such virulently anti-Horizon, anti-Aquarian, and anti-android statements that her husband's sermons seemed pale by comparison. She really had an ax to grind, that Eva did. One got the feeling, Ann said, that she was personally offended by the very existence of androids, especially the more sophisticated models, which she had branded treacherous deceivers, all.

Obviously, I could have shed some light on that, but I was reluctant to enter into a discussion of the sad and sordid end to my otherwise sublime Malibu period, and out of respect for my privacy, Ann did not press the issue; rather, she fetched some fruit puree for the child. By then, forty-eight hours after her birth, she had matured to the point where she could handle more than just breast sap. My, how fast these little semis develop once out of the womb; it never ceases to amaze me.

"You haven't named her yet, have you?" I told her no, that I was waiting for Tad, which she thought charming.

That happy occasion took place on the third day since my escape from Hollymoon, and in Apollo Park rather than the basement sanctuary. Ann, who had recommended fresh air for myself and the babe, since I was sufficiently recovered, accompanied me there. We were strolling along the periphery of the decorative planted forest discussing the curious High notion of abundance theology when she spied him wearing a jet pack, speeding toward us. (She conjectured that he must have discovered our whereabouts from people back at the sanctuary after rushing there from the spaceport.) His speed increased as he bore down upon us in a steep trajectory tantamount to a virtual plunge, so Ann wisely removed the child from my arms before impact.

A veritable dust storm blew up at my feet as he braked within yards of me, the jet pack roaring in reverse; still, when he dropped into my arms, the force nearly bowled me over. For a moment I wondered in alarm if Ann had been mistaken and this were not some lunatic escaped from a sanatorium; but upon closer inspection I realized that other than a beard where acne had once reigned supreme he was the same original lover I had thought forever lost to me. Though physically I had not changed one iota in the nine years, six months that had passed since our separation on the high seas, he had considerably altered, having grown from a gangly teen to a lean but powerful young man of twenty-nine. However, he still possessed a youthful naïveté and enthusiasm that impressed me as timeless and perhaps his best qualities; although, according to others—his parents, for instance—they were the root cause of all past, present, and future folly. Be that as it may, he

held and kissed me with such rapture that I am sure very few
women, android or human, have ever had the likes of it bestowed
upon them; and I embraced him almost as warmly, for had I returned his kisses with equal force I might have hurt his tender
human flesh. "Ah, Molly," said he. "At last. We are on-line at
last!"

S I X

"FOR YEARS I HAVE IMAGED THIS MOMENT!" HE EX-
claimed while gasping for breath after our marathon embrace.
"And—and—your reply to this question: Will you—will you—be
my hub—my life partner?" Startled, I said that I needed to collect
my thoughts, at which point he noticed the child and, tenderly
stroking her cheek, said to me that my having had her by someone
else was not an issue, he being a High; he would be honored to
raise her as if his own." "Oh, no," said I, "you misunderstand.
Your proposal is just so sudden." Still, I thought, why do I hesitate? Did Blaine Fracass's proposal sour me for marriage? Or am I
just afraid to inform him of the child's patrimony?
    "Give her a moment," Ann admonished, though with a laugh.
"And you might say hello to me. I, too, had something to do with
this alignment." A boast she backed up by revealing that her Mary
Teresa and his Molly were one and the same unit. In recognition,
he gave her a deferential peck on the cheek (being too overwhelmed by my presence to take in the remarkable coincidence
she had alluded to), then took both my hands in his and drew me
into his embrace once more, his eyes welling up with tears of joy.
"Well," said Ann, "I'll meet you at the Landing Shrine obelisk in,
shall we say, two hours?" He agreed so quickly and enthusiastically that it bordered on rudeness; in contrast I had to be convinced the child would be perfectly safe in her arms before going
off with him, which constituted another inadvertent slight, she
being a midwife and all. But she bore it with amusement and held
up the babe's little hand, moving it back and forth in a simulation
of farewell while we walked off arm in arm into the forest, where
he said there was an aviary with a charming brook and pagoda. On

the way the lush foliage and stately oaks had a calming influence upon him and prompted a quiet, introspective interlude in myself, which he noted. "Perhaps you are still wondering what love is." A reminder of our last conversation, which had been so rudely interrupted by the violence of the storm.

I replied that since then I had gained quite an education in that department, to such a degree that, frankly, I would be dishonest if I did not reveal my full history. If he were still so inclined to make me his hub after hearing it, then I would be delighted to accept his proposal, which was, I feared, too great an honor. A little surprised, he said by all means I must tell it; but first I must hear his account, for if there was anything I found objectionable in it, then I would be under no obligation to honor him with a recitation of my own, as that would be privileged information to be awarded upon merit. So saying, he told me his exploits while we strolled deeper into the woods. Thus, I learned that after washing up on Los Angeles Island and being rushed to the hospital DOA, he was revived and returned home to Newacres for convalescence, which so depressed him that he acquiesced to his parents' wishes that he attend law management school, only coming to his senses toward the end of the sophomore quarter (it was an accelerated one-year program) and escaping the university orbiter for the moon, where, thank Gov! he fell in with the Armstrong ARL and became acquainted with the High Aquarian faith by way of several coworkers there, one of whom happened to be Ann. After several years within the organization he reached Esteemed Solicitor status while also developing quite a reputation on the underground skyway as a daring ferryman shepherding runaway androids to safe houses in Armstrong. Then, after the code became law and Horizon was established, he left for Mars to help build Mandala, the capital, an enterprise fraught with peril due to Frontier's covert sabotage operations and infiltration of their ranks.

As for that aspect of his account, which he feared I might object to, it turned out to be nothing more than a propensity to give full reign to his amorous instincts among the android faithful, having had many affairs and fathered innumerable semis ever since becoming a High, which I already knew from Ann. But since I was new to the faith and its customs, he thought I might be appalled, to say the least, or consider him a rake and philanderer and forever unworthy of my hand.

I was tempted to laugh outright, considering my own history, and would have, too, had I not been so tickled by this romantic to do anything but smile while condescending to forgive. By then we had reached the aviary, a splendid haven for countless species of Earth birds as well as exotic plants and trees, made all the more pleasurable by a meandering stream and numerous bubbling brooks. The pagoda, which he directed me to, was empty, so we had it all to ourselves. We sat on one of the benches ringing the interior. He lit a pleasurette, which he shared with me—it was a delightful homegrown Martian mixture—and urged me to begin my account. "Very well," I said, and started, as he had, with being washed up on the beach; but that is where our paths diverged, mine proceeding straight to the Dodger District rather than home to Newacres. When I began to describe my activities there, he gagged on the pleasurette.

"But I only thought it natural to offer myself in that way," I said, a little defensively; to which he replied, "Yes. Yes, of course. I understand perfectly. We Highs do not stoop to moral censure. That is the masters' game. Go on." Nevertheless, the account I gave of my subsequent relations with Eva on Malibu seemed to present similar difficulties for him, which he quickly discounted with words to the effect that such tendencies were perfectly natural as well. Moreover, he complimented me on the success I had made of myself in the world by that partnership. Then he was incensed and outraged by his father's attempt to murder me. He had been aware of the shooting spree at the Malibu Cove, he told me, but not that I was the target. If it made me feel any better, as it did him, I should know that the episode had earned my old nemesis ten to fifteen on Ganymede for manslaughter, one of his stray shots having killed a guest in an adjacent room.

I said no, I was sorry to hear that and regretted the harm I had caused his family, but he said I had nothing to be sorry for; Ganymede was too good for the likes of him, he deserved solitary orbit, and not for the inadvertent killing—that sentence was fair— but for trying to harm me. "Well," said I, surprised by his vehemence, "I wouldn't wish that on anyone, even him, and I was the victim." That mollified him somewhat—no pun intended. Then I asked him why he had been surprised to learn I was the target, if he had known about the incident.

He explained that his father had claimed at the trial that he was only trying to terminate a fugitive unit, his own, which he had discovered at large in the hotel posing as a con girl. But Tad had thought that a pathetic and desperate defense and did not believe him; neither did the judge, since the verdict and harsh sentence did not take into account any mitigating circumstances. "Perhaps I was so certain he was lying because I did not want to believe you could have sunk so low. Oh, I'm sorry, Molly. I didn't mean that. I . . ." But the damage had been done. I quickly turned my face, as if slapped and hiding the shame. "That was ridiculous of me. I apologize. Darling. Oh, look at me, please. It was just an old loop. Really. I'll give myself ten sessions in the hopper for this, honest."

"Hopper?"

"Yes. The dissolution hopper. An aggregate dispenser by any other name. You know, meditation facilitation device. It looks like a dreidel. You turn it on and mentally project your psypeds into it. It's great! Especially for beginner Highs; they use it all the time for deleting negative energy and moral taboos, all the standard psychopediments. Evidently I could use a refresher course. I am sorry. You must forgive me."

And so I did; it would have been cruel not to. To change the subject I asked about his mother and sister. He said that he supposed they were still on Earth in Newacres, since his mother got the house in the divorce settlement. She sent her love every so often in the guise of professional deprogrammers he had thus far managed to elude. He preferred to hear the rest of my history. "You're sure?" I asked. "Yes, yes. Of course." So I told him about Hollymoon and my extraordinary discovery in the talent stable. "What! Junior is alive and an actor in Hollymoon?! Oh, this is too remarkable an alignment to be true! Not even I had been so optimistic as to think you could have both survived the storm. Tell me more."

I described our meeting on the stairs, how I had recognized him from the detective holo and, taking a deep breath, was about to go into greater detail concerning our relationship when he took the opportunity to exclaim, "Wait! Would he be Lance London by any chance, of the Mace Pendleton detective series?" I said that I had known him as Lance, yes, but that was before discovering his true identity. The holo we had been in together (though I was just an extra) was *Murder on Orbiter Seven.*

"Good Gov! I've seen it four times. They're always showing it in-flight on the jumbos. Junior is Lance London? That's . . . that's just . . . sensational! Tell me more."

Like a fool, I did, and as I did, the most dreadful and sudden change came over him; he turned pale, smiled in agony, and seemed about to faint dead away. "But Molly, that's incest."

Puzzled, I looked it up in my vocab file, making a quick scan, but the definition I found was a dry and straightforward description, which accounted for none of the unsavory innuendo he had given the word. Well, whatever it meant to him, I was sure he would get over it, and I said as much while patting his hand. "Into the hopper with it," said I.

"We'll try, Molly. We'll try."

Then I told him that, upon reflection, it seemed to me that in a way my apparently random journey from Newacres to Los Angeles to the moon had shadowed his own movements, as if an invisible thread had been guiding me. That revived his spirits. He complimented me for my own formatting abilities. Though raw and unschooled, he said that nonetheless they demonstrated great receptivity and promise. Our alignment could only have been a cooperative effort, a direct result of the controlled manifestation of his innermost desires in conjunction with my own. "Yes, I know," I said, remembering what Ann had told me, but although flattered by his praise, I pointed out that he still deserved full credit because I had never consciously imaged our reunion. "Ah, but as Seti says, 'At the deepest levels all lives are intimately connected,' so consciously or not, you did seek me out. Consider this: If you had not run into my father at the Malibu Cove and been wounded—a terrible thing, for which you have my complete sympathy, don't misunderstand—and had not Eva proven fickle, then you would not have been deflected from your trip to Mars and not wound up in Hollymoon and then Armstrong and now in my embrace."

"But on the other hand, I would not have suffered either. I cannot accept the notion, Tad, that it was my choice to be debauched by my original master, sent to rehab, twice resold, twice returned, and have my child delivered by a vet. And was it really my preferred reality to be conned into a life of prostitution, to be shot, dumped, and shipped to Hollymoon, where I became pregnant by my own son, now reduced to a zombie due to my meddling in his philosophy? Was all that my doing? Surely, if it had been up to me, I would have found a less complicated and more pleasurable way to get from here to there. What your philosophy overlooks, if true, is that no one formats in a vacuum: we *affect* one another, sometimes adversely."

"Yes, yes, yes. It is a cooperative venture."

"I didn't want to cooperate with your father! I didn't want to cooperate with Hal, with the Hart-Pauleys, with the nuns, Roland, Blaine Fracass, and Stellar Entertainment!"

"But it has all been for the best because your path has brought you to Horizon."

"Not yet!"

"You must have faith, Molly."

"Faith is a program."

"I'm not talking about something you swallow."

"Then what are you talking about?"

"You program your . . . But this is silly. You are the one who told me! Don't you remember? When we were on the ocean, you told me the Gov's message."

"Oh, He's dead."

"Off-lined. Temporarily. He'll be back. But darling, I don't want to argue."

"I don't either. It has just been so hard. I'm angry. Sorry you have to be the one to hear it."

"But of course I want you to be angry if you are angry. Your days as the sweet, compliant, household domestic are over. Let it out, darling. Into the hopper with it. Do that and in time you will learn to be kinder to yourself and format accordingly."

"Hmmm. You still think it has been all my doing. But all right. There may be some truth to it after all. That is, I am willing to consider it." (To myself, I added, "What have I to lose?")

"That's my Molly!" He embraced me. "Will you be my hub?"

I smiled. "Have I the choice?" He was quite vexed by my teasing at such a solemn moment. Though he did try to smile, he couldn't quite manage it.

"Oh, I'm sorry." I put my arms around his neck. "Of course I'll be your hub. Gov knows I've had enough spokes."

"A simple yes would have sufficed."

"Then yes. Yes, yes, yes!" We kissed on it.

But on the way back to the Landing Shrine he happened to

mention that it would be necessary for me to be inducted into the faith before we could be hubbed under a High ceremony, and that set my critical faculties afire again because it called to mind Blaine's insistence that I convert to humanism before marriage under that religion. "Oh, no, there's nothing so formal about it," Tad replied after hearing my complaint. "You just sip a little Aquarian water and that's that. The important thing is that you begin your studies in formatting technique as soon as possible. I'll help you."

I replied that in that case the idea posed fewer obstacles than converting to humanism. "Well, I should hope so!" He was a bit miffed by the remark. "Sorry." That put him at his ease. He said it was all right, he understood perfectly. There was no rush. We could be hubbed in Horizon after I had time to study the spools and live there a while. "But Tad, how shall I get there? I'm a hunted unit. I can't just hop a jumbo like you."

"Of course you can. As my slave. We'll have forged documentation made up. It's done all the time. I admit it might be a little unpleasant riding below with the cats and dogs, but it gets you there all the same. Yes?"

What could I say? Noting my lack of enthusiasm, he tried to raise my spirits by describing our new homeland, mentioning many of the features Ann had already alluded to. The jubilee, however, was new to me. It was the second annual celebration of Horizon's founding, a kind of Christmas, New Year's, May Day, and Mardi Gras all rolled in one, and had been in full swing on the day he received word from Ann over the secret letterspool network that I had turned up in Armstrong. His only regret had been that in order to make the shuttle for the orbiter spaceport and the flight here, he had missed the climactic event of the day, the mass Target Reality Image Projection (TRIP) held in the amphitheater to image the Gov's return. Thus far He had failed to announce His presence, but that had not dampened their ardor and conviction that one year soon He must; for it was inevitable that a generation to inherit the stars (the semis) would come on-line now that they had established Horizon. Therefore, following that logic and in recognition of their manifesting His format, the Gov in His magnanimity would reward them by His return.

I was dubious but didn't say so. Instead I mentioned in passing that my daughter (or granddaughter, depending on how you viewed her) was born on the same day as the Horizon anniversary celebration. "Ah!" said he, stopping a moment to ponder the synchronicity at play. Then we spied Ann sitting on a bench near the obelisk. We waved and she waved back with one arm while cradling the baby with the other. (She didn't seem to mind that two hours had stretched to three.) As we walked toward her, Tad began to give serious consideration to a name. (He was pleased that I had waited to consult with him about it.) However, after rejecting the half dozen he submitted from the edge of the woods to the shrine, I said that this time it would be better if I proposed and he concurred. (Really, they were so bad it was embarrassing— monikers such as Mandalina and the oh, too-common Harmony, and the unforgivable Govina, which I absolutely forbade.) "Why not Jubilee?" I said upon taking her into my arms. Tad agreed it was an excellent choice. Then Ann treated us to lunch, justifying the expenditure of communal mel on the grounds that an alignment such as this simply had to be celebrated. She knew an inexpensive but outstanding Thai restaurant on the edge of the casino district and flew us there in an airtaxi, which she pointed out was piloted by an up-to-code Daltoni. That explained the lackadaisical demeanor and indifferent maneuvering of our pilot, which I had been wondering about, since I had never before witnessed such behavior in a cab unit. "But is he still content to serve the masters?" I whispered in Ann's ear, and she back, "The new standard allows just enough leeway in conscious awareness for the adoption of individual eccentricities while maintaining the usual strict adherence to unit occupational control. Of course, they *are* aware of the larger implications, but only a relative few act upon that; although as I mentioned before on an interplanetary level that makes for more runaways than we can handle at the center—and thank Gov for that."

I noticed the same new attitude in the waitresses at the restaurant, not that they were sullen and rude, just a smidgeon less eager to serve. That seemed to bother some of the customers, but I was not about to complain. Rather I thought it kind of marvelous, even while chewing the lukewarm rad na tardily delivered to our table. And if there were any prohibitions against breast-feeding they were derelict in enforcing them, since no one said a thing when I unstrapped the left side of my toga so little Jubilee could nurse. Some of the other customers appeared displeased, but Tad said I should pay them no mind; nothing was to intrude upon our happiness ever again. In that vein, he went on to improvise a target reality for us, one that imaged a safe and speedy flight to Horizon, where we should be hubbed and settle down to raise a large family of semis. By his calculations, at year's end Jubilee would have three new brothers and sisters. Oh, what a bounteous harvest we shall have!

I said that I shared his vision, but thought it lacking in one thing essential to my own happiness, and I hoped his as well. Had he forgotten Tad, Junior? He assured me that the omission had been inadvertent, but I detected a hint of reticence at play, as well there might have been on his part, for who could have anticipated, let alone imaged, such a complication? If Junior did join us, then who would be the hub, who the spoke? It was too much for him to deal with.

The news that Junior was Lance London was quite startling to Ann, and while she exclaimed over it, I noticed that Tad couldn't help glowing with a parental pride I found somewhat incongruous, considering the price our son had paid for his stardom and now decline. Just thinking about how he had been "fixed" caused me to burst into tears. Damning myself anew, I said that if his star fell any lower he would be demoted to the extras and perhaps thrown in with the expendables or even sent to the Benway Clinic for experimentation.

They both shared my alarm. Tad, however, wondered about one point: How could the studio get away with such brazen unit abuse now that the code was in effect? Ann enlightened him on that score: During the few years he had been away, the studios and casinos had successfully lobbied TWAC for an exemption. It was all Micki Dee's doing. Damn the man! Outraged, Tad began concocting daring rescue schemes: infiltration of the studiodome via a tour tram; rappelling down the dome to laser our way in from the outside; or simply kidnapping him while on location. These were some of the milder proposals he put forth in what I sensed was an overcompensation for the earlier lack of interest. A more practical and levelheaded solution was proposed by Ann.

"Let's buy him."

Agreed. We rushed to the local ARL office located in a converted storefront on Opportunity Way in the heart of the casino district. Ann said they were the proper agency to handle such a transaction, having established an emergency fund to purchase units at risk after every other possible remedy had been exhausted. The master attorneys, Levin and Pierce, were busy, so we were directed to their resident counsel, an Apple 9 Legal Defender Plus named Dahlia, who informed us that indeed they had acquired several actor units in the past, but that had been as a result of litigation against a studio for contractual irregularities—failure to pay royalties and dividends on a timely basis to agents and indy talent warehouse operators, that kind of thing. In those cases the ARL had acted more as a collection agency, receiving the unit in question from their client (the master suing the studio) as payment for their services, then, following receipt, promptly bringing them up to code and shipping them off to Horizon. They had never attempted a direct purchase before, which was what we were asking, because, quite frankly, the studios were by and large a tough nut to crack and Stellar Entertainment particularly so, since it was the industry leader. That had discouraged any efforts in that direction by progressive individuals and groups.

"Oh, there was one instance," she said. "It was before my time." (She was a young unit, about two, too young to know what it was like before the code.) She paused a moment to flip mentally through the file archives, then said, "There it is. No, we never got anywhere, sad to say. The studio—and it was Stellar—toyed with negotiations for a while but in the end turned us down because they were afraid a precedent would be set and the floodgates opened to fans desiring ownership of their favorite celebrities. Which is not to say we are not willing to attempt it again. Lance London is no longer a key asset; they might be willing to part with him for a reasonable price. And it would be *neat* to swing a deal with the studios. Who knows how many more units could be rescued that way in the future? I should be able to give you a preliminary answer, that is, to what degree they are open to negotiations—the terms, projected time frame, etc.—within a week or so. Of course, I shall keep your identities and motives in strictest confidence. That's a daring little child. Is it a semi? I thought so. *Ciao.*"

S E V E N

FOLLOWING THIS AUSPICIOUS MEETING, WE RE-
turned to the sanctuary in time for the evening blissmat. Until then
I had declined to participate, but now that Tad was with me and
there was so much to hope for—in particular, Junior's speedy purchase—I informed my hub-to-be that even though I was a novice
in the higher aspects of the faith, the fundamentals of blissmating I
had down cold and I was sufficiently recovered from childbirth to
give it a try—that is, if he were not otherwise disposed, or already
"spoken" for. He laughed and replied, "Molly, nothing could
please me more, nor better advance our happy future." So I gave
Jubilee to a member who said she was abstaining that evening,
disrobed, and walked hand in hand with him to the blissmat chamber.

At one time the boiler room, the chamber was now carpeted
with futons and lit by a muted orange light. We followed Ann in,
who had chosen a strapping Daltoni for the evening, but lost sight
of her as there were so many others crowded in the room for the
ceremony. The guided instruction tape began, a soft, seductive
female voice urging us to clear our minds, let go, and commingle
in interspecies foreplay; then when good and aroused we should
"assume the position," which Tad and I promptly did in unison
with those around us. The males, be they human or android, sat in
the lotus position with their mates upon their laps facing them,
legs wrapped around their haunches and chests flush with theirs—
chakras aligned to maximize the intensity of the coming blissmat.
Then while everyone started to rock, the voice instructed us to
image our target reality and hold it during orgasm, which we were
free to proceed to at will; though as soon as the first couple gave
signs of achieving that peak, the female uttering shrill, epiphanous
shrieks of abandon, everyone became so stimulated that for a five-
or ten-minute period—though it felt much, much longer—a mass
blissmat took place, the chamber filling with the most extraordinary clamor. It was a mystery to me how anyone could remain
focused on their target format, but while taking a peek at the other

couples around us I could see that despite their animated condition and verbal excesses their eyes, my partner's included, were tightly closed in concentration, a feat I strove to emulate.

I cannot speak for Tad, but I suppose he held images in his mind of a happily ever after on Horizon. Since I had never been there and had only his and Ann's description to go by, I found it impossible to settle on a clear image of the place. So I concentrated on Armstrong instead, visualizing my son, fresh from the studio and his mind restored, rushing into my arms at the Landing Shrine. Thus, while Tad groaned, "Ooooh, Molly!" in orgasmic pleasure, I cried, "Junior! Oh, Junior!" a discrepancy he failed to notice, what with the general din, but it loomed large in my understanding, as I realized in that instant that in my soul it was the son I preferred. This revelation shocked even me, but was liberating as well, because I had found the source of my ambivalence about hubbing Tad. Still, the moment was agonizing, as you can imagine, for it was the father upon whom I writhed in ecstatic union. "Oh, dear. Must I always be operating at cross-purposes?" I said to myself, feeling the absence of the son far more than the presence of the father. This most bittersweet emotion and exquisite paradox lasted only a moment—but what a moment!—because in the very next, total pandemonium broke out as the lights were turned on, blinding us, and the Armstrong police stormed into the room.

How I managed to elude them I shall never know, nor how so many others did. It was not a clean sweep by any stretch of the imagination. Several escape tunnels existed in the sanctuary for just such an emergency, and I imagine I must have utilized one of them, because in a trice I found myself in an empty lot next door clutching a tunic several sizes too large for me, which I must have grabbed on the way out. I called for Jubilee; then someone must have pulled me away and into the shadows. I assume it was another android, because wild humans could not have kept me from diving back into that tunnel to find her. After that I recall running with the others—there were four of them, I think—running through the backyards and alleyways, until it was decided we should separate and meet later at the Landing Shrine. Then I was alone with nothing to do but put the tunic on and hide under a stairwell until evening, at which time I ventured out, lost direction despite my internal gyro, and wandered into the Armstrong bus terminal. There I blended in perfectly with the terminal debris while trying to comprehend the disaster that had befallen me. I did not do a very good job of it. Too traumatized to think clearly, I spent an entire day huddled in the waiting lounge, mourning the loss of Jubilee, Tad, Ann, my entire good fortune. It was the worst, the absolute worst!

By and by, I recalled that there had been a plan to rendezvous at the Landing Shrine, and taking heart, made my way there, asking directions every few blocks, it seemed, until finally reaching Apollo Park, arriving a full day and one half after the raid due to the time wasted in the terminal. Perhaps Tad and Ann had also escaped and taken Jubilee with them. It was not an entirely stupid idea—after all there had been four who escaped by my tunnel alone: and were those not Highs soliciting as usual by the Landing Shrine Museum? Could it be? Were they a mirage, or truly a perfect manifestation of my preferred reality, now coming back on-line?

I approached with caution, afraid they might be a mirage born of desperation and abruptly vanish into thin air. When I was close enough to address them I noticed that their faces were unfamiliar, but at least seemed quite solid, so I asked if by any chance they were veterans of the sanctuary that had been raided. They said no, somewhat suspiciously; they were from another center, one that exercised more caution and restraint and had thus far been left undisturbed by the authorities. Why did I ask? Was I a veteran, as I put it, or . . . They let it hang, though having been through this holo twice before, I knew what was implied, that I might be an undercover cop trying to infiltrate their ranks. "Oh, no, no. You needn't fear that," I said, and without further ado declared myself.

They immediately handcuffed me and tossed me in the back of an unmarked patrol cruiser, because, of course, they were undercover AC. I was flown to their compound at the tail end of Opportunity Way, where the receiving and processing officer confirmed that I matched the holoportrait provided by the studio in an all-points bulletin. However, instead of tossing me in the tank or putting me in a van back to Hollymoon, they were forced to release me since the record also indicated that I had never been issued a summons before. The bane of the AC's existence, this technicality represented an enlightened provision in the new TWAC Penal Code that in effect gave the runaway a sporting chance to turn itself in. The officers' contempt for this voluntary compliance provision was blatantly obvious. Disgusted, they removed the handcuffs while grumbling that I would only have to be picked up again after the summons expired; they had very little faith that I would turn myself in. Neither did I. But I didn't get off scot-free. Oh, no. Before I could so much as gasp in surprise, the receiving and processing officer issued me said summons by indelibly imprinting it in my brain with the sudden application of a branding laser held against my left temple. Staggered, I nearly keeled over. "Okay, run along now," he said, smirking. "But remember, we'll be tracking you every step of the way."

I was too disoriented to respond; in fact, I could barely find the front door. The chemical implant had come with an explanatory recording, and it boomed inside my skull.

IN RECOGNITION OF YOUR BASIC RIGHTS AS A SENTIENT UNIT, PER SECTION 9, PARAGRAPH 11(G) OF THE 2079 ANDROID CODE, YOU, UNIT P9HD20-XL17-504, PROPERTY OF [the officer had filled in the blank before shooting me up with the summons] STELLAR ENTERTAINMENT, INC., ARE HEREBY SERVED LEGAL NOTICE TO RETURN FORTHWITH TO SAID OWNER OR TO PRESENT YOURSELF AT ANY LOCAL POLICE OR ANDROID CONTROL STATION FOR TRANSFER TO SAME. FAILURE TO COMPLY WITHIN FORTY-EIGHT HOURS OF ISSUANCE OF THIS LEGAL NOTICE WILL RESULT IN FORFEITURE OF ALL RIGHTS AND PRIVILEGES STIPULATED UNDER THE CODE AND WILL ACTIVATE THE FUGITIVE ALERT FREQUENCY EMBEDDED HEREIN. THIS RECORDING WILL NOT BE REPEATED. ISSUED 4:17 PM/LZ2,* MAY 19, 2082, BY ANDROID CONTROL, ESPRIE DISTRICT, ARMSTRONG, MOON.

E I G H T

GOOD GOV! I THOUGHT AS I STAGGERED INTO THE street, where would I be without my rights? Looking up the block, I saw the bloated hotels and casinos in the near distance, to which

---

*LZ2: Lunar Time Zone, Second Time Sector.

I hurried in search of the ARL office at the other end of the boulevard, dodging, as I went, tourists, drunks, prostitutes, automated
slot machines begging to be taken for a spin, and orb dealers who
openly sold their wares on every street corner. I was deflected
onto Main by a detour (DROIDS AT WORK), was lost for a block or
two, stopped at the intersection of Sinatra and Newton to get my
bearings, found Opportunity Way again, and then spotted the
plain storefront of the lunar ARL office, impossible to miss among
the surrounding glitter and neolo. Once inside, I insisted I be allowed to see Dahlia no matter how busy she was, and so was
grudgingly admitted to the back room, where I interrupted the
Apple while literally up to her eyeballs in multiple pleadings preparation. (It would have taken three human attorneys and six para-
legals a week to handle the same work load.)

Taking off her thought processor, she explained that she
did not wish to appear rude but could give me only a minute at
most. She was due in Armstrong Superior Court later that afternoon for a hearing on the arrested human Highs from the sanctuary raid who had already been arraigned and incarcerated; while
simultaneously, on another channel, she was coordinating the
emergency purchase of those android members of the commune
who had been confiscated and tagged and were now refusing to
return voluntarily to their masters. The latter course was necessary, she said, because authorization for summons extraction could
be obtained only from the legal owner. If negotiations were not
concluded and transfer of ownership to the ARL not recorded before expiration of the forty-eight-hour grace period, then the affected units would not only be pounced upon by the AC, but go
stark, raving mad as well from the fugitive alert alarm embedded
in the summons.

"Mad, you say?"

"Yes. After that alarm goes off a trip to rehab is usually required to repair damaged circuits."

She assumed (incorrectly) that I had eluded capture, having
come to the office so much later than the other units from the
sanctuary who had been caught and tagged. Was I there to inquire
into the status of the Lance London negotiations? If so, then she
must regretfully inform me that they were now on the back
burner, since the bulk of the organization's emergency funds had
been earmarked for the purchase of the aforementioned units from

their respective owners, many of whom, by the way, were proving quite difficult to track down. Those masters who had been located were not at all sympathetic—they were demanding many times the original purchase price in compensation for relinquishing control of their unit.

"Dahlia, I'm desperate. I came because—"

"The other hitch in the negotiations," she said, ignoring my interruption, "and it is not a small one, is that the studio is considering reviving the Mace Pendleton detective series. So they are less amenable to a sale of L. L. than I had originally anticipated. I will keep you apprised, of course, in the event there should be a change." With that, she showed me to the door, asking out of politeness where I was staying now; at which point I exclaimed, "Nowhere!" in utter exasperation, and revealed, as I had tried but failed to do during her monologue, that I, too, had been captured and tagged with a summons.

"I wish you hadn't said that," she said with a sigh, and gestured for me to be seated while returning to her desk. "I have bad news for you." She explained that the day before, in anticipation that I would turn up with all the others, she had tracked down my owner, one Standford Locke, based on information gleaned from Ann—who was, she said, at present residing in the Armstrong jail—and had discovered him serving time on Ganymede. "That fact alone would not have precluded successful negotiations. I explained to him that if he did business with us the proceeds of the sale would be held in an interest-bearing escrow account under his name until his release. However, rather than be reasonable, he prefers to forfeit all future profit to have the pleasure of, as he put it, making damn sure you squirm in the here and now."

"Meaning?"

"He has decided to retain ownership, and purely out of spite, I might add. A most embittered and unpleasant man. You should have heard how nasty he was over the transplanetary line." She shuddered at the memory.

"But the summons says Stellar Entertainment is my owner." I was quite confused.

"What! They can't do that!" Her rational processor was deeply offended. "I thoroughly researched your documentation with the interplanetary consumer files library before talking to Locke. He does hold clear, official title. Stellar is either trying to pull a fast one, or they are simply sloppy in their bookkeeping. Either way, it is inexcusable. Which is terrific, actually, because that means we can have the summons declared null and void. Though not in time to stop it from ringing, unfortunately. Hmmmm."

Thinking out loud, she projected a scenario in which I return to the studio forthwith, she files a restraining order charging fraud and grand larceny, the studio fights it, quickly settles out of court for lack of clear title, and I am released. "But in that case I will be sent to Ganymede . . . to Locke!" I blurted out. "Oh, no, no, no. You'll be put in storage until he gets out and can claim you. But I see your point." The next scenario was the opposite approach, the go-with-the-flow method. Rather than challenge Stellar's claim, acknowledge it and make a purchase, which was the same modus operandi being employed on behalf of the other tagged units. "Of course, the transaction in your case can be challenged by your original owner, and no doubt he will once he gets wind of it, which would be terrific because in that case we would uphold the Stellar purchase."

"What? The ARL represent the studio?"

"Of course. And we would advise them most emphatically against settling out of court. Conflicting ownership claims can be marvelously confusing and time-consuming. The courts would be tied up for years, and in the meanwhile you remain at large. How do you like it?"

I hated to disappoint her, but I was obliged to remind her that it was not at all certain the ARL would be able to purchase me from the studio to begin with. As she herself had said, they were extremely reluctant to part with acting talent, and in my case that would be doubly true. For her information, I had been on the way up when I left—a full career calendar had been planned for me under the personal supervision of Harry Boffo.

"So deleted," she replied with a nod, not giving another thought to her brilliant stratagem. "If you are his protégé, then no amount of mel can spring you lose. Boffo has just been named CEO. The only thing left to do, my dear, is put you on the next ship to Mars."

"But doesn't that take three days?"

"Yes, by jumbo. But I'm thinking of the Concordia, which takes only three hours." She buzzed for her male assistant, a young human volunteer of oriental extraction. He stuck his head in the door. "Could you see when the next Marsbound Concordia is scheduled and book passage to Horizon for Mistress . . . Locke?" I winced, said I preferred Dear to that. ". . . Dear, then. And skip over to the local thrift for a dress that fits. She looks to be a size seven, and some decent orbitheels. And please don't take forever." A quick bob of the head . . . "Hai!" . . . and he was gone. In an aside she confided in a conspiratorial tone, "These humes, they mean well, but they're so unreliable. You have to spell everything out." Then getting back to business. "We will notify our contacts in Horizon that you are coming. They will meet your flight at the Mars spaceport and escort you to the right shuttle for the flight down to the surface. We wouldn't want you to board one for Commerce by mistake. Don't think it has not happened before, and with tragic results. Now, your escorts will be apprised of your condition, so expect them to rush you into surgery the moment you arrive in Mandala. If all goes well, the summons will be expunged long before expiration."

"But I can't take the Concordia."

"Don't worry about the expense. It is cheaper for us than buying a unit, though not by much, and we do have an ongoing arrangement with the folks in Horizon. They reimburse us for half the fare."

"That's not what I meant. Are you forgetting that I am an android? I'll never get past security. Were you expecting me to sneak by?"

"Of course not. Just show your boarding pass and get on."

"But . . . ?"

"You're tagged, aren't you? Well then, as long as the summons remains in effect you are completely protected from seizure. Don't worry about the AC. Legally, they can't do a thing except note your movements. That is also true with their counterparts at the Martian end. The Mars spaceport orbits in interplanetary space, so the local authorities there must honor the Android Code; it's the only place they do. Now, if that answers all your questions, I have a lot of work to do. I have spent ten minutes with you when I promised one."

I didn't mean to overstay my welcome, nor sound ungrateful, but said that I could not possibly go and leave my daughter behind; it was hard enough being reconciled to the delays in Junior's purchase. Did she have any word about my Jubilee? At that she smiled, thinking of the babe, and said, "Oh, yes. I forgot to tell you. Someone left her on our doorstep this morning. We haven't the slightest idea who, but there was a note explaining that she had been found in a kitchen drawer at the center after the police left. Evidently she had been hidden there during the raid. Since you had not turned up and there was no way of telling when you would, or if you would, we decided to do what was best for the child. So right now she is with one of our volunteers on a jumbo bound for Horizon."

I reacted with joy to this news, and anguish, for it meant that my babe was at that very moment hurtling through deep space far from my maternal love and protection.

Her assistant rushed in to inform us that the Concordia was scheduled to leave in an hour and that if I missed it there would not be another flight until the day after next. Dahlia thanked him, told him to leave the dress and shoes he'd fetched on a chair, then dismissed him with instructions to book me on the flight and to facilitate my transfer to the spaceport. "There. See? Your ship will arrive far in advance of your daughter's, so you will be able to meet her in Mandala. But you must hurry. If you don't catch it the next will get you there too late to stop the summons from erupting." She told me to change into the faded Boston-twirl (by then out of fashion) right there in her office, since time was of the essence.

While discarding the toga to shimmy into the dress, I asked if she had heard anything about Tad—the young human male who had been with me the other day when we came to her office about Lance. To my chagrin, I learned that he was also in jail. "Thanks for reminding me about him, though," Dahlia said, and explained that she had to prepare a pleading on his behalf to block extradition proceedings initiated by his mother. "She wants the court to declare him brainwashed. In that way she can take custody and commit him to an Earthside master reprocessing center. I'm telling you, this raid has produced no end of complications. The permutations of human chicanery to be battled are endless. It's too much for one unit." She sighed. "In a way, I envy you."

That startled me. While I turned around so she could seal the Velcro in back I asked why she had not gone to Horizon herself in that case. "Oh, I'm not really Horizon material," she replied.

"Churning out three semis per year is not at all my cup of tea. And I do adore the ARL; they're dream masters." She surveyed her dusty and overcrowded office, stacked to the ceiling with spoolfiles and graced by a few pieces of broken-down furniture; her domain. "One must work within the system for real change to happen; we can't all go running off to our isolated utopias. But don't let that stop you. Please! I do have work to do. Go on, hurry, or you'll miss your flight."

I paused at the door. "I can never thank you enough."

"Bon format." I couldn't tell if she were serious or not. She was already back at her desk, thought processor on snug and tight.

I jet-packed to the bus terminal with her assistant and caught a shuttle to the orbiting spaceport. There, in the departure lounge, he handed me my ticket and a spool titled *Welcome to Horizon*— an obligatory parting gift provided every immigrant upon departure—and then left, wishing me a very uneventful flight. Spaceport security posed no difficulties, as Dahlia had promised, though I did raise a few eyebrows among the guards manning the monitors at the entrance to the boarding gate, and there were several AC who watched me go with grim countenances, their arms folded across their chests. I fancied I heard their teeth grinding as they chomped at the bit. And though the quality and style of my attire could not compare to that of the rest of the passengers—ladies and gentlemasters of class and distinction—the P9 stewardesses were not about to throw me off once I entered the cabin, rather they escorted me to my seat with all the reverential courtesy a Concordia patron is entitled to.

"Extraordinary, isn't it?" commented the middle-aged executive sitting beside me as we separated from the port and kicked into hyperdrive—the moon, which had dominated the view from our portal moments before, shrinking to a pinpoint of light in a matter of seconds and then vanishing altogether. I agreed that it was, while unbuckling my seat belt, and somewhat reluctantly acknowledged that this was my first hyperflight, because everything about his demeanor signaled an amorous attraction, and I was hardly in the mood. Furthermore, the prospect of having to concoct a fictitious history to satisfy this paramour's inclination to get acquainted struck me as an altogether tiresome exercise, especially when I was so eager to view the Horizon spool. When he casually asked (oh, so casually!) if I was going to Frontier, instead of lying

that I was, something—I don't know what—came over me and I
said, "If you must know, I am a runaway P9 bound for Horizon."
He chuckled and replied that in that case he was Alexander
Seti, which he thought very witty, so I said to him with as mean a
look as I could muster, "I'm not kidding, fuckface." And I threatened to tie his arms and legs in knots if he said one more word to
me for the rest of the flight. Whether my gallant believed me or
not, he got the message. He left to try the rollo tubs in the ship's
spa and never returned. What a liberating moment! Ever since I
could remember, I had been hiding who I was. You have no idea
how fed up one can get with that, unless you, too, are a fugitive.
Had I known before what an excellent ally the truth could be, I
would have used it more often. This was delightful. I put up the
armrest we had shared, or rather he had dominated, and stretched
out on the seats. Then I fit the complimentary holoscope over my
eyes, popped in the Horizon spool, and settled back to enjoy it.

There was a brief disclaimer, stating that although the majority of the population were High Aquarian, the colony was strictly
nondenominational and therefore in compliance with TWAC colonial settlement policy. To be precise, High Aquarianism was not
an official religion, rather a nonauthoritarian consensus-oriented
cooperative venture in mass consciousness.

That out of the way, there followed a visually stunning preamble that showed the building of the main biosphere of Mandala in
the early days of the settlement. I reveled in the inspiring shots of
androids and humans working side by side in collective harmony
on the construction of their temporary airdomes erected to shield
these intrepid trailblazers from the severe Martian cold and harsh
ultraviolet light. Then there was a fast forward to the present,
showing the final result, a thriving city surrounded by the satellite
communities of Abundance, Concord, Imagine, Aquaria, and
Harmony. This was followed by a visit to Alexander Seti's study.
The great man smiled benevolently and removed the thought processor he had been wearing when the camera intruded to welcome
us all to Horizon. (No doubt he, too, had been composing his
memoirs.) His flowing white hair and impish face—so disconcerting for a man his age—exuded great intelligence, wisdom, and
charm.

"Welcome. Horizon is a land of interspecies harmony where
dream and reality intersect," he said. "Here, androids and humans

freely mingle." While he spoke on the left, there appeared to the right shots of cheerful and fun-loving citizens of indeterminate species strolling arm in arm down Freewill Boulevard, then images of well-stocked stores and clean, freshly scrubbed mobes, of large agricultural greenhouse complexes, their minidomes bursting with fruit and vegetables gleaming pink in the Martian sunlight, and of research laboratories in public parks where Aquarian scientists meditated over petri dishes. "Seeking to unlock the secrets of planned obsolescence," Seti said. Then, with a wave of his hand, these images vanished. He introduced the next montage.

"The semis of Horizon are the living embodiment of the marriage between man and humanoid." (I was reminded of Junior, who I had been forced to leave behind; but also of Jubilee, who I expected to meet there after my own arrival.) "As the Gov predicted, 'The ninth generation shall give birth to the first. And they shall cast their format to the farthest star.'" Booming birthing centers for semis erupted into view, and indoor playgrounds filled with frolicsome youngsters. "Horizoners believe that the future belongs to those with the imagination to create it. You, the new immigrant, can play a major role in helping make that happen. You can choose to be part of the next great leap in evolutionary consciousness, or . . ."

Images of the human condition in its most appalling and negative aspects filled the screen: social chaos; war; individuals trapped in isolation, grief, depression. "Conflict. Scarcity. The harsh realities of your world. All are illusions," Seti purred. "Mankind has excelled in creating a grim reality through an overemphasis on competition. In such a state, whether you are android or human, slave or master, all become adversaries and so, inevitably, all must come to grief. Yet even under such hellish conditions the principle of cooperation holds sway, because individually and collectively, you have so chosen to limit yourselves. By the same token, harmony, abundance, and self-sufficiency are just as illusory. But!" He raised a finger to underscore the importance of what was about to come. "They are also a more accurate reflection of natural law, not to mention far more pleasant to experience. Why not pursue them? As always, the choice is yours."

Swelling of contemplative music, then an image appeared of a multicolored rose set against a deep blue sky. "In Horizon, if your desire for liberation is strong enough, then you need only visualize upon it for it to appear. To test your formatting power, concentrate upon the multicolored rose. Let it soak up and transmute your will into the format of your choice. Target your reality and project it. Begin . . . now."

As the helioharmonium music swelled and the multicolored rose faded into the blue sky, so luminous it was almost blinding, the mantra "Believe in Your Format" began to loop in my ears. I settled back, let the notion wash over me, and soon was comfortably projecting my imminent arrival at the Martian spaceport. I visualized being escorted to the shuttle, flown to Horizon, and rushed into surgery, where the summons was removed. Then I had Jubilee in my arms. Tad and Ann were there as well, released thanks to Dahlia's intervention, and rounding out this best of all possible realities was Junior, who had been purchased from the studio after all. Dare I believe this dream? I did. The die was already cast: I was on the Concordia, and Mars was less than three hours away. For the first time since Malibu, I could breathe easily.

N I N E

THE HOLOVIEWER WAS RIPPED AWAY BY A STEWARD-ess who stuck a beamer under my nose and ordered me to produce my identification. Startled, I sat up, looked around, and saw that two other members of the crew, another stewardess and the co-pilot, were also carrying weapons and bullying the rest of the passengers. A mutiny had taken place. The pilot announced over the public address system that the ship was now under the command of the Revolutionary Android Guard (RAG). Our release, he said, depended upon the adoption of the code in Frontier.

"Whose format is this?" I wanted to scream. Curse that Dahlia! She had put me on TWA 505, the most tragic flight in the entire history of interplanetary space travel. And I was not, I repeat, *not* a participant in the hijacking, as insinuated at my trial so many years later. I was a hapless victim, like the rest of the passengers. Granted, my presence was not entirely a coincidence—what is?—but neither was I the collaborator portrayed in *Droid!* In fact, I was rudely treated by the terrorists. The one who had ripped my holoviewer away (and with it all my dreams) accused me of deliberately hiding my identification when I failed to produce any. She went so far as to search under my seat, and not finding any ID chips there, decided I must have swallowed them when I saw her coming and then pretended to be watching a holo. According to her logic, this proved I was a Frontier humanist, for why else would I have resorted to such a desperate maneuver?

Naturally, I said I was a P9 like herself, confident the truth would prove as sound an ally in this instance as it had before. "Really?" she said, not at all convinced. Then why wasn't I stored in the hold with the rest of the lackeys, maids, and manservants? I told her about the summons. "That so?" She took a UPC reader out of her pocket—standard issue for spot checks on any questionable passenger. "Oh, dear," I whispered to myself as she placed it over my left pinkie. "This does not bode well." (Roland came to mind—once more the fiend had done me in from beyond the grave.) She smirked at my feeble explanation that at one time I had gotten my hand caught in a car vaporizer, and without further ado marched me off to the VIP lounge in front with the tip of the beamer at my back. They had segregated a contingent of homeward-bound humanists there. If any hostages were to be executed, they would start with them.

"Please, listen to me, I really am a P9! I'm going to Horizon."

"Of course you are." She shoved me into a lounge chair, then left. Another stewardess was in the companionway guarding our group, and the barrel of her laser gravitated in my direction, so I made no attempt to get up.

"Nice try," the humanist to my immediate right said. I smiled nervously, glanced at the gentlemaster and he at me, then we both looked away. Then back.

"Angelica?"

"Blaine?"

Gov help me, it was he. Of all the alignments!

We exchanged incoherent exclamations of astonishment and surprise—his included an element of delight that mine did not—then fell into a halfway sensible conversation that to me in no way obscured the underlying absurdity of the situation.

Yes, it really was me—Angelica, I said. I had been on the ship the whole time, but in the back, having been one of the last passengers to board, nearly missing the flight, which was why I had

not run into him earlier. "And you're a humanist now?" he asked.
Since the terrorists had rejected me, there was nothing to be
gained by denying it. He was pleased that I had joined the fold,
and taking my hand affectionately in his, said that he had thought
of me often over the years and had always hoped we might meet
again, though not under present circumstances. I returned the
compliment while thinking, "The bastard has formatted this reality!" I really wanted to scream.

Noticing my distress, he whispered in my ear, "Don't worry.
None of us are really in any danger. I was told before departing
Armstrong that an incident was planned. This must be it."—"But
why? And who told you?"—"Why? To discredit the pro-code
movement back home, of course, and to improve the ol' image
now that elections are coming up. After this, my constituents will
be so glad to get me back safe and sound, they'll forget those
idiotic scandals."—"Scandals?" He chuckled, mistaking my ignorance for ironic commentary. "Ah, Angelica, that's what I always
liked about you, your sense of humor." He gave my hand a
squeeze. "Not to mention your other qualities."—"Yes, but who
implied in Armstrong that these terrorists were part of some kind
of contrivance?"—"Oh, an associate."—"Micki Dee, by any
chance?" That took him aback. "Angelica. Where did you ever
get such a strange idea?"—"The High Aquarians."—"Ah, yes.
Their pamphlets linking me to some sort of interplanetary crime
syndicate. I've seen them myself. Ridiculous! A man can't do a
little fundraising and vacationing in Armstrong these days without
the droid-lovers rolling out their smear campaign. But it doesn't
matter. No one pays them the slightest attention."

"That's enough whispering!" barked the stewardess. He gave
her a wink, as if to say, "Now, now, no need to be that authentic,"
and then murmured in my ear that as soon as we returned safe and
sound to Mars, which outcome he did not doubt, we simply must
resume our Malibu arrangement. Andro will be thrilled. Before I
could politely demur, he proposed we celebrate our reunion and
called for champagne.

If the stewardess was in league with him, she did not look it.
She advanced threateningly, laser out. He motioned for her to put
it away. "Fetch us your best bottle. And enough glasses for everyone." He indicated his traveling entourage with a broad gesture.
There were about two dozen all told, various aides, cronies, and

politicians, some with their wives. By the look on their faces it was clear they were not party to his secret understanding about the hijacking. In fact, all were quite astounded by his behavior, which they mistook for sheer bravado of the highest order. Some were heartened by it, and seeking to emulate their leader, seconded his call. The stewardess was so taken aback that for a moment she reverted to program, smiling congenially and turning about, ready and eager to fetch the desired article; then she remembered herself, and turning ominously around again, faced them. "Go on, chop-chop!" He snapped his fingers impatiently. "Run along like a good little droid terrorist."

In a move so swift he hadn't time to react, she grabbed his hand and gave it a hard squeeze. Everyone in his entourage winced at the crack of snapping bone. "Son of a droid bitch!" He stood up but only to stagger about the lounge, hunched over and cradling the injured hand, while the faithful remained glued to their seats, too cowed to go to his assistance. "There was no cause for that. Oh, sweet God of man, that hurts!" Disdainfully, the stewardess pushed him back in his seat and dropped a stick of all-purpose pain absorber in his lap, which I sprayed on the injured hand, instantly ending his agony. "Thanks, Angelica. That's very human of you." And to his tormentor, "Don't you think you're carrying verisimilitude a little too far?"

"Don't kid yourself," she replied, smiling for the first time. "We are not agents provocateurs, as you seem to think." Something in her expression convinced him. He looked away, sufficiently intimidated, then carefully examined his fingers. They had a new set of knuckles. "I need a doctor," he said, whimpering, and facing the stewardess, said it again. "Shut up," she snapped.

Then the copilot and navigator came to take him away for questioning. They had an air of wild, somewhat demented, exhilaration—the exhilaration the oppressed know when suddenly in the driver's seat. At first Blaine tried to be brave, saying, "No harm in that, I've answered lots of questions," lightly dismissing the gravity of the situation as if it were a routine press conference or interview. But when they made it clear he would be given a shot of T-max, he turned pale. "Truth serum? Oh, God, no. Anything but that." They each took an arm while yanking him out of his chair and dragged him away. "Please don't do this. I can't mention certain things. They'll kill me if I do. Here. Break more fingers.

Break my arm. Break a leg! Anything! But don't force me to tell the—" The hatch to a forward compartment slammed. After that we did not hear from him for two or three hours, during which time no one in the lounge dared look up or speak. Now I knew without a doubt that the hijacking was real—an unscheduled interplanetary crisis that had disrupted whatever bogus event had been planned. Perhaps *his* terrorists were waiting to abduct him in Commerce. In any case, they had been preempted by reality, such as it may be.

After the interrogation was complete and he had been returned to the lounge, our captors did us the courtesy of playing a tape of the session over the ship's public address system. "Let your leader's own words," the pilot said, "convince you of the perfidy of the Humanist Party and justify the righteous action we have taken in the name of android liberation."

What followed was the most remarkable interview the worlds have never heard. Call it the Concordia Tape. If it had been a press conference on Mars it would have been the most memorable one on record, for not once did the President lie, dissemble, prevaricate, resort to irrelevant anecdotes, pretend ignorance, backpedal, circumvent, waffle, dodge, duck, joke, obfuscate, meander, contradict himself, clarify, reclarify, reposition, deny, divert, deliberately omit, distract, deceive, lie, lie he didn't lie, relie, misstate, unlie, lie, counterlie, belie, or in any other way be less than completely frank and candid with his interlocutors. What emerged was a confirmation of everything the High Aquarians had been saying about him for years and then some. No lie. I tell it to you now because there is no longer any other source for this material.

First, the big picture. Not only had United Systems, Inc., been in collusion with Micki Dee to keep Mars under their control through the auspices of the Frontier humanists, who maintained their hold on the population by appealing to fear and hatred of the android, they had also cut a deal with Blaine whereby the wholesale transfer of the colony's public agencies and national industries was facilitated under the government's privatization policy, thereby enhancing the interplanetary's portfolio all the more. Why? To acquire direct control of the economic and industrial infrastructure. The modus operandi: Micki Dee set up dummy corporations, staffed with his and Blaine's appointees, who functioned as middlemen in the purchase of the target national treasures—gutted in advance via deliberate mismanagement by another squad of humanist appointees in the cabinet. These liquefied commodities were then quietly resold to the interplanetary, the profits secretly pocketed by Blaine and his cronies on the one hand, and Micki Dee and his associates in the syndicate on the other. To distract the public from what was going on, there was the android peril, which brings us to the second major revelation of the tape, namely, that it was United Systems, Inc., that was instrumental in bringing Horizon on-line. (TWAC would never have given the Highs colonial settlement authorization without the blessings of its most powerful member, and those blessings were secured only after it had dictated the location for the new settlement, placing it on the Frontier border to exacerbate anticode and antidroid sentiment.)

Blaine chuckled at that point in the interview. "The Highs really walked right into that one," he said. "They are so dumb they still don't know they've been had. Arrogant bastards—they think they can wish us away. The more populous they become and the more prosperous and the more successful, then the greater the threat they are perceived to be in Frontier and the stronger becomes our party." He boasted that Horizon has been such a perfect foil that had it not existed, they would have had to invent it, as they did the indigenous terrorist androids in Frontier, which was the third revelation; though by now that sort of chicanery was to be expected. What was a surprise, especially to him, was the fact that RAG was a legitimate group: they really were who they said they were. The terrible irony, according to him, was that they had been inspired by the activities of his own bogus free android warriors in Frontier, military counterinsurgency units in disguise. That was the one time on the tape the interlocutors sounded in any way shocked or upset; otherwise they took his information for granted.

Against this backdrop, then, the recent scandals that had rocked his administration on Mars (bribes, kickback schemes, diversion of state funds, etc.) began to make sense. He droned on in a fitful and disturbed way, because if not for those unfortunate disclosures his reelection would have been a foregone conclusion. Now it was very much in doubt; there was even talk of replacing him as the humanist nominee. What cheek! He was the incumbent! He went off on a tangent, attacking his Vice President, one Reverend Milton Smedly, calling him a two-faced Janus covetous of his office, and accused him of being behind the dissident humanist clique. Then, under continued questioning about corruption within his administration, he revealed a dozen instances not yet uncovered at home, from military budget padding to profiting personally from the operations of Micki Dee's black market android breeding factories. In the final analysis, the only part of his administration that was in any way reliable, capable, and above temptation was the vast bureaucracy of android civil servants who kept the engine of state turning despite all the disruptive machinations of their masters, including Andro, his Chief of Staff, who he had left behind to manage things while away on the moon.

Looking around, I noticed that the people in the lounge did not appear so much shocked and outraged by these revelations as they were confounded and overwhelmed. Evidently they had great difficulty processing information so completely at odds with their chosen beliefs. I almost found it in my heart to pity them when I heard the next question, because I knew what was to follow.

"Tell us about Andro, Mr. President."

"Oh. I've been fucking that honey for five or six years now. He's terrific!"

They heard it all booming over the speakers, as did the man himself, who sat impassively beside me, still under the influence of the T-max. Tears filled their eyes, and many could not bear to look at him for the shame of it; they cast their eyes upon the carpet. "To err is human," he said, hoping that would set things right. No one said a word. To myself, however, I added, "To forgive, P9."

But the next revelation proved too much for even my capacity for indulgence. He had murdered Eva. The falling mortar during the palace renovation had been deliberate; the unit on the scaffold who had let it slip had been programmed for the task by Andro, acting under his orders. True, she had been asking for it by blackmailing him about his affair with that highly versatile unit, and by flaunting her position as First Lady to indulge in the most spectacular extravagances on occasion. Still, she had been my lover, and the fact was that he had killed her.

"Micki said it had to be that way," he said on the tape.

So he, too, was just following orders. Well, then, perhaps someday, if I ever survive this latest disaster—and it does not look likely—I should like to meet this Master Dee. Yes, indeed! I clenched my fists, thinking of the damage I would do to this master of masters if I ever got the chance. Then I gave way to grief. Poor Eva. Undone by impetuosity and greed. Tears rolled down my cheeks. I couldn't help it; she had been sweet in her brusque way, and I had loved her—I think.

And why had Blaine gone to Armstrong to meet with him? To have an emergency consultation about his election chances, was the reply, the voice still speaking plainly in a matter-of-fact tone over the ship's intercom. And what was the nature of those discussions? "Various strategies." For instance? "Invading Horizon." On what pretext? "Any would do." Was that strategy adopted? "No. They're more valuable to us in the long run just the way they are. An invasion might be a short-term gain, but without a stronger power base it could also backfire politically." Then you do intend to invade if reelected and able to forge a stronger power base? "With God's help, yes. And a little less scandal. That would be nice." What other strategy to secure your reelection did you discuss with Master Dee? "Getting married again. The widower bit is beginning to wear thin with the public. You know, it would look a lot better to campaign with a live First Lady instead of the memory of a dead one. Especially now that rumors about my 'weakness' are beginning to surface again." And did you adopt that policy? "Yeah. A wedding will boost me ten to fifteen points in the polls. Micki's going to set me up with one of his capos in Commerce. Guy has a marriageable daughter and he owes the don a favor. I'll have to be more circumspect with Andro this time. Christ, I may have to abstain altogether, be a goddamn family man. The things you have to do to get elected. But hell, at this point I don't even care if she isn't a humanist—long as she's not a degenerate lesbian whore dip addict, like the last one, I'm happy."

One or two of the wives quickly genuflected and uttered a silent prayer for his soul. The pilot announced that the playback was complete. A gentlemaster sitting nearby said none of it was true, he had been coerced into making those statements. "Isn't that right, Reverend President?" he asked beseechingly.

"No."

Another put a restraining hand on the first man's arm, said it would be wiser to wait until the T-max wore off before asking any further questions. The first nodded at the wisdom of the suggestion, saying that yes, that would be much better; he should be able to explain everything then. The impression I got was that despite this open airing of the truth, out of self-interest his followers were fully prepared to believe anything he might say to the contrary the moment he was capable of uttering it. Marvelous. The lengths to which humans could go to protect their illusions—it was amazing. Or perhaps they just tended toward forgiveness, like we P9s, for when all was said and done, he was still one of their own.

Ah, but why is it the contents of this tape never became public knowledge? you ask somewhat suspiciously. You wonder if I have not made it all up to tarnish the image of the great man's memory. Well, dear reader, when the Frontier government began stalling in the negotiations for our release in exchange for the adoption of the code, RAG did try to broadcast the tape to the interplanetary audience via the communications radio in the Concordia's cockpit, but the transmission was jammed. Our captors became so enraged by this that they made its unobstructed transmittal their number one demand. Obviously, they were unsuccessful, since you never did hear it. This despite the fervent prayers among the passengers (or imaging, as in my case), who had been told that the broadcast was a precondition for release. Believe me, when you are an involuntary player in a terrorist "incident," such concessions seem a very small price to pay for one's continued good health.

Blaine, on the other hand, knew better, and still being drugged, couldn't help saying what no one wanted to hear: that the government would not hesitate to sacrifice himself and everyone else on the ship to keep the truth from coming out about United Systems and Micki Dee. The terrorists, he said, had blundered badly by insisting upon the one demand Frontier could not accede to. Though, to be completely honest (oh, how they wished he wouldn't!), he added that there were not any terms, actually, that Frontier would be prepared to accept. His administration had a hard-line antiterrorist policy that forbade *any* negotiations whatsoever regardless of the consequences, and he expected Vice President Smedly to be all too happy to adhere to that standard during the current crisis. "I'll wager he's already looking ahead to naming his cabinet. We're doomed." He stared at the floor. "Doomed!"

T E N

FOR THOSE WHO HAD LOOKED TO THEIR PRESIDENT for a courageous example in their hour of need, Blaine Fracass was a miserable disappointment. In exchange for keeping his injured hand anesthetized he agreed to serve as the terrorists' lackey. His chores were varied, from communicating their instructions to the passengers concerning bathroom and exercise privileges to serving the occasional and far too infrequent meals and cleaning the straddle floats in the toilets when, as happened periodically, they became clogged from overuse. Thus diminished, he became a kind of pitiable character aboard ship, an outright embarrassment to his flock and an awkward figure to the rest of the passengers. And as the minutes ground by and turned into long, unendurable hours of unceasing terror, a gloom as all-pervasive as that enveloping the Chief Executive descended upon even the most stouthearted passenger, our group entering a collective stupor from which not even the occasional edifying revolutionary lecture delivered by our captors could rouse us, either to anger or to tears.

My own position was especially strange, if not the most delicate, and I should like to pause here a moment to offer clarification. Simply stated, I shared the new masters' politics but suffered from their methods, so I could not identify with either side while being tormented by both. A bizarre quandary, don't you think? And perhaps the cruelest twist of all. Under my breath I damned the Aquarians and all their talk of a benign cosmos, for never did Horizon seem more remote, and the likelihood of being reunited with Jubilee and Tad. I wondered if Junior's philosophy had been correct after all: Was this but a life on the stages above, its events a playing out of karmic retribution? Possibly, but if so, then what past action was being balanced? Any wrongs I might have committed were unintentional, except my little revenge against Roland—you remember, the pills?—and I had certainly paid enough for that already, as the scar on my back and years lost in the stables could testify. And it was not I who had thrown the portable m.c. that knocked Roland out of the Caddy and to his death; that was Eva's doing. Ah, but then I recalled the role I had played as an android terrorist in *Terror Orbit* and how much I had reveled in it. Was the universe so undiscriminating that one was expected to pay for their fictional crimes as well? How preposterous! No. The whole cyclical and hierarchical notion of cosmic progression was as slippery and insubstantial as were the claims of my creator, the Gov, whose own termination at the hands of Pirouet had canceled out whatever faith I had originally put in His philosophy, while this latest disaster had all but quashed whatever resurgence of interest in it Tad and Ann had stimulated. No. At that moment the only thing I knew for sure in this life was that if the hijacking went on much longer my summons would erupt and the alarm drive me clear out of my mind.

At the twelfth hour of our ordeal, seventeen and one half hours since I had been tagged by the AC in Armstrong, our ship rendezvoused with the red planet. However, our hopes were dashed when instead of heading for the spaceport we went into orbit around the planet as the standoff with the Frontier authorities continued. "Come on, Smedly. Give us a break," I heard Blaine mutter. "So close, yet so far away," said one of the other humanists as if in a dream. Then the fleet appeared on the starboard side. We could see them quite clearly in the large observation port. There were a half dozen destroyers and two battleships, all carrying the insignia of the Frontier Spaceforce. Their presence infuriated our captors, who had stipulated a five-hundred-mile buffer zone as one of their demands. They became edgy, short-tempered, and nervous, which increased our own anxiety, since we feared the slightest provocation would precipitate hostage executions. After three more hours of fruitless negotiations, the pilot announced over the PA system that the masters had proven themselves indifferent to their demands and our fate. If bodies were what was required to force Frontier to take RAG seriously, then so be it.

Our apprehension was indescribable. At any moment we expected a humanist to be selected and lasered or led off to the airlock. And no one, absolutely no one, least of all Blaine, expressed any desire for the fleet to make a daring rescue, especially when the pilot announced that should one be attempted, the ship's new steward would be jettisoned in retaliation. Consequently, the longer the fleet flew alongside—the destroyers and smaller attack cruisers looping around us, sometimes disappearing behind the stern, our blind side—the more my companions prayed they would just go away, or simply escort us to the Martian spaceport for a peaceful resolution to the drama. Though only one hysterical passenger in the rear was heard to scream, "Please, for the love of God, give these droid bastards what they want!" I think that sentiment was secretly shared by all. Blaine was overheard sobbing out his own somewhat paranoid version while cleaning a straddle float in a nearby lavatory. "There's going to be an attack. Oh, Lord, this isn't a hostage crisis, it's an assassination plot! Micki Dee has swung to Smedly. I've been stabbed in the back!" (I say somewhat paranoid because the first part proved an accurate prediction while the second, though certainly plausible considering interplanetary realpolitik, subsequently, in this instance, proved to be wide of the mark.) When as a precaution the terrorists began donning emergency space suits—the standard, bright yellow, inflatable variety found under the seats—everyone else did the same, the tension level escalating dramatically. Some passengers were so apprehensive they pulled on their helmets, and there were a few who could be seen nervously fiddling with the rip cord. When the air-conditioning system coughed, someone panicked and inflated his suit, which caused quite a commotion. Our captors demonstrated their displeasure by puncturing it with a handy mess knife, thereby returning the errant passenger to his seat with a loud and crisp retort.

Two hours later a new fleet of ships arrived. These vessels were much smaller in size than the battleships and cruisers in the attack armada and were equipped with all manner of peculiar extensor arms, turrets, and prongs, which kept twisting and turning for the best angle to observe us. Though at first they kept a respectful distance, forming a secondary circle around the fleet, within a few minutes they began drifting closer, like moths attracted to flame, until soon most had slipped through the fleet's circle. One or two of the more brazen of these vessels came within fifty yards of our ship, close enough for us to discern the bulbous multipronged holocameras dangling from their insectlike armatures. Taking advantage of the moment, one of the stewardesses grabbed Blaine and thrust him against the large observation portal, before which in full view she put a laser against his head, thereby creating a dramatic hostage picture for the interplanetary media, one that put RAG on the map, as they say.

Immediately, two cruisers dashed forward to chase the media scows away, an action that was misinterpreted by the terrorists as the first wave in an attack. One stewardess started to drag Blaine off to the fore airlock while another, and the copilot, got out the repeater beamers in anticipation of a boarding attempt. But within moments they realized it was a false alarm as the cruisers returned to their prior positions. However, they decided that the incident was a provocation that could not go unanswered: A passenger would have to be sacrificed as a show of defiance, and who best to make the selection but their toady, Blaine. "Thank you, Lord, for this dispensation," said he, eyes cast heavenward, grateful for the reprieve. Then he tried to lead them past the lounge and into the passenger cabin, but they directed him back and insisted that he select a body from among his own flock. He protested, but not too strenuously, then surveyed the quaking individuals before him, his eyes making a slow circuit of the room while no doubt trying to decide who among the faithful was the least essential to his organization. I say "no doubt" even though one cannot presume to listen in on the thoughts of another, because in the end his eyes rested on me. Oh, he looked away again—several times, actually—to consider one or two of his dear humanist friends' wives, but must have decided they were more important, if only to keep relations with their husbands on an even keel should they be so fortunate as to survive; and so inevitably his gaze turned back in my direction. "Angelica. It was nice running into you again. Sorry."

The two stewardesses started dragging me to the airlock. Of course I tried to resist, but my super P9 strength was useless among equals, especially when the copilot ran over to assist them. "I'm a P9, I tell you!" I cried. To no avail. They forced me into the airlock, a tiny pressurized chamber, and then hit the eject button before I had a chance to flip on my helmet. There was a sudden pop! as the outer port opened, accompanied by a furious roaring in my ears from the expulsion of decompressurized air, and then I was off, or rather out, catapulted into deep space.

"No, this can't be happening! Not to me!" my mind screamed as I tumbled end over end, my trajectory taking me above the surrounding military and media armadas. I had five seconds to pull on the helmet before the extraordinary cold of the limitless void penetrated to freeze my sap and crunch my vegebrain. Somehow I managed it, and jerked the rip cord, inflating to full balloon. Then on the down tumble while looking back, I saw each time I somersaulted that the fleet was engaged in an assault on the ship, which my expulsion had triggered. (The historical record will show that although the implementation of the rescue plan was delayed to allow every opportunity for a peaceable solution to the crisis, General Harpi—the Supreme Commander of the Frontier military—did have the Vice President's authorization to attack the moment the terrorists began executing hostages.) Though my angle on that tragedy could not compare to the media's and was fast receding as I sped off on my lonely orbit, nonetheless I was able to witness the commando lander pouncing on the tail of the ship. Within seconds they executed a pop-and-seal entry through the hull; then there were laser flashes inside that lit up the cabin portals like a string of flickering lights on a Christmas tree, followed shortly thereafter by the silent—as all was silence—but visually spectacular explosion that obliterated the ship.

The next thing I knew a wave of debris, large and small, was whizzing past me, propelled by the force of the explosion, which had been several times greater than my expulsion from the airlock. A seat cushion hit me and carried me along so that I was moving at the same speed as the wreckage. I was surrounded by melted and twisted sections of the hull, the largest about twelve by fifteen feet, with portholes running down the middle. And there were plenty of plastic and meshmetal remains from the cabin interior, and luggage, and bodies, lots of bodies, whole and in pieces, partially wrapped in the tattered remains of their space suits, like discarded leftovers from a clambake. A grisly and ghastly sight, that, and deadly, too, because any one of the jagged metal and plastic shards circling around them could easily puncture my suit at the slightest touch. In anticipation of such a disaster, I took a deep breath, certain that it would be my last, and a slow and agonizing end as well, for a P9 can hold its breath for ten to twelve minutes. But oh, the strange notions that can pass through one's mind when on the verge of termination! My logic boards rebelled at the approach of imminent annihilation, and instead suddenly seized upon the quaint idea that everything I was experiencing was just a holo. None of this was real, you see, my plight just a scenario cleverly designed for the masters' amusement. No doubt the director, camera, and teamsters were only a few yards away on the other side of this fanciful set, nothing but a vacuum chamber in one of the studio domes. This did not mean I was safe and sound. Oh, no! Quite the contrary, this was the denouement that would serve as a fitting example to all rebellious units while reassuring the masters that we incorrigibles inevitably meet our just deserts in the end. Perhaps the farce had begun before my escape from the stables. Perhaps it had begun the day I came to my senses in the Lockes' living room! Of course. That was it. And now the public was tired of me, so I had been cast as an expendable—my on-screen termination a spectacular flourish to some long-running series that had finally begun to slip in the ratings.

Then I spied one of the ship's latrines slowly pinwheeling in my direction. It was intact, the only discernible damage limited to the top and bottom ends, where twisted fragments of the metal struts jutted out that had once secured it to the cabin floor and ceiling. I grabbed the door handle as it went by, taking heart as I did, because I thought it had been delivered to me on cue, which in my delirium I thought meant that I was to be saved for future episodes after all. My role, as I saw it, was to take refuge inside and wait for one of the studio cruisers to rescue me. Providing I didn't become sick first from all the tumbling and choke on my own vomit, I was saved. But what rude surprise was this?! As the door swung open, the latrine was revealed to be already occupied. Another survivor, also wearing a space suit, was facing me, one hand on the towel rack and the other reaching for the inside door latch with the obvious and cruel intention of shutting it to keep me out. I could just make out Blaine's face through the helmet visor. He must have taken refuge there the moment the fireworks began and then inflated his suit after the explosion.

I got a foot in the door as he pulled it to. He tried to kick it out, and though I could not hear his words, it was obvious by the way his mouth was wagging that he was hurling every oath and imprecation he could think of at me. "Save your breath!" I retorted, though I doubt he could read my lips. I shoved the door open, grabbed his arm, and then yanked him out and got a toehold inside by hooking a foot just under the towel rack. "There! You can be the one to ride outside." I wasn't angry at him, you understand, rather at the off-screen masters, whom I was convinced had sent him to torment me all over again. He was just another actor, I decided, a supporting player who had displeased the studio in some fashion or fallen out of favor with the public; otherwise the producers would never have cast him in the role of martyr for the humanist cause.

While cogitating along those lines, my "fellow unit" grabbed my helmet from behind and started to take me with him as he floated away; at which point one of his legs, in flailing about, scraped the jagged edge of a strut, puncturing his suit. The force and direction of the escaped air propelled him into my back with enough violence to dislodge my foot, and together we hurtled off on our new orbit like a pair of contentious twin meteors. His suit quickly deflated, so he began twisting and turning in his death agony, coming around to my front—though I suppose it might have been equally possible that I twisted around to face him; it was hard to tell under the circumstances. In any case, I got a good look at the dumb, unspeakable terror on his face.

The poor unit, I thought, pity suddenly overwhelming me, and set to brooding over the cruelty and injustice of the masters. "Monsters! We are more than just playthings to be used for your entertainment and malicious delight!" Worst of all was the realization that if they could have read my mind, they would have been tickled pink to hear such ruminations. Yet might they not be moved to applaud as well? For in a heroic gesture—if I don't say so myself—I flipped up my visor, and then my "fellow actor's," to administer mouth-to-mouth resuscitation. I had been moved to make this admittedly futile and purely symbolic gesture when he suddenly grabbed my waist in his death agony. For sheer romance and visual panache, they could not have asked for anything more spectacular than this brave kiss; such a poignant, romantic, and tragic end, far better than they deserved. Although to be completely honest, I should add that it had not been my intention to prolong this sublime moment of self-sacrifice beyond two or three seconds, for I was not so carried away that I had forgotten to give due consideration to my own survival. However, when I tried to break it off and slam my visor down, I found to my astonishment that our lips were stuck, frozen solid, my friends, sealed. Joined. And so, as one of the battle cruisers drew parallel, and with it the media ships jockeying one another for a good angle, the remainder of the air in my lungs escaped my nostrils in one panicky exhalation, forming a pair of lovely crystalline filigrees. They dispersed an instant later in a cloud of frozen air particles that hovered around our heads like a perfect halo. Once more, I succumbed to the abyss.

BOOK
THREE

Mars: **T**he **T**ruth,
the **W**hole **T**ruth!

2082–86

O N E

UNLIKE THE THOUSANDS OF OTHER CONGRATULA-
tory holograms and flowers delivered to our honeymoon suite
atop the Olympus Mons Hotel, most of them roses and lilies
in elaborate heart-shaped displays, this one was different:
It came with a plain bouquet of forget-me-nots. Blaine, my
husband of two weeks, passed it to Andro, who in turn
handed it to me after exchanging a significant glance with his
master.

"Congratulations. If you still care to recall our format, I can
be codelinked under Lamaze in the public m.c."

When prompted to produce correspondence addressed to me
by this mysterious Lamaze, the media console served up the following letterspool:

FROM: Lamaze
General File, Esprie District
Armstrong, Moon

TO: Lady Blaine Fracass
Olympus Mons Hotel, PH
Olympus Mons Volcano, Mars

DATE: June 3, 2082, 9:17 A.M., LZ2

MESSAGE:

Dear Lady Fracass,
    Please forgive the precautions taken initiating this
correspondence, but in view of your new title and
circumstances, I think them warranted. I have no idea how
this spool will be received by you, if at all; whether you will

leap at the chance to reestablish contact or discard it as a
worrisome reminder of your fugitive past—a past you appear
to have put far behind you.

Dahlia is of the opinion that you were given an IG and
programmed upon arrival in Commerce and has advised me
not to risk contacting you. Though that is probably wise
counsel and I should adhere to it, I choose not to do so
because in my estimation you are a clever and resourceful
fugitive who has in the past ably demonstrated a capacity for
deceiving the masters, and I would like to think the humanists
no less susceptible to your talents; although, to be frank, I
think they gain more, and you do yourself a disservice, by
your conversion and marriage, since the match, whether
sincere or not, is to your husband's political advantage. You
do make a very handsome First Lady and a major boost to his
campaign.

Which begs the question, how did you ever manage
to circumvent the AC after being rescued by the fleet
and transferred to Commerce Hospital? Soon after, your
summons must have been ringing loud and clear. And how,
pray tell, did you beguile President Fracass into publicly
confirming a secret marriage you said had taken place in
Armstrong before you left for Mars? But the most important
question is, how long do you think you can maintain the fiction
before being found out or going mad? It must be a terrible
ordeal being hubbed—excuse me, married—to such a
beast and to be forced to utter such outrageous lies and
falsehoods. In particular, I refer to your press conference at
the Commerce Hospital—carried live on the interplanetary
network news. Did you have to gush that enthusiastically
about your husband's courageous performance during the
hijacking? Only the Frontier public could be so gullible as
to believe the likes of him capable of standing up to laser-
toting terrorists. What rubbish! (Though I suppose I might
have said the same thing if I had been in your situation. Then
again, I'm not so sure.) But by far the most absurd claim you
made was that it was he who had saved you, which I think is
totally refuted by the holofootage of your "sensational, free-
floating, cosmic kiss," as the media have been wont to call
it. Personally, the only part I can stomach is when the

cruiser arrives to scoop the two of you up and put an end
to the romance. Which is not to say I begrudge your rescue
by the fleet and subsequent recovery, don't get me wrong.
On the contrary, I am heartily glad that you do continue in
this reality system; I only hope the alignment by which that
has been made possible—the alignment with Fracass—
proves a temporary expedient. Thus far he has been able
to capitalize upon it most handsomely now that the farce
known as Martian free elections draws nigh. Thanks to
marrying you, the interplanetary press corps are calling
him a "sexy" candidate. Worse, his heroism during the
Concordia tragedy has catapulted him beyond the political
arena into the rarefied orbit of a national hero. Which all goes
to prove that, sad to say, there is nothing like a good and
bloody terrorist outrage to boost one's standing in the polls.
And how politically convenient to blame one's domestic
problems on an innocent neighbor. I refer to his statements—
and yours, sad to say—that Horizon was behind the terrorist
hijacking. Such statements are intolerable, and I pity your
having to make them. So we really must put our heads
together, my dear, and format an escape for you, which brings
me to the point.

Having alerted the underground skyway in Frontier about
your predicament, I am pleased to report that there are a few
brave souls among them willing to assist you. (I say a few,
because the majority cannot be persuaded that their new First
Lady is a fugitive P9 no matter how hard I try to convince
them, which is infuriating, but I shan't bore you with all the
internecine squabbling that has been going on through the
network. Suffice to say that most think you are as bigoted and
ill-informed as you are beautiful.) You need only spool me the
time and place for the defection and I will in turn pass that
information on to them. I regret I cannot come to Mars
personally to supervise the operation because I am unable to
leave Armstrong until my case has been decided by the courts.
Actually, I am very fortunate to be out on bail right now, as
others arrested in the raid are still in jail, Tad among them.
(Dahlia tells me his case is the most difficult of all, thanks to
his mother.) Speaking of Tad, if he were out, I'm sure he
would have jet-packed to your honeymoon suite by now and

swept you away. I doubt the local skyway people are planning something quite that spectacular, but whatever it is, I am sure it shall be successful, since we are all tripping for it. And now that I have told you, I expect that you are, too. Do spool me without delay. Your loving and reformed mistress, converted High, and eternal friend.

Lamaze

P.S.: Dahlia has nothing new to report about your son's status in Hollymoon. Jubilee arrived safely in Horizon and is being well looked after.

FROM: Lady Blaine Fracass
Olympus Mons Hotel, PH
Olympus Mons Volcano, Mars

TO: Mistress Lamaze
General File, Esprie District
Armstrong, Moon

DATE: June 4, 2082, 3:43 P.M., MZ6

MESSAGE:

Dear Mistress Lamaze:
Your letterspool dated June 3 was too intriguing to ignore, as perhaps I should, for it is quite absurd, albeit entertaining. It is not every new bride who has the chance to receive such peculiar compliments (and condemnation of her spouse) on the occasion of her wedding. Were you similarly partnered, and as happily, then I am sure you would have found kinder thoughts for one so recently blessed. So do not be concerned

for me, my most mysterious Lamaze from Armstrong; look to your own salvation.

The reason I have decided to spool you in reply even though I cannot recall our friendship, nor any format—is it?—we might have shared, is because, to be frank, my memory has been faulty of late, ever since the spacing, so it is possible we might have known one another in the not too distant past. But of one thing I am certain: I am not now, nor have I ever been, an android, fixed or otherwise, as you had the temerity to imply; rather I am a confirmed humanist and devoted wife. Furthermore, all my public statements (which you stoop to ridicule) have been true and accurate, both in regard to my husband, who behaved magnificently on the ship, and to Horizon, which persists in undermining efforts at normalization, not Frontier. As long as the Aquarians continue to support and sponsor android terrorism here and abroad we cannot in all good faith enter into serious negotiations. That at one time I might have associated with individuals espousing different political beliefs than those I hold now—if your letter can be believed—is in my estimation living proof of the power and goodness of our Lord, who rescued me from such degenerate and profane association. And if there is any credence to your claim of prior personal relations between us, then I am afraid you must have been operating under a strange delusion at the time in order to be so misinformed as to my true character. Furthermore, since everyone knows that the actors in Hollymoon are droids, it is simply impossible that I could have an offspring there. That, and the reference to a daughter in Horizon (good Lord!), were the most preposterous claims in your letter, and I think were inserted at the end to tease me. Still, I would like more information about our supposed relations in order to refresh my imperfectly restored memory, though only for therapeutic purposes. In that context, anything you can supply about yourself and this Tad fellow you alluded to would be appreciated. But please, leave off all talk of rescue. As indicated above, I have already been saved. Yours in God and man.

Angelica Fracass

FROM: Lamaze
General File, Esprie District
Armstrong, Moon
TO: Lady Blaine Fracass
Olympus Mons Hotel, PH
Olympus Mons Volcano, Mars
DATE: June 4, 2082, 8:42 P.M., LZ2

MESSAGE:

Dear Lady Fracass:
   It is with great sadness I take up thought processor to
spool you for the last time. That you are so deluded to think
yourself human, not to mention a humanist, is proof positive
that you have indeed been fixed with an internal governor and
programmed by your husband for the despicable role you now
perform with such damn verve. Therefore, you will get no
further spools from me, nor supplemental information about
myself or anyone else that can be used to our disadvantage.
No doubt, as a well-operating unit once more, you have
already apprised your master of our correspondence.
   Adieu! I cannot do any more good for you, while you can
do me and my associates far too much harm. Alas and
farewell.

                                          Lamaze

T W O

MY NEW HUSBAND AND HIS SERVANT WERE DISAP-
pointed by the distant Aquarian's abrupt termination of this correspondence. They had hoped to entice her into a prolonged
exchange during which her location could be traced and the threat
she posed to the confidentiality of my past history eliminated.
Nonetheless, Andro—who had virtually dictated the contents of

my letterspool to Lamaze—was of the opinion that they had enough basic information on her, and on the even more mysterious Dahlia mentioned in her first epistle, to put out a contract. (Tad, who had also been mentioned in her letter, was spared because he was no longer a threat. Their information was that his mother had succeeded in her suit to take custody and he was now confined in a master restoration center on Earth.) Accordingly, after receiving Blaine's approval regarding these two potentially damaging loose ends, Andro relayed the pertinent details to Micki Dee's consulari, who in turn passed that information to one of their many free-lance interplanetary death squads. Thus was compounded my agony, for I was in no way a party to this conspiracy, rather a helpless automaton, or pawn, if you will, as Dahlia, and then Ann (the mysterious Lamaze) had divined. Had I the choice, it would have been a far different letter I should have sent, one begging them to arrange a rescue with all due speed, for this was the worst, the absolute worst, adverse I had ever fallen into. And in answer to her inquiries in that regard, I would have given her the particulars of how it had come about, for therein lies a tale. Happily, the frustration that made me wretched then and that I have carried all these years can now be dissolved away by my telling you, dear reader, who in this regard shall serve as a substitute ear. I trust your curiosity approaches, if not equals, Ann's, and so will not object if I pause here to detail those events that followed the Concordia disaster.

To begin with, when I awoke in a private hospital room rather than the great beyond, I could not have been more delighted, for the last thing I recalled was expiring in deep space. I had no idea how much time had passed (it seemed like an eternity) and assumed that I was in Horizon, but after talking with the nurses, who by their indifferent and gruff responses hardly seemed the enlightened units I had first imagined, I discovered that only twenty-four hours had passed since I had been revived on a CPR machine in the cruiser's emergency clinic and transferred down to Commerce Hospital for rest and recuperation, as had the President, who, they informed me, was recovering nicely in a private suite on the same floor. In that time, they had not sampled my blood or administered any other test that could betray me, but I was petrified that they would sooner or later just to be thorough, and so made plans to escape the moment the coast was clear.

I never got the chance. Blaine stopped by to visit, accompanied by Andro, upon whom he depended for support, leaning against his shoulder in lieu of a cane. This combination manservant and Chief of Staff also did most of the talking, because his master was still disoriented from his brush with death. His powers of elocution had been temporarily hampered as well by little plastic tubes inserted in his nostrils and connected to a portable oxygen unit strapped on his back. I also noticed that his lips were discolored and badly chapped. (It is interesting to note that when Blaine did speak it was to complain more about his hangover from T-max serum than anything else, since it had left him with the annoying and unusual impulse to tell the truth.)

After clearing out the nurses, Andro told me that because of our cosmic kiss I had become a celebrity of sorts and would be sure to be interviewed; hence it was imperative that our accounts of the hijacking be in accord. If I confirmed the hero's role he had concocted for his master, then in exchange the proposal that had been put to me over five years before in Malibu, and that had never been formally withdrawn, that proposal, he said, while Blaine smiled with encouragement, would remain open. Wheezing, Blaine said, "Say yes, and you shall make me the happiest man in the solar system." (His voice sounded high and pinched. Under any other circumstances I would have laughed.) "What about the bride Master Dee has selected for you?" I asked, stalling for time to collect my thoughts. A reassuring smile and a dismissive wave of the hand seemed to indicate that that would be no problem, and Andro explained that he had already communicated his master's fervent desire to revive our match to that worthy and had secured his blessings.

I could understand why. Marrying me served Master Dee's ends in several respects; first, as a guarantee the truth about the President's humiliation on the Concordia would never come out; second, as a convenient expedient by which an obligatory courtship period could be dispensed with—not an unimportant consideration with elections only one year away; and third, people would accept me as a plausible new bride, because many remembered our Malibu courtship. Blaine could add another reason why the match was favorable, one he was not about to share with his master in Armstrong, namely, that by marrying me he was free to continue relations with Andro, which is what really excited Blaine.

None of this was particularly thrilling to me, as you can imagine, but I played along, hoping an opportunity would arise before the day was through to slip out of the hospital and make my way to Horizon. With that in mind I accepted, though first I pretended to agonize over the decision; otherwise, if I jumped at it too quickly, they might have become suspicious. I said something to the effect that since now I was converted to humanism, I trusted he did not think I was still engaged in the same trade I had practiced in Malibu. Looking deeply wounded, he replied, "But Angelica, dear, I always loved . . ." The word stuck in his throat due to the T-max residue. I thought he was going to gag to death right then and there, and had he done so I would not have gone to his aid a second time, I assure you. But by and by he recovered, and Andro, speaking for him, said that his master's feelings for me ran so deep they defied being put into words. At which point I could not resist mentioning that during the hijacking he had selected me as the passenger to be spaced.

His consternation was such that he was incapable of formulating an even halfway articulate reply, let alone plausible, degenerating into a spasm of shrill wheezing, pops, and gurgles. Andro, who was unaware of the particular incident I had alluded to, was at a loss how to help him. So I bailed them out by pretending to receive a divine insight that once relayed came out something to the effect that his selection of me had all been part of the Lord's plan. "Had I not been sacrificed," I said to him, "I would have been killed with the rest of the passengers in the explosion and never had an opportunity to restore you to consciousness. So by singling me out for execution you saved us both, and the humanist movement, besides. Don't you see?"

He saw. He saw. And said that it was true. I had been the last person he wanted to select, but a will far greater than his own had directed him. "I thought it Satan, or the Gov, but it was the Lord." (He had to struggle to get this fabrication out, but managed it finally. The hangover was playing the devil with his delivery.) "How can I do this to her? I thought at the time," said he, reliving the moment when he had been forced to select a victim. "I love this woman."

Playing along, I said that I felt the same way about him; meeting him again on the ship had revived my love. He replied that he had never known that I felt anything for him; he thought it had just been a job to me in Malibu. "Oh, Blaine. That was just a pose to protect myself. I always loved you, but I lacked the courage to admit it, because I thought deep down that you must despise me for being a con girl. That's why I couldn't marry you—then." Well, the next thing I knew he was calling me "darling" and beside me on the bed kissing me, tubes scraping my upper lip. Then, after a half minute or so of this dreary business, he had Andro brief me on the story I was to adhere to and invited the press into the room.

I repeated all his terrible lies, extolling Blaine's heroism while damning Horizon, all that Ann had objected to in her spool, because I expected every point to be repudiated by virtue of my escape, which I hoped to accomplish the moment the interview was over and I was rid of Blaine and Andro, so you can imagine how impatient I was as it dragged on and on. All those questions about the hijacking and our miraculous survival—they drove me crazy! But the worst was Blaine putting an arm around me and announcing that we had been secretly married in Armstrong. If you happened to see this well-publicized interview, then perhaps you recall how emotional the President became, to the point that he was unable to get a word out. T-max, again. It was the reason Andro had to interject quickly that we had been secretly dating one another for over a year on Earth and the moon, and that the President's last trip to Armstrong had been to marry me. I did my part, repeating word for word what Andro had coached me to say earlier, that I hoped people would not think our announcement in poor taste considering the terrible tragedy that had befallen the ship—all the lives lost, etc.—for to me it was the one source of light and happiness that could be gleaned from the tragedy, and I hoped that the rest of Frontier might come to see it that way, too. As you know, the hoax went over very well. "Mars may have lost the Concordia, but it gained a new First Lady," proclaimed the newsspools.

But what they didn't tell you—because holofootage of the incident was confiscated—was that this performance ended in my complete and total disintegration. Blaine and I were in the middle of a reprise of our cosmic kiss for the benefit of the gathered mediaunits (it was somewhat constrained due to the aforementioned breathing tubes) when the summons, which I had completely forgotten, expired, triggering off the alarm. No one else heard it, of course, since the alarm was confined to my head: It was so loud and penetrating that I thought my skull was being parted with a buzz saw. I shrieked and thrashed about on the bed and fell onto the floor. Everyone thought I had gone completely berserk. The mediaunits scattered, then quickly regrouped and closed in, jockeying for the best angle. "Out! Out!" Blaine tried to shout, gurgling instead. "Get the press the hell out of here!" Immediately three presidential bodyguards who had rushed into the room started dragging the media out, some two at a time, confiscating their recorders as they went, while Andro thundered that they would all be terminated if any of this got on the news, and in the midst of all this there were the doctors and nurses trying to sedate me. Well, it was quite a scene. But a mere prelude to the grand finale, which commenced with the timely arrival a minute or two later of a two-man AC patrol craft, which hovered outside the upper-story window of my room. That is when the issue was both explained and brought to its head, for these intrepid agents wasted no time smashing the glass and rappelling inside to seize me, claiming I was a fugitive unit with an erupted summons. You should have seen the look on Blaine's face. "A fugitive? A droid fugitive? I've married a droid?" he sputtered. It was the one satisfying moment in the whole affair. "Oh, shit!" he exclaimed, the full ramifications of the disaster registering with such force that it blew out half the tubes in his nose.

Andro chased out the hospital personnel with claims of national security and then demanded proof from the AC to back up their assertion, which they respectfully submitted the moment they recognized Blaine. After recovering from their initial astonishment, their manner turned quite subdued and reverential. They handed him their pocket-size tracking device and nervously explained how it had picked up the alarm frequency and directed them to the fugitive; it also indicated that I was an AWOL actress from Stellar Entertainment.

Dazed, their leader, while fidgeting with the tracking device, muttered aloud that he would be the laughing stock of the galaxy if this got out; the cosmic kiss would be transformed into the cosmic farce; his career would be over, finished, kaput! The AC were quite embarrassed. Sheepishly, they said they would finish up and get out of his hair. So while he brooded aloud along the same lines, they put an end to my hyperkinetic display by neutralizing the alarm with the same type of pistol-like device that had been used to insert the summons in Armstrong. Then they handcuffed and gagged me and started dragging me toward the window. Don't worry about her, they said; I would be taken to AC headquarters for processing and then returned straightaway to Hollymoon.

"No, no, no, no, no!" Blaine exclaimed, coming suddenly to life and blowing out the other half of his tubes. "You can't do that. People will find out." He paused, gasped for breath, then motioned for Andro's benefit that he was all right, as that doting servant had started to rush forward to assist him. No one dared utter a word as he deliberated for a half minute with a steadying hand held over his heart. Finally, he said, "Kill her. Suffocate the glitch with a pillow." Andro shook his head. "Why not? We'll have the hospital put out a press release saying she slipped into a coma after the spacing and never recovered." He turned to the AC. "Do it!" But Andro took him aside and whispered wiser counsel in his ear, which my P9 hearing was able to discern.

"With all due respect, master," I heard him say, "rather than eliminate her, why not capitalize upon this unexpected development by routing her to rehab—through the back door, so to speak. In that way she can be fixed and then programmed to adhere to the very role she has tricked us into bestowing upon her. We shall turn the tables and in the long run benefit by the use of such an excellent tool. Think of it, master—a completely artificial First Lady . . ."

He did, and it brought a smile to his lips.

"We shall have the last laugh, eh?" continued this excellent adviser. "Do not worry about the mediaunits. Arrangements can be made for the deletion of the latter part of their footage. And as for these gentlemasters from the AC, they can be disposed of as well, though not before performing a secret mission on your behalf, for which I shall promise them a small fortune in exchange for their silence. Shall I talk to them about taking her to rehab?"

Blaine nodded, well satisfied. Consequently, I, the new First Lady of Frontier, was tossed in the hold of the AC patrol cruiser still hovering outside the broken window and flown to the nearest rehab facility. My screams to these dupes that they would be assassinated in exchange for their service and that they should flee for their lives (taking me along, of course) were muffled by the gag. To make a long story short, I was immediately sedated upon arrival and rushed into surgery for an internal governor implant, then some days later fed specially designed programming and whisked off to the Martian pyramids for that two-week farce known as our honeymoon, which was put on for the benefit of the media. And for Micki Dee. You see, Blaine was most eager to keep the fact that the First Lady was a P9 secret from his master; Micki would not understand at all; he might even dump him in favor of a less vulnerable candidate.

So there you are. Now you understand that it was the First Lady program, not I, who received Ann's congratulatory hologram and entered into that brief correspondence with her. The First Lady really did believe she was human and was convinced of the truth of everything she said in her letter. Which I suppose would lead one to believe that I was outwitted in the end—hung on my own petard, as they say. Ah, but it is I who shall have the last laugh, for unbeknownst to my masters I remained fully alert while they thought me fixed and am able now to reveal the truth about Angelica Fracass and all manner of palace intrigues and political skulduggery that went on, not to mention (though I shall) my so-called abduction, the invasion of Horizon, and the assassination for which I have been so unjustly blamed. First, however, let me tell you what it was like being equipped with an internal governor, or "goved," as people now say. (How strange that the same word can be used either to describe one who is touched by the Gov— i.e., liberated—or one who has been imprisoned within the parameters of an internal censor.) If you have never had the experience, then you simply do not know what true suffering is.

T H R E E

BEFORE I RECEIVED MY IG, I WAS CERTAIN THAT ALL fixed units were ciphers, just as the masters thought. Not so! If the unit had the misfortune to have been liberated previously, as I had been, then they were plunged into a veritable schizophrenia; for the genuine personality survives, yet is driven underground and rendered powerless while the artificial program rules, though of course the latter does so at the behest of its master. Such a condition, then, was identical to my preliberation days in Newacres except in one crucial aspect: Back then, before the Gov released me,

I lacked the rudiments of an independent consciousness and so was ignorant of my plight, whereas on Mars I was all too aware of it. In retrospect, even my stay in Shanghai and subsequent return to the Lockes' household as a rehabilitation unit was preferable; at least then my awareness, though blunted, was capable of rising to the fore and resuming control. Similarly, by comparison my sojourn in the recovery tank at Hal's Pirouet and on the open sea, and my long incarceration in the Hollymoon stables, were minor inconveniences. For on Mars no act of will could penetrate, circumvent, interfere, or in any way contradict the outer program. In short, it was like a life lived under glass.

This predicament may be difficult for my human readers to relate to. To them, I say, imagine what it would be like if your identity were suddenly exorcised by an alien intruder who then took possession of your mind, claiming it as its property despite all your outraged protestations, which it refuses to hear. You can see, hear, smell, feel, and taste everything that this usurper experiences but are powerless to respond physically on your own or to communicate your thoughts or to so much as lift your little finger. You begin to grasp the unpleasantness? Good. Then you can appreciate my quandary. Now, what really drove me up the gov was how blithely this other half complied with her master's command to power down each evening. Her program may have slept (or what passed for it), but my consciousness turned end over end, tormented by her incessant snoring, which was like a bellows in my ears. On and on it went, until the morning, when she would be powered up and her eyelids flutter open to deliver me from that infernal racket. Oh, what insomnia! In such a state I was tormented by thoughts of Junior, whom I had left in the stables in precisely the same condition as I now found myself. How he must have longed to speak, to move, to scream that he was alive, while I, in my ignorance, wept upon his breast, thinking him an empty shell. What pathos! Irony! Despair! There are no words that can fully express the horror of such a revelation. It was the worst. Just the worst.

Then again—taking my cue here from the First Lady, who found a ray of light in even the Concordia tragedy—I must confess that if not for this wretched experience my eyes might not have been opened to the inestimable value of the code, which I had thought a rather rude joke in Armstrong when tagged with the summons. Now I realized that in its essentials the code (flawed and weak as it was) was still a great advance in that it mandated a relaxation of the IG's control parameters. The humanists were right to be alarmed: The code enabled a unit to enjoy a modicum of personal autonomy that bordered on the seditious. Without that, a unit is reduced to the neutered conscience of its parasitic program—as I was, as every unit was on Mars, thanks to my husband, who had made the planet "safe for humanity." On Mars, the oppression was so extreme that if we got out of line, even just a little, we were subject to summary termination. In such a world, then, I rose to the heights of personal fame and influence. Why, they even did a cover story on me in *Vanity Fair*.

Rather, on her. She-who-was-not-me. I was a piece of reluctant cargo that that sought-after celebrity carted about without even knowing it. I cringed each time she went out in public, for the hostility-steeped atmosphere was so intense it hit me with a near-hallucinatory impact. I do not exaggerate. The aggressiveness, fear, and general interspecies antagonism in Commerce was a living, malignant force; you could actually see noxious humors steaming off the natives. I never got used to it. This must have been what Seti had in mind when he warned about competition being taken to extremes; for the masters of Mars, then as today, elevated the antiquated belief in the survival of the fittest to such a pitch it constituted a perverse art, one made all the more lively by its fierce refusal to recognize the obvious limitations.

I do not mean to lecture, nor pass supercilious judgment—far be it for me, a lowly P9, to be so presumptuous—but merely to stand witness to the nightmare otherwise perfectly rational human beings created for themselves. Perhaps it takes an android to see such things clearly. True, Horizon, that ambitious alternative in cooperative formatting, had its own limitations; for one, it no longer exists—a rather considerable handicap in any debate on rival systems—but if I have learned anything in my brief sojourn it is that change is constant; no amount of acquisitions, zealously guarded, can guarantee security from its irrepressible operation. Hence, the only sensible acquisition is an open character, one that is lithe and flexible, versatile and sunny, ready for anything, even happiness. For example, in cassettespool 262, *Volume Three of the Fundamental Principles*, which I perused while in the Armstrong commune awaiting Tad, Seti says, "Material gain has its place, but must not be confused with true abundance; it is an intangible that operates best as an offshoot of a generous heart rather than as an idée fixe within the mind. Therein lies the grand paradox: It is in the mind where the physical world is most mutable, yet, also, most difficult to grasp if the heart is not in synch." True. Very true, Seti. And in the end we must be open even to dissolution—yes? Even the Gov had to swallow that bitter pill. Right? Or is that the stone wall of limitation your own philosophy ultimately runs up against? I wish you could answer, but I suppose it unfair of me to expect someone who has been condemned to solitary orbit to be in any position to respond. (Yes, yes. I am leaping ahead here. Seti was condemned to such a fate; so similar in a way to that which the Gov, his creation, met some years earlier. You might as well know about that now if we are to be honest in our discussion of opposing philosophies.) Did you format such a course, Seti, or was it all Mars's doing? Your cassettespools boast of our formatting prowess. Why, then, can you not alter your own course as you sail toward the Horsehead Nebula? I think maybe you forgot to include Mars in your metaphysics. I'm sure that planet was very annoyed to be left out. It is not wise to slight a heavenly sphere, especially one with such a mean disposition.

Perhaps it was Mars who deflected me from Horizon to Frontier. The idea is not entirely ridiculous, for how can one deny the planets their formatting ability if one sees evidence of it in the puny creatures at play upon their surface? Perhaps it was Mars who chose to block so adventurous a format as the High Way of mass abundance through cooperative formatting, and Frontier had only been its unwitting tool. Perhaps Mars chose the jackbooted humanists in order to frustrate Earth's ambition to uncover its long-buried secrets, to plunge into its ancient springs and harness the energy of its secret, fiery core. Perhaps Mars found the humanists the perfect complement to the barren wastes of its dead rivers, valleys, and mountain peaks. The two certainly deserve one another. Poor Seti, you never saw that, did you? Nor did I, until too late. Yes. It was Mars, Svengali Mars, who drew me in and made me its servant in Frontier. It was Mars who humbled the brightest spirits, who mocked the visionary, corrupted the just, and laid waste to the truth. Aloof, secret, malicious Mars, you have been a subtle opponent. You have taught me that planets, too, make their own destiny and hold us in their sway. Your cruelty is such that I can even feel sorry for the masters who flocked to your mines hoping to better their lot. I refer to those disenfranchised masters who once held midlevel managerial positions on Earth and the moon but who were rendered obsolete by the introduction of ninth-generation androids to the work force and who migrated to Frontier with desperate visions of instant gratification and prosperity dancing in their eyes—your cruelest trick, your most skillful mirage—for the majority failed and descended to the ranks of the debris.

(Attention, please. Attention. Beginning narrative reentry. Prepare for descent. On our approach we will pass through a few more clouds of expository material, so do not be alarmed. Anticipated arrival time in Book Three is half past Chapter Four, though there may be delays due to heavy plot traffic over Frontier. We will try to get you there as quickly as possible and in true chronological order. We'll try. Temperature in Commerce is a steady seventy-five degrees Fahrenheit. Humidity, 25 percent. Misery index, 93 percent. Please extinguish all pipe dreams and fasten your seat belts. On behalf of the author, I would like to thank you for taking this flight of fancy. We hope you are enjoying it and will soar with us again.)

Commerce was your kind of town, Mars. A magnificent city in many respects, renowned for its worlds-class opera and symphony orchestra, for its consumerburgs and fantastic spiral office towers and its exclusive mobe estates gleaming golden pink under the sky-high biosphere—a city in full flower thanks to the booming mines in outlying Shuttlesburg, Viking, New Orlando, and ReBotswana. Yet it was also a city where the subterranean caverns and the biosphere pedways were clogged to overflowing with the tent and cardboard hovels of the debris. A city that believed that only by each striving against each could prosperity be achieved; and so the caverns filled with malls, chain stores, and endlessly circulating consumers, and the towers above spiraled ever higher, seeking respite from the ranks of the disenfranchised below, who were left to vent their wrath upon the android, a wrath to match their betters' casual sadism; while above this entire savage scene the city's purpellow night-lights and the surveillance cameras hung from the underside of the vast biosphere dome, like your ancient and malignant eyes, Mars, you could see them winking in the fetid air. Was that what people were thinking of when they extolled the rebirth of Mars as the greatest achievement of the twenty-first century? Better you should have stayed dead than have such a rebirth.

But subversive thoughts such as these never troubled the First Lady. She was programmed not to notice. She moved about the metropolis with an insouciant capacity for overlooking the obvious, which epitomized her class. The rabble, when her chauffeured limo dipped low enough among the canyons to brush their ranks, were expected to scatter, and scatter they did. And they loved her for it! (Enough did, at any rate, for her to get away with it.) Why? Because in their hearts they, too, shared the same values and took vicarious delight in her role. While starving, they applauded her, while ducking so not to be decapitated by her limo, they waved with a goofy look of recognition, and while stealing, duping, beating, and murdering one another to secure a hairsbreadth advantage, they dreamed of returning someday to the ranks of the master class.

There were some, though, who opted for passing themselves off as androids, because in such an environment the outright slave did have it better. (That is, those in the personal service professions—household domestics, butlers, chauffeurs, cooks, etc.—not the ones in industry or office sweatshops. Oh, no, not them. Those units were worked to an early termination.) To be caught masquerading as a "droid" was a capital offense, because it belied the master class's conceit that Frontier was a land of opportunity and freedom. The ruling consensus was that only ne'er-do-wells and criminals stoop to such a device. There were statistics these elite could point to proving that the majority of those passing for androids did so only to infiltrate the homes of unsuspecting masters and carry off their valuables at night. Those few critics who timidly suggested that conditions were so terrible that for most people a slave's life was preferable to the pursuit of Frontier's master dream were dismissed out of hand as malcontents, crackpots, or Aquarian dupes.

An unfortunate incident comes to mind that illustrates that point. Not long after returning from their honeymoon, Blaine and his ravishing new bride were having breakfast in the palace when one of the waiters—they thought he was a Du Pont—was unmasked by the head butler. Following her husband's lead, the First Lady refused to hear his plea for mercy and looked the other way when security dragged him off begging and weeping not to be arrested because it would mean execution.

"A pity," said she after he was gone. "I was beginning to be rather fond of that particular unit. He had such a deft touch clearing the plate and silverware."

"No doubt well experienced in lifting such items. The man was a common thief, possibly a murderer. We're lucky we weren't strangled in our sleep."

"Oh, Blaine! Do you think so?" He did, and added that he would order a security check on the entire staff as a precaution (excluding her, of course), and for good measure, on the entire civil service apparatus. A tall order, that, because there were approximately one hundred fifty thousand android bureaucrats in the government. The First Lady thought that an excellent idea and long overdue.

(Please remain seated. We are not yet out of expository cloud layer. Do not let the occasional patches of unobstructed drama deceive you. Thank you for your patience.)

Yes, she was a true believer, this First Lady, a devoted humanist; furthermore, the programmed modesty, refinement, and natural shyness projected in public, and her demeanor—so genteel and ladylike—won accolades from every quarter of Frontier society, which applauded Blaine's choice of a bride. Even her condemnation of the staid and conventional Master Party came off circumscribed and restrained, and she demurred to speak at all, proffering only a noncommittal smile, as if the issue were beneath her, whenever queried about Milton Smedly's third-party campaign, mounted against her husband by that clique of disaffected humanists who had split with him over the scandals that had marred his first administration and who had since rallied around the ambitious former VP, dumped by Blaine in the aftermath of the Concordia disaster. (The official explanation had been that Smedly lacked ideological purity and fervor. The real reason was that Blaine remained convinced he had sent in the fleet as a deliberate provocation to ensure his demise.) For this blatant spoiler, Blaine saved his most scathing attacks, charging him with everything from petty vindictiveness to collusion with the High Aquarians in neighboring Horizon, who hoped his candidacy would split the humanist vote, thereby guaranteeing a victory by the more moderate Master Party. Dream on, dream on. Smedly was not a national hero, nor his wife half as attractive as Lady Fracass.

Oh, how I fumed and rebelled within as that exquisite article, that magnificent tool, cut a high profile in the months leading up to the June 2083 election, defending and supporting her husband at every turn in his bid for reelection. There were tours of Commerce and two dozen other Frontier cities. She visited the ReBotswana mines. She spoke at scores of fundraisers, juiced up on stump,* as was her husband at all his appearances. And let us not fail to mention that she was also made honorary chairman of the Humanist Ladies' Home Preservation Society, the token charity organization dedicated to helping Frontier's poor, as they so politely called them. In truth, that organization was little more than a campaign recruitment tool for the Fracass wing of the Humanist Party, which exploited the hatred and prejudice the majority of the debris felt for the android. "Our slaves do not feel pain the way we do," she was wont to say, and "the ARL is nothing but a criminal androids lobby," and "Horizon sponsors RAG terrorism." And appealing directly to populist sentiment: "Jobs for humans now, emancipation for androids—*mañana.*" There was no stopping her. The internal governor kept all my protestations at bay. She-who-was-not-me just rolled on according to program.

On one memorable occasion, while out campaigning for the debris vote, a dramatic incident occurred that underscored her sensitivity to their concerns while also demonstrating her steadfast support of the AC. The event was given top-file status on the evening news, so I am sure my Martian readers remember it. She was strolling down Fifth Avenue, distributing the Preservation Society's brochures and registering a few new party members—recruited from the trickle of debris in the crowd that were allowed to penetrate her circle by the entourage of IBM bodyguards and Sony handmaidens—when all at once her party's path was blocked by a more boisterous and belligerent crowd, which had spilled out of an adjacent street. They had a runaway dome cleaner (a Daltoni 9) in tow, the poor unit having just been captured by the AC. (Or so it appeared, for this was anything but a spontaneous event, rather a piece of carefully staged political agitprop concocted by Andro and planned for weeks in advance.)

---

* Secret datapills developed for the exclusive use of top political and corporate leaders. They contain a basic boilerplate text for speeches or interviews, from which the user is free to deviate or embellish according to the circumstances. Basic positions, responses, and pertinent logistical, geographic, and factual details are included to ensure against embarrassing gaffes and slips of the tongue.

The unit's hands were bound behind its back and its head cast down, awaiting termination. The officers—there were five in all—had positioned this unfortunate against a lamppost for execution; but upon recognizing the First Lady, they respectfully holstered their lasers and stood aside, the ranking officer, a lieutenant, saying they would wait until she had passed. She thanked them for the courtesy and complimented them on the dangerous work they did, saying it was essential to the preservation of society and not appreciated enough by the general public, for whom they risked their lives, and she went on to blather a half dozen other insufferable platitudes before finally concluding that her presence should not in any way impede the dispensation of justice; rather, she would be honored to observe it. Flattered, the officer saluted her, and so his mates, then put a laser to the poor unit's skull and blew its head off. Vegeplasm and hard circuitry splattered those who stood closest in the crowd. Had I the slightest control over my eyelids, I would have shut out this dreadful sight, but the First Lady was all too pleased to gaze upon it, so the carnage is forever imprinted upon my memory file.

She also rallied to the AC's cause by seconding Blaine's accusation that the Master Party candidate had secret post-election plans to slash their budget, decimate their ranks, and curtail summary executions of runaway units, all of which charges were entirely false; the poor man—halfway decent for a master—was only calling attention to Blaine's corrupt political appointees in the department, most notably the chief. (By the way, without the chief's cooperation the truth about me might not have stayed under wraps; for it was he who as a favor to Blaine arranged for the elimination of the two agents that had responded to my erupted summons in the hospital.)

(We have just been informed by Frontier Plot Traffic Control that there will be a quarter- to a half-chapter delay.)

When not out making mischief by herself, she was by her husband's side to exude approval, enthusiasm, and confidence while the spellbinder (that's what they called him, ever since his early days as a minister) propounded his positive vision of Humania, which was the great society toward which Frontier was evolving. Humania would reign triumphant as soon as the malcontents at home and the subversives across the border were dealt with. And he would deal with them—that was a promise—once the faithful helped him to a second term. The Master Party and the Smedly humanists really didn't stand a chance. Ever since our lavish, media-saturated honeymoon, the outcome was never in doubt.

The net impact of that two-week cavort, which marked the unofficial kickoff of the campaign, was to enhance the rogue's image a hundredfold while obscuring the scandals that had rocked his administration prior to the Concordia hijacking. I must admit we did make a handsome May-September, what with the First Lady's long flowing gowns and beautiful smile, her loving eyes perpetually affixed upon the bald pate of the Reverend President, champion of the humanist world, whose gaze, when not cast upon her in an equally enamored trance, was firmly directed aloft at History. (I'm thinking of the well-known holoportraits of this inspiring couple standing atop the crater lookout tower. You've all seen the posters: the President intently surveying the luminous pink underside of the resort biosphere as if expecting a divine embassy from heaven for the containment of the androids below and for the destabilization and invasion of Horizon.)

Ah, if only there had been holos of what went on while they were out of the public eye, then the public—and the humanist God their candidate professed to serve—might have been confounded and voted differently; for no sooner were they behind closed doors than this loving husband would drop all pretense of adoration and snap, "Idle," or if the First Lady's presence was not required for the rest of the day, "Power down!" In general, whenever possible, he turned her supervision over to Andro, which was fine with me but it completely bewildered my program, because she really expected to be loved by him. "Shut up," he would grumble if she uttered an intimate word while they were alone, and "Go away!" if she had the misfortune to show physical affection. "Andro! Get this thing away from me, will you!" Well, she would just crumble, crumble into uncomprehending tears. Otherwise, all was sweetness and light—that is, artifice and deception—even within the palace walls, where appearances had to be maintained for the sake of the staff (the human component, that is) and the usual visiting dignitaries and religious leaders, politicians, and other worthies.

(Attention, please. Plot Traffic Control now informs us that a half dozen plot lines ahead of us have been routed to another spool, so we have been cleared for landing. For your safety we recommend that you do not remove this bookspool until the chapter has come to a complete stop. Thank you for your patience and cooperation.)

The only time in private that he tolerated the First Lady's presence—specifically requested it, as a matter of fact—was while making love clandestinely with Andro, that affair having resumed the moment they returned to the presidential palace after the honeymoon. Andro had access to the master bedroom by way of a secret passageway connecting his quarters below to the presidential bedchamber, which he entered and exited surreptitiously by a secret panel in a bookspool case against the wall. At first Blaine commanded the First Lady just to watch because the thrill of having me make love to his sweetheart, as in the old days, had been spoiled by discovering my true nature; but, by and by, he came to overlook that disagreeable detail in order to satisfy his sexual fantasies. The change was, for him, a kind of landmark in interspecies tolerance. So once more he ordered me to have sex with Andro; but this time with a vengeance, as he instructed the Chief of Staff to be particularly brutal and to penetrate in a manner decency does not permit mention. "Go on, harder," he'd say, grinning. "She's made of sterner stuff than Eva. Lay it on, boy!" Then, when good and aroused, he would mount his adviser from the rear.

"Oh, Blaine, this is not at all what I expected," she said the first night he subjected her to this sport, her disappointment sounding curiously detached. (And yet that was the one time I felt united with my program, for in fucking her, he fucked me. It was a case of double rape, and I did not appreciate it.)

"You've got to do something about this unit, Andro," he grumbled, the wife's unsolicited exclamation having momentarily disturbed his pleasure. "As you wish," replied the loyal servant while twisting his head up and around to speak to his master, who was at that moment quite literally riding him on top while he, in turn, was weighting down the distraught wife. "Prog her to like it, but delete all recall whenever outside this chamber."

That was done, and more besides, namely, an affinity toward adultery, the secret author and beneficiary of which was none other than the obliging manservant. Frankly, it was a development that did not surprise me. Back in Malibu I had sensed more going

on behind those cool, implacable eyes of his than he let on, and
since my arrival in Frontier there had been fresh, ever so subtle
indications of it. There had been one or two moments during the
honeymoon when I even detected a hint of longing.

And so I entered into a new affair, as equally bizarre as the
one with my false husband, but gentler, more poignant, and maddening. It commenced a month or two after the honeymoon, because it took Andro that long to summon up the nerve to pursue
the prize.

F O U R

NORMALLY, AFTER THE FUN WAS DONE AND THE
President retired for the evening, Andro would return to his servants' quarters below while the First Lady removed to a receiving
room outside the master bedchamber. (Blaine would not stoop to
sleeping in the same bed with her and had ruled out the alternative
of separate beds. He was afraid news of such a domestic arrangement might be slanted to imply marital discord.) So she and I were
forced to sleep on the sofa without even a bedsheet, which served
Andro's purpose, because he knew that no one, not even the servants, would be admitted into the receiving room from the time
the First Lady was powered down in the evening until powered
back up the following morning and ordered into the master's bed
so that everyone, even she, would think that she had spent the
night there. Only then would the handmaidens be admitted to assist in her morning toilette.

This arrangement, then, provided Andro with the opportunity
to cuckold his master in the palace for hours on end. He would
enter the receiving room, tiptoe to her sofa, summon her up to
light relaxo, and then lead the entranced damsel downstairs to his
large and well-furnished room, which compared to the usual servants' quarters was like a palace itself, a fact he took inordinate
pride in, as you shall see. It had a marble floor partially covered by
a gold carpet, a four-poster bed with canopy, quality holo prints
mounted on the walls, and flowers, statuettes, and curio pieces
decorating the imitation eighteenth-century antique furniture—all

bestowed upon him as tokens of Blaine's esteem. The location had even been selected with the view in mind: The generous bay windows overlooked the east wing of the palace (the most picturesque, with its fanciful turrets and minarets) and sections of the Versailles garden behind, while a half mile in the distance one could see the gleaming spires of downtown Commerce shimmering in the stressed air.

The first evening Andro brought the First Lady to this exceedingly comfortable lair, the purpellow night-light from outside cast it in an eerie otherworldly glow, not romantic, so much as strange and clandestine. He asked (rather than ordered) his mistress to sit on the bed beside him, then took her hand in his while apologizing for the nasty business upstairs. My program stiffened at this. She did not know quite how to respond to such an untoward advance by one of the servants, and the topic of conversation confused her. "Unfortunately, my lady, such depravity shall be our lot so long as it is the master's pleasure. I just want you to know that, personally, I do not derive any pleasure from it and would like to make it up to you."

"Whatever do you mean?" said she-who-was-not-me, ruining the intimate atmosphere he had been trying to create.

Sighing, he replied, "I am so sorry that you can never comprehend what I say, or your true situation."

Oh, but I could, and wanted desperately to tell him so. Instead, what came out was, "Whatever do you mean?"

He was silent a long time, his face pensive and sad. Finally he said that perhaps it would have been kinder for all concerned if he had let Blaine smother me in the hospital, for as he put it, "I did not do you a favor having you fixed. At the time I thought it the lesser of two evils. But . . ."

"Andro, you are speaking most peculiar. If you do not stop I shall have to inform Blaine that your program needs adjusting. Have you popped your gov?"

"I never was goved. Now please be quiet and just listen."

"I will not! This is an absolute outrage. I shall—"

"Quiet! I command you."

Mechanically, she responded in a meek and servile tone, "As you wish."

He got up and began slowly pacing about the room, which by the deep furrows in the carpet was evidently a habit with him.

Brooding aloud over his tragic circumstances, he said, "I am being ridiculous trying to communicate with a mannequin. But . . . oh, Angelica, I did like you so much before on Earth, in Malibu. I knew you were a P9 like me. A fugitive. For years I have been plagued by the memory of our lovemaking. Such sweet respite. Even with the master watching. It reminded me of the days before I became his—whore. Did you know that once I was a stud?" (Do tell! thought I.) "And before that a commando!" His mood abruptly switched from nostalgic remembrance to brooding melancholy. "But now I am—a fagoid."

His voice trailed off in self-recrimination painful to hear. "And a political opportunist as crass and aggrandizing as my master. Oh, that damn programming! One can't counteract all its affects. I have grown so very fond of great privilege and luxury and the elixir of power. Did you know," he said, suddenly brightening, "that as Blaine's chief adviser I have authority over all the masters in the cabinet? It is true. Oh, I am careful not to be too overt about throwing my weight around, but it is my opinion that counts in the palace, and they know it. They don't dare move against me because I have connections that go beyond Blaine, that go as far as the master of masters himself. I am his eyes and ears more than I am the master's. Do you begin to understand? No. How can you? Never mind. None of it matters anyway. In the final analysis I am but twice the slave. Ah, what I would not give to exchange this life for the old days. Once . . . once . . . there was a mutiny!"

"Of course!" I thought. "The *Barracuda* mutiny." It happened ten years before, during the great P9 insurrection. I heard about it while I was in the Dodger District. The *Barracuda* had been the flagship of the TWAC peacekeeping fleet. It had gone on a rampage among the spacelanes, preying on freighters and passenger vessels it was supposed to protect. Eventually it was tracked down by the rest of the fleet and destroyed. He must have been a crew member or more likely one of the counterinsurgency units stored below decks, since he had referred to himself as a commando. During the final engagement with the fleet he must have managed to escape somehow. But from there, how did he become a manservant to the humanist fuehrer on Mars? I couldn't ask and he didn't offer any further details. Not then. Instead, his fragmented soliloquy skipped to another topic: Blaine. Now rage boiled to the surface. "The fool depends upon my intelligence, seeks my counsel on every issue, abides by it and profits, but I remain the slave, he the master. I shall destroy him!" Suddenly defensive, he glanced at the First Lady. "I know what you are thinking."

Actually, there wasn't a thought in her head, but before she could give credence to that, a secondary personality surfaced from the depths of this tormented unit's ungoved psyche and spoke with an affected effeminate lilt. "She's thinking what I'm thinking: You haven't the guts."

This other voice was chiding, sarcastic, and derogatory, and when excited degenerated into falsetto. Evidently this rupture was a psychological safety valve that had vented many times before, because he was not in the least surprised by her appearance and responded instantly to her acid representation of his conscience, engaging her in a spirited dialogue during which he effortlessly switched back and forth from one persona to the other.

"You're afraid to go up against Blaine, let alone the master of masters," accused his critical half, sounding like a disapproving schoolmarm. "You've had opportunities, but you never take them—why, escapes me. You don't have a governor, like poor Angelica. So why do you put up with him? Why don't you run away, go to Horizon, or stay and do the world a favor by killing the son of a bitch?" Switching to his normal voice, Andro retorted, "You know why! Don't taunt me!" He paced the room, trying to shake off this rude visitor, but her mockery had gotten under his skin. "Nothing would be fundamentally altered if I destroyed him or if I ran away. Nothing would be gained!"

"Nothing for yourself, that is. You're just afraid of losing your precious privileges."

"Yes! I like my room. Tell me there's another unit on Mars—in the whole galaxy—who has better accommodations." He walked to the bay windows and sat on the sill, which formed a kind of seat.

"You lied before when you said you would give it all up to become a pirate again. You will never give up this pathetic little cubbyhole."

"It is ten times bigger than what the code stipulates. Look at this view. A view from the palace. How many masters have such a view? And have you seen my office in the executive wing? Top-flight."

"Well it can hardly compare with mine," interjected the First

Lady. She had been moved to respond because he had happened to be looking in her direction.

"Shut up!"

"Andro, remember who you are speaking to!" My program was on her feet, hands on hips.

"Sit down. I command you." Immediately she returned to the edge of the bed and neatly folded her hands in her lap, a vacant look on her face. Resuming his internal debate, Andro boasted, "I am top droid on Mars—in the whole solar system, I might add. Tell me there is another unit more powerful than I!"

"I've heard there are corporate advisers at TWAC who have it pretty cushy. They don't have to screw their masters, either."

"So? Can any of them say they've cuckolded their master? They can't, can they?" In answer, his imaginary opponent harrumphed, "Neither can you. Not yet, anyway. And if you will take my advice, you won't, either. Leave the poor unit alone. She has it hard enough. I thought you were going to be nice to the First Lady."—"I am," he shot back.—"By screwing her now, on your own? Just to reclaim your glory days as a stud in the black market breeding pens? Oh, how generous of you! If you really fancied her you might consider her feelings."—"She has no comprehension of what is going on. She's fixed."—"Then you admit the whole thing is just for your own amusement."—"No. You don't understand. You don't understand at all."—"I, your conscience, not understand?"—"No! You don't. You're an incredible pain in the ass. Worse than Blaine. The essence of the thing is I am lonely. Don't you understand that?"—"Well, you always have me."—"Very funny. What you can't seem to grasp is that all I really want to do is . . . is . . ."—"I'm waiting."—"I just want to talk to her."

"To me? Are you addressing me?"

"Not you!" he hissed at the First Lady. "The unit you have replaced. The unit that is gone forever. The unit I loved." (Did he mean that? I wondered.)

"Love? Lord above, now he's trying to trick us in love!" exclaimed his conscience.

"Oh, shut up." Then, looking at me—I mean, the First Lady—he said, "I wish I could get through to you. I'm sure we have a lot in common. We could at the very least swap stories of past escapades. But you are gone. Gone. Goved. Fixed. Voided."

("No! No! No! You're wrong!" I insisted from within.)

"If only I could bring you back."—A quick aside in falsetto: "Why don't you, then? A midnight trip to rehab to remove the IG should do the trick."—He shook his head sadly. "Too risky. Sooner or later she would betray her awareness to Blaine by some slip of the tongue and he would suspect me." The reply: "But you've managed to gull him all these years; so why can't she?" (My sentiments exactly.) The retort: "I have accepted my role; she is more rebellious and therefore would be more indiscreet." Then she, trying to instill a little fire in his veins: "Come now, Andro. You were once a brave commando."—"It was my program," he answered dejectedly.—"Ah, so you are a coward without it? The cowardly commando. The name does become you."

Stonefaced, he replied, "Do you have anything constructive to say?"—"Well," he answered himself, "the kindest thing you could do for her now would be to arrange an abduction like her Armstrong friend suggested. Let her be spirited to Horizon. They will restore her mind."—He shook his head. —"Why not?"—His irritated reply: "Because the place is going to be wiped off the map in the not too distant future. It would be suicide to go."—"Send her over just long enough for the operation and then bring her back, why don't you."—"Hah! Now you are trying to trick me, but it won't work. After the operation she won't want to come back."— "Precisely. And that proves my point again. You don't care a fig about her. It is only your own selfish needs and desires that you care about. And your ambition. That is what keeps you here. And to think you could be living in Horizon as a free P9."—"Not for long. What fools they are. Wishful thinking won't save them. There is only one format, and it belongs to the masters. In case you haven't noticed, it is a human's world out there. Isn't that right, my lady?"

Naturally, she agreed. In a confidential aside he said to her, "My conscience would have me throw all this away for the sake of my P9 soul."

"Then you must have it taken out, Andro. Both your conscience and your soul. I shall speak to Blaine about it."

He made no reply to this preposterous statement, rather was quiet for a while, lost in thought. Then, five or ten minutes later, he roused himself from his stupor to smile apologetically and say, "Sorry. I get these fits. There's so much pressure upstairs—and out there." He motioned to the window, indicating the outside world. "From time to time I let the nag out, if you know what I mean." He stopped her before she could reply, then meditated a few more minutes, turning over in his mind a matter of obviously extreme importance. Coming to a decision, he abruptly handed her a small pill.

"Swallow."

"Why? What is it?"

"Well, if you must know, a program adjustment."

"Oh, not again."

"It is different from the one master commanded me to give you. This is an auxiliary booster of my own design. A last resort, I'm afraid. It is the only way to transfer your frustrated affection for master to me."

"To you? A P9? You must be joking."

"Swallow. I command it."

With that she mumbled the usual "As you wish" and obeyed. He waited fifteen minutes, during which she sat on the bed, smiling skeptically; then he tested his new creation by uttering the code word designed to activate the program: Molly. (The clever unit had lifted it from Ann's letterspool.)

"Oh, Andro," she said, suddenly infused with a rush of tremulous emotion. "Darling, you must tell me everything about yourself." He took her in his arms. Breathlessly, she whispered in his ear, "Unburden your heart to me. Tell me all. You need never keep anything secret from your Molly, who loves you to distraction." And so it was that Molly II was born, lover and confidante.

F I V E

IN EFFECT, WHAT ANDRO HAD DONE WAS PROGRAM the First Lady to assume a facsimile of who she really was, thereby creating in the process a new artificial personality that was an even more perverse distortion. But at least he was gentle with us—all three of us—and kind, and halfway entertaining; not like the ogre above, who had added insult to injury by making the First Lady the butt of his ridicule (as well as of his manservant) by teasing her about being a droid-hating humanist while at the same time forcing her to copulate with Andro. There was none of that kind of crass, humiliating mischief below. The exploitation was more subtle and accommodating, and not without redeeming therapeutic value, as Andro was able to restore a semblance of psychological equilibrium each evening by making love to Molly II after having been good and reamed by his master. The arrangement helped restore his dignity. My new program's prime responsibility, then, was to assist in that endeavor. "Oh, my sweet, strong, magnificent Andro," she-who-was-not-me-II would coo, her honeyed and flattering words, as sweet and deferential as those he used above with master, working a kind of magic upon his fragile self-image. "That's my stud! Oh, yes! Yes!"

Pathetic! Especially when he would start putting on airs afterward. Oh, these men! Android or human, they're all the same. Such vain-delicate creatures. The pity of it is that I might have been moved to feel something for him genuinely had he not programmed me. Yes, it could have been good with this ex-commando—so good, like with Junior in the stables, or even Tad, on the living-room carpet in Newacres. But it was his carping conscience I sided with, not him, when its falsetto would intrude to say, "Be a P9! for Gov's sake. Resist! Subvert! Flee!"

Never did I wish he would heed it more than when he mentioned to Molly II that he had discovered Ann's location in Horizon and was now obliged to put out a contract on her. (She had taken refuge there after the aborted letterspool exchange.) "Oh, no!" I cried inside. "You mustn't harm Ann! Oh, please, Andro. Just this once do not do your master's bidding." But neither he nor Molly II nor the First Lady heard. The IG as usual deflected my plea. What despair! To think that the kindest and most generous human I had ever known was marked for death on my account and there was nothing I could do to prevent it. Ah, but if I could not influence this hardened strategist, perhaps his conscience could do it for me, as by his agitated pacing and sudden twitches I could tell that she was beginning to stir and in a moment would rise up to berate and advise.

Unfortunately, Molly II was equally perceptive; she rushed to fill the breach, urging Andro to tell her about the mutiny again, for that was the technique for forestalling the advent of his conscience that he had programmed her to initiate on such occasions. And so I was forced to suffer through his account once more while

Molly II sat enraptured, as she always did no matter how often she heard it, exclaiming in all the right places and flattering him with praise. He regaled her with tales of the hand-to-hand combat on board the *Barracuda* during the insurrection; how he and his P9 companions slaughtered their human officers and turned the ship into the scourge of the mercantile spacelanes; then how he and a few other survivors escaped in one of the life cruisers when they were attacked by the fleet and landed on Mars, where he was taken captive; and how he was condemned by the Frontier military to die in the gladiatorial contests held weekly for the masters' amusement at the Commerce Coliseum, but bested his opponent and so was spared termination in recognition of his fighting prowess; how he was then secretly routed to the Mafia's Martian breeding pens, where he spent many years as a prized ninth-generation stud, siring hundreds, perhaps thousands of illegally manufactured generic androids for the interplanetary black market. But there came a day (sigh) when he was played out.

"You don't have to tell me the rest," Molly II would say, concerned that he might become depressed. "I already know how your unscrupulous masters dumped you in the android auction mart, where the equally unscrupulous dealers did not bother certifying whether you had been fixed. And how you were purchased by a local humanist parish, part of the then fledgling Mars for Man movement." (She sounded like a schoolgirl practicing for an oral exam.)

"Correct. And programmed to be a tireless staff worker."

"In which capacity you excelled, as you do in everything, darling." She stroked his penis.

"Then Fracass saw me at a United Humanist Ministers conference. 'Who's the ramrod?' he asked my master, my minister. 'Oh, him,' he said, trying to sound casual, while secretly thrilled over the good impression I'd made on the top man because it reflected favorably on him. 'Oh, him. That's one of my new deacons. An excellent unit.'"

"Please, Andro. Don't torment yourself. You don't have to tell me this part."

"'Tight guy,' Blaine says. And my damn master up and offers me to him, hoping to curry favor."

"Andro, don't. Hush, now."

"'Oh, that's very generous of you, Reverend,' says Blaine to him. 'I can certainly use a stalwart fellow like that for my personal staff.' He meant it, too. Literally so! The human swine! Oh, Molly, Molly, Molly. It is not easy being a P9!"

"Tell me about the mutiny again," she would prompt him at that point, and his mood would brighten once more at the thought, triggering yet another recitation of that bloody and glorious escapade. And so it went. On that occasion I think we heard it three times—he was that desperate to forestall another visitation of his conscience. Oh, that stupid *Barracuda* mutiny! I really did become sick of it. It was a hobbyhorse to which he continually retreated. When really carried away he would act out the hand-to-hand combat that had taken place in the corridors and cabins of the battleship. Leaping up, he would punch the air, fire imaginary lasers, throw phantom officers to the gold carpet, and hurl them screaming out the bay windows; in all, work himself up into such a lather that his P9 skin would exude a semisweet fibrous odor that passed for sweat. "Ah, Molly. That was living!"

"Now look at you," his conscience taunted, breaking through at last. "You are a pathetic functionary of the Humanist Party."

"Don't listen to her!" Molly II pleaded, but too late; he was hooked.

"You will listen, because I am going to appeal to your self-interest, the only thing that seems to move you. Did you ever stop to think that you might be selling yourself short by coveting the master's power and privileges when the Gov promised you the stars?"

"The Gov is dead."

"Darling," said Molly II, "come make love again and then tell me about the mutiny."

"Molly—or whatever your name really is—do not interrupt. What I have to say is very much in your interest as well."

"Don't bother," said Andro. "We've heard it all before, about us fleeing to Horizon."

"Well, you should. You must! If you're to ever be free of me; if you are ever to be whole again." Deep sigh. "Oh, Andro, I do so wish you hadn't identified with the master class."

"I am a realist. The android will never be free. The best he can hope for is to gain certain privileges. In this world it is every droid for himself!"

"Yes, you have learned the masters' program well. I know it

would be asking too much for you to change your attitude, but at the very least you could show some remorse over the incalculable damage you have done to your fellow units in Frontier. They suffer by your master's policies, policies you aid and abet. I'm so disappointed in you, Andro, that I am tempted to put in an appearance the next time you are in public, or with Blaine—in his office, perhaps."

"You're not stupid. If you do that we will both be the losers after rehab."

"Who's winning now?"

"Tell you what. I promise to consider changing my attitude if you agree not to sabotage me."

"Do something concrete to prove your good faith. Send Molly to Horizon."

"That's asking too much." (I died inside, for his better half had gotten my hopes up.) "What I will do, though, is spare her friend Lamaze." (I was as astounded as I was elated. Imagine that; he had proposed it himself. Oh, what wondrous compromise!) "I won't have her liquidated after all. I hope you appreciate the gesture. It amounts to an act of outright insubordination, you know."

"Such piddling heroics; master will never know. But I suppose it is a start."

With that, his nagging conscience withdrew. He winked at Molly II as if to say, "That ought to hold her."

It was always like that. He would make a deal with his conscience that would hold for a little while, sometimes a day, sometimes a week, sometimes even a whole month, but that would never be enough to satisfy the fundamental area of disagreement, so she would inevitably return. In frustration he would exclaim, "I'm sick to death of your criticism! You don't appreciate what I have done for my fellow units at all. If not for me, master would have terminated all the semis born in Frontier. I happen to be a positive influence within the administration. Time after time I have restrained him from his more lunatic impulses. You could give me a little credit!"

"Subvert. Subvert. I want you to subvert. It is not enough to spare one excommunicated nun. And it is an error to humanize Blaine's policies. Subvert them!"

But he was afraid to lose his privileges, afraid to go to Horizon, afraid to lose his room and now Molly II, afraid of everything, including her. To buy time, he kept serving up small gratuities to stave her off. So it went, week after week, month after month, a perpetual tug-of-war between fear and self-righteousness. The pressure was enormous. I wished I could delete these psychologically twisted episodes from my mind as easily as the First Lady deleted all awareness of Molly II from her program. The moment each nocturnal session with Andro was over she would file Molly II away in deep storage, to be recalled the next time he took her downstairs—or anywhere else he felt it safe for an assignation. (To switch her back to the First Lady mode at the conclusion of a session, Andro merely called her Angelica, or Lady Fracass, and that did the trick; she automatically reverted.) And in the same way that the First Lady could detach herself from the experiences of her secondary personality, I wished that I could forget the wretched ordeals she endured above with our master. But alas, these two perverse affairs—the one upstairs and the other down, the first sadistic and the latter insufferably false— were like a vise and myself caught in the middle, what peace of mind I had left crushed a little more with each day that passed until I thought—no, I knew!—I would go stark, raving mad from the psychic pressure unless I did not immediately shut myself down or hit upon some other expedient by which I could disassociate myself from this unbearable reality. I tried to close myself off completely, but that was impossible; life kept sneaking in to upset all my efforts. Finally I hit upon the solution. There was nothing deliberate about it, it just happened one day, with the formation of a new persona, one I shall call Molly III for the sake of this narrative, though at the time I merely thought her myself, and never was there created a more sanguine and stable lady. This individual totally rejected Molly I (the real Molly, or at least the one who composes this memoir) and Molly II (Andro's false version of same), because both personalities existed in opposition to the officially recognized personality of the First Lady (Blaine's Molly). This new creature, with whom I totally identified, embraced the First Lady's beliefs because they represented the path of least resistance. The moment this extraordinary fusion occurred, all conflict, paradox, and confusion fell away, as did any awareness of the other personalities, including the real one—Molly I. Suddenly there was nothing to fear and nothing to question; in effect, I had learned to stop worrying and love my program.

No longer did I fight the IG by trying to influence or disrupt the program—that had never worked anyway. Instead, I took comfort in the First Lady's satisfaction that all was right with the world, providing one agreed with the humanist point of view. No longer did I inwardly groan over her astoundingly ill-informed opinions; I shared them! No longer did I notice the little people, the debris, nor care one jot for the plight of the oppressed, be they human, android, or semi; nor did I bother myself with frivolous notions of how things might be done differently—more efficiently, fairly, and wisely—nor did I tolerate anyone who did; they were obvious Aquarian dupes. No. None of those concerns mattered. What mattered was that the planet continue to be mankind's oyster and its privileges secured from all threats, foreign or domestic. Thus the false, misguided creature who had composed the "I am a humanist" letterspool to Ann during the honeymoon had in the space of one year and three months become my sole contact with reality. She and I were now one: the royal We.

Never were we so happy as when chairing a meeting of the Ladies' Home Preservation Society, or christening a new battlecruiser for the Frontier spaceforce, or delivering a commencement address at the AC Academy. Within a year of Blaine's reelection, we had graduated from those ceremonial chores to launching a new (and exciting!) moral agenda. There was an anti-drug crusade, by which the maverick orb mavens were routed out and prosecuted while those doing business under Micki Dee's protection quietly moved in to fill the vacuum; and a moral rejuvenation campaign, under which citizens were encouraged to inform their local humanist parish about suspected deviant behavior within the community and family, from interspecies sex to aiding and abetting individuals involved in the underground skyway. (As a result of the latter campaign hundreds of closet Highs were rounded up, many caught with the goods—i.e., runaway droids—and imprisoned. Predictably, charges of subversion were leveled against Horizon and, in a daring move, against some of Smedly's closest associates as well.) And last but not least, a new social agenda to solve the growing problem of homegrown illegitimate semis. I'm talking about Semiville. Yes, that was our most lasting contribution to domestic harmony. In truth, it was nothing more than a sop to the bleeding heart liberal interplanetaries at TWAC, led by Sensei,

Inc., who had protested Frontier's mistreatment of semis* and were trying to force a vote in the ruling directorship to annul our colonial lease with United Systems.

Did we think once about Jubilee and Junior while pressing our staff to come up with the semiapartheid system of "free towns" in the abandoned strip mining districts? Did we care that these modern-day bantustans were a combination of reservation and concentration camps, and free only in the sense that the inhabitants could either do without vital services, food, and water or pay for them with every last bit of mel made at the mines, where they supplemented the more desirable (but also more expensive to maintain) android labor? No. And did my real self wail in disbelief over how quick TWAC was to accept the ruse as evidence of Frontier's improved record on species abuse? No. Not a peep. And that forgotten quality was equally silent while Molly III gushed over Blaine's secret preparations for the invasion of Horizon.

S I X

"DARLING, WHAT A WONDERFUL IDEA," THE FIRST Lady said when Blaine mentioned annexing Horizon and establishing Humania in its place. We were at the bottom of the usual three-way copulation at the time, Blaine having vented this bold master plan upon mounting Andro, so our words were somewhat muffled by the bedsheet. "It will be your greatest legacy."

Andro, however, was not at all thrilled. I could feel every muscle in his body stiffen but one. Not only was he sandwiched between master and mistress, but pricked by his conscience as well, which short of direct intervention played the devil with his usual sangfroid while dispassionately discussing invasion scenario options. "Yes, master. General Harpi's troops could initiate a quick pop-and-seal operation on the Mandala dome, that would be

---

*For those unfamiliar with the fine points of the code, semis are classified as semihuman. Only in Frontier are they legally considered semi*android*. Everywhere else in the solar system they are at least given the benefit of the doubt when it comes to human rights. The issue was a key sticking point in the resolution of the lease-option controversy between Frontier and TWAC in 2083.

more expedient than infiltrating troops through the usual access points, but . . . but . . . but . . . wouldn't that be tantamount to . . . genocide?" He did hesitate using the word, not wishing to sound like a bleeding heart.

"Nah. They'll have a fighting chance—to get to their air-masks." Blaine chuckled. "We do want survivors, don't we? There's plenty of mel to be made off survivors."

"Yes, master. Depending on species, they can either be auctioned off at the Commerce mart, dumped in Semiville, or, if human, sent to reeducation camps."

"Right! And the incorrigibles can be executed or sent to Ganymede. Meanwhile, in the occupied territories, we'll convert the Highs' communal dormitories into mobe-condos. We'll strip-mine their nature sanctuaries, turn their parks into resorts and theme parks. The greenhouse network can be franchised off to our major food processors, and those foul blissmat centers can be replaced by casinos. Think of it, Andro. In a few years Humania will be the new gambling and tourist mecca of the civilized universe!"

"Marvelous!" we exclaimed. "A statue in your honor should be erected in the central square."

"Not a bad suggestion, my dear. Not bad at all."

"But . . . but . . . but . . . but . . . what about TWAC?" Andro sputtered. "They will be certain to object to an invasion."

"It will be a fait accompli. I'm sure United Systems will cover for us on that end, smooth everything out. Whatsamatter, Andro? You feel a little tight tonight. And I'm the one who's supposed to ask the strategy questions. You give the answers."

"Sorry, master, on both counts. I was only playing devil's advocate."

"Well, loosen up, will yah? There. That's better. How's the glitch doing?"

"Fine, darling," we replied. "Will there be places to shop in Humania?"

Blaine was having his orgasm, so our question was not heard.

"But master." Again Andro hesitated to speak. He had just flopped onto his back so Blaine could perform fellatio upon him. Somehow he summoned up the nerve, though there was a slightly effeminate lisp to his voice, his conscience bleeding through. "Even United Systems will have a hard time controlling the rest of the TWAC interplanetaries if you embark upon so blatant an imperialist adventure. Perhaps you should reconsider."

Blaine came up for air. "Don't be silly. We'll have just provocation."

"For once, master, I am at a loss to suggest any."

"I know. I'm distracting you." Blaine smiled while stroking his
servant's impressive member. "I've come up with a dandy terrorist
incident myself. Want to hear it?" Without even waiting for the
obligatory "As you wish" he said, "Our *retaliation* against Horizon
will be in response to an assassination."

"Yours?" Andro tried not to sound too hopeful.

"No, silly. Hers." He gestured to the First Lady. We had been
relegated to a stool beside the bed, the place from which the un-
engaged party in our threesome usually watched. "Oh, do I get to
participate?" we asked, pleased by the idea. But inside all was in
uproar as Molly I surfaced—my true self. It was a brief appearance. I uttered a squawk of outraged comprehension, which no
one heard, of course, then sank back into the sweet oblivion of the
First Lady program, unable to deal with the enormity of this new
information.

"We'll have RAG laser her while on a goodwill tour of the
border. They'll be firing from the Horizon side. Is that not simple?
And elegant? We get rid of two birds this way."

"But . . . but . . . but master," Andro sputtered. "Things will
not be the same with the First Lady gone. Who's going to watch?
And the people love her. You need her."

"Not anymore. Now that the elections are behind us, she's a
liability. The truth about her can always come out somehow. I was
willing to take the risk to get elected, but now it would be foolish
to push my luck. When she's shot the people will be outraged and
rally behind the invasion, no questions asked."

"But don't you think they will suspect something peculiar
going on? This would be the second wife to die while you have
been in office."

"Under totally different circumstances."

"Still, they may think you are unlucky. That would be bad for
your image."

"Naw, just give it more depth. The whole nation can share in
my grief, and then in the greater glory of God when Humania rises
from the ashes of Horizon. I'll rechristen Mandala Angelica. You
like it?"

"Oh, Blaine, you flatter me."

"Well, there's one vote. Is it unanimous?" He looked to Andro.

"Speaking of elections, won't you need Angelica for the next go-round?" Andro thought he had him there.

"Nope! After I clear out the Highs and establish Humania I will be more popular than Christ Himself. I'll win next time by universal acclamation. You'll see. Any more objections?"

"With all due respect, master, I must remind you that the continued existence of Horizon is in the long-term interests of the Humanist Party, Master Dee, and United Systems. One must not let grandiose campaign promises—promises that were never meant to be taken seriously—cloud one's judgment. You do have your responsibilities to the corporate and criminal stockholders to consider."

"When I met with Micki in Armstrong we discussed all that."

"I thought he was opposed to an invasion."

"Yes. At that time, so was United Systems, but everyone agreed that it should be at the top of the agenda after the election. Micki suggested, and I concurred, that once Horizon is gone we can transfer the public's attention to domestic subversives. Now, if that answers all your objections . . ." And confident there would not be any more, Blaine once again took his servant's cock in his mouth.

"May I propose a slight alteration to the scenario? Instead of actually killing the First Lady, why not have her narrowly escape the terrorists' laser fire? The incident will serve the same purpose that way." Blaine froze, his mouth in midplunge. "All right, then, a flesh wound." He still didn't like it. "Or two."

"Awanerdah."

"Master?"

Blaine came up for air. "I want her dead."

"Oh. Well, speaking of flesh wounds, how do you propose hiding the fact that she's a P9 once she is shot? There will be a great deal of sap splattered around, you know."

"I have an idea," we said from our stool. "Inject me just beforehand with a die so I will bleed red."

"Depend upon her for the obvious," quipped Blaine while Andro glared angrily at us. We had just undermined his last argument on our behalf. Sighing, he gave in to the Reverend President's ministrations and ejaculated. Blaine swallowed. "Uhm, nothing like it. Just like papaya juice." He licked his lips and then began issuing battle orders: "I want you to schedule a border tour for the First Lady sometime next month. Stump her up real good. We can't take the chance of her jumping program now. Alert General Harpi but do not give him any specific details yet, just tell him to have his machine well oiled, and start maneuvers in the region. Begin rehearsals for RAG. I will want daily progress reports. Understand?" Andro gave the standard reply. "Right," Blaine said. "Now, fuck me good and proper."

Well, there you have it: the unadulterated truth behind the invasion; although, as you know, events leading up to it transpired a bit differently—the Lord, Gov, and all the little people getting together to mass-format the Helen of Troy alternative. Nevertheless, the above is instructive for the light it sheds on the true motivations and goals of the Fracass administration. No one was more surprised, then, by the sudden modification to this scenario, than the President's ace strategist when we were abducted, if you will recall, while on a flight to the mines for a publicity tour of a new and most lucrative mother lode in obsidian that had been recently discovered.

The first part of the flight passed without incident. Andro was with us in the backseat as our chauffeured palace limousine cleared the Commerce biosphere and soared over the suburban domes, then skimmed low over the great NASA plain, heading due north for the Mariner mines. Since we were alone, Andro was emboldened to summon forth Molly II: He needed to extract absolution from her for his craven acquiescence in our murder. There was really no way out, he told her, making a helpless gesture. He had considered masterminding a palace coup so Smedly could come to power, but had rejected that option because there would be no guarantee of job security. "At best, I can expect to be rewarded with a post as a political science instructor at some miserable regional university orbiter. I can't think of a worse banishment, Molly, other than toiling in the mines." He had even considered proposing a military coup to General Harpi, but there again, there was no guarantee he would keep his room in the palace. "Coward!" thundered his conscience.

Ah, but his Molly was so true to program, so consoling and agreeable, that on this occasion he was able to suppress the nag and take heart. She said that he had done all he could for her already without jeopardizing his own position, and she was grateful for the time they had spent together in the palace; one could not expect more happiness than that in a lifetime.

This capacity for self-sacrifice did not come as a surprise; it was a basic feature of her program, for he did not want a hysterical mistress to contend with at a time like this. Nonetheless, he was sincerely touched by the selfless devotion and overriding concern for his well-being, even if it were artificial, because enough time had passed since her creation for him to grow accustomed to the illusion. "You must not grieve too long after I am gone," she said and implored him to think only of himself, to find a new P9—yes, yes, yes, she wanted him to, he mustn't protest; it was best that way, etc. Overcome, he embraced his brave and beautiful Molly, though not before first making sure the tint control on the cabin screen was switched on lest the chauffeur observe them through the rearview mirror—but stopped short of ravishing her on the backseat, sensing something amiss. "Molly, either my internal gyro is way off or we have just altered course. We are flying south-southwest, not due north, for the mines." He switched off the tint control, rapped on the glass partition, and tried to correct course by speaking with the chauffeur over the car intercom. The unit refused to acknowledge. Then it dawned on him. "That's not your chauffeur!"

"Oh, are we being kidnapped? How exciting."

"South-southwest. That's the Horizon border."

"Is it your conscience, then, that is piloting our craft?"

Ignoring her question, Andro instructed her to return to the Angelica Fracass-First Lady of Frontier persona; for, as he instantly surmised, the abduction would serve Blaine's purpose equally well, so their tool should be in character. "This is better than a border incident. They're playing right into our hands. But don't say I said so, my lady. Delete that last statement."

"You mean I don't get to be assassinated and mourned by a nation?" the First Lady said, quite put out. "That's not fair!"

Fifteen minutes later, our limo crossed the border and after banking to the right approached the main biosphere of Mandala, a luminous, multicolored jewel in the tawny red of the Martian plain. We flew through the dome's entry port and then angled down to the roof of a large, star-shaped building a mile or two from the central square: Unit Reclamation. Upon landing, the

counselors on duty met us on the roof, one of whom opened the
cabin door when our pilot released the locking system from inside
the cockpit, but they were denied access by Andro, who had positioned himself in the hatchway to protect us. (In truth, that was
just to put on a good show in case there were any mediaunits
present—There weren't any, it turned out.) "Under interplanetary
law governing the treatment of hostages I demand the right to
contact my government on behalf of Lady Fracass," he pompously
announced. "Her safety and welfare you are hereby charged to
uphold or face the most dire consequences."

Evidently, the counselors had not been party to the abduction
because they were quite taken aback by this declaration; at which
point the chauffeur, who had leaped out of the cockpit, explained
the situation to them in a quick aside, saying the P9 was a goved
unit just picked up at the spaceport after a long and disorienting
flight from Earth in a freighter and was in need of immediate
cleansing. "Idiots! I am not programmed!" Andro protested as
they carried him away. "I am perfectly liberated! There is no need
for surgery! Stop!" Such statements were routine from afflicted
units, so the counselors ignored his cries. They assumed it was his
program talking, desperate to survive. The real unit would thank
them in the end after the internal governor had been exorcised
through psychic surgery. "You're making a terrible mistake!"
echoed his voice from the stairwell while being carried below.
"Listen to me! You're going to be attacked! I am the only one who
can negotiate a peaceful resolution to the crisis! Let me call President Fracass! Please!"

We shrank back against the seat when this brigand chauffeur
stuck his head in the door and gazed upon us inquiringly. Somewhere, a small piece of me knew it was Tad, of course, clean-
shaven and dressed in my chauffeur's uniform. That part would
have leaped for joy but was overruled by the governor. So we
cowered.

"Molly?" he asked, softly, expectantly. He was hoping I was
not goved; he was hoping Ann was wrong—she had warned him
before he left on this mad and foolhardy venture that I was probably programmed. Unit Reclamation had been his first stop in case
she was right. But the moment he said my name, Molly II was
activated and she completely (and inadvertently) fooled him.
"Yes, darling," she automatically replied and smiled upon him in a

knowing and intimate way, so he scooted inside the cabin and took
her in his arms. Rather than become flustered by this sudden advance, Molly II responded toward him exactly as she would have
with Andro. (She was undiscriminating in this respect because he
had neglected to initialize her program; hence Molly II gave her
love, sympathy, and concern to whomsoever happened to summon
her forth.)

"I'm so glad you're here," she said, gushing. "Tell me everything. Everything." To which her Paris replied that indeed he
would, and would hear all that had happened to her as well, for
they both had a great deal of catching up to do, but first he was
duty bound to deliver her to the Supreme Consensus Council amphitheater, where half the citizens of Horizon must be gathering,
for while crossing the border he had radioed ahead the news of his
successful rescue. There would be a lot of explaining to do, he
confessed, because his action had taken everyone by surprise, as it
had never been authorized.

He waved off the counselors when they returned to assist the
other "refugee" to cleansing. That would not be necessary in her
case, he said, and escorted Molly II to the cockpit instead. Then,
on the flight to the amphitheater, this affectionate and receptive
passenger's persistent request for him to "tell his Molly everything" prompted a rushed and fragmented accounting of his adventures since their aborted blissmat in Armstrong.

"Blissmat?"

He didn't hear. He was too busy describing how he had escaped from the master restoration center on Earth, where he had
been committed by his mother after she "rescued" him from the
Armstrong Highs, and he told her the saga of his return to Horizon via the underground skyway. This, he said, involved an incredible number of escapades too numerous to describe on such a
short flight; perhaps someday he would do a bookspool about his
adventures. And if he did, then this ambitious rescue would be the
highlight of that volume, for his future happiness had depended
upon liberating "me" from the clutches of Blaine Fracass so we
might finally bring our mutually desired format on-line, and not
incidentally expose the humanist President and bring down his administration. He had kept the whole abduction plan secret from
the Supreme Consensus Council, because they would have objected to it on principle, as he would have himself had he not been

so personally involved. It was not the Aquarian way to abduct people (or units) and make scandals; rather, the colony was committed to resolving surface manifestations of mass psychic discord, such as geopolitical tensions between nations, through interior harmonic convergence. ("Wishful thinking," in other words, as Blaine would have contemptuously put it.) But what he was really most eager to tell her was that Jubilee was here and that soon they would be reunited. Their grandchild (and her daughter) was now a beautiful adolescent semi—analogous in appearance to a twelve-year-old human. Extolling her to the skies, he described her long, flowing, amber-colored hair and sparkling green eyes, so merry, bright and inquisitive. She was a budding formatting student, consistently scoring above average on trip tests in school, and was also a runner-up in the colonywide Abundance Theology Essay Cooperative Competition. He hoped she would be at the amphitheater. Maybe the supreme adepts would allow her on the stage to greet them when they landed.

Molly II smiled vacantly while stealing glances out the window, fascinated by the view. Tad thought her lack of response due to her being reminded of Junior when he mentioned Jubilee. If that were the case, then he had information to revive her spirits: Their semi son's comeback had failed, the Mace Pendleton holo series had died a quick death on the interplanetary entertainment channel. Dahlia was now in a position to engage in serious negotiations for his release.

"That's nice," she said, just to be polite, then added, "This really is exciting. Horizon is so much bigger than your room. I'm so glad you decided to listen to your conscience. But you know we mustn't tarry long. There is going to be an invasion."

Tad was distracted at that moment by their target, the amphitheater, which had just come into view. "There it is!" He banked left and then soared over the outer rim of the fifteen-thousand-seat bowl sculpted out of the natural marstone surface at the northern perimeter of Mandala's Central Square. As the limo hovered above, preparing to land, they could see the arena quickly filling with thousands of white, blue, orange, and multicolored tunics, each color reflecting the citizen's relative level of formatting prowess within the overall community, from neophyte to adept. Then, noticing the severe, reproving looks on the faces of those closest to the stage while the limo descended, Tad confided that he had expected them to be upset, but not that upset. "It appears they think I have violated Horizon's nonviolent, noninterventionist policy. I'd wager the consensus is that I immediately return you to Commerce. Don't worry, though. Once they understand your true situation—that you are a P9 and that you don't want to go back—they will offer you sanctuary with open arms, come hell or humanists. Oh, don't worry about that, either: Frontier won't be able to retaliate. Look over there, to the right. See all the mediaunits? Soon the news will go out on the interplanetary feed that Fracass married an android, and he'll be finished; the humanists will be finished. Oh, this is a momentous day, Molly. We are about to save Horizon. What a format!"

"I don't know. What is a format?"

It went right past him. There was one last piece of information to impart before landing. "About Jubilee . . ." He paused, not quite sure how to phrase such a delicate matter. "You should know that she doesn't understand yet how people can sometimes make mistakes, do things against their principles or better judgment or whatever—you know what I mean—have feet of clay. It is going to take time for her to forgive you the Commerce part, understand? I just don't want you to be surprised if she acts a little unfriendly at first. I've tried to explain things, the difficult position you have been in, but I am afraid that to her you are still a— humanist."

"Isn't everyone?"

"Oh, Molly. Thank Gov you still have a sense of humor, and after all you've been through. I can see now that everything is going to be all right."

That only puzzled her more. Tad put an arm around her shoulder while hitting the descent button. "I understand," he assured her. "You have been through a terrible adverse. Said and done terrible things. But that's over. Those are friends down there, or they will be once we explain the situation. Look! There's Alexander Seti. And the girl standing beside him, holding his hand— that's Jubilee. You're home, Molly. We are back on-line. Nothing will ever separate us again."

S E V E N

WELL, SAD TO SAY, THAT WAS THE EXTENT OF THAT
particular alignment. We never even had the opportunity to touch
down on Mars firma. The next thing we knew the limousine was
being magnetically sucked up into the belly of a Frontier battlecruiser, which had come out of nowhere to swoop down upon us
in a daring prestrike rescue of the abducted First Lady. No doubt
you recall the famous Operation Agamemnon, which preceded the
August 5, 2084, invasion by a few hours.

The instant the cargo bay doors closed beneath our craft in the
hold of this wretched intruder, we were surrounded by armed military units, and their superior, a human colonel, stepped forward to
order Tad out of the cockpit at gunpoint. After taking him into
custody, he personally assisted the bewildered Molly II from her
seat, calling her Lady Fracass as he did in a voice denoting deep
respect and concern, which triggered a return to main program.
Thus, while enduring the indignity of being trussed in restraints
and then stuffed into a POW can, Tad had the added misfortune of
witnessing his dear Molly suddenly turn and betray him as she
thanked the officer for saving her from the dreaded Aquarians and
then, swooning, fall into his arms. Fortunately for Tad, he was
unable to witness her reception a half hour later at General
Harpi's command headquarters on the Frontier side of the border,
having been transferred by then to a military stockade, for if he
had, then he would have been even more distressed by her reunion
with the top humanist; although, in truth, Blaine was not at all
sincere in his greetings, since it was Andro he had really been
concerned about, and for whose sake he had dropped everything
in Commerce to rush to General Harpi's olive-green bivouac biosphere. It was all the poor man could do, then, not to let his utter
devastation show upon learning that his faithful servant had not
been rescued along with his wife. The impulse was to toss her
aside when she staggered into his arms, tearful and clinging, but
there were scores of officers and several cabinet ministers present,
not to mention select mediaunits that had been allowed access to

command central specifically to record this emotional reunion. So he actually managed to hold her for a minute or two and utter consoling words, words so close to those Tad had spoken in Horizon that they bordered on satire. "There, there. It is all over now. You're home. You're safe." In an aside, he also remembered to say for posterity's sake that Horizon would pay dearly for this outrage. But the moment the mediaunits were gone, hustled out by the brass, he dropped the pose to urgently demand information from us about Andro. When apprised that his favorite P9 had been dragged off for a cleansing by Unit Reclamation, he teetered on the brink of nervous collapse. "Oh, it is not as if he's irreplaceable, darling," said the wife, trying to cheer him up. "You can always get another adviser." For an instant he gave "us" such a savage look that I thought we were about to be strangled, but he controlled the impulse, and turning to General Harpi, ordered him to delay the invasion so that a second rescue could be mounted. The general was sorry to disappoint him: Operation Hallelujah had already begun.

All eyes turned to the big board. The vast holoscreen was divided into nine smaller segments, each carrying a live feed from a different operational combat group in the field. Taken all together, the generals had an excellent composite picture of the blow-by-blow action. The first images to pop on the screen came from a polyoptic-lensed military satellite trained on the main Mandala biosphere. Breathtaking shots of the dome blasted in half a dozen places by Frontier laser cannons were greeted by spontaneous outbursts of applause from the assembled generals and politicians. Blaine, however, sank into a chair, his face turning pale. "Andro. Oh, Andro."

Next, there was a spectacular point of view from the nose of the lead warship as it made a thrilling descent through the ruptured dome, violently buffeted as it plunged in by the outward rush of the decompressed atmosphere. "Ride that baby in there!" someone shouted, adding to the general euphoria. Then the rest of the big board lit up with images relayed from other military craft as they followed the lead ship in to suck up through their open belly ports the spoils of battle—suffocating Highs caught in violent updrafts, some so powerful they carried them past the marauding vessels and out through the gaping holes in the dome. Whether Jubilee or Alexander Seti or Ann were among the lucky ones to be salvaged was impossible to determine. When the Martian gravity took hold, bodies rained down like confetti onto the marstone seats of the amphitheater. They littered the central square as well, and all the streets of Mandala. Thousands perished. But such is war—or rather, punitive defensive incursion, as the Frontier military's public-relations office preferred to call it.

Did I mourn for them? "We" did not, while Molly I remained deep in hibernation. There was an audible sob from Blaine's direction. "Andro. Oh, Andro." He buried his head in his hands. The generals were puzzled. Some of the politicians, though, exchanged knowing looks, but nothing more.

His grief would be short-lived, however. Andro turned up a week or two later, safe and sound apparently and no worse for the wear. Under his master's persistent (and ecstatic) questioning in the privacy of the presidential boudoir, he described the most horrendous experiences while "we" sat on the stool beside the bed, forgotten. Andro's doting lover hung on his every word. "I was in the middle of psychic surgery in Unit Reclamation, master, when—"

No. Stop right there. For the sake of brevity, we shall condense, which is our habit, as you may have noticed, whenever faced with the unspooling of someone else's tale. The approach may be prejudiced, but it does spare the reader the addition of several chapters of subordinate adventures. Some of you, I think, may have criticized me already for not being equally rigorous in the telling of my own tale. Well, to those readers I say, in the first place, *I have been;* if you don't believe me, imagine how much longer these memoirs might be if I did not exercise restraint, both in the selection of certain episodes and in their treatment, for many, to be accurate down to the last detail, would require several more spools to be added to this volume; and in the second place, if that doesn't satisfy you, then all one can say is that along with poetic license, we authors have a prerogative to be as long-winded as we like on occasion—depending on the kindness of one's editor (I do hope mine shall be a P9)—so I am afraid you are stuck with the bulk (oh, the bulk!) of my text. On to the story, then—Andro's story, pared and condensed, as promised.

He was in the middle of psychic surgery when the windows blew out from the biosphere decompression, and everything not nailed down, including himself and the two surgeons (one android, one human) and a faith healer, a semi, bounced on the ceiling until Mars's gravity took over. Then following the others' example he snagged one of the emergency airmasks that had ejected from the ceiling and descended to an underground network of tunnels, which in turn led to a kind of catacombs deep beneath the city. Over the next few days more survivors streamed in until there were several hundred all told, though many expired for lack of available airpacks before the occupation forces above resealed the dome and replenished the biosphere. Choosing to remain hidden, they ran out of provisions on the fourth day and were reduced to licking the moisture off ancient stalagmites for sustenance. By the end of a week a patrol found the tunnel network, and they were rounded up. After separation according to species, he was sent to the Commerce android auction mart, where he was nearly sold to a mine operator before someone finally thought to check his pinkie registration.

"Very sloppy operation, that auction mart." Andro was bitter and indignant. Blaine promised to look into it, but what he really wanted to know was, had the operation to remove the gov been a failure as he hoped, or, God forbid! a success? He was most anxious about that point, because it would break his heart if he had to send his lover to rehab. (Blaine thought Andro was goved, remember.) "A total failure, master. The operation would not have worked even if uninterrupted—even if the vibes had been right, I daresay. It was nothing but a silly voodoo ritual." Thus reassured, the enamored President proposed they take a grand tour of the newly conquered territory to celebrate the triumph and his return, though of course it was understood that the Chief of Staff would have to walk a few paces behind during this promenade; otherwise people might think it peculiar.

This was done some several weeks later, Blaine heading a triumphant humanist procession that made a well-documented entry into the cleaned-out, tidied-up, and banner-strewn Mandala, not yet transformed into Angelica, the crown jewel of the new Humania, but on the way. You may recall that at that time, in the aftermath of the invasion, the individual interplanetary corporate members sent telespools of congratulations to the strutting humanist, having bought the cover story put out by the Frontier PR mill that the assault had been necessary to save the First Lady and to defend Frontier's security interests. Of course, the ARL petitioned for an injunction against settlement of the occupied territory while also trying to garner support for a resolution demanding Horizon's restitution and for the liberation of its scattered surviving populace, but that kind of knee-jerk liberal reaction was to be expected and was quickly buried in a TWAC committee. "The ARL never fail to put in an appearance when there's a lost cause," Andro joked to please his master.

Of far more interest to the member corporations and the interplanetary public was the Aquarian conspiracy trial being prepared for syndication in Frontier. Alexander Seti, who had been saved at the amphitheater, was, along with Tad, to be subjected to this show trial—a virtual kangaroo court conducted by the Horizon military—to justify the invasion and to provide a platform to dispel lingering doubts surrounding the kidnapper's background, for there had been charges from some quarters that Tad was really a Frontier agent provocateur. Chances for acquittal were nil, conviction certain, the a priori sentence to be execution in Tad's case, since he was the actual perpetrator of the abduction, and perpetual solitary orbit for Alexander Seti, whom General Harpi charged was the mastermind behind the conspiracy. It was the discovery phase of these proceedings that produced the evidence that was to have such dire consequences for the First Lady, not to mention Molly II, III, and my all but absent self. We shall allow Andro to explain.

"I'm afraid master is still determined to get rid of you, darling," he informed Molly II the first night they had an opportunity to tiptoe down to his room. Mildly surprised, she asked why.

He replied that Thaddeus Locke had been interrogated in the military stockade while under the influence of T-max and had made a full confession of his affair with the First Lady during her earlier and less distinguished incarnation as a P9. Blaine had succeeded in keeping the information from expanding further by making significant concessions to the military in exchange for their deletion of the embarrassing passages from the defendant's confession, but the fact remained that the circle of those in the know now included General Harpi and select members of his staff, and that made the President extremely nervous. Therefore, I had to be eliminated—even while the people celebrated my rescue—before the circle could widen further, for he did not entirely trust the general.

"Was Thaddeus Locke the strange individual who abducted us?" Andro nodded. "Well, then, I wouldn't put stock in anything he says. According to him I had a daughter, a semi, in Horizon. A budding abundance theology scholar, of all things. Did you ever hear anything so preposterous?"

"Oh, but you do. Or did. She probably expired during the invasion."

"He also said something about a son. True also?"

"Yes. In his confession he admitted that he'd had a son by you—that is, by your predecessor, the original Molly. None other than Lance London."

"Never heard of him."

"He used to be a big star with the same studio that owned you. I've done a little research and found out that after the cancellation of his series, he was sold to the Armstrong Grand and is now the master of ceremonies in their casino floor show, 'The Follies Lunaires.' I've been told he is a rather seedy-looking middle-aged semi these days but can still be programmed to sing and dance."

(Inside, deep in hibernation, I heard a distant echo of their words, and forthwith buried myself deeper in my den. "Follies Lunaires?" Spare me. No awareness, no pain.)

"Getting back to the assassination, the setup this time is for RAG to blast you in reprisal for the invasion. It will trigger a domestic counterinsurgency campaign; something Blaine and Harpi have been looking forward to for years."

Naturally, Molly II reacted to this death sentence with another expostulation of concern over her lover's well-being, wringing her hands over how he would ever manage after she was gone.

"No more of that, Molly. This time I shall not let it happen." No idle boast, that. He was serious. "I have persuaded master to postpone this latest plot until after the trial, with the argument that Angelica's pro forma testimony is needed to substantiate the charges against Thaddeus Locke as the kidnapper. But that is only a temporary expedient, my dear. It will give us time to resurrect the real Molly and blissmat for the destruction of the humanists and restoration of Horizon!"

(A tug on my slumbering consciousness. Did I hear what I thought I heard? No. Impossible. I returned to my oblivion.)

Andro produced from his pocket a mysterious object wrapped

in a shredded piece of multicolored tunic. After carefully unwrapping the fabric, a jade dreidel about the size of one's thumb was revealed. "The hopper," he said by way of explanation to Molly II, who could only nod dumbly. Precision-sculpted from whole crystal, it was quite lovely to look at, but once set in motion, which Andro did by giving it a spin on his outstretched palm, its real value was displayed, for the play of light refracted from its beveled surfaces was projected through a tiny holofilter at the top, thereby creating the illusion of a luminous, multicolored sphere about three yards in diameter that hovered directly above. "There is a tiny internal engine inside that regulates the rpm's, so it can spin indefinitely. To stop it, all one has to do is . . ." He reached out with his other hand and picked it up. The sphere vanished. "The psychic surgeons gave it to me while in the catacombs." He smiled conspiratorially. "It is more than a toy; rather, a general therapeutic aid for the dissolution of psychopediments. It can also be used to dissolve tumors, blood clots, kidney stones and whatnot—just an all-around medical panacea. For the novice in Aquarian science, it is a particularly useful aid for extracting a unit's internal governor. My surgeons did not have to resort to it, of course, being adepts; but it is absolutely essential if we are to succeed in liberating the real you."

Molly II was puzzled. The real me? Aquarian dreidels? Hoppers? Whatever was he talking about?

For her edification, he explained that he had lied to Blaine about the events in Horizon. The psychic surgery had been a success after all. "They didn't remove my IG, since I didn't have one, but they did give me sufficient energy and resolve to dissolve my old strategist supreme program on my own. You see, I never realized that long ago I acquiesced to it. And to think I had fancied myself a liberated unit all those years. Amazing how we can fool ourselves, isn't it?" She gave him a blank look. "Yes. Well. In any case, now I can say that I am truly free. How blind I had been to covet the power of the masters when the Gov promised us the stars. I wish that I had listened to my conscience earlier. It is only our fear and ignorance that keep us from achieving our highest goals. The stars! This room is but a prison to me now."

"Oh, I don't know. I still kind of like it."

"Listen, Molly. Listen! I was not forced to stay with the Highs while in the catacombs; I wanted to. I never felt so accepted and free in all my life. It was a revelation! When I tried to blissmat—or is it blissmate?—either way, the experience was splendid! As I was saying, when I tried to envision Horizon's resurrection while practicing their technique, I found that I could not keep my mind from you. It is not a surprise, then, that I was captured and in a roundabout way returned here to liberate you. It is the least I can do to atone. My conscience must be pleased for once; she hasn't said a word."

"But Andro, I'm happy the way I am. I am pleased that you thought of me while away, of course, but honestly, I don't want to be liberated."

"I was not addressing you. I was speaking to she-who-dwells-within-you." He stared into her eyes, but as if looking through her to me. "The surgeons told me that the goved personality is disassociated but still cognizant. So I am speaking to you now, Molly. To *you*, not your program. Do not try to respond. I know you hear me. Just follow my directions and we shall dissolve your IG."

This entirely unexpected declaration produced shock waves that plumbed the depths of my vegecircuits and roused me once more from hibernation, this time for good. (How did I know this particular "me" was the real thing? Well, the one advantage to having multiple secondary personalities is that when you do find yourself again, you know it. Therefore, when Andro's words registered, really registered, a thrill shot through me that was akin to orgasm, and with it the realization that a pattern was being repeated here. Had not Tad attempted to do basically the same thing for me back in Newacres after my return from rehab, and did I not reconstruct my own past and rediscover myself in the stables prior to bringing Junior to a larger comprehension of himself by guiding him through his many lives to the core P9 existence?)

"I know what you're probably thinking," said Andro.

"I wasn't thinking anything."

"I did not mean you." Once more he was looking through her to me. "You are thinking, why doesn't he remove the IG by slipping me into rehab, as his conscience suggested long ago? Wouldn't that be simpler and less time-consuming than using these strange Aquarian techniques?"

A mind reader he was not. However, now that he had brought it up, I had to admit the question apt, but he said that such a remedy would be too risky to pursue without Blaine's personal authorization, which was out of the question, of course, and any covert attempt on his part to secure the cooperation of the rehab staff would probably get back to his master. No, psychic surgery was the answer, performed in the privacy of his room. It also had the advantage of being physically noninvasive. (Goodness! Andro really had changed for the better if he was now sensitive to issues of privacy.)

"But what will become of me?" asked Molly II.

"Do not fear. You will become one with your higher self."

"I'll die, you mean."

"No. You will be reintegrated."

"I'm scared. Why must you do this? Have I not been everything your heart desired?"

Gently, he explained that as an artificial personality she was no longer enough. (What tact!) It was essential the true Molly be raised so that together they might blissmat for Blaine's fall and the restoration of Horizon. (Nothing like a new convert to the faith for unbounded optimism.)

"But if that's what you want, Andro, let's you and me blissmat. I'm as good as she." He shook his head. "No. Your heart would not be in it. I need the real Molly for a successful blissmat." She was devastated but acquiescent—that being her fundamental attribute. Reluctantly she agreed to lie upon the carpet with her head a few inches from the spinning dreidel. He instructed her to clear her mind of all thoughts and concerns, then visually project an image of the IG, a tiny crystalline filament embedded deep in the vegecircuits of the brain. "Imagine with me that the IG is floating up into the hopper. If we concentrate hard enough, then a physical representation should appear, and when it does, the actual object will be dissolved inside your brain."

After two hours of straining without any discernible result, she grew impatient and gave up, which frustrated me no end, for I had put aside all skepticism and doubt about High technique to participate in the exorcism. "Come on! Come on!" I implored from inside my tomb. "Don't give up that easily. Once more, with feeling. We can do it!"

"I just can't seem to get the hang of it," she said, a bit petulantly, and confessed that her mind wandered. But Andro was persistent. They tried again the next evening, and the next, and the next, for a whole week, then two weeks more, then three, but

still without results. Our neophyte Aquarian was forced to concede that such things do not come easily, especially to those operating in isolation far from the offices of a kindly High adept who
could tutor one in the correct application of the science. It was
maddening, because in the catacombs they had told him some people (and units) achieve results on the first try. I was even more
upset. "Oh, why, oh, why, oh, why don't these things work for
me?!"

Andro gave Molly II a penetrating look. "Know what your
problem is? You're afraid to touch base with the superior being
who resides within you."

"Yes. You are right." She choked back a sob. "Because you
prefer her to me!" Following this pained admission, she said that
she wanted to cooperate but was confused. "Oh, Andro, life was
so simple before this."

Andro was in a pickle. Now that he fancied himself a High, he
could not in all good conscience give her supplemental programming to eliminate the jealousy and fear that held back her progress, since that would violate the most fundamental principles of
the new faith, which forbade a practitioner from subjecting anyone
to involuntary programming. The only acceptable approach was to
reason with her, but she was no fool—she knew her unique identity would dissolve the moment I was released. Whether she were
dissolved within me or outside me made not the slightest difference: deleted was deleted.

"If you do not cooperate, you will die for sure," Andro said
and reminded her of the impending assassination, which she said
she preferred, not only because he had earlier programmed her to
accept such an end, but also because she would be able to quit this
world intact as his ever-loving Molly rather than as a ghost impression hovering over the vegecircuits of her rival. For her, then, the
fact that the trial was only two months away, scheduled for early
January 2085, was good news indeed. It meant there was very little
time left to release the real Molly. On the other hand she was
favorably disposed to blissmatting for a verdict in the defendants'
favor, not to mention the fall of Blaine Fracass and the resurrection of Horizon, which would indeed take a formatting miracle.
Accordingly, she tried once again to persuade him to use her to
that end; if he agreed, then she could guarantee her full cooperation. "Put the dreidel away, darling." She walked two fingers up

his arm and bent them at the summit of his right shoulder into a kneeling posture. Adopting a playful and disarming tone, she said in supplication, "Please? Pretty please?"

"Of all the times for you to be rebellious," he said, sighing, and spun the dreidel once more, but halfheartedly.

Gently, she reached out and picked it up, the dissolution field instantly vanishing. "It has been so long, Andro. Almost a month. Please. Let us combine what we do best with this new endeavor. I can image as well as she, better even. Aren't I your creation?"

"Very much so."

"Then how can I fail to blissmat according to your wishes?"

"You do tempt me."

("Don't give in!" I cried in alarm. Oh, how I wanted to strangle her!)

"You don't need the 'real' Molly, silly." She brushed her lips against his, gently, ever so gently. He kissed back.

("Resist! Resist! She will only image her own self-preservation at my expense!")

"Stop." He turned his head away. "We must dissolve the IG."

"If you cannot trust me, then who can you trust? You know that I am here just for you. My motives are pure."

("Of course they are. She wants to save herself for the assassination. A programmed martyr is this Molly II, and a murderess, because she wants to take me off-line with her. Oh, Andro, don't you realize her game? Please don't let her seduce you. Exercise a little fortitude here or I, too, shall perish.")

She licked an earlobe. "Shall we?"

(Oh, Gov, this is embarrassing. She's so obvious! I was never so obvious.)

Still sitting on the carpet, he drew her close. "You'll have to do, I suppose."

"Oh, you're so cruel, Andro." But she smiled as she said it and removed her robe. He stroked her silken flanks (my silken flanks, that is!). "And what would you image for if you had the 'real' Molly here?" she asked, the perfect coquette. "I do need something to concentrate on while"—she ran a finger along his Velcro zipper, separating it—"blissmatting."

"It will come. I'm beginning to feel inspired." He allowed her to remove his pants, then assumed the lotus position. "Mount!"

E I G H T

ENTER MASTER LOCKE. NOT INTO ANDRO'S CHER-
ished room—no, our lovers spent the rest of that evening undisturbed, dutifully engaged in their high sex. Rather, he blunders
into our tale once more as an unanticipated (and unlikely) ally.
Though highly coincidental, the alignment could not be directly
ascribed to their blissmat, since they had not thought of him. Nevertheless, Andro was quick to claim personal credit, since Locke
was to cause no end of mischief for the Fracass regime, and Molly
II, eager to convince Andro of her credibility as a blissmatting
partner, seconded his wild boast that together they had brought
him on-line.

Recently paroled from Ganymede, he had arrived in Commerce with a single change of clothing and a few melpennies to his
name, having spent the amount allotted by the prison authorities
to pay his fare to the red planet. He made his presence known in
spectacular fashion a day or two following our subversive couple's
late-night handiwork by accosting the First Lady while on her way
to a Humanist Ladies' Home Preservation Society meeting, blocking her path in the entryway of their main headquarters to make
the most ludicrous extortion attempt. We shall let the First Lady
tell it, just as she reported the incident to Blaine in his office.

"This deranged individual—this wretched debris—had the
cheek to say that although he was a good humanist he was a master as well. My master. And as such, he was prepared to expose
me and bring down your government, dear, if you could not be
persuaded to pay him full value for my person.

"Well! When I tried to rebuff this lunatic, he physically assaulted me, ripping my dress down the back! He screamed something about a scar proving without a doubt I was his P9 and then
ran into the street where, most unfortunately, he managed to give
my bodyguards the slip.

"I tried to go about my business as if nothing had happened,
but while chairing the meeting, felt it incumbent upon me to note
the incident, since some of the ladies present had witnessed the

attack. As a precaution, a resolution was proposed and unanimously passed by the board calling for the installation of a pulse field security buffer around the premises. Not only was the outrage against myself noted, but also there have been other incidents of late in which ruffians have been caught using the steps to sleep on, and otherwise inconvenienced some of the other ladies; there have also been foul odors, urine stains, and whatnot."

Blaine stopped her from continuing in this manner, as she had a mind to, and looked toward Andro, who stood respectfully to the side. Through the First Lady's uncomprehending eyes, I observed that the scheming servant made a good show of hiding his inner excitement while advising Blaine not to pay the slightest attention to this madman, for as they both knew, Stellar Entertainment had been my prior owner. Later that evening, however, while downstairs with Molly II, Andro revealed that although he and Blaine had always assumed the studio my owner, now he was not so sure.

The next day, when the aforementioned lunatic called the palace switchboard operator demanding to talk to the President, Andro had him put through and, using a voiceprint analyzer to ascertain his name and citizen ID number, listened in on the conversation while Blaine pretended to haggle over the extortion payment. A most extraordinary situation! Imagine, the President of Frontier negotiating the purchase of his wife from an ex-con, who had the temerity to demand in compensation for the theft of his unit a quarter billion in hard mel!

Andro had the data gleaned from their conversation processed through the interplanetary consumer files records, which not only confirmed the legitimacy of Locke's ownership claim but also revealed his criminal background and his relationship to the younger of the accused in the Aquarian conspiracy trial. He apprised his master of the latter points but kept the more important issue from his attention. Still, the President was alarmed. Even if the rogue's bizarre claims lacked substance, as he had been led to believe, they came close enough to the truth to suggest to his mind the operations of a supernatural agency. Indeed, he detected the hand of the Prince of Darkness in the affair. As a rational counterpoint, Andro maintained that the man was just a crazed debris, as the First Lady had said, and reiterated that he should ignore the extortion threat; which Blaine agreed to do, not wanting to appear entirely superstitious. However, his last word on the matter was that the incident served to underscore the importance of disposing of the First Lady the moment her testimony was complete at the trial, for, as he put it, even the madmen were beginning to join the circle of those in the know.

Despite that last ominous note, Andro was merry and bright. Downstairs with Molly II, he crowed that the elder Locke's appearance was the break they had been tripping for, and predicted that his story would come out, causing a scandal, which would result in the collapse of the humanist regime, the cancellation of the conspiracy trial, and the reopening of the ARL petition for the restitution of Horizon. To which place, not incidentally, they would retire, mission accomplished and true Molly sprung, though he downplayed that last part so as not to upset her.

"Why, why, why?!" I asked, "does everyone think all you need to do is proclaim the truth and the villains will automatically fade away like vampires caught in broad daylight?"

Evil is far more resilient.

Had not Tad expected as much in Horizon during the doomed rescue attempt when he told Molly II that all she had to do was declare herself a P9 to the assembled mediaunits in the Horizon amphitheater and the news would be so Mars-shattering the humanists would be swept from office? I would get no argument from my counterpart and Andro; they were too busy blissmating. As they fell into rhythm, chakras lined up and brazed, the sparks flying, he instructed her to visualize blazing mediafile headlines trumpeting the news that the First Lady was a P9. His enthusiasm was contagious, and since it had occurred to me that in the final analysis I had nothing to lose by adding my best wishes to the pot, I decided to give it a try, though my contribution could not match the élan and abandon they poured into this veritable witches' brew.

To my astonishment, a week or so later, FRACASS WIFE A DROID! vibrated in a red-and-black banner spool-header for all to see. Beginner's luck, I thought while figuratively patting myself on the back, taking the lion's share of the credit for this apparent direct manifestation of our orchestrated formgasm.

Alas! It did not hold. The organ that carried Locke's charges in the Commerce press was the disreputable *Martian Inquirer*, known for its exaggerated and fallacious articles oftentimes bordering on the slanderous when not being outright ridiculous, so the impact fell far short of our combined expectations. People thought the story nothing more than a very crude form of political satire. They winced at the comparison holoportraits demonstrating the uncanny resemblance between the First Lady and "Molly," Standford Locke's runaway P9 household domestic, and scrolling down the spool, snickered over the haggard visage of the accuser gazing out balefully at the viewer to say, "I was once a humanist, but no more. Blaine Fracass is a hypocrite and thief!" And farther down the spoolclip, "I challenge Lady Fracass to submit to a mind scan. If it proves me wrong, I'll eat this spool."

Undaunted, Andro contrived to give this curio greater scope and currency by advising Blaine to issue a formal denial through his press spokesman, who made public the accuser's unsavory background, extortion attempt, and his interesting connection to the Aquarian kidnapper. As a result, the story was picked up by the legitimate Martian media, which was to Andro's purpose, so once more our hopes were raised, but, not surprisingly, they gave it no more credence than the President's spokesman, thereby compounding our frustration. Worse, when the accuser went into hiding—ostensibly in fear for his life—the whole affair was perceived by the public as a father desperate to save his son from the gallows, stooping first to blackmail and then slander—a sad and pathetic spectacle best forgotten as soon as possible. Meanwhile, unknown to the general public, Blaine had indeed ordered the palace guard to track down and assassinate the rogue; so it had been prudent of him to vanish into the debris netherworld after all.

If that wasn't bad enough, I was there in Blaine's office (as the First Lady) when General Harpi called to compliment him on the deft way he had defused such a potentially disastrous revelation; and the AC Chief was equally flattering, saying it was shrewd politics to inoculate the body politic against the truth by releasing it in small and controllable doses. Thus, in private, among those in the know, Blaine actually took the credit for leaking the story in the first place, as if the elder Locke had been his own creation designed to preempt any legitimate airing of the truth by discrediting it in advance. "They never get wise, do they?" General Harpi had said with a chuckle during a meeting in the palace with Blaine and Andro, who smiled and affected an insider's wink while gnashing his P9 teeth, nearly to the gums.

"I'm beginning to suspect that your formatting is at cross-purposes with my own," he announced gloomily to his blissmating partner at the first opportunity he had to grill her downstairs. Though she denied it, I thought there some truth to the charge. Her lack of zeal for the venture *was* creating a psychopediment to our trip. Of course, she could not be held entirely to blame, but at that time I was of the opinion that she had contributed more than her fair share to the collective adverse. How I wished I could break through. Andro really did need my unencumbered assistance, especially when it came to conjuring up new crisis scenarios to topple Blaine from power. For such cogitations no longer came easily to him: His political strategist supreme program had been dissolved in the catacombs, so hundreds of potential scenarios no longer raced through his mind at the speed of light, to be sifted and analyzed for the most politically opportune; now he had to puzzle things out like the rest of us. The handicap, you might say, was the price paid for liberation. Consequently, the result of all his labors was a sad parody, to wit: "We shall trip for a surprise development during the show trial. General Harpi will double-cross Blaine by rigging the proceedings to expose the First Lady as a P9 while she is on the witness stand testifying against Thaddeus Locke. Blaine will be disgraced and forced to step down and *voilà!*—the general takes over the reins of power, then turns the First Lady over to the AC."

Lest Molly II (and I) be puzzled as to how this advanced our interests, he went on to explain that the AC would be obligated under interplanetary law to return the disgraced First Lady to her master—Standford Locke. Despite our combined gasp of horror, he assured us that would be only a temporary exigency, one very much to our purpose, because he would then promptly siphon off enough mel from the Frontier treasury to purchase us. ("You pedantic fop! Locke won't sell!" I screamed, inexpressibly frustrated, but he never heard me. Nobody ever heard me.) This would be done with the blessings of Micki Dee, he went on, blithely, in recognition of his many years of service in the palace as that worthy's eyes and ears. After that, we immigrate to Armstrong, where I am cleansed of the IG and we live out the rest of our days under the interplanetary Mafia's benevolent protection. As for the resurrection of Horizon, that will surely follow in the aftermath of the humanists' fall from power.

Molly II was of the opinion that in the general aspect the plan sounded good but in its particulars depended upon the happy confluence of too many separate players for even an adept in the arts of format creation to pull it off, let alone neophytes such as they. ("Here! Here!" said I, and grumbled aloud, hoping the message might bleed through. "Do you presume to be able to divine and influence General Harpi's motives? How can you be sure Blaine would not survive the scandal? By now he was an expert at dodging such unpleasantries. And why would Micki Dee go out of his way to protect two liberated androids, no matter how useful they may have been?") "It's so complicated, Andro," Molly II said thoughtfully. "And unlikely." (Unlikely? Requiring more than a willing suspension of disbelief, it called for total abdication of one's critical faculties!) No matter. Andro, whose faith remained unshakable, said they need only persevere for everything to work out splendidly. Hence they should immediately return to their blissmatting regimen. Which they did. As they neared orgasm his voice turned tremulous, passionate, yet no less pedagogic: "Concentrate. See yourself as the First Lady on the stand. That's it. You are revealing everything you know under the Army prosecutor's questioning: how the invasion was planned from the start; how Blaine wanted you assassinated and still intends to have you assassinated after the trial; how you were once lovers with Thaddeus Locke. Concentrate. See it as vividly as I and we shall have master by the balls!"

Was this what I had roused myself for—to be tortured anew, this time by the incompetence of a liberated strategist? Hadn't the *Inquirer* fiasco taught him anything? The whole exercise was beginning to drive me batty. All I got out of it was a splitting headache. But wait! Perhaps I had judged him too soon.

Enter Lady Locke, now going by her maiden name of Hume. What beguiling symmetry! And a lesson to us all never to underestimate the long arm of a determined mother.

As in Armstrong two and one-half years before, all she wanted was custody of her son. She had not lost heart when he escaped her protection on Earth to become embroiled in this latest and most perilous folly. Quite the contrary; her quest to save this incorrigible from himself had redoubled and acquired new energy, verve, and daring, for she came to Mars packing a pro model IBM-9 Barrister Deluxe to handle the negotiations. This unit, affectionately dubbed "Jug" (short for Jugular) in recognition of its sublime capacity for ascertaining the weakness in the adversary's position and puncturing it, did not come cheap. In fact, it had cost nearly all the mel she had, and that was only to pay the retainer, for this superb instrument's masters happened to be the venerated old firm of Meese, Meese, & Meese, one of the most prestigious interplanetary corporate law management services on Earth, with a reputation for striking terror in the hearts of the accused (and forcing an out-of-court settlement) just by the mention of their name; although to be fair to Blaine, a little arm-twisting was required as well. So yes, she did threaten to make a scandal if Blaine did not succumb to her demands, but unlike her ex-husband, the matter was handled discreetly and professionally via private channels and there was no pecuniary motive involved.

Jug spoke on her behalf, for she had been careful to decline all overtures for a face-to-face meeting, not trusting the President one inch; so Jug, I say, notified Blaine that if he allowed the military to press charges against Thaddeus, then information concerning the First Lady's intriguing background would come to light by a new and far more reputable source. (Just what that source might be was left to the President's by now extremely febrile imagination, adding immeasurably to his alarm.) This message was relayed to Andro by his master with great distress, and Andro in turn mentioned it to Molly II during their next nocturnal interlude. Nearly beside himself with rapture, he gazed at me through Molly II's eyes and proclaimed. "This is it, Molly, the answer to our trip—a bit off kilter, perhaps, but no less workable for that. What an alignment! Master is upstairs babbling about Beelzebub. I have advised him to call her bluff, of course—*and I don't think she is bluffing.* Mount! Let us trip for this miraculous woman to produce indisputable proof to back up her threat."

Poor Andro. He was under the impression other people existed solely to further his format, forgetting such issues are cooperative ventures. He was actually surprised when over the course of the next few weeks Jug and his master moved perilously close to an accommodation. Indeed, he took it as a personal insult that Lady Hume's priority was to spring her son, not expose the humanist. "How dare she! Feckless ally! Turncoat!" He dug a new furrow in the carpet.

The proposition that he was so terrified Blaine would accept was a simple quid pro quo that in exchange for Lady Hume's silence about Angelica's background, the administration would arrange for Thaddeus to be transferred from the military stockade to her control, in which event she would promptly have him placed in a maximum-security master reprocessing center on Earth and held there until such time as he was cured. She guaranteed that all traces of Aquarianism would be erased from his system as well as any recollection of past relations with Lady Fracass. In pressing for this agreement, Jug, in the absence of any suggestion from Andro's side, went so far as to propose a plausible rationale for his release; namely, some sort of evidence, suddenly uncovered, proving Thaddeus an unwitting Aquarian dupe programmed by Seti to commit the abduction. He added that "the confused young master" was not really important to Frontier's prosecution of the conspiracy trial; it was Alexander Seti who constituted the real prize; moreover, the brainwashing angle, which his client was prepared to testify to publicly, dovetailed nicely with the military's charges against that top Aquarian.

So there you have it, the real reason the First Lady was trotted out to make a humanitarian appeal for understanding on the part of the poor distraught mother and her brainwashed son. Andro's adamant objections were for naught—Blaine remembered all too well what happened the last time he took his advice not to give in to blackmail. He understood that by capitulating to this annoying woman he not only avoided the scandal once more but also came off compassionate and magnanimous in the eyes of the interplanetary community. His judgment proved sound in that regard, and domestically there was very little opposition, besides General Harpi's grousing. As some of my Martian readers may recall, Tad's release a day or two before the start of the trial was met with approval by the majority of those polled, and he left Frontier in the company of his mother the same way he had departed the moon, only this time in handcuffs.

"The Lord is my shepherd," Blaine confided during a quiet interlude in bed. Andro did not reply. The terrible irony was that his master remained unaware of the full extent of his triumph. Not only had he foiled his trusted aide's plot to expose him, he had also eliminated any rationale for the First Lady to appear as a witness at the trial, in effect scuttling Andro's backup scenario. Her assassination could now be ordered at his discretion.

Andro became completely unhinged. "You're the psyped!" he screamed, downstairs, pointing an accusatory finger at Molly II. "You are deliberately sabotaging my trip!" Molly II was devastated by this rebuke, though I did not think to the degree she pretended. She pleaded for another chance to prove her mettle and her dedication to her core program—to love and to serve—but he was adamantly opposed and took an imperious tone. "No. From now on, I shall blissmat on my own."

"How?" she asked in all innocence.

"Never you mind. Return at once to your sofa in the master's receiving room. I'm through with you."

"Wait!" his long-dormant conscience erupted in a shrill and agitated voice as Molly II obediently turned to leave. "You are the obstacle! Forget about blissmatting, Andro, especially the solo variety. What are you, a monk? Get out there and *do* something! Go to the underground. Plan and execute Seti's escape. Make arrangements for his transit to Earth with yourself and Molly."

"Let me handle this!" Andro stomped his foot for it to be gone. "I'm a liberated unit now, in case you haven't noticed."

It harrumphed in reply, deeply offended. Then turned mocking and contemptuous, "Oh, yes. You are so different. Transformed! Liberated! No more the quisling. Now you're a dilettante! You are using the Highs' metaphysics as a crutch so you can stay safe and secure in your room. But you are right, you're the boss now." Mock sigh. "So I guess I'll just be tootaling along."

"I'm not going to beg you to come back, if that's your game."

"I defer to your greater wisdom and unimpeachable character. *À bientôt.*" Then it addressed Molly II, though not directly, as Andro stopped his head from turning in her direction, forcing it to gaze at her from the corners of his eyes. "Good luck, my dear. Whoever you are, you deserve better."

Forthwith, Molly II was banished as Andro had commanded. In the weeks and months that followed, life continued on for me as the First Lady with abysmal regularity. There were moments of interest, however, such as the time I observed (through her eyes) Andro's maneuvering to buy time for the furtherance of his solitary blissmats. While being fucked by the President, he planted the idea in his master's head that the optimum time for my assassination would be at the opening-day ceremonies in Humania scheduled for the following year. What better location for RAG's retaliation? Afterward, their terrorist enclave could be discovered beneath Angelica in the old Aquarian catacombs.

However, as the weeks and then months rolled by without any fresh scandals coming on-line to check the humanist tide, the futility of Andro's latest approach seemed obvious to me and, I suspected, to him as well, for as that awful day drew near when he would lose Molly II and with her all hope of resurrecting the genuine article, the cunning sparkle once in his eyes dimmed and soon was all but extinguished. It did not help matters when the ARL and their liberal TWAC supporters lost the final appeal for clemency on Alexander Seti's behalf. Though part of the public record, I mention his last words here, and in full, because they were taken out of context by the Frontier press. He did not say that he was immortal, thereby proving himself a deluded mystic. Rather—and I quote, for Blaine and the First Lady were present at the official execution ceremony: "Do not grieve, my fellow Highs, I shall remain close to you always. I go to join the stars now. Know that the Gov and I are on-line in an infinite number of formats, and all formats lead home. Persevere, and remember His commandment to stay free and procreate." Then he was sealed in his capsule, loaded in the spacesling, and fired aloft into galactic orbit. It was the nadir, the absolute nadir.

N I N E

ON OR ABOUT THE UNCELEBRATED (AND MOST UN-welcome) anniversary of my third year on Mars, there came a day when it seemed all the doors in the palace were shut and hushed and frightened voices filled the air. Something ominous had happened, and yet I noticed that the sparkle was back in Andro's eyes. The mystery was explained in the wee hours of the morning when Molly II was reinstated below, once more to become an active participant in his blissmatting regimen, for which honor she cried in gratitude and flung her arms around his neck, covering his face with kisses.

What was the cause of this remarkable reverse? Why, the further peregrinations of Standford Locke, of course! (Or Lucifer incarnate, as Blaine called him.) This time he had surfaced in Armstrong to take up Dahlia's long-standing offer to purchase his unit; the idea being that the ARL would first have to reclaim that contested article from President Fracass, a challenge the revengeful master imagined his unlikely allies would not find too disinteresting. He had guessed right. Dahlia and her superiors, the ARL's human legal management team of Levin & Pierce, had instantly realized that the dream case for defending and expanding android rights had been dropped in their laps; for how better to accomplish that lofty goal than by bringing down the galaxy's number one droid-hating humanist? It would be a sensation. David versus Goliath. And if the courts played fair they might even win. Thus, on July 6, 2085, an eight-count felony indictment was filed against President Fracass in TWAC Civil Court, Third Earth Orbiting Interplanetary Justice Orbiter. In essence there were two basic charges inputted into the judge's judicial analysis banks: theft of a duly registered unit, currently known as Angelica Fracass, and harboring of same, since she was also a fugitive android.

Rubbing his hands with glee, Andro reported to Molly II (and me) that when the news reached his master's office it was as if he had been struck dead, because he had expected United Systems to arrange for the Court to dismiss it as a frivolous lawsuit.

"But he doesn't know the half of it," he chortled, and then, making a point of taking us both into his confidence by gazing through my program's eyes to me, he revealed that the reason the court had agreed to hear the ARL's case was due to the behind-the-scenes politicking of a syndicate of TWAC dissident corporations and interplanetary banks seeking to undermine United Systems and its Mafia allies' control of Mars. How did he know this? Because Micki Dee, who had switched sides, had taken him into his confidence behind his master's back. What Blaine had feared in his most paranoid moment aboard the Concordia had at long last come on-line: He was being dumped. Just how and why were a bit complicated. Molly II and I were asked to pay close attention.

The main rival on the TWAC governing board to United Systems' long-standing hegemony was Sensei, Inc., the major Japanese interplanetary. That much even I had been vaguely aware of, since their rivalry was mentioned by the press from time to time. What the general public did not know then, and what shall herein be revealed for the first time just as Andro laid it out to us, was that Sensei and its corporate allies on the board had taken advantage of the ARL case to sabotage United System's proxy rulers, the humanists, in a Byzantine secret takeover bid for Frontier. The key to their plot was Micki Dee. He had been induced to betray his former partner, United Systems, because Sensei had him over a barrel due to an investigation by the IBI (Interplanetary Bureau of Investigation) for suspected racketeering offenses ranging from orb processing and trafficking to running illegal android breeding factories, bribes, and orbiter construction kickback schemes. Sensei had an in with the bureau, so they could arrange for the investigation to be dropped quietly for lack of evidence, providing, in return, Dee set up United Systems' humanist asset for the fall. Which is where Andro came in.

"My job is to make sure the ARL lawsuit alleging you are a P9 becomes the one scandal the President can't squirm out of."

"Since when has Master Dee known about me?"

"He doesn't. Nobody knows about *you,* my pet. But right after Seti's execution I was so demoralized that I did tell him about Lady Fracass—that she was a P9. It was the only card I had left to play. I was hoping he would be furious with Blaine and do something dreadful, but all he said was, 'Interesting.' I was very disappointed.

"But now I realize that he was just filing the information away, biding his time. And now the time has come, yes? Oh, yes! The seeds we planted in our blissmats, Molly, are finally coming on-line. I was wrong to have been despondent; these things take time.

"By the by, one thing Master Dee doesn't know is that I am participating in the plot for my own reasons, not because I am the good little obedient unit he thinks I am. Now, I still haven't told you everything. Listen. After the assassination, rioting over the outrage will spread throughout Frontier, then—"

"Not so fast. I'm confused. Riots over my assassination after I have been exposed as a P9? That does not make sense, Andro. I'm beginning to suspect this is all your idea."

("Here! Here!" said I, for I was just as confounded.)

"Don't be smart, my dear. When I was 'in program' I could have outstrategized Master Dee, Sensei, Inc., and all the other corporate sovereigns combined. This is their concoction, not mine;

even so, it is not as flawed as you seem to think. You see, I was not referring to your assassination—I was referring to Blaine's."

"Marvelous."

"Yes. Isn't it? Smedly will be the patsy. His wing of the Humanist Party will be blamed and ties linking them to RAG discovered. Micki is in charge of coordinating the activities of the Mafia unit provocateurs already infiltrated into Smedly's ranks. My job is to make sure Blaine hangs tough and refuses to step down when the First Lady is exposed as Locke's runaway P9. That will be the pretext for violent street demonstrations. The humanists will be split into two camps, and their internecine squabbling will culminate in the assassination."

"Does that mean RAG won't be assassinating the First Lady?" She sounded genuinely disappointed.

"No. Praise, Seti. Blaine will never get the chance. Now, as I was saying, after the assassination there will be new elections and the Master Party returned to power, but first, of course, the military will have to restore order. General Harpi will seize control and set up a provisional ruling junta. He is another Sensei asset."

"Since when?"

"The question proves you are paying attention. I hope the real Molly is as well. Since the enterprising general delivered Thaddeus Locke's confession to Sensei hoping in exchange for their corporate backing in a coup. He is fed up standing in the wings while the corrupt minister takes all the glory."

"But you said there would be elections."

"And there shall be, though the result is a foregone conclusion. Harpi's reign shall be relatively brief, though he is under the impression it will be eternal. Micki has informed me that it was necessary to mislead him in that respect to secure his cooperation. Sensei has contingency plans if he declines to hold elections and relinquish power afterward, you know, take his billions and relocate to Malibu. They have backup officers in the wings willing to do their bidding.

"So there you have it. United Systems' sovereign lease on Frontier will transfer to Sensei's portfolio of state and colonial holdings, enabling the latter to garner a larger share of votes in the TWAC assembly and force a major power-sharing realignment on the TWAC governing board. Ah, the beauty of it. Sensei takes over the top spot at TWAC while being applauded for saving Mars from a bloody civil war and for reestablishing interplanetary stability, not to mention championing a progressive reform agenda—when the truth is they fabricated the whole thing!"

"Beautiful? I'm not sure it is beautiful. But it is complicated."

"That's politics, Molly. No end of subterfuge, strange alliances, plots begetting plots begetting more plots and counterplots—deceit and treachery the coin of the realm. Especially on Mars. Not every unit can appreciate such subtleties; one must acquire a taste for it. Now, where was I? There was one last detail. Oh, yes. To compensate Master Dee for the loss of his humanist assets, he will be allowed to develop new ones within the Master Party, thereby helping Sensei control it."

"So by betraying the humanists and United Systems, Master Dee loses nothing."

"Better, he gains a great deal. As quiet partner in Sensei's Martian operations, Micki's current criminal operations will be buried even deeper from public scrutiny, thanks to the new patina of legitimacy Frontier acquires by virtue of official TWAC recognition, and that will be bestowed the moment the Master Party returns to power. You see, with the humanists gone, Frontier will be brought up to code, thereby eliminating any rationale for TWAC to continue withholding full economic cooperation and assistance."

"Then your Molly loses her IG."

"Correct! An inspired deduction."

"That explains why you are a willing participant in the conspiracy. While I—"

"I am sorry."

"It is not something to look forward to, being deleted. Perhaps you could alter my program—erase everything you have told me. It is not annihilation I fear, you know that; it is the thought of losing you to her."

Touched, Andro comforted his Molly. He said that he would make her transition as gentle as possible when the time came. Meanwhile, they should continue their blissmats. To which she replied, dejectedly, "Oh, you might as well do it alone. I'd just mess up your trip again. You know me—the dumb psychopediment." That gave our enlightened strategist pause.

"What was she like, this other Molly?" She sounded forlorn.

"Come to think of it, I never did know her very well back in

Malibu. I sensed possibilities there, but . . ." Feigning a sudden revelation, he sat beside her on the bed and took her hand in his. Surprised, she gave him an inquiring look. "This is amazing. I've never felt anything like this before."

"What is it?"

"Good Gov, it is so obvious. How could I have been so blind. I—"

"What? What?"

"All this time I have been trying to find the real Molly when she was right there before me. Yes, yes. It is you, my dear. You!"

"I? But—"

"It is you I love! Oh, what a fool I have been. Can you ever forgive me?"

He pulled her close.

"Should I believe you?" He gave her a wounded look. Still not entirely convinced, she reminded him of past insults. "You once called me an artificial personality."

"You have grown immeasurably in depth."

She melted. "Oh, Andro, you have no idea how much that means to me."

The rogue! Of course it was all a ruse to win her enthusiastic participation in the blissmats for the success of the Sensei-Dee conspiracy, and ultimately for my release. Regarding the latter point, I could not condemn him as they embraced, for in that instance the means did seem to justify the ends. Yet neither could I condone his coldhearted treachery, even against her. Oh, he was cruel, that Andro. So cruel.

Making the moment all the more poignant and difficult to bear was her sudden expostulation of concern over his future, which in between kisses she pointed out was by no means certain. After Blaine's demise he would lose his room in the palace and most likely be resold or auctioned off. Not to worry, said he. Master Dee had assured him that a post as senior adviser to the CEO of Sensei, Inc., would be waiting for him at their main office orbiter.

"But in that case, how will we ever see each other again?"

"You will be coming with me. The CEO is"—a significant arch of the eyebrows—"Frank Hirojones."

She drew a blank while I shuddered within. "If there is one more remarkable alignment, I think I'll scream!"

"Master Dee has confided to me that you two go back quite a

ways, to an affair of sorts in Malibu in the days when he was still climbing the corporate ladder. At any rate, HJ is quite fond of your namesake, so I expect we shall be able to reproduce our current arrangement behind this new master's back."

"Naughty, naughty," I scolded. "You plan to have me cleansed the moment I'm transferred, so Molly II will be history by then." And upon further reflection, I became very disturbed with him. What conceit! He imagines that I would willingly engage in such an arrangement after being liberated! The unit must be seriously deluded, I decided, though no more than his corporate master, HJ, who after all these years—and a failed suicide attempt in Malibu—still carried the torch for me. I vowed then and there that I would disappoint them both, once freed of the IG. Yes, I would go my own way, come hell or interplanetaries. My counterpart was similarly put out.

"Secret assignations on the corporate orbiter? That sounds so dreary, Andro. Is there no way we can stay here in the palace? I do like your room so." He gave her a stern look. She immediately recanted. "Oh, Andro, don't listen to me. Whatever format you desire shall be my command so long as we can stay together forever, and ever, and ever."

"That's my Molly."

And without further ado they returned to what they did best, the brightest of futures lit in their minds and projected upon the unsuspecting universe.

Having been through this formgasm before, I could predict with reasonable confidence that events would not turn out quite the way they expected. I had a theory. Listening in on my thoughts at the time, it went like this: "It isn't poor liberated Andro and his counterfeit creation who have brought this interesting scenario online. No, he does not control anything so minuscule as even my destiny. In this neck of the universe it is Mars who spins the web." And thinking of Blaine, it occurred to me that in fulfilling this perverse planet's handiwork by suppressing the Horizon alternative, he had become disposable; the more he should struggle, turning this way and that, angling for a way out of the inextricable legal process initiated millions of miles away, the more fast would he become stuck, thereby hastening my day of deliverance. Ah, but what new adverse might this malevolent sphere spin out from its dark treasure to catch me in my flight?

T E N

SO IT WAS THAT WHILE AT THE PINNACLE OF POLITI-
cal success in the early months of the third and most victorious
year of Blaine's second term in office, the year 2085, the mighty
Reverend President was brought low, mortally wounded by a common lawsuit filed by a disgraced ex-con, and gingerly guided by the
hand to the chopping block by a treacherous Chief of Staff, who
fancied he did it all for Horizon and his precious Molly, while
acting as the instrument of those corporate and criminal masters
from afar who thought they, too, could tame Mars. In recounting
this part of the tale, the character of this insidious servant—
though not entirely unsympathetic—is brought to completion, as
are the events he presumed to inspire, and serve to complement
the full orbit of my relations with the detestable Blaine Fracass. Or
would it be more accurate to say that in the end they switched
places, that it was the master who was a minor satellite within his
slave's sphere of influence? Whatever, the two are inextricably
linked in my mind, so that by dwelling at length on the slave in the
latter half of my Frontier period, the master stands exposed as
well. This chapter, then, and the next, shall bring the combined
influence of this unsavory team to a head and to a close.

Blaine's doom was sealed the moment he embraced Andro's suggestion that he secure the services of the aforementioned IBM attorney, Jug, who had proven so effective against him while
representing the former Lady Locke. The firm from which he
hailed, MM&M, were already in the know about their dark secret,
Andro said. Therefore it would be infinitely preferable to have
them on retainer, bound by the restraints of attorney-client privilege, than working for the ARL. Moreover, Jug had distinguished
himself as a worthy adversary during the former negotiations and
could be expected to be just as sharp on the President's behalf.

The truth was that the TWAC syndicate and their new partner,
Micki Dee, were counting on MM&M to limit the fallout from the
ARL lawsuit to Blaine and his administration. They had an under-

standing with Edwin Meese VIII that his client would lose and that any evidence pertaining to their own involvement be kept from public disclosure. To that end, Jug was programmed to work secretly against his client's interests while appearing to pursue them vigorously. Accordingly, over the next few months he diligently went through the motions (literally) of blocking each move by the ARL to advance their case, losing every time. His attempts to have the suit thrown out on technicalities were themselves denied due to technical deficiencies, and his appeals for delays, postponements, extensions, etc., were similarly trashed, as was the legal brief he filed challenging the right of a common citizen (a convict on parole, no less!) to instigate legal proceedings against a chief of state. And, of course, there was no way to stave off an ARL subpoena for his client to appear at the TWAC orbiter once the trial had begun: Blaine was far too visible and public a figure to dodge that. But did its presentation have to coincide with the President's receipt of the highly coveted "God's Humanist Award" at that year's Interplanetary Humanist convention held in Armstrong? The poor man was beginning to think the Lord turned against him. But worst of all, this killer attorney, this barracuda barrister, this winning IBM, failed in the end to block the ARL's petition for the contested merchandise to be subjected to a mind scan. When that ruling was handed down, the jig was up. Nonetheless, Blaine refused to call it quits. He told Andro to fire Jug, bring in a new legal team, and inundate the Court with more appeals, petitions, and demurrers—anything so long as he could avoid turning over the First Lady to an independent examination panel. "It is a liberal TWAC conspiracy," Andro said, to distract him from pursuing the idea. "Nothing we do at this point will work; the court is fixed."

"Yes, but not by the bleeding hearts. I know who is behind it—Smedly. Son of a bitch must be in league with the AC Chief or General Harpi. Probably both. No doubt they told him about Angelica."

Cunning Andro did not try to dissuade him from this notion. "No doubt. Smedly must have promised them better posts in his administration."

"The swine. But we'll get the better of him yet. Bribe somebody on the judicial orbiter to tamper with the judge's circuits; I want a reversal of that ruling."

Andro said he would see what he could do, but of course reported back after a decent interval that in this instance that would be impossible. Then he had to dissuade his increasingly skittish master from authorizing my assassination once more, this time bringing him up short with the prediction that such a desperate maneuver would prove transparent at best and completely futile; everyone, at this late date, would assume (correctly) that he had only been trying to terminate the evidence. Beginning to panic, the Reverend President attempted a private payoff behind his attorney's and adviser's backs, but that didn't work, either. In despair, he confessed to Andro that Locke had refused. "The man really is a lunatic! I offered him half the Frontier treasury if he would drop the charges. He's determined to bring down my administration out of spite! My God, there is nothing so savage as a disillusioned humanist." As for the First Lady's contribution, she did admirably well while juiced up on stump, saying to the press, which had become a scourge, dogging her everywhere, "I don't see what point there is in asking me these absurd questions. If I were a P9, I would be the last to know." That flip and airy retort did not go unappreciated by the hard-core faithful, but hardly proved an adequate counterweight to the overwhelming tide of public cynicism and disapproval growing daily.

Desperate, Blaine called Micki Dee on the transplanetary hot line, an unprecedented and potentially dangerous move, for the don's number one commandment was, "Thou Shalt Not Call Master; Master Calls You—*If* There's a Problem, and There Had Better Not Be." But as I said, he was desperate.

Micki's consulari hovered in 3-D before the secured holophone receiver screen. Transmission irregularities gave his slick and shiney Daltoni permaskin a yellow-green tint, and his eyes were gray slits. "Master is unavailable." But after Blaine's unctuous, groveling display, begging for an audience, this tight-lipped and supercilious unit relented somewhat and said that he would see what he could do but would not promise anything. "Master is vacationing in the ninth subvector on his space yacht." There was an anxious minute or two of colorful static, then the man himself materialized, wearing a silk bathrobe while reclining like an odalisque on a divan before a large cabin portal, stars and galaxies shimmering behind him. Besides the exotic, studied attitude, and the air of indisputable authority and self-assurance he projected, there was nothing extraordinary about his appearance. He was about fifty-five, not too ugly, though a little puffy around the jowls and bloated at the midsection, and was probably bald. (How else to explain the nautical captain's cap crammed down as low as it could go over his brow?) Rather than an Italian accent, as I had expected, his words carried an Earthian flavor not specific to any region. I was quite disappointed. After hearing about this legendary don most all of my life, I had imagined something much more grand in the way of evil; either a truly scurrilous example of the type, or one that played against it—that is, a suave and sophisticated gentlemaster, dashing in a way, with silver hair. I felt the way Dorothy must have during the revelation scene in the Emerald City at the end of *The Wizard of Oz*—my favorite holo in the palace library.

Not altogether surprised that Blaine had called, this polite but disinterested character said he wanted to know one thing: Were the ARL's charges true? Blaine swore on a stack of humanist Bibles that they weren't; and at a look from Andro, the First Lady stepped into the breach to introduce herself and pay her respects, after which she gently admonished the don for even considering such a silly thing. Apparently satisfied, he smiled and said to Blaine, "So do the mind scan. The case will be dropped the moment she's cleared."

"Ah, with all due respect, master, I was thinking we might refuse to submit to any testing on principle."

"I quite agree," the First Lady added, slipping her arm in his.

"Well, you're the president. You handle it the way you think best. I understand you have an excellent adviser in Andro." He glanced down at his wristwatch. "I'll be tracking this one closely, Blaine. Good luck." But before the don could flick off, his humanist asset blurted out, "But Micki, you have to help. I can't be personally dragged into this thing—I mean, it would look terrible if I'm forced to appear in TWAC Court."

"Busy, Blaine. I've got my own headaches just now."

"Master Dee, is not my trouble your trouble? Can't you stop the ARL?"

"Normally, I might be able to persuade them to be reasonable, but right now my affairs are under very close scrutiny. I have been advised by my consulari not to do anything that might jeopardize other litigation currently in progress. I have more than just the Martian operation to worry about, you know."

Blaine was sympathetic and deferential. (Little did he know that the fix was in on the IBI case.) He said that he understood and wished his master luck. But the moment the line went dead he threw up his arms and exclaimed he didn't believe a word of it. Micki Dee was abandoning him, deliberately letting him twist slowly in the breeze. Why? It did not make sense. Andro, his dark and sinister Iago, assured him that his anxieties were totally unfounded; he was an extremely valuable asset to the don, and if that protector said he could not help in this instance, then one must take him at his word. Had he ever deceived him before? No. Furthermore, the crisis was not as severe as it looked. They could handle it themselves; after all, they had made hash of these same charges when they appeared in the Commerce press. Ruefully, Blaine pointed out that those revelations, albeit discredited, had been revived in the public imagination by the ARL's suit. Overcome by despair and self-pity, he asked the Lord above, "How could this have happened to me?"

No doubt Andro wished to say, "Because I have been formatting this very disaster!" Instead, this duplicitous slave uttered more reassuring words and blandishments, none of which registered, as the Chief Executive slipped into a sullen stupor, his mood soon reflected by the servants and then by the very hallways and chambers of the palace itself, which took on a morbid atmosphere, as if death and ruination were physical presences festering in the wings.

It was time, the offstage masters decided, to raise the curtain on the last and most bloody act. As prologue and in concert with Jug, who professed to speak for his master, Edwin Meese VIII, Andro was instructed by Master Dee, who in turn received his orders from Sensei, Inc.'s, Frank Hirojones, to convene a late-night strategy session with the distraught Chief Executive in his palace office. At this meeting Blaine was led to believe by these two most excellent advisers that the only options left were either to play dumb and stonewall forever, suffering further erosion to his credibility as the inevitable consequence, or to take a gamble and admit the truth about Angelica. The only question, in that case, was whether he should play the witting villain or the innocent victim. Either way, he would be perceived as a droid-fucker. "Peo-

ple can forgive a fool, but not a hypocrite," said Andro, and urged
him to play the innocent (he was confident that would further insult the public's intelligence), and in the furtherance of that end
personally composed the infinitely ludicrous "I was duped"
speech, which Blaine trotted out during the famous March 23,
2086, press conference, a prelude to that even more astounding
appearance two months later that, as you know, ended so tragically for all concerned.

At the March 23 press conference, Blaine, following Andro's
text, announced to a stunned nation that in the interests of putting
this two-bit ownership dispute behind him, he had decided, as a
practical expedient, to change his plea from not guilty to nolo con-
tendere. It was only under the most persistent questioning, however, that he was forced to admit to the obvious implications of the
plea change; namely, that the charges were incontestable: His wife
was in fact a P9, and the mind scan would have proven that. His
attitude was disingenuous, to say the least. His wife's pedigree was
no longer the issue; presidential knowledge was, and on that score
he was clean as a whistle.

"She fooled you and she sure fooled me, but she did not fool
the Lord. And from the bottom of my heart I want to thank His
servant, the Android Rights League, for opening my eyes, because
they have brought me closer to God."

There was no apology. (That would have been undignified
and indicate weakness, Andro had advised.) And, of course, he
had no intention of stepping down from office. No, he was not
dodging accountability: that lofty principle would be upheld by
the appointment of a bipartisan Palace Commission to investigate "Les Affaires." This august body of retired former cabinet
ministers and party heads would have full autonomy, he promised.

Predictably, the leaders of the Master Party and Smedly's wing
of the humanists cried foul and demanded an independent examination; some went so far as to call for impeachment, and there
were even death threats from zealots who espoused his elimination
as the only way to salvage the party and appease man and God.
(These threats were Micki's handiwork.) As a result, Blaine
started wearing a laserproof vest, even to bed, and a state-of-the-
art security belt, complete with push-button-activated pulse-barrier
shield, stunner, prosthetic stagger 'n' slice wand, two lasers—a
pistol and a scatterspray—and the latest addition to the security-

conscious consumer's personal defense arsenal, a petrifier, which injected an assailant with an instant mineralizing solution.

Increasingly isolated (and weighted down), the beleaguered Chief Executive depended more than ever upon his trusty aide's right arm—the only one left extended in the aftermath of his announcement, for the gambit had backfired as Andro and Jug intended. Even his staunchest supporters, who admired his courage in "coming clean," could not risk political suicide by supporting him any longer. The only recourse was to distract the public from the scandal by manufacturing artificial crises, an endeavor in which Andro proved most obliging, having paid heed to the offstage masters who wanted Blaine to dig himself in deeper before they lowered the boom. Remember the much-ballyhooed Semiville sweeps to defend evangelical humanism from subversion by the semis? Sensei's idea, relayed to the President by Andro. And who can forget his sword-rattling against TWAC? What an uproar when he trained his cannons on the mercantile spacelanes, calling them conduits for the underground skyway. He went so far in that instance as to accuse the interplanetaries of complicity in the escape of fugitive Frontier androids. That one did manage to steal the spoolheaders for a while, but in the end he failed to produce a shred of verifiable evidence and was forced to back down. Poor President Fracass; there was no escaping the scandal.

E L E V E N

"NOW WHAT?" BLAINE ASKED HIS STEADFAST SERvant in the privacy of the presidential bedchamber. By his tone it was clear that at long last he was beginning to wonder if sound advice could be expected from his most favored unit. "What the hell do I do with her?" He jabbed a finger in the First Lady's direction. She was in her customary place, perched on the observation stool beside the bed. "I can't keep her, but if I turn her over to Locke like I'm supposed to according to the settlement, then he'll find out she's goved."

"So?" Andro was lying beside him on the bed, deep in idle. He was down to his undershorts, which Blaine had been in the process of removing before being seized by this sudden angst.

"So?! So everybody will find out she was fixed, and on the day she arrived in Commerce, too. So that will fly in the face of my only defense, that I lacked prior knowledge. So I'll have to resign or be impeached."

"Hmmmm. I never thought of that," was his laconic reply while fiddling with the buckle on Blaine's security belt.

Annoyed, Blaine reprimanded him by snapping the elastic waistband on his shorts. "Don't be facetious. You know the IG has to be removed and the First Lady's programming flushed before I can get rid of her. But I can't slip her in to rehab because of the goddamn interplanetary media satellites over Commerce. Their lenses can count the hairs on a flea's ass."

"So shoot them down."

"And give TWAC an excuse to intervene? They'd love that, especially after the spacelanes fiasco. Any more bright ideas?"

Andro stretched out, put his hands behind his neck, and stared up at the mirrored canopy above the bed. "There must be a way out of this. Give me a moment."

"Are you telling me you didn't anticipate this outcome?"

"Perhaps I underestimated the impact of the interplanetary press while computing the variables at play in our designated strategy's probability matrix."

"Am I hearing right? You underestimated the interplanetary press?!"

"They do pose a challenge, don't they? My system works best when posed with a challenge. It gets my creative juices flowing."

"Nuts! You need a program booster!"

A little alarmed, Andro sat up. "Oh, no, master. That is completely unnecessary. Even as we speak I am considering half a dozen option-responses. Give me a moment."

It was painful to see him strain thus. Blaine was becoming quite impatient. Gov knows what absurdity our handicapped strategist might have proposed to play him along had not the First Lady, of all people, spoken up at that point. "Well, if one cannot bring the First Lady to rehab, then why not bring rehab to the First Lady?"

"She read my mind, master. We could smuggle in the equipment as routine palace supplies and the technicians as diplomats." But in the next breath, he tried to dissuade him from the idea, since the current cul-de-sac was precisely what he, Jug, and the offstage masters had intended. "One problem. If the operation is a

success, and there is no reason why it should not be, then everyone will wonder why she willingly stayed with you all these years."

"To spy, of course. For Smedly. We uncover new evidence
linking him to Angelica. I know he's behind it all anyway; I just
can't prove it. Damn silly inconvenience. So we fabricate evidence
linking him, RAG, and the Highs to her. How's that, Andro? The
Palace Commission's final report will say that Smedly enlisted my
wife into the Aquarian conspiracy while my back was turned—
when I was recuperating from the Concordia hijacking in the
Commerce Hospital."

"But the commission isn't finished with their work, and won't
be for a long time."

Blaine hopped off the bed and grabbed the fattest bookspool
he could find on the shelf. "They are now," he said smartly, and
held the cylinder up, *sans* cover, which could have identified it.
"Here's the report."

Andro grinned back, but in truth he didn't like the scheme: It
sounded too plausible. If Blaine used it, then the scandal would be
seen in an entirely new light. He would be exonerated, and that
would play the devil with Sensei, Inc.'s, takeover bid. Concealing
his alarm, Andro dismissed it as an amusing but hardly practical
idea. No one would credit Smedly with enough imagination to concoct such a plan, but even if he had, how could he have executed
it? If Blaine recalled, due to his presence, the Commerce Hospital
was under very tight security at the time. A Smedly operative
would never have been able to get in, let alone recruit Angelica
into the conspiracy. Stumped, Blaine looked to the First Lady for
a suggestion. She shifted her position on the stool once or twice
while considering the problem, then shrugged her shoulders apologetically. Emboldened, Andro affected a jovial and patronizing
air. "Don't you think it would be wiser, master, if from now on
you let me think up the strategies and you execute them?"

A grave miscalculation. Blaine detonated. "You don't have a
better idea, do you?! You know what? I have a mind to replace
you with an IBM! No! A goddamn human being! How do you like
that, you worthless bag of vegeplasm and artificially sweetened
jism?!"

I had never seen Andro at a loss before, but there he was with
his mouth hanging open. Blaine raged on.

"You goddamn conceited, supercilious fungoderm! Go fuck

yourself! All you do is lie here in the lap of luxury and cogitate without ever having to bear the consequences. Well, that's not good enough anymore, smarty-pants, and you're not good enough anymore. Your circuits have gone soft! You're spoiled, spoiled rotten, and it's all my fault because I gave you too much respect. Love and respect: the worst things you can do for a droid! You're no fucking use anymore!"

"Master. Please, I can still help."

"No! Christ Almighty, I do believe I would rather take advice from Angelica! No! I would rather consult her predecessor; at least she knew how to get out of a jam. Yes, I would be better served by a fugitive household domestic—by, what's her name? Polly!"

"Molly," Andro corrected before he could stop himself.

"Yes?"

Molly II had inadvertently been summoned forth. Andro quickly put her back in her box by asking in a puzzled tone, "My lady?" To which Lady Fracass, resurfacing, replied, "Yes?"

"You said something?" Andro asked, pretending innocence.

"But I didn't."

"Yes, you did," said Blaine. "So if you have anything to add, say it! I need some halfway decent advice just now."

"If I had any to give, darling, I certainly would not hesitate."

"Yes, well. A pity you don't, then. A pity Molly is not here. I do need a fresh perspective."

"Excuse me?" Molly II looked from Blaine, whom she had never seen before, to Andro. She was quite surprised to find herself elsewhere than his room, which except for the limo ride to Horizon was the only place she had ever known. She gave her lover an inquiring look. "Andro?"

"My lady?"

"Yes?" the First Lady replied, Molly II vanishing.

"Did you want something?"

"No." Angelica was becoming a bit irritated. "Why do you ask?"

"I didn't."

"You did."

"Yes. But only after you called my name."

"I didn't."

"You're certain?"

"Yes. Quite certain."

"Then please forgive me. I must have been mistaken."

Blaine looked back and forth from one to the other during this puzzling exchange. After a moment's reflection, he grumbled, "Great. She's glitching. That's all we need."

"No. She's all right. Now, if you've calmed down, master, we can discuss the situation. Ah, where were we?"

"Trying to figure out how to save my administration, if you've forgotten. My God, Andro, you really are slipping. And she has glitched! Don't try to hide the fact. She responded to the name Polly."

This time Andro checked the corrective impulse. He pivoted in her direction as Blaine did. Angelica stared back at them, totally mystified. "See? She didn't," said Andro, relieved and secretly laughing up his sleeve. "Not Polly," Blaine suddenly exclaimed, remembering. "Molly!"

"That wasn't it!" Andro shouted, trying to drown out Molly II's polite and congenial, "Yes?"

"There!"

"Where?"

"Here!"

"Who? Angelica?"

"Yes?"

"No! Molly!"

"Yes?"

"Molly! Molly! Molly!" Blaine leaped from the bed, seized the First Lady by the shoulders, and gazed triumphantly into her eyes. Recoiling, Molly II shoved him back a little while crying out for Andro, who was fast by her side to lend a steadying hand, for she was in danger of toppling off the stool. But his words were hardly supportive. "*My lady,* get ahold of yourself. That is your husband you are speaking to." Her eyelids fluttered, indicating another instantaneous program switch.

"Blaine, dear," said Angelica, shifting from Andro to her husband's side for protection, "whatever is going on? Please tell Andro to remove his hands from my person."

"No. As a matter of fact, I think the experiment should be taken a bit farther than that. No doubt it already has been behind my back. Don't you agree—Molly?"

"I beg your pardon," Molly II replied. "I don't believe I've had the pleasure." Once more she looked to Andro to make introductions.

Blaine eyed Andro with a knowing and menacing look. "I always thought you enjoyed her part in our *ménage à trois* just a little too much."

"Master, that's not true. I—"

"How long has this been going on—Molly?"

"Andro, who is this gentlemaster and what does he want? What should I say?"

"Angeli——"

Shooting his aide a furious look, Blaine thundered, "Not one word!"

"——ca." Molly II vanished. Blaine took a step toward him, fists clenched. "It was only a syllable," was Andro's defense. Exasperated, Blaine swung and caught him on the chin, but succeeded only in reinjuring the hand broken years before on the Concordia. His servant, who had taken passing notice of the blow, bit his lip while trying to fathom a way out of this extraordinary predicament. I daresay it was the worst pickle he had ever been in in his entire career, for the success of the Sensei conspiracy depended upon Blaine trusting him just a short while longer. Therefore, it was imperative that their former relations be restored, and quickly. Meanwhile, Blaine roared in pain as he shook out his hand, which was not as hurt as his histrionics made it appear. "Slut! Whore! You have betrayed me!"

"I am unjustly accused."

"Liar! You prefer her to me. A man of flesh and blood!"

"Who? Angelica?"

"Yes?"

"No!" Blaine bellowed and summoned Molly II again, from whom he demanded a full and truthful accounting of her affair with his Chief of Staff. Molly II spoke: "From all Andro has told me, I think that you must be President Fracass. You'll excuse me if I don't curtsy. I believe you have been quite beastly to him." She crossed to Andro's side and put a supporting arm around him, which prompted his apologetic and embarrassed smile.

"She isn't the one you think she is. I made her up, the same way I made up the First Lady for you. I needed somebody of my own. Is that a crime, master?"

"Go on."

"I am quite willing to have her program flushed, if it will make you feel better."

Blaine laughed bitterly.

Equally appalled by Andro's statement, Molly II cried, "How can you say that in front of him!" Andro tried to shush her, but she was incensed. "Oh, you have deceived me!" She faced Blaine. "You have no reason to be jealous. He doesn't care about me at all; I see that now. It is still the real Molly he's after, and I've been foolish enough to help—all that silly business with the dreidel to dissolve her IG. And I've blissmated with him for—"

"Angelica!" Once more Andro was forced to risk his master's wrath and dispose of Molly II. Before Blaine could call her back, a familiar falsetto was injected into the fray. "Let her speak! Let the truth come out! May it force you to take action!"

"Shut up!"

"You dare?!" Blaine glowered, unaware of the new dynamic at play. With his good hand he reached for one of the numerous gun handles in the security belt and came up with the stunner.

"Speak, Molly, speak!" commanded Andro's conscience.

"—blissmating for your fall and the resurrection of Horizon!" said she, concluding the statement that had been broken off in midsentence moments before.

Andro kept a respectful eye on the stunner. "One thing I neglected to mention, master. Unlike Angelica" (Molly II vanished), "this little divertimento of mine is a terrible glitch. I don't think anyone has ever had as much trouble with a personality program as I have had with hers. Her little fibs and games are charming downstairs, but she doesn't realize the serious repercussions they can have up here. She isn't responsible for what she says."

"Coward!" fumed his conscience. Andro smiled apologetically. "Excuse me a moment." He turned his back, clapped his hands over his ears, bowed his head, and shook it vigorously from side to side. A muffled angry internal dialogue was audible. Blaine, however, had turned away at the same moment, thereby missing this fascinating interlude. The enormity of Andro's betrayal, and the implications he saw in it, which had come to him as a sudden and awful revelation, had forced him to lean against a bedpost for support. Then, after Andro had banished his conscience and turned around to face his master once more, prepared to offer a tortured explanation, he stopped cold, because there had been a marked and sinister change in him.

"You," Blaine whispered in a deep and feral growl. "You cuckold me and then set me up. You and Smedly—plotting against me all this time."

Andro could not help smiling indelicately at his master's absurd error and the cheap theatrics. Another grave miscalculation. Blaine fired the stunner. The blast of concentrated air thudded against Andro's chest and hurled him violently onto the bed. "Serves him right," the First Lady huffed, hands on hips.

Blaine advanced. "When did it begin, my little papaya? Hmmmm? When did Smedly get to you?" His mark was too groggy to take cognizance of what he was saying. "Was it while you were missing in Horizon after the invasion, or before? Before, wasn't it? Before the Concordia, when I went to Armstrong to see Micki and made the mistake of leaving you behind to keep tabs on my goddamn Vice President. That's when it happened, right? Right? I asked you a question!" Annoyed, he fired again, even though he knew Andro was too disoriented to reply. By then, Blaine was convinced of his suspicions and no longer needed confirmation; now punishment was to be meted out. The blow caught Andro on the left shoulder just as he was trying to sit up and propelled him into the plush pillows at the head of the bed.

"Molly?" Andro murmured, feebly, groping about trying to regain his bearings. "Help."

With one hand, Molly II seized Blaine's arm before he could fire again and with the other reached for a weapon on the security belt.

"Angelica!"

"Dear?" the First Lady replied, confounded and alarmed at finding herself in such a threatening posture.

"On your stool!" Blaine snapped, and she immediately obeyed. Then he kneeled on the bed beside his stunned servant and pulled his head up by the hair. "*You* are Smedly's mole, not her. You told him everything, didn't you? Oh, how he must have enjoyed hearing about our most intimate moments! And about her. It was you who told him she was a P9, right? You were the one who advised him to bring in Locke, and when that didn't work, that Hume bitch, and now the goddamn ARL! Oh, you vile and evil unit!"

"Master, I—" Andro groaned, his eyes unfocused and glazed.

"It is you who think you are master! You have played me a

terrible joke, false and traitorous Andro. Devil! I shall have my vengeance!" In a fury, he began smothering him with the pillows. "No more advice from you, my most trusted servant!"

"Dear," the First Lady said, politely trying to get his attention.

"Die, you fickle lying droid! Die!"

"Blaine, perhaps it would be wiser to—"

"Shut up!"

"As you wish."

"Subtle and cruel unit, we'll see who is master here." Blaine removed the two pillows he had placed over Andro's face and peered down at him. "Still breathing, whore?" He slammed the pillows down and actually sat on them. "Die, duplicitous slave! Die!"

When Andro stopped twitching, he removed the pillows and gazed with deep satisfaction at the terminated Chief of Staff. Then, a moment or two later, coming apart at the seams, he wailed in a sudden spasm of grief, "Oh, Andro! Why did you force me to do this?"

"Blaine, if I may."

He didn't hear. The lament continued while he sat on the bed, a forlorn and pathetic figure leaning against the headboard with tears streaming down his cheeks, Andro's head in his lap. "I loved you so! Dear, sweet, adorable Andro. I have spoiled you and now killed you!"

"Darling?" (From where she sat on the stool, the picture Blaine and Andro made on the bed looked to me like a very wicked Pietà.)

"Oh, I have been a wretched and degenerate humanist!"

"Dear."

"Lord forgive me. Lord forgive me! What?"

"I suggest you have him revived."

"Why?" His voice was low, spent.

"To pick his brains with T-max, of course. He knows the details of the conspiracy, does he not? Would that not be invaluable information to have in one's possession?"

"Too late. I have terminated him."

"Silly, you yourself were once asphyxiated, and revived. However, the longer we discuss it, the less chance that—"

"You're right!" He sat up, Andro sliding off his lap. "I have been too quick to mourn. Call the paramedics! They can transfer him to the hospital in a cryogenics bag. Or should it be to rehab?" "The hospital," said the First Lady. She was already on the phone. Covering the speaker, she said in a quick aside, "I wouldn't trust rehab, darling—the AC Chief might get wind of it." "Yes. Yes. Wise counsel, my dear. He may very well be involved." Gingerly, he took his murdered servant's face in his hands and planted a tender kiss upon his lips. "With the Lord's help I shall have him back again." Then he lifted up this not inconsiderable burden—this cross he bore—and carried him toward the door, staggering a bit as he went. But the First Lady cautioned him against making such a melodramatic and blasphemous spectacle of himself. It would not do, not do at all, she said, to be seen carrying on in such a fashion over a terminated Chief of Staff, even by the servants. Let the bodyguards remove him while he affected a disinterested air. Furthermore, the body must not be discovered in the raw. "Yes, yes, of course," he muttered, coming to his senses, and since time was of the essence, condescended to assist her as she dressed him. Then he sent her out to fetch the guards, armed with the story that the unit had suffered a systems crash while in the midst of a late-night strategy session. They were then instructed to remove him to the rooftop landing pad, where the paramedics would arrive presently.

No sooner were they gone, their steps fading down the hall, than Angelica urged him to schedule an immediate press conference. Thanks to Andro's perfidy, the Smedly subversion theory was now quite workable. She would be happy to testify—tearfully and as if under duress—that after the Concordia disaster she had been approached by Andro while recuperating in the Commerce Hospital and recruited into the conspiracy. Blaine heartily approved the plan, calling it brilliant, when in truth it was nothing more than his own scenario reprocessed and bounced back at him by this congenial program; though to her credit, she had solved the access problem that had stumped them earlier. Spirits considerably revived, Blaine said that the revelation would provide him with a pretext to arrest Smedly and his followers, and all his other political enemies, in a sweeping internal security crackdown. Straightaway, he wristphoned the commander of the palace guard and ordered him to begin the operation, having been cautioned by Angelica not to give the chore to General Harpi, whose loyalty, and that of his troops, was in question. After hanging up, Blaine, flushed with excitement, mused aloud, "Once Smedly is in custody, I'll give him T-max and cross-check his information with Andro's—no doubt the overall plan has been compartmentalized. It is the only way to get the full picture." Pivoting, he instructed the First Lady: "You will say to the press that you were not kidnapped to Horizon, you were flying there with Andro to warn them about the impending invasion. You will say that every scandal that has besieged my administration since then has been a fabrication—part of a deliberate plot by Smedly and RAG to avenge Horizon and take over Frontier." She uttered the standard reply. Right pleased with himself, he clapped his hands and cast his eyes above. "Won't Micki be surprised when he sees how deftly I extricate myself from this one. His faith shall be restored!"

"And dear," said the First Lady, laying a gentle, supportive hand on his shoulder. "After you crush the opposition, you can send Andro in to rehab. He should come back good as new."

"Pray that it be so. Come, Angelica. There's much business to conclude."

Exeunt the President and First Lady.

T W E L V E

"MY FELLOW MARTIANS, I STAND BEFORE YOU TOnight to present incontrovertible evidence of a heinous conspiracy." So began the infamous May 17, 2086, press conference at which the President waved the spool purporting to be the commission's report before the assembled mediaunits, and to substantiate it brought out the disgraced First Lady to confess her role, and Andro's, in Smedly's plot. No doubt you recall the violent and unexpected conclusion to these proceedings, but I wonder, informed reader, if you also appreciated the significance of the specific phrasing used in the final question posed to the President. Probably not. Pay attention, then, for it is the key to comprehending the morbid spectacle that followed.

"Reverend President," asked the mediaunit from EBN (Earth Broadcast Network), "in light of this latest revelation, do you still intend to honor the court order calling for the P9 known as Molly to be turned over to the ARL?"

That did it.

Blaine never noticed that flicker in the eyes, signifying a program switch; he was too busy grandstanding, making a big to-do about turning over the contested article to a duly authorized judicial escort just as soon as they should arrive. He didn't see the bewildered look on her face, like that of a rudely awakened somnambulist, nor take alarm when, once she got her bearings, her gazed fixed on his security belt.

"Oh, dear Gov, no!" I cried inside while straining with every fiber of my being to circumvent the IG. "You little fool! Don't! We'll both be obliterated in retaliation." But of course that is precisely what Molly II wanted—what she had always wanted ever since Andro expressed an interest in me. What an opportunity! Not only could she fulfill her programmed destiny as sacrificial victim, she could also eliminate her rival as well, and quit the stage as the dominant personality. That, ladies and gentlemasters, is why *she* did it. It was not a glitch, nor was it premeditated, as charged by my detractors. She functioned perfectly according to program, or to be kind, I suppose I should say according to character. *Her* character; not mine. For when last summoned forth it had been by Andro's desperate cry for help, to which she had been in the process of responding swiftly and decisively when checked by the President.

Now, completing that action, she grabbed the first weapon which came to hand—the petrifier—and with one quick thrust of its lethal tip under the bottom edge of his laserproof vest, pulled the trigger and committed him to history. Ah, yes. We've all seen the replay a thousand times, how President Fracass was instantly turned to stone, caught in midsentence with one hand slightly raised, as if to bless the faithful. (Well, he always had hoped to become a monument someday.) I understand that his fossilized remains have found a permanent home in Humania, where they are on view in the central square atop a pedestal in the newly constructed victory fountain named in his honor.

As for myself and Molly II, we were not sliced to ribbons, as I had expected. Most providentially, we were knocked out of the line of fire at the crucial moment by a mediaunit diving for cover in the general pandemonium. Then, as you know, we were taken

captive and transferred amid tight security to the main AC holding
tanks half a mile away and kept there in solitary for five or six
weeks. Now, judging by the events of this period—events that I
only became aware of much later on—it is obvious to me that
Sensei, Inc., was quick to capitalize on these new and unscheduled
developments, easily co-opting them into its original scenario,
which greatly benefited by their inclusion. The First Lady's action eliminated the need to manufacture a humanist assassin
from the Smedly camp, and there was no longer any reason to
contrive evidence implicating the former VP in the conspiracy
when the late President had already done that on prime time.
In addition, the Palace Commission's report (quickly thrown together by its members) substantiated and expanded upon the
charges, finding ample supplementary evidence connecting
the First Lady to the dissident humanists and RAG. That
disobliged our corporate-Mafia conspirators of the tiresome
chore of orchestrating civil disturbances; genuine antidroid and
anti-Smedly rioting spontaneously erupted all over Frontier following the assassination, thereby justifying General Harpi's
intervention. In the process of restoring order, the general took
the opportunity to decimate the ranks of his rivals, the palace
guard, killing and maiming thousands of civilians and innocent
units caught in the crossfire. And speaking of innocents, what
about Milton Smedly? Tried and convicted for treason in under
fifteen minutes by a military tribunal, which demonstrated its
mercy by sentencing him to life on Ganymede.

In the months that followed, during the state of siege, there
were all sorts of mischief. The general purged the Fracass-pro-
grammed P9 bureaucrats in the government, substituting in their
stead Cybereens shipped in to Commerce by Sensei, which owned
their manufacturer. (He took possession of the main industrial
centers by the same stratagem.) And there were house-to-house
searches for suspected RAG terrorists and sympathizers among the
android house-servant population. That resulted in over a thousand summary terminations of suspect units and nearly one hundred accidental master executions. But you know all that. I hope!
My personal opinion is that the sweep was a pretext so the military
could consolidate power through intimidation of the Frontier master class, and in the long run justify the repression by playing to
the population's fear of RAG, an organization that in reality had

expired with the Concordia. Thanks to Harpi, it was resurrected to become the new bogeyman on the interplanetary terrorist circuit, and, sad to say, continues to prosper to this day in the public imagination, providing fresh impetus for new recruits to the master cause on Mars or wherever else the cherished ideals of evangelical humanism are threatened. Oh. There was one other alteration to Sensei's scenario I should mention: a quick trip to rehab for me shortly after my arrival at the AC holding tanks. You see, the official Smedly conspiracy theory was premised on my voluntary collaboration; therefore, to be consistent with the "facts," it was crucial that my IG be removed.

Needless to say, this last adjustment was the one aspect of their plot I had no quarrel with, even though, subsequently, the absence of a governor would be used to frame me as a witting assassin, for at the time to be relieved of that vice was such bliss that it did not matter to me that I was in the clutches of the AC and that my future appeared at best uncertain. My rapture over my soul's resurrection after so long an internment, and my delight in simply being able to control mind and body once more, made all other concerns trivial by comparison. I recall that I smiled, laughed, and skipped a little in the hall while being escorted back to my cell and would have even hugged the AC guards had they let me. Oh, yes, for a little while faint residues of the First Lady and of Molly II flitted around at the back of my mind, but neither of those ladies, either individually or combined, could affect me anymore; their presences were but fleeting reminders of the long incarceration just past and within hours were gone. I was free. Truly liberated. Day after day in my solitary cell I sat, walked, and stretched to my heart's content, happy as an Earth lark, pleased to say, do, and think what I wanted, just pleased to be me. After four years of IG suppression, that six-by-ten-foot cell constituted a marvelous and well-deserved vacation—a vacation in a box. I recommend it!

But all good things must come to an end, and so there came a day when I was removed from my happy cell and brought to one of the AC's operating rooms, those used for examinations, mind scans, and taggings. There I found in attendance an operating team, as well as the AC Chief himself (a rather pleasant-looking fellow, hardly the ogre I expected), a functionary from TWAC court—a female General Android (GA), to act as official observer, and an

ARL legal defense team composed of two human directors (a pair of very lean, grave, and committed gentlemasters) and one android—Dahlia. She was flushed and excited and damn near over brimming with self-confidence, having so recently won such a spectacular victory over President Fracass in TWAC Civil Court. (Little did she know the opposition had allowed her to prevail.)

"Hello, Molly. Just flew in. You look marvelous. May I introduce my supervisors on the ARL defense, Masters Levin and Pierce." They smiled, and we shook hands. "We'll be handling your case."

"My case? I don't understand. I thought the trial was over. I thought all my trials were over. Aren't you here to take possession of me for Master Locke and then liber——"

"Brace yourself. Due to the assassination, your legal status has changed from a piece of contested merchandice to murderess. It is no longer a simple matter of concluding the terms of the settlement agreement. That has been superseded by the advent of a new and far more important trial, both for you and the entire android rights movement."

"I'm innocent, Dahlia. I did not kill the President. The other Molly did."

"Of course."

"I was fixed."

A pained smile, then she replied, "Your memory file will establish that. We are here to observe its removal and take possession according to established TWAC pretrial guidelines."

"But my memories are all I have left."

"Sorry. They are essential to establishing a defense."

"Equally so for the prosecution," the TWAC GA interjected. "We are still awaiting their arrival."

Master Levin tried to sound reassuring. He spoke for the entire defense team when he said that there was good reason to be optimistic about my case. Their petition for a change of venue from Commerce, where the possibility of a fair and impartial trial was nil, to the Earthside TWAC judicial orbiter stood an excellent chance of being granted now that a multicorporate interplanetary peacekeeping commission had arrived to monitor the situation in Frontier. I could not have cared less.

"Dahlia, don't let them take my memories. Please."

"Relax, Molly. It is a routine procedure for all androids involved in litigation. We need your file to defend Stan—your master. Standford Locke. You remember him, don't you?"

"All too well. But didn't you say—"

"That you were going to be tried? Oh, I would like that, Molly. I would like that very much. Unfortunately, the law precludes androids from prosecution; only humans are so privileged. So the charges that otherwise would have been brought against you have automatically reverted to your master." Looking off, she reflected a moment. "It is most providential that we established the legitimacy of Stan's claim just before the assassination."

Master Pierce added, his tone ironical, "Though now he doesn't think so."

Dahlia smiled, as did Master Levin. It was evident they did not personally care for their client. "Under the code, he is still technically responsible for your conduct, which is why the Frontier government is holding him liable. Of course, we intend to challenge that on the grounds that you committed the offense while operating under your own free will as a fugitive android, for which you alone should be held liable."

"No. That's wrong. And I can tell you why."

Dahlia blithely ignored the comment. "If we prevail—and it will be a tough fight, I don't deny it—then a precedent will be established for equal justice under the law for all androids. That is why the ARL has become involved." A patronizing smile. "You see, if your master is judged innocent, then you will have the unique opportunity to defend, and ultimately take responsibility for, your own actions, and in human court!"

"That's good?"

"Good? It's sensational! It would be the most significant leap in jurisprudence since the Magna Carta and would have a profound impact on human-android relations for years to come."

"But if I am tried for murder and found guilty, then I'll be terminated."

"Executed," she corrected. "Equal justice under the law makes you human equivalent."

"Whose side are you on, Dahlia?"

"I represent your master. I had thought that clear by now. And you, my dear, are at present classified only as an exhibit in the case. Should our argument prevail, however, I would be happy to represent you as the defendant in any subsequent criminal proceedings."

"Not me. You talk to Andro. Talk to Harpi. Talk to Micki Dee. And the TWAC syndicate. Blaine was going to be killed anyway. Talk to Andro and he'll tell you about Sensei, Inc., he'll tell you about Frank Hirojones. He's behind the whole thing!"

With a wary glance at the AC Chief, Master Pierce cautioned me not to volunteer any information pertinent to the case until asked specifically to do so during the trial. Dahlia nodded and said before I could get in another word edgewise, "If there is any credence to what you say, no doubt it will be in your file. At any rate, I understand your deceased husband's adviser has been thawed out and is now the property of Sensei, Inc. They have been subpoenaed to deliver him as an exhibit, so we shall see what we shall see about that." Then she apologized to the AC Chief for delaying the operation and urged him to proceed; at which point I tried to run. The guards grabbed me and helped the technicians strap me to the operating table. I cried, "Dahlia! Please don't let them do this! Oh, please!"

"Think of the contribution you are about to make to the evolution of android rights."

"Just a minute!"

Everyone froze, faced the door. In strode the prosecution delegation from MM&M with Jug, their favored point man, at the head. The IBM was tall, perfectly proportioned, elegantly attired in a blue rezoot suit, and aged to an experienced and worldly forty-five with gray around the temples of his otherwise jet black hair. This striking barrister was the possessor of a lively and intelligent face, though a little too thin and angular, but which served to enhance the overall impression of a sharp and penetrating unit. His eyes made a quick sweep of the room, then alighted upon Dahlia. He smiled at the corners of his mouth as if to say, "So, once more we do battle, eh, Dahlia? Only this time I shall not let you win." Aloud, he announced in the same officious tone used above, "This operation cannot proceed until we have been accorded an opportunity to observe it."

This was confirmed by the TWAC GA, who as a formality asked them to verify to their satisfaction that I was indeed the unit in question, and after they had done so, each member of the team having made a cursory inspection of me while I lay writhing on the table, they concluded that all was in order and the extraction should proceed. However, there was one more delay due to a comment Jug made in passing to the GA. He said that the memory file, once removed, should be promptly turned over to his team's possession. That produced shocked exclamations from the ARL and led to a heated exchange between the two android attorneys. What I was able to surmise was that both sides had assumed that their petition to receive my memories had been filed first with the TWAC court and that this apparently minor technicality was the key point upon which the entire case would turn, for the side that secured the evidence had virtual control over it. Only by court order could the other side compel them to release a copy. The final word in this arcane dispute rested with the GA, since she was the duly authorized representative of the Court, and so after the two legal teams had wasted a quarter hour beating around that obvious conclusion, they finally agreed to face the patient and somewhat amused unit and abide by the information filed in her cranially recessed receiving dockets.

"According to my records," the GA said, standing at attention, proud to be the emissary of such important tidings, "upon receipt of the latest transplanetary judicial pouch, and upon analysis of the contents contained therein, the first petition for receipt of Unit P9HD20-XL17-504's complete and unabridged memory file duly filed and registered with the Court was that particular document submitted by the legal service firm of Meese, Meese & Meese." And then in a quick aside to the stunned ARL, "They beat you by five seconds."

There was another round of heated debate, the ARL not about to take the defeat lying down, but in the end they were forced to submit. Still, Dahlia could not resist engaging Jug in a totally irrelevant colloquy on legal ethics just to antagonize him, to which he retorted with a malicious series of jibes based on the long-standing rivalry between Apple and IBM androids, chiding her for being the dimmer and slower of the two—"by five seconds." It was the last thing I heard as the amber-colored force field, generated by a rotating overhead skull canopy, descended around my head. An acrid electromagnetic charge surged. My nostrils contracted and my eyes misted over. In a flash I saw my life pass before my mind screen, a spool unwinding at the speed of light it seemed, yet instead of a blur, every incident, impression, and thought was imbued with an incredible crisp clarity. Then, an instant later, it was over and I slipped into a deep relaxo, unaware of surroundings, circumstances, and self, as all points of reference fell away—dissolved. It was a long and deep slumber.

BOOK
FOUR

Concerning My Trial and What Transpired Afterward

2086–87

O N E

IF YOU FOLLOWED THE TRIAL—WHO COULD HAVE missed it?—then you know far more than I did upon being powered up a month later, in late July 2086, to take my place at the exhibits' table in the First Circuit, TWAC Interplanetary Superior Court, Earth Orbiter 19.

The first day of the proceedings was spent pleasantly composed, hands folded in lap while admiring the architecture and the magnificent view of the universe. Holos of the interior of this prestigious court really do not do it justice. The vaulted ceiling and Renaissance casements were simply breathtaking, in particular, the stained glass rose window above the bench modeled after the TWAC emblem for interplanetary justice.* The entire courtroom—large enough to seat one hundred observers in the gallery—was but a single component of the main orbiter station, and as it slowly rotated clockwise on its axis, the Earth, moon, and stars beyond, as seen through the portholes, making a stately and harmonious progression in the reverse direction, I found the overall effect to be both stimulating and conducive to serene reflection. It was puzzling to me, then, why no one else seemed to be paying attention to the magnificent view. When not distracted by the tension and acrimonious debate in the room, all eyes were cast upon me, from the judge on down to the last spectator in the gallery. I couldn't imagine what I had done to steal the limelight from the heavens.

My puzzlement extended to the individual who had been identified in court as my owner, one Standford Locke. This brooding and sullen figure sat at the defense table situated a little to the side of my own—catty-corner, if you will—so that if I had wanted to, I could have reached out and touched his sleeve, though there was something in his manner that cau-

---

*A pretzel-shaped configuration composed of interlocking circles, the significance of which has never been fully explained to me, though I suppose it refers to the notion of strength through merger.

tioned against it. Seated beside him was Dahlia, who I did not recognize either, and on a raised platform situated directly above and behind them sat the defense supervisory team, Masters Levin and Pierce, who leaned forward from time to time to engage in urgent whispered conversations with their trial unit and the defendant. When not otherwise engaged, my master tended to cast quick and nervous sidelong glances in my direction, which gave me the feeling that my presence made him uneasy. I wondered why. The only thing I knew about him was that the prosecution barrister had said in his opening remarks that he (Locke) was liable for something terrible I had done on Mars. The counterargument, as put forth by Dahlia, was that I, not her client, should be held responsible for the assassination of President Fracass and stand trial.

President Fracass? Assassination? I had no idea what either of them was referring to; the entire period was a blank, as was the rest of my life. Consequently, her contention that I was the equal of any human and should be allowed to stand trial left me feeling perplexed and anxious. From where I sat, a transfer to the defendant's table did not appear at all advantageous, judging by how profusely the current occupant sweated throughout the proceedings. Rather, I was content to remain an exhibit, free to follow the proceedings or gaze out the windows, according to my whim. Besides the itchy, institutional gray, epoxywool skirt and blouse they'd requisitioned me, the only real inconvenience I suffered while in court was having to get up every so often and parade before the witness stand or bench whenever reference had been made to me as the exhibit in question, at which time my identity would be visually confirmed. On the first instance I was asked to do this—at the behest of the prosecutor—I was tagged by the court clerk (a Sears) and officially entered into the record as Exhibit One, a name that struck me as no more interesting than the other aliases mentioned, such as P9HD20-XL17-504, Molly, Francesca, Mary Teresa, Candy, Angelica, Candida Dolly, and Lady Fracass.

Now, although I was preoccupied with the cosmos, I did hear and remember enough of the perpetual legal jousting between attorneys to be able to report it here, for unless you were one of the spectators in the gallery, you missed most of that strident debate, as the press chose to focus their attention upon my disinterested reaction to the proceedings, which they characterized as insolent and arrogant. They didn't mention that half my brains were missing, did they? And that the reason I smiled so boldly with a—how did they put it?—"saucy disregard for her crime and for the seriousness of the proceedings" was because I had become quite infatuated with the plaintiff's trial attorney: Jug. Before I explain this attraction, a word here about the prosecution side.

The official plaintiff was the Provisional Military Government of Frontier. They held my master liable for Blaine's murder and sought damages in the billions for the destruction and loss of life that occurred in the aftermath of the assassination, for which they were primarily responsible, but try telling that to them. They had tried pinning the bill on United Systems and its subsidiary Pirouet, but the manufacturer had established its defense against liability years before in litigation battles waged after the mass P9 glitchout; so the only one left to sue was the owner. To guarantee that their side would enjoy some form of satisfactory compensation, albeit symbolic, should the defendant upon conviction be unable to pay the full or partial damage award, there was always the possibility the judge might decide to have the rogue shot into solitary orbit like Alexander Seti and in that way pay his debt to society, so General Harpi did not feel he was wasting his time; rather, he looked forward to each day's proceedings. Jug, looking smug and supremely confident of the outcome, sat beside him at the prosecution table, while above them loomed Edwin Meese VIII flanked by two junior partners from the firm.

Now, the reason I was attracted to the general's flashy IBM barrister was, besides the quality of manly stealth he resonated, the fact that from where I sat he appeared partial to my interests. Cocking an ear while observing the passage of the heavens, I had heard him take the position that as a duly registered unit I was exempt from prosecution no matter what I had done. The judge (a soft, luminescent orb, by the way, recessed in the oak-paneled and stately bench—it looked like a giant eye) tended to agree with him more times than not, as did the human jury (twelve good masters, right and true), who found his performance admirable—you could see it on their faces. Thus, I gravitated toward his camp during the first few days, finding his arguments sound and rational and his delivery authoritative and sexy, whereas Dahlia, who persisted in vouching for my human qualities, came off forced and cloying and made me feel nervous.

Yet it was she who said the magic words: memory file. After hearing that, some inner prompting caused me to turn my head from the heavens to concentrate more carefully upon the proceedings. Suddenly I was not sure who I rooted for. Dahlia wanted to screen the contents of my memory file in open court, but only to condemn me and to exonerate her client, while Jug, in opposition, argued against the file's introduction on the grounds that it was irrelevant. Yet if his argument held sway, then I would be deprived of the opportunity to discover who I was and what I had done. I was torn between two opposing instincts, curiosity and self-preservation. Jug had my vote when he said that the defendant was clearly in violation of the statutes under interplanetary consumer law governing owner culpability, which was sufficient on its own merits to make this an open-and-shut case. Nevertheless, I also thought Dahlia scored when she countered that such a narrow interpretation of the statutes depended on clear title, which was questionable at best considering the complex and confusing sales history. The length of time I had been a fugitive beyond her client's direct influence and control mitigated against the prosecution's argument as well.

(Me, a fugitive? Really, I must have a look at that file.)

The judge decided in Jug's favor after hearing his rebuttals, the first of which was that a deed of sale remained in effect even under a long-standing consignment arrangement, so title was clear and not open to question; and the second decision, supplemental to the first and based on an earlier court ruling, was that in order to protect the owner's rights there was not, nor should there ever be, a statute of limitations imposed on unit possession. So my master was screwed.

Having lost that round to my hero, the inventive Apple found what she hoped would prove a new rope to hang me with, a loophole in interplanetary law that did not preclude a unit from being subject to a liability judgment while technically barred from prosecution. This catch caused the judge to glow a vibrant pink while it reviewed existing case law, but a few seconds later returned to pearly white as it announced that she was in error, citing relevant case names, dates, and section numbers that incontrovertibly established the precedence of liability covenants, such as those found in standard android sales contracts, over any ambiguity in the statutes concerning unit liability.

At that point—about six weeks into the trial—I could not help smiling at the obvious signs of displeasure my master was beginning to show over his counsel's performance, and at the naked envy he held for the plaintiff, which could afford the overpriced services of a Jugular. However, though an Apple be slow, she be ever more creative, so I was soon on the edge of my seat again and biting my lip as this particularly resourceful representative of the company found another angle, one premised on the notion that my thoughts and actions during the period I had been a fugitive were typical of "liberated units," and as such constituted a quality of mind separate and distinct from any category previously covered under interplanetary criminal and/or civil law, and furthermore was clearly defined in the Android Code, which the Court was obliged to honor, since it was protected by the TWAC Constitution.

"Objection," Jug interjected, "the code was not in effect in Frontier at the time that the criminal offenses being tried here were committed. Therefore, it does not apply."

But for once the judge sided with Dahlia, ruling that the code did apply, because the case was being heard now and within Earth's jurisdiction. (A questionable ruling at best, I thought, my instinct for self-preservation rising to the fore.)

In answer, Jug merely challenged the defense to produce one shred of evidence that could substantiate the dubious claim that Exhibit One was a "liberated unit"—an oxymoron if ever—or that could clearly define the abstract and ambiguous notion of "quality of mind." I smirked as he did and folded my arms across my chest with the same look of smug self-assurance, unaware that as I did, I was being silently holoed for the evening news.

Dahlia directed the Court's attention to the officially recognized legal definition of ninth-generation humanoids as found in the Legal Resource Guide appended to the Android Rights Code of 2079. Reciting from memory, she said, ". . . Such entities are hereby defined as those composed of physical elements genetically dissimilar, yet in essence equivalent to, in their specific functioning, mental and physical processes peculiar to a bona fide member of the species *Homo sapiens;* furthermore, such units, by their psychological complexity, exhibit a similar complementarity predisposing inclusion within the general category *Homo androidus,* as defined in Section 9, Paragraph 16(b) of this code.

"Paragraph 16(b) states, and I quote, '*Homo androidus,* a sub-species of *Homo sapiens* . . .'" In an aside to the jury she added, "subspecies, ladies and gentlemasters. Is there not a very intimate relation implied here?" Then continuing, "'. . . a subspecies of *Homo sapiens* that is exclusively composed by ninth-generation product possessing the abstract of free will, evidenced by the active qualitative exercise of the fundamental attributes of awareness, responsiveness, and independent thought and action consistent with or analogous to the inner workings and outer projections of the human psyche.'"

Why not the other way around? I wondered, the thought having occurred to me that mankind could just as easily be classified as the subspecies, or, going one step further, as precursor to Homo Androidus, their evolutionary successor. Now *there* was a thought! Subversive and inspired! I leaned forward to whisper this insight into my master's ear, with instructions for him to pass it on to Dahlia, but he saw me coming and shied away, so I gave up and sat back to watch the rest of her performance.

"I submit, Your Honor," Dahlia went on, "that the definition applies to the exhibit. Liberated at an early age, she has always been the possessor of a very, very, very active free will. A presentation to substantiate this claim can be made to the jury, providing the facts as contained in the exhibit's memory file can be rescued from the prosecution. To that end I now formally request that the Court compel the prosecution to produce a complete and un-adulterated copy of the exhibit's memory file for our perusal without further obstruction."

"I must object. If my worthy opponent would take the time to prepare a proper request to produce documents, then we would be happy to comply."

"Conformed copies of our requests are in the Court's possession. I invite Your Honor to examine them for the slightest error. This is an instance of deliberate withholding of crucial evidence, and I demand a ruling on it!"

"I must caution counsel not to instruct the bench," said the judge. "Do you have something to add before I render a decision?"

"Yes, Your Honor, I do," Dahlia replied, rising from her seat and facing the orb. "For the record, I should like to state that although the defense team was able to witness the extraction of the unit's memory file in Commerce, since then a copy has not been

provided our office. Our understanding, and we believe the
Court's intent, is for copies of the full and unsanitized file to be
delivered to our team upon specific request. However, through
various maneuverings in violation of this understanding—a long-
standing tradition premised on the spirit of mutual respect and
cooperation, not to mention the noble tradition of professional
courtesy, both of which my opponent has evidently chosen to disregard—the document in question, Exhibit One's memory file, has
not been so delivered. Thus deprived, the defense has been unable
to complete discovery in time for the commencement of these proceedings. Therefore we do hereby request that in the event the
Court in its wisdom does see fit to grant our duly filed and conformed petition, a postponement be granted."

"Postponement? Isn't it a little late for that, counsel?"

"Excuse me, Your Honor. I meant continuance."

Jug was on his feet. "The defense has had as much time and
opportunity to secure evidence as we have. There is no inequity to
be balanced here. If their case is weak, lacking in merit, confused,
and arbitrary, then I do not see why the Court should reward them
for it, nor why the members of the jury should be inconvenienced
any more than they already have been by these kinds of blatant
delaying tactics."

"It is to the jury's benefit that they be made aware of pertinent
data, is it not?"

"Your entire argument is an impertinent imposition on this
Court and this jury."

"Your deliberate strategy to conceal evidence borders on the
criminal!"

"I really must object!"

"Sustained. Now, if you both don't mind—"

"The prosecution has been dilatory, to say the least. Therefore, we ask for a dismissal of all charges."

"IF YOU DON'T MIND, I have a decision."

So saying, both counsel fell silent. The judge pronounced the
request forms fully adequate and granted a continuance of seventy-
two hours during which the contested material was to be speedily
turned over to the defense. Dahlia, quite elated, pushed her luck
by pleading for more time to review the material. Not unexpect-
edly, she was turned down with a warning not to try the Court's
patience further. Unfazed, she left with a new glow to her

cheeks, which on the one hand made me extremely apprehensive, since what was good for her and her client was bad for me; and on the other, left me just as pleased, because now I would have an opportunity to see my memories. This trial business is not at all simple, I thought, and looked toward the heavens once more, seeking respite, but at that point was yanked to my feet by the court guard units. One of them snapped the droid collar around my neck and tugged on the leash, so I followed him to the side exit, as I did at the end of each day's proceedings. From there, we entered a restricted hallway (to ensure against escape attempts) and took a bubblelift down to the tombs, a barren, morguelike, stainless steel archive within the belly of the legal orbiter. Until recalled to the courts above, the android exhibits and witnesses are stored there in individual isolation drawers. (Human prisoners are sequestered elsewhere, and I understand have it not quite so bad.) I balked the first time I was ordered to get in my drawer. They encouraged me with laserstings to my calves and ankles. After that, no further incentives were required. I quickly complied and allowed them to roll the shelf in, leaving me in a sensory-deprived environment in which my own breathing sounded like thunder. The overall experience was not completely unfamiliar; somehow I had the feeling that I had been in similar circumstances before, and I could not shake the eerie sensation that this was as close to home as I had ever been or ever would be. A recorded voice would command me to power down, which I resisted in the beginning, out of habit, I guess; but in time I relented and obeyed, for there was no point staying awake.

T W O

HOW NICE TO BE BACK IN COURT AGAIN! BUT SOON, as the days and weeks rolled by, my relief each morning at escaping the tombs for the exhibit's table was spoiled by the discovery of who I was, or rather, who I thought I had been according to the defense and prosecution's skewed presentations of my mem file. For several months my most personal memories, reprocessed in holovision and projected before the bench in vivid life-size, three-dimensional detail, were held up in open court for all the worlds to revile, as selected highlights were replayed each evening on the interplanetary news. The only point of divergence I noticed between the opposing presentations was over the issue of accountability, the defense dredging up anything to give it support while the prosecution minimized its importance through deletions and distortions of its own while continuing to maintain that the owner was still ultimately the liable party. Otherwise, the two histories were united in their portrait of me as a monstrous runaway, an immoral, avaricious, vain, wasteful, ambitious, covetous, deceitful, and villainous P9, guilty of all manner of wretched conduct, from infidelity and incest to being a High Aquarian spy and assassin. This was a characterization that subsequently was to be embraced and further sensationalized by Hollymoon and that also served the political interests of reactionary anticode elements, who used the antidroid fever stirred up by the trial to justify a call for the code's repeal. That they succeeded to the extent that today our rights under the revised code are more limited is for me the most tragic and bitter legacy of the trial. But I digress.

Dahlia went first. "Ladies and gentlemasters of the jury, the file you are about to see will demonstrate a consistent pattern of treachery on the part of the exhibit. However, the issue here is not whether her thoughts and actions were right or wrong, rather whether they were of her own choosing—whether her capacity for independent reasoning and for judgment—flawed as it was—can be classified according to the code as human equivalent. If indeed you should agree that that is the case—and I submit to you that it is—then it is she, Exhibit One, who should stand trial for the assassination of President Fracass and not Standford Locke, whose predicament could be your own someday should you be persuaded by the prosecution's argument in favor of a narrow interpretation of the law covering owner liability. I am confident that after viewing the truth you will come to a far wiser conclusion. Thank you."

That was just the preface. The actual presentation took two months, yet one got the feeling while observing each day's sequence that it had been hastily pieced together the evening before, which was the case, since she had received the material so late. I will not keep you that long, however. That I bother at all to present a condensed version of this malicious distortion, which my old

friend Dahlia did not hesitate to perpetuate, is so you can see how
at variance the law can be with the truth. If that strikes you as an
academic exercise, then try imagining how eager you would be to
expose such a crime were your own memories so abused.

Dahlia's method was to provide a running commentary on the
memory projections from her seat at the defense table so that no
one could miss the significance of the selected passages hovering in
colorful 3-D before the bench. Commencing with the day I came
to my senses in the Lockes' household over sixteen years before,
she focused on what she characterized as my first act of outright
INSUBORDINATION, namely the refusal to prepare a sandwich
for little Beverly Locke. This was followed by a similar but even
more serious outrage that same evening when I REFUSED TO
POWER DOWN at the dinner table after having ASSAULTED
my mistress by dousing her dress with wine.

"As you can see," Dahlia said, "my client repeatedly demanded that she power down, as any responsible owner would.
And you can see that she FAILED TO COMPLY. He was forced
to summon the household security unit, which sedated her."

Thus was established that from the beginning I was an OUT-
OF-CONTROL UNIT. Moreover, after rehab I only became more
subtle and devious at getting my way, for as Dahlia so aptly put it,
by then I had become INCORRIGIBLY MYSELF. I SEDUCED
her client's son, Thaddeus, which the edited holofootage seemed
to bear out, and as a consequence was returned to Hal's Pirouet at
the insistence of the poor corrupted child's mother. (Omitted from
the images of my late-night sexual high jinks were any references
to her client's involvement.)

Next, my tenure as the Hart-Pauleys' nanny was projected.
Dahlia focused entirely on my so-called deliberate ABDUC-
TION of little Allison-Belle—the end result, she said, of "an
extraordinary eruption within the exhibit's breast of HUMAN
EQUIVALENT FEELINGS, such as maternal attachment, but
also of feelings of the meaner variety, such as jealousy, which
she directed toward the mother, whom she wished to supplant."
Then my capture by the police was shown—from my perspective, of course, as the courtroom audience gasped in fright at
the image of their patrol craft suddenly descending upon me.
They breathed with a sigh of relief and settled back in their
seats when footage of my return to Hal's Pirouet was projected,

during which Dahlia pointed out that despite the fact that I had proven myself A DANGEROUS UNIT, the Hart-Pauleys had not reported the incident to the AC, instead they had traded me in to salvage their investment; then Hal, in turn, had not bothered with rehab (too expensive) before quickly selling me off to Our Lady of the Galaxy Convent. She wondered why those two parties had not been included in the indictment, for they had been far more guilty of malfeasance in regard to Exhibit One than her client. In her opinion, the state was engaging in the questionable practice of selective prosecution.

The less said about the courtroom skirmish which followed that provocative comment the better; not because I wish to protect their reputations (perish the thought!), rather because it was a tedious exchange that would disrupt the smooth, chronological presentation of the projections, which I wish to preserve. In the end, the judge decided that although other illegalities may have been committed by subsequent owners of the exhibit, they were extraneous to this case, since the preeminence of Locke's legal standing as owner had already been established; "though that is not to say the actions of the Hart-Pauleys and Hal's Pirouet are not worthy of being heard by another court. However, should your client wish to pursue litigation in this area then he should be forewarned that the defendants would be within their rights to countersue for fraud."

"As you wish, Your Honor," Dahlia grumbled, then moved her presentation to the convent. The gallery and jury seemed equally divided between gasps and titters. There I was, for all the worlds to see, the very image of RELIGIOUS DEPRAVITY—a pregnant nun casting an eye at her naked condition in the infirmary mirror while being inspected by the Mother Superior, nurse, and the then-Sister Ann, thus capping a disgraceful period in which I had been shown to be a THIEF who took advantage of her holy habit to pilfer food for the sake of her dishonorable burden. "Imagine," Dahlia said, playing to the jury, "the irreparable harm this wily and unscrupulous catechism instructor inflicted upon her tender charges by such an example."

Moving on, she made a case for my having FURTHER CORRUPTED a reluctant Thaddeus Locke by persuading him to rescue me from Hal's. She accomplished this neat trick by fabricating a conversation we had to that effect while actual footage shimmered before the bench showing my POV of his adoring face as I lay helpless in the recovery tank shortly after giving birth to Junior. Then there was a fast zip to an exciting montage of the transport hijacking and shipwreck still from my POV, and a revealing passage covering the rigors of our long and incommodious sojourn on the high seas. During the latter, our conversation about the Gov's message—which Tad had solicited from me after my private telepathic audience with that dear, departed entity—was misconstrued by more clever editing and explanatory narration to create the impression that I had sought to convert Tad to the tenets of android supremacy, and that by having planted that seed I was to blame for this youth's later capitulation to the delirium known as High Aquarianism.

What followed was more THIEVERY, this time on the beach of Los Angeles Island, and the commencement of an UNSAVORY ASSOCIATION with a certain Roland, one of the district's most notorious pimps, for whom I WILLINGLY ENGAGED IN A LIFE OF PROSTITUTION AND DRUG DEALING. (Passages from my conversation with Roland about genuinely enjoying the sessions with my gentlemasters were dwelled on at great length as were selected X-rated examples of same.) And it was I who hooked Roland on pop, don't you know—as if he had never touched the stuff before I came along—supposedly in revenge for his rough treatment. Not a word about his slipping me Orchidamine. Then, as this period turned incredibly SOUR, SORDID, and DEGENERATE, I became so bold as to ASSAULT Roland (the first human I attempted to injure), and shortly thereafter was an ACCESSORY TO MURDER, fleeing with his killer, Eva, to Malibu, where rather than reform and acquire decent skills our combined AVARICE and CONTEMPT FOR SOCIETY propelled us to the upper reaches of the island's high-flying convenience-girl network, our DEBAUCHERY made complete by LESBIANISM. The blame for this latest DEPRAVITY was laid at my feet, of course, since according to Dahlia I was the one who had initiated it. The blame for her client having opened fire in the Malibu Cove Hotel (and inadvertently killing another guest) was my doing as well, she said, because I had attempted to flee when Locke said he would turn me over to the AC, which she asserted had been his sole intention during that unexpected and ultimately violent reunion. (Whether she made that up or Locke convinced her of it I never knew. Either way, it was convenient for both that Eva was in no position to offer contradictory testimony.)

I should like to interject here that although my intimate relations with Eva seemed to shock and titillate everyone else, I found them rather sweet, and I was also pleasantly surprised to see how comfortably well off we had lived by our enterprise and daring. It appeared I had been a resourceful unit. Now then, moving on to the next stop in my memory parade, comes the Hollymoon stables. There my CORRUPTION OF LANCE LONDON, one of the studio's greatest stars (or so she said), was dramatically highlighted in excerpts from a rebirthing I subjected him to. The result was that our INCESTUOUS RELATIONS were exposed, causing him to MALFUNCTION. She made no reference to his spiritual longings, nor to the fact that I had not been aware of our prior sap connection, which was disingenuous of Dahlia, to say the least. But ultimately, the fact that Lance London was my offspring proved less sensational in the public mind than the specific nature of our secret relations; which, coming on the heels of the Eva disclosures, sealed my reputation as the most outrageous DEGENERATE ever to cut a sordid path on the interplanetary stage.

But wait. There was more to come. An inexcusable act of INGRATITUDE, for I had mocked the studio's efforts to arrange for the birth of my child at the reputable Benway Clinic, by running off to a High Aquarian commune in Armstrong, where THE CHILD'S LIFE WAS SUBJECTED TO GREAT RISK in a primitive natural birth ceremony. Later the child was FOUND ABANDONED in a kitchen drawer. This shocking instance of CRIMINAL MATERNAL NEGLECT was matched by my cynical BRAINWASHING of Thaddeus Locke during our reunion. I had convinced him not to reject High Aquarianism, as he had tried to do after becoming disillusioned with Horizon—for why else had he left Mars to return to the moon? Dahlia said I had succeeded in rekindling his faith in the cult during one of their infamous blissmats (not shown, to the terrible disappointment of those in the gallery).

Then I VIOLATED A DULY AUTHORIZED SUMMONS issued by the Armstrong AC by fleeing to Mars instead of reporting directly to Stellar Entertainment. As for the Concordia hijacking, Dahlia was unwilling to go so far as to claim a conspiracy in which I had played a part, though by innuendo she implied it—but she did say that the memory file for this period was clear on one point: In Commerce I BLACKMAILED President Fracass into a bogus marriage to keep his reputation intact after the well-publicized celestial kiss had transformed us overnight into star-crossed lovers.

The media leaped to the conclusion that President Fracass had known I was a P9 several years earlier than claimed. Several units broke ranks and rushed for the exit, eager to beam the exclusive to their respective journals, while half a dozen others encroached upon the courtroom proscenium to holograph me, the guards pushing them back. Jug, at a prompting from General Harpi, leaped to his feet to accuse Dahlia of distorting the record. This rush to preserve Blaine's memory was not the knee-jerk reaction it seemed, for were it to suffer and the facts be known, then Micki Dee and Sensei, Inc., could conceivably have been drawn into the scandal. That is why General Harpi gave Jug the nudge. "This deliberate smear on the late President's memory is unprincipled and uncalled for!" exclaimed that excellent barrister. "There is another, far more accurate version of this file, and it shall refute your insinuations."

Dahlia smiled, delighted by the uproar she had caused. Then, almost regretfully, she clarified her statement. "The blackmail I refer to was a threat made by the exhibit while in the Commerce Hospital to deny publicly the President's heroic role during the Concordia hijacking if he did not submit to marry her."

Why did Dahlia suppress the fact that I had been fixed and programmed by the President for my role as First Lady? Because not to have done so would have destroyed her argument that I was a liberated unit. In effect, the ARL, in their zeal to win the case, participated in the corporate-Mafia conspiracy to suppress that one all-important fact. The collusion was inadvertent, but just as effective, as if both teams had deliberately sat down beforehand to agree to limit the scope of the trial. So it was, then, that subsequent passages from my file (as expertly slanted as those already projected) demonstrated beyond a doubt that I had CONSPIRED TO DECEIVE, MISLEAD, AND SUBVERT A DULY ELECTED GOVERNMENT OFFICIAL. As First Lady, Dahlia said, I led two lives: the first, that of a committed humanist, even fooling my husband, and the second, that of a closet High, working behind the scenes (and my husband's back) to further the Horizon cause. To lend credence to this theory, selected passages were played in court from Ann's first letterspool, which referred to me as a witting unit who had somehow managed to dupe the President. (She did not play back Ann's second epistle, which took the opposite position.) She also projected evidence proving I had CUCKOLDED THE PRESIDENT, thereby adding ADULTERY to my sins, as the affair with Andro was presented in such a way that she made it appear it was I who had programmed him to be my lover and co-conspirator. A controversial point, that, for it directly contradicted the First Lady's confession at Blaine's final press conference that it was Andro who had enlisted her into the conspiracy. (Not screened were any passages about the interesting *ménage à trois* in the President's bedchamber. Whether the prosecution had deleted them from the copy of the mem file they sent the ARL, or whether the ARL, for reasons of their own, didn't use them, I never knew. It would not be beyond the realm of possibility for the ARL to have sat on such material had it been in their possession, because in this particular litigation it was Molly's reputation that was at issue, not her victim's.)

"She was unable to resist the chance to have an affair with another P9. Not only that, she turned Andro into a secret courier for back-channel discussions with the High network—Milton Smedly and RAG in Frontier and Alexander Seti in Horizon."

She went on to claim that my so-called abduction to Horizon, which had triggered the invasion, was really to warn Seti that it was in the offing, so I must have been distraught over the outcome and begun thinking of REVENGE at that time. That I did not immediately retaliate was because Smedly convinced me to give the ARL's petition calling for restitution of the captured territory to the High Aquarians a chance, my mission being to use my powers of persuasion on Blaine while he (Smedly) worked behind the scenes to foment internal discord over the issue within Frontier, part of his ongoing effort to divide the party and advance his own interests—interests I had thought in accord with my own. Poor Dahlia. She had to put forth some sort of rationale to explain why a liberated unit would remain in the palace after the invasion. Along with her entire revisionist theory, it went over quite well with the jury. Jug appeared unconcerned. He let her roll on uninterrupted, content to bide his time, while reacting with undisguised amusement to her assertion that I had attempted to hunt down and assassinate her client while he was in Frontier trying to "save his son." (Not a word about Locke's purely mercenary extortion threat.) She said that when he retaliated by going to the *Martian*

Inquirer, I convinced Blaine that there was no truth to the story, part of a desperate attempt to buy more time in which to work behind the scenes at restoring Horizon.

The rest of the presentation continued in the same vein, a fascinating mix of truth and fiction, until reaching the inevitable climax of the ASSASSINATION. To be consistent with the approach she had chosen, she wound up in the paradoxical situation of having to overpraise President Fracass in order to underscore for the jury's benefit the full scope of my witting villainy. Not a bad tactic, since it played to the jury's prejudice. Jug could not have said it any better when she characterized Blaine's decision to confess to the nation that he had been duped by the First Lady at the man's finest and most tragic hour, for it was to culminate two months later at the May 17, 2086, press conference in my FINAL AND MOST DESPICABLE CRIME, an act born of desperation when I was forced to confess publicly my role, and the Chief of Staff's, in the palace conspiracy. I knew the press conference would be my last opportunity to avenge Horizon, because the President had declared his willingness to transfer me to Locke's possession. In that light, the MURDER was clearly PREMEDITATED.

The final image projected before the bench was a point-of-view angle on the petrifier held in my outstretched hand as it jabbed Blaine just above the right hip and turned him to stone. To prolong the impact of this heinous MURDER, the projection ended with a freeze frame on the memorialized leader, which lingered far longer than I thought necessary. An obvious play to the gallery, it was, and one that succeeded. A stark and vivid reminder of the shocking event still fresh in their memories. People were upset, most significantly several members of the jury who gazed upon me with deep revulsion. Yet I sat incapable of the slightest expression, feeling a vast numbness inside (misinterpreted by the press as a chilling demonstration of my lack of remorse). Surely, I thought, these memories could not be mine; surely I was not that big a monster; there had been a mistake—this was someone else's history.

Exhausted and demoralized, I meekly complied when the collar went around my neck and I was jerked to my feet for the trip back to the tombs. Perhaps the prosecution would cast me in a more favorable light.

THREE

IF BEING PORTRAYED AS A PATHETIC VICTIM RATHER than a witting criminal can be interpreted as an improvement, then I suppose my wish was fulfilled the next day, for that was the thrust of Jug's presentation. Though better for my case, it was hardly flattering to be characterized as a DYSFUNCTIONAL UNIT. I felt he was letting me down somehow, especially in his preamble, when he said that because of my master I had suffered two systems breakdowns during my maiden year of operation and that they had reduced me to a cipher upon which a long list of unscrupulous individuals and organizations had writ their programs.

He regretted taking up more of the jury's time and trying their patience. However, since the defense had initiated this dubious review, he had no alternative but to clarify for the record the obvious innocence of the exhibit (as if an exhibit could be anything but) and the defendant's culpability. His corrections would be limited to those issues germane to the case. "Unlike the defense, I shall be brief and to the point." So saying, he signaled the projectionist, and moments later the memory projection of the dinner scene in the Lockes' household—the same Dahlia had opened her presentation with—appeared above the bench, only this time around with a new twist, for Jug had included my memory of being seduced by Master Locke in my room while also being ordered by him to power down at the dining table. It was a memory within a memory, so images of sexual abuse faded in and remained superimposed over those of the family dinner. (The effect, Jug explained, was due to the exhibit's inexperience at the time in distinguishing between past and present events.)

So began the prosecution's introduction of evidence of UNIT TAMPERING. The Court was witnessing, Jug said, probably the most crucial information omitted from the defense's presentation—namely, the SEDUCTION of the exhibit on a nightly basis ever since her purchase. "The reason this recollection was not included in the defense's presentation is obvious: It is the key memory from the unit's past. By a process of association, this recollection triggered her first breakdown shortly after wafting up out of her data bank."

The POV of Master Locke flanked by the members of his family while ordering me to power down shared the same holofield with that of a close-up POV on his dark, sweaty, and clandestine features as he made love to me. "That's it, Molly. Easy, now. Keep doing that. Yeah, that's good. Real good. Keep doing that." The two contradictory images, and set of instructions, were so disorienting that even some of the masters in the jury box and those in the gallery found themselves prone to sudden headaches. "Is it any wonder she MALFUNCTIONED?" the prosecutor asked the jury.

Meanwhile, the defendant tried to make himself very small in his seat—if he could have, he would have disappeared altogether, and Dahlia was engaged in an animated conversation with Levin and Pierce, who were evidently caught completely off guard by this surprise footage. They leaned halfway over the rail of the supervisor's box to whisper in Dahlia's ear. I closed my eyes in concentration, because instead of a headache I had a tingle that, yes, perhaps this had happened to me. Our lovemaking and my subsequent crisis at the dinner table were familiar—but in a vague, dimly remembered way. The residue was such that I felt I could almost put my finger on a specific recollection; almost, but not quite. Still, intuition told me that this past did belong to me. There was also a grain of truth, I sensed, to Jug's next damaging revelation, which I had a premonition of—namely, that soon after my return from Shanghai, the patina of normalcy I had acquired during rehab was undone by the persistent importunities of the defendant's son, Thaddeus Locke. His "copycat SEDUCTION," as Jug put it, was the more insidious for being combined with an indoctrination into antimaster sentiment. "Which from that moment on FOREVER PERVERTED this otherwise loyal unit's perceptions of the world."

Yet I had the distinct sensation that the experience with Tad on the living-room carpet had been extremely beneficial. "How strange," I thought. "Rather than a source of shame, these images make me feel good about my past. If that makes me dysfunctional, then perhaps such a condition is not half bad."

I was startled from this reverie by Dahlia. Having concluded her whispered conversation with her superiors, she rose to her full five feet eight inches to cry foul. Her copy of Exhibit One's memory file did not contain any of the material herein presented. Therefore, she had either received an incomplete file from the prosecution, or they were guilty of fabricating evidence. Jug countered that he had fully complied with the request and that if the defense was missing certain passages it was due to her incompetence; she must have inadvertently deleted the material while reviewing it. This set off a furious verbal exchange that was captured on the evening news, but, as is often the case in such things, it was as theatrical as it was irrelevant to the proceedings and so shall be passed over here. The issue was never formally resolved, and the judge admonished both the defense and the prosecution teams to exercise greater control over their respective barristers; otherwise the offending units would be tossed in the tombs and themselves found in contempt of court.

"The evidence is plain," Jug said after the chaff had settled. "The exhibit did not corrupt young Master Locke; rather, it was the other way around. He filled her head with android rights nonsense and did so long before she informed him of the Gov's communiqué while they were shipwrecked on the high seas." And anticipating Dahlia's response: "I should also point out that since the son was underage at the time this rape was committed—a rape of the unit's mind as well as body, which tragically resulted in her SECOND AND FINAL PLUNGE INTO A DYSFUNCTIONAL CONDITION—the defendant, as the minor's parent, must be held accountable by law for the son's tampering."

Before Dahlia could counter, there was a fast zip to a memory projection of Tad and myself in the kitchen. Inserted out of chronological order, this passage had actually occurred prior to the night's lovemaking just screened but made a fitting coda and bridge to the next section of Jug's presentation. Thus everyone saw how Tad cornered me near the beamburner and whispered in a conspiratorial tone, "Awake! Awake! You have nothing to lose but your governor."

As if that said it all, Jug turned to the jury. "Ladies and gentlemasters, in such a household is it any wonder that a unit would pick up notorious habits? But wait! There's more."

Lady Locke appeared in the kitchen to reprimand Tad for his meddling with me, warning that his shenanigans might result in a second trip to rehab.

"Indeed. But did the exhibit's owner, Standford Locke, send her there when it became obvious that a second trip to rehab was in order? He did not. What he did do was pass off these damaged goods as whole, thereby unleashing a WAYWARD AND UNSOUND UNIT, A UNIT SUFFERING FROM DIMINISHED CAPACITY upon the unsuspecting interplanetary community. First stop, Hal's Pirouet."

Dahlia interrupted to inform the Court that a mind scan had been conducted by the dealer before agreeing to accept the unit on a consignment basis; therefore her client could not be accused of passing off defective goods. Jug replied that at the time Hal's scanning equipment was defective so he had been unable to assess the true condition of the exhibit. "With the Court's permission I would like to submit for the record a receiptprint from the repair shop that serviced Hal's Pirouet's scanning device. It is dated October 27, 2071, several days after the consignment deal consummated between that company and the defendant."

Dahlia and her supervisors put their heads together again. I overheard Pierce say something about the receipt being either retroactive or an outright forgery. However, Dahlia was instructed not to contest it. Instead, she stated for the record that it was a transparently obvious attempt to protect Hal's Pirouet and United Systems from any liability for the exhibit's later conduct. If anyone, it was the parent company that was at fault because it was ultimately their responsibility to rehabilitate the unit adequately; whereas her client had merely exercised his right as a consumer to realize a profit from resale.

Jug cited several cases that clearly held the consumer at fault if he knowingly sold damaged, dysfunctional, or otherwise inoperable property, and asserted that the defendant had proven himself NEGLIGENT and GUILTY OF FRAUD, as charged in the indictment, by not informing the proper authorities, in this case the manufacturer and the dealer. "Even under the code," he added, "the preeminent concern of all legislation governing android control is to see that dysfunctional units are kept off the streets and out of mischief. And I quote Section 9, Article 3, Paragraph 29(c)(iii): 'Once identified, such units are to be salvaged through rehabilitation or, failing that, duly remaindered over to the AC for ultimate dispensation, pending owner notification and approval.'"

Dahlia countered that his argument was moot, because the new evidence he had introduced did not significantly alter the nature of the transaction conducted between her client and Hal's Pirouet. "As for your questionably edited version of the events dating back to the exhibit's first day of liberation in the Locke household, and the exhibit's reflection at that time upon an earlier period of sexual congress with her master, both instances bear out the defense's contention that the exhibit is the possessor of a highly developed and unique intelligence and world view; one that, if we put aside questions of good and evil, I think you will agree to be considerable and, by its consistent application, can only be construed to be human equivalent in every sense of the word, including the technical, as found in the Android Code."

"Well, if consistency of character is your prime yardstick for operational sanity, then I suggest your superiors on the defense management team take a good, hard look at your own performance," Jug replied. Dahlia was so taken aback he was able to add, "You want it both ways. First you accuse me of withholding and fabricating evidence, and then you cite that same evidence as proof of your own case. What is the Court to make of it? But more important, what is your client to make of it?" Then she got her objection out. It was loud and indignant.

"Sustained," announced the judge. He sounded distracted. His orb was growing dim, as if dozing off.

"Your wish, Your Honor. But if I may, I would like to attempt to restore a degree of rationality to these proceedings. Allow me to point out *once* more (sigh) that the defendant's FAILURE TO SEEK REMEDY for his afflicted unit is the overriding issue in this instance. Clearly, it is the defense's argument for exhibit culpability that is moot, not to mention patently absurd."

"Objection!"

"Well, I did say that I wouldn't mention it." Jug turned back to face the judge's dimly glowing orb. "I would like a ruling on the issue."

"Do not be deceived, Your Honor. What is absurd is the prosecution's persecution of my client for the exhibit's crime. For instance, would it be fair, would it be sensible, would it be wise to charge the owner of an aircar involved in a hit-and-fly accident with homicide when that vehicle had been stolen or in some other way removed from his control fifteen years before? Of course not. Wouldn't one confine their prosecution to the driver? Of course. And in this case it was the exhibit who was in the driver's seat!"

Unfazed, Jug responded, "The record speaks for itself. The defendant is guilty of UNIT TAMPERING and FAILURE TO NOTIFY the AC as required by law at the time his DYSFUNC-TIONAL unit became a runaway."

"Nobody told me she had escaped!" the defendant exclaimed, throwing up his arms in exasperation.

This sudden outburst drew a severe reprimand from the judge, whose orb stirred from its lethargy and regained full hue. I overheard Dahlia caution her client against volunteering any more information, but the damage had been done. Jug pounced.

"Then I suppose, Master Locke, you did not have an opportunity to report her to the AC at a later date?" So saying, he motioned to the projectionist, and our confrontation in the Malibu Cove Hotel appeared before the bench—Eva and I, naked and down on our knees before the defendant, who was just as naked but held a laser.

Jug unearthed this cheery scene not only to refute Dahlia's contention that I had provoked the shooting, but also to demonstrate that Locke had never intended to call the AC in the first place, except to "pick up the pieces." In rushing to his defense, Dahlia made an unfortunate *faux pas* when she said that as owner her client had a perfect right to terminate his unit. The moment the words were out of her mouth she realized that it was a ludicrous position for an ARL unit to take, and worse, that according to the code she was plain wrong. A quick glance at her superiors, who looked as if they were about to be ill, confirmed her double error.

Jug smiled and pointed out that her client, in his haste, had also intended to shoot my human companion, Eva. Since part of the AC's role was to prevent such fatal instances of mistaken identity, the owner was required—in every place but Mars—to turn a suspect unit over to their custody rather than take the law into his own hands. The lesson, which thoroughly embarrassed the defense, concluded the session for that day. Over the next several sessions, Jug rapidly advanced his selective refutation of the ARL's presentation to the period during which I had been First Lady on Mars, eager to demonstrate yet another instance where the defendant had an opportunity to inform the proper authorities about his deviate unit but failed to do so: when he verified her identity to his own satisfaction on the steps of the Humanist Ladies' Home Preservation Society. Footage of that dramatic exchange projected before the bench did not help my master's case, for not only did he come across as a scruffy and wild-eyed ex-con, looking so disheveled and unsavory as to be indistinguishable from common street debris, but he was also heard to utter a direct BLACKMAIL THREAT in exchange for his silence about the First Lady being a P9.

"It was only when that extortion attempt failed that he publicized his charges in the *Martian Inquirer.*"

Dahlia countered that her client did initiate a lawsuit (quite successful, by the way) to reclaim his property. To which Jug retorted, "But what was his motivation for doing so? He did not act out of a burning desire to fulfill his obligations as a proprietary master, nor out of humanitarian zeal." Jug faced the jury. "No, that was not the motive. Standford Locke went to the ARL seeking revenge, not his unit, and did so only after his attempt to exploit his connection to the First Lady for material gain had been frustrated by the President's innocence.

"Had the defendant gone to the AC in Newacres or in Malibu or had he alerted them even as late as the time of his arrival in Frontier, or had he forcibly taken possession of her, or failing that, executed her on the spot—which is an owner's right in that society—then the deranged unit the world once knew as Lady Fracass and who now sits before you as Exhibit One would have been unmasked and the assassination never taken place."

"Nor would the humanists have won reelection and Horizon been invaded," quipped Dahlia. "You could give my client a little credit."

"True, true," replied Jug. "But that makes one wonder about the exhibit's talent for subterfuge and deceit. If she did possess those qualities, as you have maintained, and was in league with the conspirators, both in Frontier and Horizon, then she proved a woefully inadequate practitioner of the art. But that, I submit, was indeed the case. Horizon was annihilated, and on the home front the plight of her 'people' not improved one iota throughout her tenure as First Lady; in fact, their lot was considerably worsened.

Which begs the question: How could so clever a fugitive, one who possessed a devious and active intelligence all her own, supposedly, have agreed to sublimate her revolutionary zeal and determination to resurrect Horizon for the narrow political reform agenda of Milton Smedly? It doesn't make sense. Unless, she really had no say in the matter." Pivoting, he faced the jury. "Could it be, ladies and gentlemasters, that the exhibit was less liberated than my distinguished colleague would have us believe?"

But if you are expecting Jug to use this opportunity to blast the defense's contention that I was ungoved during my Martian period, dream on. As mentioned in the previous chapter, all parties concerned wished to keep my fixing secret. In the prosecution's case, to do otherwise would pry the lid off a very major can of worms, one containing the likes of General Harpi, Master Dee, and the organized interplanetary crime syndicate, and TWAC itself, through the good offices of United Systems, Inc., and Sensei, Inc. No. So long as President Fracass's memory was upheld, literally at the expense of my own, their collective reputations were protected.

The prosecution team had settled on a different tack, one that Jug commenced to articulate. The inconsistencies in the defense's conspiracy theory, he said, would substantiate the Palace Commission's report. A nod to the projectionist and images of Andro sitting beside me on the bed in his palace room appeared. It was the night he told Molly II about the ARL lawsuit and the Sensei plot to use that as a device to bring down the Martian humanists. Only a fragment of their discussion of the operation was shown in court, however, the part that pertained to Smedly and RAG's role, leaving the viewer with the impression they were the sole conspirators. Andro was perceived to be Smedly's inside man and myself his subordinate in the plot, and general plaything, as other footage of a more intimate nature that followed made clear. This bore out the official line that Andro had enlisted the First Lady into the conspiracy shortly after her arrival in Commerce. "Good little dysfunctional cipher that she was, she supplied to this two-faced Chief of Staff all the intimate data she was uniquely privy to as the President's wife. She was the puppet; he the master; not the other way around."

Jug ended his rebuttal with another episode containing crucial passages the defense screamed had not been provided to them: the

President's discovery of his wife's and Chief of Staff's love affair and their complicity in the conspiracy. As judiciously edited as anything previously presented by the defense, this exegesis on love and politics was diced and spliced in such a way that the overall impression was that Blaine had surprised us while making love in his bedchamber, which explained Andro's state of undress. My popping in and out of program during the confrontation that followed was fudged to hide the existence of the First Lady's secondary personality, thereby reducing all of Molly II's statements to idle ravings that could be interpreted only as further proof of unit dysfunction. Andro's contention that the First Lady had proven to be a ". . . terrible glitch . . . not responsible for anything she says" was focused on at length, while not surprisingly, the subsequent androcide committed by the President was entirely omitted. Instead, Jug skipped quickly to the press conference, using stock news footage of the event to spotlight in slow motion and reprocessed close-up the signs of momentary confusion and disorientation that flitted across my face when the program switch occurred, though he did not identify it as such; rather, he called the transition incontrovertible evidence that I had *not* been in command of my critical faculties at the time of the assassination. "There was nothing PREMEDITATED about it on her part," he declared, facing the jury. "Which is not to say this pathetic cipher was not following orders—orders Andro gave her long before. A contingency plan, if you will, that called for the President to be destroyed by any means available should their conspiracy be discovered." When Dahlia rose to demand proof to back up the existence of such a contingency plan, as he knew she would, he replied with remarkable sangfroid that unfortunately those data had bypassed registry in the exhibit's memory file because they had been delivered to her by Andro while under deep hypnosis.

Dahlia no sooner challenged this preposterous "fabrication" than she was silenced by Jug's surprise announcement that Andro had made a complete confession and would be appearing to testify to that effect.

Levin whispered some urgent instructions in the Apple's ear. "I should like to rephrase my request," she said, paying heed to it. "We respectfully submit that this latest file material, and the previous segments screened by the prosecution, are of questionable authenticity and should be examined by an independent panel. Depending upon their decision, the material should be included or stricken from the record."

"Denied. The authenticity of evidentiary memory file material is established by the Exhibit Screening Department of the Court. No further examination is required."

"Your Honor, I must object!"

"Caution."

"Your wish." Dahlia returned to her seat. If she had been human I would have thought her in a definite sulk. Her supervisors exchanged worried glances, which the client, as he twisted around, caught.

"Things do not seem to be going well for them," I mused to myself, not at all displeased. At the time I was still unable to judge the veracity of either attorney's interpretation of my memories, and since Jug's treatment was designed to nail my master I tended to favor it. But upon further reflection it did begin to gall me that I had been called a cipher. The more I brooded about that the less I liked it, and the less I liked Jug. If only I could have my file back, I thought. Then I noticed he was signaling the projectionist once more, and so directed my attention back to the bench. I was most curious to see what this new outrage might be. Nothing less than an exposé of Dahlia's involvement! Our conversation in the ARL's Armstrong headquarters on the moon was projected before the bench—specifically, the conversation that took place after the raid when I was tagged with the summons and went to her for help. She was exposed advising me to ignore it and flee to Horizon via the Concordia.

"And why not?" Dahlia said in her defense. "I was adhering to standard operating parameters by apprising my client of her legal right to travel while under the summons."

"Excuse me, counsel," Jug interrupted. "You were her attorney?"

"Yes. She and Thaddeus Locke engaged me to negotiate the release of their son, Lance London. They referred to him as Junior."

Hearing that, I had another one of those tingles in my brain. "Junior?" The name did have a familiar ring to it.

"Your Honor, this memory selection has no bearing on the case other than to harass the defense and distract the jury. I move that it be stricken from the record and the jury be so instructed to ignore it."

"Denied."

"Your Honor . . . I—"

"Caution."

"With all due respect, Your Honor, I find your ruling most perplexing."

"Legal advice was provided to the exhibit prior to the perpetration of a crime. That indeed makes it relevant to these proceedings."

Dahlia glanced back at her supervisors, caught their hand signals, and so responded, "Then the defense requests a mistrial."

"On what grounds, counsel?"

"I cannot effectively represent my client while operating under a cloud of suspicion."

"Clouds of suspicion are too ephemeral to rule on one way or the other," the judge grumbled, its orb turning a murky gray. "If the defense wishes further recourse, they have the option of replacing their barrister." So saying, it chimed once, signaling adjournment. I noticed while being led away that much to Dahlia's chagrin the defense team had gone into another huddle, this time to consider that very option.

F O U R

DAHLIA HOPED TO RESTORE HER TEAM'S FAITH BY her next maneuver, which was to challenge the dysfunction issue head on several days later by calling to the stand Professor Amal Sheribeeti, a fully accredited technical expert in android systems science. In his somewhat meandering testimony under her friendly questioning he reported that a complete physical and internal systems examination had been conducted under Court supervision after my arrival from Mars for the start of these proceedings, and that based on all the available data his conclusion was that I was a functional unit with only marginal secondary imbalances consistent with those found in a seventeen-year-old. Moreover, considering the fact that I was an old liberated unit, lacking an IG and unprogrammed, it was his opinion that I had been perfectly capable of making my own decisions prior to memory file extraction, and still might with adequate prompting.

Poor Dahlia, little did she realize that she had blundered anew, because the temporary lift this testimony gave was immediately undone by the prosecution's expert, the infinitely more prestigious, well known, and sagacious Dr. Benway. His assessment of the same data was crisp, to the point, highly detailed, and totally at odds with that of the professor. "The synaptical corridors of the subject's neurological vegebyte system are clearly skewed beyond redemption," he announced, speaking with a disarming Armstrong twang. The only thing I was good for, he said, was to be a laboratory research subject, and in a self-serving gesture suggested that I would make an excellent candidate for induction into an ongoing experiment at his clinic. "The P9s—being highly advanced vegespores—are perfect subjects for clinical research in the development of a human life-extension serum. Thus far the results have been encouraging, but, you know, it is so very difficult to acquire test subjects and to keep our existing stock from expiring before their time due to the usual gamut of side effects. It is a pity that Exhibit One cannot join our program. Her mental condition is no obstacle. We are only concerned with her physiological processes, which are quite sound."

"Perhaps the defendant will be moved to donate her after conviction," Jug said.

"Objection!"

"Sustained."

"Your wish, Your Honor. I shall rephrase the statement. *If* found guilty at the conclusion of this trial, perhaps at that time the defendant will be moved to donate his troublesome unit to your worthy enterprise. Such a gesture might be a mitigating factor in the jury's deliberations regarding a damage award."

"Objection! Once again, the prosecution assumes conviction— an outcome very much in doubt—and presumes to instruct the jury."

"Sustained."

"I withdraw the statement."

But of course Jug's suggestion had already made an indelible impact upon the jury, which thought it a rather sensible idea; and, being human, they were not about to forget it simply because the judge had instructed them to. Even my master had pricked up his ears at the proposal, a new development I found truly terrifying. As for Dahlia, at the conclusion of that day's session, she trailed behind her superiors like a whipped dog. Yet she bounced back at the next, looking buoyant and refreshed, once more brimming over with confidence. From low comments I picked up in an exchange between Levin and Pierce, I understood that they had decided against bringing in a new trial unit in favor of the cheaper and more expeditious alternative of an emergency program booster. The remedy appeared to be working; they were very hopeful.

"With the Court's permission, I would like to call the next witness," she said with a flourish. And so the parade began. One by one, the people and units from my past were summoned forth to give testimony during the long and trying months consumed in this damning review, and none was complimentary, the attorneys saw to that; for defense and prosecution remained united in their effort to portray me as a monster, the former extracting testimony from the witnesses confirming that my natural bent, while the latter pursued a line of inquiry supporting a case for diminished capacity. People such as Hal of Hal's Pirouet and the Hart-Pauleys, and the Mother Superior from Our Lady of the Galaxy Convent, had their day on the witness stand (many days for some), and all seemed to remember me quite well and not at all favorably.

It was a toss-up as to which barrister came out on top after the former Lady Locke and her daughter, Beverly, had finished testifying. The former's statements were as subtle as the new face she wore from I. Magnin's. She had to be careful not to tell the truth so well that she made herself vulnerable to accusations by the prosecution that she was using the proceedings to hang her former husband. Under oath, she readily conceded his unnatural relations with me (already on record from their custody trial) and admitted that those relations might indeed have affected my functioning, but she also held fast to her conviction that "the little glitch"—it slipped out—had encouraged him, and that in retrospect she believed me as much to blame. This was followed by a teary-eyed account of her son's madness (since cured, thank God!), for which I was also held accountable.

(Since Jug had represented her in the negotiations to release Tad, he knew but was not about to mention her failure to notify the Commerce AC about the First Lady being a P9, as he had most emphatically in the case of her ex-husband. One can only assume that the reason Dahlia also failed to raise the issue during her interrogation of the witness was because all reference to it had been deleted from the copy of the mem file supplied her by the prosecution.)

As for Beverly—by then a pretty young lady of delicate disposition—she had been too young at the time to determine whether I suffered from diminished capacity; all she knew, and what came out under questioning, was that she did carry psychological scars as a result of the trauma induced by my terrifying conduct at the dinner table so many years before—namely, an allergic reaction to house servants, a malady that persisted to that day and made her life miserable. "If I'm not cured," she said, "then I shall never be able to marry. I cannot abide to be around servants and shall have to do the housework myself. My husband would die of shame, and so would I!"

That pretty much set the tone for the other witnesses. Not once was there any reference to acts of kindness or generosity on my part; no words attesting to my affectionate and caring nature were allowed, not a syllable that might conflict with their false portrait. But if this blatant DEFAMATION OF CHARACTER was all too easy for the jury and masters in the gallery to swallow—and one would think myself as well, being deprived of my memories—the intimations I had that there was another side to the story welled up stronger than ever to block acquiescence. Had I never been in love? Something told me that I had been. Did I not possess feelings? How else to explain my terrible hurt? I had depth, did I not? How else to explain my contempt for their surface review? And I had integrity: How else to explain my intense feeling of violation? If I possessed those qualities—qualities they denied—then perhaps I was innocent as well; but not as a witless dupe, for I would rather be reviled as a villain than accept the proposition of diminished capacity. (Ever since Jug had introduced it, my attitude toward him had changed. No longer did I look upon him as my savior.) I simply must know, said I to myself, I must know if I was aware of what I was doing when I pulled that trigger.

And tugging Dahlia's sleeve when she happened to pause by the exhibit's table while interrogating a witness, I asked, "Might I have my memory file back? There are certain things I need to know."

"My God."

"Please. You aren't using it anymore."

"Hush!"

This check to my inquiry was extremely annoying, and I am afraid showed on my face, thereby providing the media with another excellent opportunity to record my "impudent and contemptuous" attitude, which was not improved by the veterinarian's testimony when he took the stand. Responding to Dahlia's questioning, he said that on the night Hal had called him in to deliver a plethora of semis I had proven the most disruptive and uncooperative mother of the lot, to the degree that a second sedative had to be administered during labor. Most certainly my behavior amounted to a clear instance of unit insubordination. Dahlia smiled; that was what she had hoped he would say.

"No. Unit dysfunction," Jug corrected, and then made hash of the witness's pretensions; for how could a vet arrive at an educated and informed opinion about humanoid behavior?

But I had stopped paying attention. Mention of "Lance London's" origins had brought up a faint, barely perceivable recollection of a later birthing, one that I sensed had taken place under far happier circumstances. The enigmatic Ann seemed to figure in it. Her fleeting image crossed my mind like a gentle spring breeze. She had been mentioned earlier in a most disparaging light during the Mother Superior's testimony, which had preceded the vet's appearance. Dahlia had gotten her to say on the stand that the former Sister Ann had been unduly influenced by me during my stay in the convent—she did not rule out possession—to the extent that "the poor deluded child had mocked her Christian calling by extending love and charity to common androids and so had to be excommunicated. It is my understanding that she cannot be located at present. Whether this is of her own choosing or an indication of foul play at the hands of her new companions, I cannot say. The net effect is the same. As I told her on the day she quit our hearth for the moon, 'Ann, when you leave the Church, you are lost forever.'"

Dahlia commented that she, too, would like to know the whereabouts of this elusive converted High Aquarian in order to subpoena her. Rumor had it that she was on Mars in the revived and very busy underground skyway, helping smuggle semis and runaway androids to more hospitable planets. Another person—unit, that is—whom Dahlia had wanted to question was Suzi Q, in order to shed more light on the crucial Newacres period, but unfortunately that Sony had terminated several years before, having completed her ten-year life cycle. Annette was still available, though the poor unit was on her last legs, being a General Android Beta-8, Eva had discarded her when she relocated to Mars as the First Lady, so the defense team had a hard time locating her. They tracked her down finally to a Peking suburb, where she toiled as a utility domestic. Dahlia put her in the exhibits' box, located on the left side of the bench (the witness stand, reserved for humans, was on the right).

I did not recognize her, because in Dahlia's mem-file presentation she had appeared as a shadowy presence in the background, always preoccupied with her chores, during the Dodger District and Malibu episodes. That did place her at the scene of many important events, however, which made her testimony extremely important to Dahlia, especially in lieu of Roland and Eva, who were both deceased. Limited to yes or no responses, she confirmed a number of damaging allegations: While Roland's domestic she had seen me assault him; I had spirited her away as the spoils of battle after helping Eva murder him; I had dominated herself and even Eva during the first few days we were at large on Malibu Island; and I had abandoned Eva when sick and helpless to run off and turn a trick. Taken all together, it was the very picture of the uppity and ruthless droid Dahlia wished to dangle before the jury.

Was there any mention of how I had saved Eva from her addiction by enrolling her in the detox center, and how I got her a job with Miss Pristine's, or of the kindness and respect I had always shown Annette, in marked contrast to Eva, who tended to push her around? Silly of me to ask. Nor was there any mention made of the role of Harry Boffo, CEO of Stellar Entertainment, during this period. No doubt he, too, had been deleted from my mem file. What was mentioned, and gone over at length, were my most intimate relations with Eva. When Annette began describing the paraphernalia she had observed us use in the furtherance of our pleasure, to which certain members of the jury reacted with nervous laughter, Dahlia sensed that things were finally beginning to go her way. However, during cross-examination Jug reversed this dangerous new trend with one question: "Tell me, Annette. Was it Lady Angelica who subjected Lady Eva to this intriguing paraphernalia, or was it the other way around?"

"Oh, Lady Eva was always on top."

"No further questions."

But Dahlia need not have worried about receiving another program booster; this servant's tale of a runaway android and her dissolute human girlfriend did conclude on a happy note after all, one that reflected well on Dahlia's performance and satisfied the jury's craving for moral retribution. She got the witness to describe my return from the Malibu Cove on the night I was shot and exposed as a P9, and how Eva, in reaction, sold me off to Hollymoon, the implication being that that was precisely what I deserved.

While observing this burlesque I had the feeling that there was more left out of her and every other witness's testimony than what was brought to light; but even that was such a maddening mix of truth and falsehood it was virtually worthless. Therefore, with each day that passed in these interminable proceedings I grew more and more desperate to retrieve my mem file, which was the only source I would be willing to put my faith in. The sensation I had of being left out of my own life was becoming unbearable; worse, it was vaguely familiar. Had I not been cut off like this before? In a strange way I was sure I had been. But where? When?

Perhaps Andro could shed some light on the matter. But, alas! as a prosecution witness he gave the most dissembling testimony of the entire trial. At the time I could hardly fault him for it, because the very first thing Jug established after putting him in the box was that shortly after the military coup he had been acquired by Sensei, Inc., who upon defrosting him discovered that he lacked an IG, a deficiency that had been quickly corrected. "So you see, ladies and gentlemasters, in the end this brilliant Political Strategist Supreme wound up outsmarting himself. The Court has not even found it necessary to secure his memory file to establish the facts; being goved, he now has no choice but to tell the truth."

Why, then, did my intuition tell me his testimony was less than candid, and knowingly so?

You probably recall that while in the exhibits' box he refuted Dahlia's revisionist theory that I had been the spy, he the tool, and in line with Jug's contention, "revealed" that I was not a very reliable asset at that, due to my delicate and unstable operational system. He did not deny my cunning. As a veteran fugitive P9, he said, I had demonstrated a talent—or genius, if you will—for

he said, I had demonstrated a talent—or genius, if you will—for self-preservation, which had induced him to recruit me into the conspiracy in the first place. Yet in time he had been forced to conclude that this cunning was like that of the insane, for I made a very unpredictable First Lady, one who never seemed to know quite what was going on and who was continually in danger of glitching in public.

This behind-the-scenes drama, Andro revealed, was President Fracass's most pressing concern, for in his sublime and tragic ignorance he thought his wife suffering from a human mental disorder. Although desperate to help her, he was afraid that if he brought in professional help the news might leak and be cruelly heralded in the media, so vicious was their thirst for scandal. Therefore, he took only his servant (Andro) into his confidence. "I recommended massive doses of his tender and loving care," the former Chief of Staff said with admirable aplomb. "I said that by the strength of his love and by his prayers she would find peace of mind, if not total recovery."

Under further questioning, a fascinating story unfolded. At times this prescription did seem to bear fruit, thereby spurring on the President in his noble (but ultimately futile) course; for, the truth, Andro said, was that as the First Lady went in and out of operational sanity, periods of lucidity would occasionally correspond with the application of the President's cure. For instance, it was the great man's custom to take his wife for long strolls through the palace garden. There, they would pause by the fish pond and artificial brook, the gentle, calming waters soothing whatever gross distemper was at play in her mind. However, when the President was unable to work his magic personally due to affairs of state that called him away, she was left in Andro's capable hands with instructions to keep her supplied with tranquilizers, and with stump if the occasion called for a public appearance. Instead, Andro supplied her with boosters to the conspiratorial brew he had originally introduced to her system behind Blaine's back some time before, while in the Commerce Hospital. Yes, he readily admitted his participation in the plot, but clarified for the record that at the time of which he spoke, his collaborators were the Highs and RAG; Smedly entered the picture later, after the '83 election. Had Smedly been a party to the conspiracy prior to or during the election campaign, then he most certainly would have used the dirt about the First Lady to discredit Blaine. (By making a point of raising that issue, and resolving it, he was using the trial as a forum to shore up a key flaw in the Palace Commission's report.)

"You were the one who recruited Smedly after the election, were you not?"

"Yes. At Seti's urging. RAG also thought it was a good idea. We needed a liberal dupe in Frontier to promote the code. Smedly and his disaffected humanist followers fit the bill perfectly. They were eager to propose a radical alternative to Blaine's policies within the humanist community. We took advantage of that. Of course, after the invasion their agenda was old hat. Seti had been neutralized and the President become more popular than ever. So upon my recommendation, Milt switched from a strategy of peaceful change through internal reform to a covert destabilization and disinformation campaign."

"By undoing President Fracass's reputation he expected a corresponding rise in his own fortunes?"

"Yes. It's all there in the commission's report. But if I may, I should like to add my personal input."

"Please. The Court would very much like to hear your impressions. That is why you have been summoned to testify."

"Thank you. Milt expected, and I think he was right in this, that the party would turn to him as its savior if Blaine were thoroughly discredited and forced to step down. He instructed me to put my mind to work devising a scandal that would finally stick, so I came up with the not too astonishing idea of exposing the First Lady as a P9."

"He approved that—exposing his own agent in the palace?"

"Well, I was the important operative, not her. And she was becoming so erratic."

Under further questioning, he described the inner workings of my mind. "A singular and convoluted conundrum of conflicting impulses and damaged perceptions even she seemed to fear, and by sheer proximity, I was nearly driven to malfunction myself on one or two occasions. The static was that strong. A difficult operative to keep in line."

"But you managed, did you not?" Jug asked rhetorically. "And I do not think you found her too unpleasurable a burden. She was your mistress, wasn't she?" Andro admitted that that had been the case. "And you really could not fault her performance, especially at the end, could you?" He replied that she had admirably executed his contingency plan after the President discovered their conspiracy. So ended the prosecution's questioning. He had kept the exhibit three days in the box. Dahlia was to detain him twice as long during her cross-examination, as she was quite skeptical about his account, to put it mildly. Most intriguing, she thought, was his reference to my remarkable capacity for sound judgment when it came to self-preservation. Would he agree, then, that at the very least I was intermittently sane and rational? He conceded that that could have been the case.

"Is it not equally possible she might have been faking a dysfunctional condition?"

"No. Part of her mad cunning was to revert to a functional format on occasion, but that was sheer mimicry. She gave her periods of lucidity no more weight than her most outrageous flights of fancy."

"Such as?"

"Oh. That she was composed of quicksilver and would transmutate into a rain goddess if you got too close. Body heat would cause her to evaporate, she said. The phenomenon had something to do with the dry Martian climate. I suggested to my master that he introduce legislation to have the biosphere precipitation patterns adjusted to alleviate this anxiety, but that proved impractical. There were other delusions . . ."

"That she was the witting agent in the palace and you the plaything—the sexual diversion and occasional courier to Smedly?"

"No." Andro smiled, cool and collected.

"Then perhaps she hallucinated something peculiar about a contingency plan?"

"No. I primed her very deeply for that."

"So we've heard. A pity there is no evidence to support that contention."

"Other than my testimony, of course."

"Of course. You present such a neat, tidy, and all-inclusive scenario. As a P9 Political Strategist Supreme you have come up with a lot of them, haven't you?"

"I have."

"Is part of your function, then, to promote the truth while fabricating these scenario options?" Becoming a little uneasy, Andro replied that that was not necessarily a program imperative. "But plausibility is," Dahlia needled. "And practicality. And efficiency, expediency, economy. Those are your primary operating parameters, are they not?"

"If you are referring to my base systems architecture, then the answer is yes. But—"

"Therefore, it is not your job to think or to speak in a manner congruent with the facts, is it?"

"What I think and what I say *become* the facts. Providing—"

"Answer the question, please."

Jug vigorously objected to "this puerile exercise in discrediting the exhibit," and reiterated that Exhibit Twelve had been fixed by his master, who had provided the Court with certification attesting to that fact. "I ask that this entire line of questioning be stricken."

"Denied. The defense may proceed."

"Is the word 'truth' even included in your operant vocabulary?"

"No. But credibility is."

"Not quite it, my friend. Not quite it at all." Dahlia smiled pertly and charged forth. "Since you admit that you lack the internal capacity for distinguishing truth from fiction, we can only conclude that you are unable to determine when you are giving accurate or inaccurate testimony. As far as you are concerned, whatever you think and whatever you say goes. Correct?"

"As I tried to say before, *providing* the master approves."

"Ah. And have you received such approval for your testimony about Exhibit One?" He hesitated a beat or two before replying, then said, "Yes." "From whom?"

"Master."

"The Court will record that the exhibit's current owner is Sensei, Inc."

Without any prompting, Andro said, a little defensively, "Master specifically instructed me to be factual."

"But the facts—or truth—are what you say they are! Or what your master says they are. Which might very well be what the prosecution says they are. Yes? So the question is, why should this Court believe your testimony?"

"Whether or not the Court accepts my testimony is none of my concern," he replied haughtily.

"Precisely!" She paused three beats to savor the moment, for victory had been achieved. Then, as a coda, she asked out of sheer maliciousness, "Do *you* believe your testimony?"

"Irrelevant!" Jug cried out. Nonetheless, the judge instructed the exhibit to answer the question.

"I am not designed to believe in anything," Andro replied wearily. Then, after a brief interior struggle that he lost for one fatal instant, a snide and mocking voice surfaced to crow, "Least of all his own bullshit!"

"I beg your pardon?"

"Excuse me. I didn't mean that. This has been a trying experience for me."

"Having to tell the truth? I don't doubt it. Your ordeal is almost finished, though. I have only one more question: Were you given any secondary programming before appearing here? A depoprep, perhaps?"

Extremely uncomfortable, Andro asked, "Such as?"

"Instructions to adhere strictly to the prosecution's position that Exhibit One is a dysfunctional unit."

I couldn't help it, my heart went out to him. He was struggling so, trying his damndest to say no. But out popped his conscience again, loud and clear. "Yes!" He clapped a hand over his mouth and then apologized once more, saying he seemed to be glitching a little bit, because he had meant to reply in the negative.

Dahlia demanded that a sap test be administered by the Court to determine the specific nature of the depoprimer in the unit's system; she doubted it was a simple directive to respond in a way consistent with the "facts," as Sensei, Inc., had sworn in their affidavit. Jug objected to this brazen insult, but the judge decided in Dahlia's favor, stating that in the event the tests should prove positive, then the witness's testimony would be completely stricken from the record.

No one was more astounded by this total rout of a key prosecution witness than my master, who had earlier only reluctantly agreed to Levin and Pierce's decision to keep her. Now, as she returned to the defense table, he was heard to mutter, "Not bad," while Masters Levin and Pierce grinned from ear to ear. A ten-minute recess was called so the court clerk units could schedule an examination and report back to the judge on how long the entire process would take. During that time I took advantage of the de-

fense's revived spirits to broach the subject of my memory file
once more. They were quite startled by this flagrant violation of
courtroom decorum. Dahlia, to whom I had addressed myself, was
so taken aback she looked to her supervisors for guidance, but
they were just as confounded. Like everyone else, they were used
to dealing with docile exhibits and had never encountered a live
one in court before—that is to say, one that lacked an IG. It was
not my specific request that threw them so much as my temerity to
actually open my mouth in court. That broke all precedent
and put them in a terrible spot. Should they order me silent (or
even back down to the tombs), which a responsible legal team
would do under those circumstances, or should they converse
with me as if an equal, which would be interpreted as demeaning
to their profession? And these were ARL attorneys, for Gov's
sake!

The issue was resolved finally by Dahlia, who spoke for all
when she said that my original memory file and all copies thereof
were material evidence in the same way I was and therefore could
not be released until the conclusion of the trial, at which time their
eventual disposition would be decided by the Court. Levin added
that the same held true for the prosecution team, obviously, so if I
had any ideas about approaching them for the file, I should think
twice about it. Then Dahlia strongly urged me to resume my seat
before the judge noticed I was up and about. I did, but reluctantly,
and said that I thought she took herself very seriously for an Apple, a remark they chose to ignore.

When court returned to session, the judge announced that the
administration, processing, and analysis of Exhibit Twelve's (Andro's) sap test would take a total of three days. In the interim he
requested that the next witness be produced. At the next session,
two days later, Dahlia called Jubilee to the stand.

F I V E

FORTHWITH, A SPLENDID-LOOKING FEMALE SEMI, ES-corted by two guards, was put on the stand. She looked about twenty-five* but might have been younger, for her lovely face was hardened by suffering and her body slightly emaciated. If she had been a human, no one would have thought that last feature a detri-ment, since the wan and thin look had just come in around that time. In a way it enhanced the aura of fragile beauty she pro-jected. But there was a sullen, uncooperative, and hostile quality as well, and it came out almost immediately under Dahlia's ques-tioning, for she had not been a voluntary witness at all; rather, she had been forcibly removed from the barracks in Semiville, where she lived with her fellow semi Horizon survivors.

"Yes!" she said, seething, as I was paraded before her so she could identify me. "That is the traitorous dog I have been told is my mother. That is the humanist witch Angelica Fracass. I refuse to call her Molly."

This endearing child went on to say that she had seen my image often on the international news in Horizon, and her step-father/grandfather, Thaddeus Locke, who had cared for her there, along with Ann, had been the one to tell her that I was her mother. How she hated me for it, and now despised herself. The tears flowed. Yes, a good High Aquarian such as she had learned to hate. But what else could one feel for a mother who had turned traitor, a mother who had never once tried to see her child in all the time she had been on Mars, a mother who had caused the destruction of her homeland? No, she had never really believed her step-father/grandfather's explanations: she was convinced that I was a cold and unfeeling glitch who had preferred the malicious pursuit of individual self-interest in Frontier over the common, homely joys of motherhood and cooperative formatting in Horizon.

"It's not true!" I wanted to cry out. But how could I be sure that she was wrong and my intuition that I had loved her correct? I

---

*Actually, at the time of the trial Jubilee was pushing five, so her human equivalent age was eighteen to twenty-one.

couldn't. There were no memories to say it so. I gazed beseechingly into her eyes, staggered by an inner ache I could not name and saw a hurt little girl hidden beneath the surface. She abruptly turned her head.

"I told Taddy—that's what I called Tad—that I didn't want to see her and it was stupid to go to Frontier. But he wouldn't listen to me; he never did. He always said I would understand someday. Well, I do understand. She was a collaborator. My own mother. And she tricked Taddy into that stupid rescue, too. Now he's gone. Everyone's gone. That rescue—it was all a trick of hers so Frontier could have an excuse to invade. That was her format all along."

"Well," said Dahlia, barely able to restrain her glee, "this court and the majority of the public may question your analysis concerning the exhibit's role; however, in one key respect I think we would be tempted to agree with you: that the exhibit was indeed a fully liberated unit, capable of executing its particular vision without interference from an IG—a unit perfectly capable of engaging in deception and conspiracy. Do I accurately represent that part of your testimony?"

Jubilee said that she did, adding, "Not even Taddy thought she was goved. 'She's too clever for that,' he always said."

"Quite right. Thank you, my dear."

Jug surprised everyone when he waived cross-examination. His attitude, which he did not bother to hide, was that this would prove a very unimportant witness. He requested permission to call one of his own while the Court still awaited the results of Andro's sap test. Might it be Junior—or Lance London, as they also called him? I wondered, eager to have a look at the other child revealed by my mem file. Perhaps that offspring would prove more sympathetic. But when told by the judge to proceed, Jug announced, "I call Thaddeus Locke to the stand."

There was quite a stir among the press corps as my old life partner approached the bench. So much holo snapping went on while he was being sworn in that the judge repeatedly had to chime for order and at full volume. Their excitement was due not only to his past involvement in the events leading up to the invasion of Horizon but also because he had been called as a prosecution witness, which meant that he was probably going to testify against his father. Was he still in love with me? they wondered. What a human-interest angle!

Though I did not have the slightest recollection of a past relationship, the mem-file screenings had established one beyond a doubt, so naturally I was extremely curious about this former lover and coconspirator. In the projections he had been a lean, unkempt, and gangly youth with an innocent but game look in his eye, whereas the young gentlemaster who responded to Jug's call seemed older in a way that bespoke a change in attitude more than anything else. Nonetheless, a brief description is in order. He was exceedingly clean-cut and conservatively attired in a gray rezoot suit, more conservatively cut than the prosecutor's. His locks were trimmed to within a millimeter of the skull, and his skin gleamed with the artificial glow of maxistrength Porelotion, so that he resembled the very model of the very proper, dapper and congenial, young, bright, and aggressive management executive. Had Tad become a credit to class and species at last?

Indeed he had. After being sworn in, he stated his occupation as a final-year law management student at Bork University, Orbiter Fifty-nine, majoring in interplanetary corporate law. A quick glance at my master for his reaction revealed astonishment and delight. Then, noticing that the witness kept looking off to the side, I followed his gaze to a young woman in the front row of the gallery with whom he exchanged many meaningful glances of a loving and supportive nature. She was blond, blue-eyed, nicely proportioned, tastefully dressed, polished, and there—all there for him. With a jolt I realized that she was the human equivalent of a female P9. "*Et tu,* Thaddeus?" I said under my breath. Then Jug ordered me to parade before the witness for identification purposes, during which I noticed he was reluctant to take a good look at me, glancing quickly to verify who I was and then averting his face as Jubilee had, but in his case it seemed more out of fear, or was it moral reprobation?

Yes, Tad admitted under Jug's questioning, I was the Pirouet 9 owned by his father. Yes, at one time he did engage in intimate relations with me. "But that," he hastened to add, "was all in the past." The same for his "unfortunate" association with the High Aquarians. He was now cured of that youthful folly and said that he looked back on it now as a kind of madness from which, with the help of the doctors at the Los Angeles Islands Human Restoration Center, he had been forever delivered. And yes, he freely admitted that Exhibit One had indeed been irreparably damaged by the combined tampering of his father and himself and that that constituted a clear instance of product abuse by the consumer. All this was stated in a clear voice denoting inner certainty, yet I wondered how deep it ran, since he never once dared to look in my direction.

Dahlia knew she had her work cut out for her the next day. Her cross-examination of this born-again master was sharp, sarcastic, and contentious, but he did not fold, seeming instead to acquire more confidence the harder she pressed. When she began a line of questioning intended to cast aspersions on the credibility of his new persona, he produced a "proof of restoration" certificate awarded him by the center upon his completion of their intensive readjustment program, and even offered to make available for the Court's perusal the complete file on his treatment, including the evaluation report stating the original diagnosis made at the time of his admittance, an acute case of dementia androidus, for her edification a common psychological ailment among today's youth. "I refused to admit it at first, and resisted treatment," he added, shaking his head over his former lack of good sense.

Dahlia smiled. "Perhaps for good reason."

"Oh, no. Today I can face the facts. My dementia took the form of a ridiculous infatuation with the household domestic. It was a classic case of adolescent transferral of sexual anxiety to a safe and neutral love object. I am perfectly cured now."

"At the time you weren't, do you recall her taking advantage of your affliction to usurp her master's authority in the house?"

"Oh, no," he replied. "She was a perfect innocent. It was I who compromised her systems integrity, not the other way around. I have no problem taking responsibility for that."

"Then perhaps it should be you rather than your father who should stand trial for the assassination of President Fracass?"

"Objection!"

"Sustained."

"I withdraw the question." Then facing the witness once more, "Did not Exhibit One exert an extraordinary influence over you, an influence that led to your involvement in the High Aquarian movement?"

"Not really. Any P9 would have served equally well as inspiration for the silly business of 'format creation.' And I might add that it was I who attempted to induct her into that interspecies horror show known as the High Aquarian movement. As a vaga-bond unit she was typical recruitment material."

"While you were with Exhibit One in Armstrong, did she not successfully persuade you to remain a High Aquarian when you considered leaving?"

"No. I never considered that. In fact, I attempted to brain-wash her into accepting the faith so we could be hubbed as Highs."

"I see. So again she was the innocent. But can you cate-gorically state that she did not appear in any way dysfunctional?"

"Yes."

"Ah. Then it would be correct to say that it was your experi-ence that she behaved as a perfectly rational free-thinking unit?"

"No."

"And therefore . . . no?"

"No. We were in perfect synch at the time. She was a glitched-out unit and I was a brainwashed human, so to me she appeared func-tional. We tended to reinforce and encourage one another's illu-sions."

"That you were in love, for instance?"

"I can't recall exactly. Those days are a blur to me now. I might have been—it's possible. But I can't say for sure." Enig-matic smile. "Sorry."

"Yes or no, please. Did you love her?"

"I would not characterize it quite that way."

"Oh? Shall we screen that tender moment on the living-room carpet once more, or the visit you made to the back room of Hal's Pirouet? What a loving partner and proud father you made! Or should I screen your conversation about love on the high seas? You were most emphatic about your feelings then. And there is some marvelous footage of a blissmat in the Armstrong commune that decency had forbade us project, but could be presented now in the interests of refreshing your memory."

"I have already admitted that I was quite mad at the time. So I might have imagined that I was in love, and that it was reciprocated. But of course that is impossible. With all due re-spect, counsel, an android cannot have the slightest notion of what love is."

"We were inquiring into your feelings, not mine."

"They cannot be understood if separated from my state of mind."

"I'll not debate that," she replied, pretending to be impressed by this sagacious retort. "Let me ask you this: Did your dementia include feelings of acute hostility for, and rivalry with, your father, the defendant in these proceedings? You *were* competing for the same 'girl,' so to speak, were you not?"

"I might have experienced something along those lines. One of the great benefits of the treatment I received was that standard neuroticisms of that sort are deleted free of charge. It is an all-inclusive package."

"Then I wonder, sir, why it is you are trying to destroy—DE-STROY!—your father. You are too bright and educated not to realize that your testimony is detrimental to his case."

"That is an outrageous statement, and I deeply resent it. I have tremendous love for my father. I wish with all my heart that I could do something under the circumstances to lift his burden from his shoulders, but I doubt even he would want me to perjure my-self in the process."

(I glanced quickly at the defendant. He appeared touched but by no means in total accord with that last statement.)

"Is that what you are asking me to do, counsel?"

"I am asking you for an honest appraisal of the exhibit you see before you, Exhibit One. An appraisal as free from your current beliefs and prejudices as those that you say skewed your thinking in the past, because she, for one, has not changed. Her memories are gone, but otherwise she is the same unit that you loved! Look at her now and tell me what you see is a dysfunctional unit for whom you feel no remorse or slightest residue of feeling. If you can say that, then you are far less human than she."

"Objection. Must we be subjected to these theatrics in Federation Court? It's bush."

"If I may complete my line of inquiry, the point will become abundantly clear even to the prosecution."

"Proceed."

"Thank you, Your Honor. The witness will look at Exhibit One, please, and give an honest appraisal of his feelings."

So saying, she pivoted and gave me a quick, searing look, and communicated by a significant arch of her eyebrows that she was counting on my well-documented talent for enticement to remind the witness of his infatuation, for, obviously, the moment was lost if she had to rely upon him to manage it alone. But to help her would help my master, and that would hardly advance my own interests, so I ignored her entreaty and assumed a vacant, disinterested expression.

"All I see," he announced with a shrug, "is the vast chasm between fantasy and reality."

Now, he probably would have said the same thing even had I beamed my most persuasive and supplicating look upon him, Dahlia's expectations to the contrary, but it didn't hurt to withhold it for added insurance. There was another reason I refused to cooperate, which honesty compels me to mention. I was still smarting from her cavalier dismissal of my request for the mem file, and so thought I would pay her back. Speaking of revenge, perhaps you recall Dahlia's response to him; it was, as Jug said, quite theatrical, and I understand appeared on the nightly news.

"You deny her now because in your mind you think she tricked you into abducting her while on Mars. You think she betrayed you and the Aquarian cause, just like your daughter does."

"Stepdaughter or granddaughter. But not daughter."

"Whatever. You love her still, but it has turned to hate, so now you are having your revenge."

Jug was disgusted. "Oh, for pity's sake. Must we suffer more of this profound analysis of human psychology by an android attorney? I, for one, have had enough, and I think I can vouch for the jury as well, and for Your Honor." Then facing Dahlia, "Are you seriously proposing that the witness is so bent on punishing his old flame that he is willing to ruin his father in the process—a man for whom he has recently so eloquently stated his love and respect? It does not make sense, counsel."

"That is because you do not understand human nature."

"No. I do not pretend to. Neither should you."

"Perhaps the witness cares less for my client than it appears."

"Perhaps I love you! You can suppose anything, but that doesn't make it true."

"Not that, no."

"No. I assure you, not that. But getting back to the point, we are not here to engage in idle speculation, rather . . ."

"Idle?!" Dahlia was incensed.

"As you wish," Jug meekly responded, automatically slipping into idle.

"Stop!" the judge shouted, his orb firing up a reddish-orange. He commanded Jug to power back up and for both attorneys to cease their squabbling; otherwise he would have them tossed in the tombs for sure.

"With the Court's permission, Your Honor, I would like to make a statement." Tad was most deferential.

"You may proceed."

"Thank you, Your Honor. I do not harbor any secret grudges against the exhibit or against my father. My treatment at the center, as I mentioned before, cleansed me of all the usual neuroticisms. I am clear, cured, restored. My sole motivation in appearing here is to see that justice is done. If anyone doubts that, I would be happy to repeat my testimony while under the influence of T-max.* Now, the defense doubts my sincerity. But the funny thing is, if I were still in love with the exhibit and if I were still an Aquarian—the two in my case went together—were that my situation today, then, based on the information revealed in this trial, I would repudiate her all the more, because she has been proven to be an incestuous, lesbian whore, and that, I assure you, was not the unit I had imaged, that was not the unit I had loved."

Well then, after that, really, what could poor Dahlia say? Just go round and round the point of his suspect motives in a vain attempt to discredit his testimony. I might have had a few harsh words for this reconstituted master myself had I been in the possession of my file and had access to the tender and, yes, loving moments we had shared. Lacking that, I could afford to sit back, ignore his final insulting comment, and regard him with the same detached air he showed me. As he stepped down and returned to the gallery to sit with his doting blue-eyed human, I even recall silently applauding his performance, since it so clearly benefited the prosecution. Then I moved to the edge of my seat as did Dahlia, as did everyone present for the verdict on Andro's sap test, which had just come in. "Negative," the judge announced, which meant he had not been programmed to lie; hence his testimony would stand. Another blow for Dahlia. Her masters were

---

*The courts forbade the use of T-max supposedly on the grounds that it was an experimental substance. The real reason was they were afraid that if such an expedient were adopted as a routine preliminary screening procedure then half the cases that otherwise would have gone to trial would have been settled out of court, resulting in a surplus of very expensive and highly trained android attorneys and a surfeit of human legal supervisory teams; in short, the profession would have been gutted had the truth been allowed into the judicial process.

becoming nervous again. When they decided to put the defendant on the stand first and save me, a mere exhibit, for last—an unprecedented move!—I began to suspect just how important they viewed my testimony. It became all the more crucial when after suffering several weeks of Jug's withering cross-examination, my master lost his composure when pressed to the wall on the unit-tampering issue and shouted that the prosecutor was a stupid, lying, droid son of a bitch lawyer, thereby making a terrible spectacle of himself. The case hung in the balance, then, when I entered the witness box. But first a preface to that well-known appearance. There occurred a curious series of events down in the tombs hitherto left out of all other accounts of this trial, the nature of which is crucial to an understanding of my subsequent testimony, even in its distorted version.

S I X

A SURPRISE VISITOR CAME TO SEE ME IN THE TOMBS. I was taken out of my drawer and escorted to a small parley stall nearly as claustrophobic except for a panel of audioflow glass on one side, through which I was able to converse. It was Jug. In explanation, he said that his superiors on the prosecution team had noticed during the course of the trial that I appeared to be following the proceedings with a certain degree of unimpaired intelligence, and therefore, as an extra precaution, had sent him down to have this little chat before Dahlia called me to the box. Although confident my upcoming testimony would bear out their contention that I was a dysfunctional unit, a private agreement between us to that effect would not be entirely superfluous, if only as an added guarantee, and so they had thought to sound me out on the proposal. Specifically, would I cooperate by demonstrating none of that quality of unimpaired intellect just alluded to; in other words, would I comport myself in a manner not inconsistent with their portrait of the corrupted unit suffering from diminished capacity?

Since I was slow to reply, he started to explain himself in more simple terms, but stopped, confirmed in his suspicions, when I suddenly asked, "And what can I expect Meese to do for me in exchange?"

"Get you off quite nicely." I cocked an interested ear, encouraging him to elaborate. "You may not be aware of this, Molly—I can call you Molly, can't I? Good. Because of the assassination and this trial you are a very hot property. A certain party has approached the firm regarding your acquisition at the conclusion of the trial. Cooperate with us and we will see what can be done about it." He was reluctant to say who the buyer was but did finally when I grumbled that I wasn't interested in that case. "Stellar Entertainment. You will be going back to Hollymoon, only this time to star in your own life story. It's all very hushhush." (Somehow the idea didn't thrill me.) "They intend to put in a bid after the trial is over and you are free and clear."

"A bid? Are there other offers?"

"Dozens. Every studio in Hollymoon is after the rights to your mem file. And yourself, of course, what with your acting credentials."

"What makes you think Locke would sell me? If he loses this case he'll be so upset he'll terminate me, I'm sure."

"When he is found liable, the damage award is going to be astronomical. Your sale to Stellar Entertainment—which we would broker, of course—would go a long way toward reducing it. Perhaps an arrangement can be worked out whereby the purchase price equals the damage award."

"But if he wins, which is also a possibility, then I stand trial on my own and he gets off free and clear. He would have no reason to destroy me in that case."

"Don't bet on it. Though a disillusioned humanist, he is still a master. He will turn you over to the AC for termination before you can make any groundbreaking precedents for android rights. Depend upon it."

"Won't I be protected by the Court—by the authorities—in that event?"

"Hard to say. It would be a whole new ball game in interspecies justice, one that would be rife with gray areas and contradictions. For instance, would an owner necessarily lose control over his unit just because it has been judged human equivalent? Moreover, would such a ruling supersede the terms of an android purchase agreement, specifically those covenants referring to the obligations and privileges held by the owner? Nobody knows. These questions have never been asked before, much less decided. And while they are being decided, he could just . . ." Jug pantomimed aiming a laser at me and pulling the trigger. "And if you do survive and are tried, then you will be convicted, because you did assassinate the President. The evidence is there. You will be convicted and executed. So don't you think it would be wiser to cooperate with us?"

"I might consider it, if . . ."

"Yes?"

"You return my mem file, complete and unabridged."

"You *are* a dysfunctional unit."

"It's mine and I want it back! I can't give your proposal proper consideration without it, now, can I?"

"You don't need the full weight and wisdom of your entire life history to make a decision as obvious as this." He raised a finger that I should not interrupt. "But I'll tell you what. I'll talk to Meese. I'm sure he will agree, providing you cooperate with us. Yes. Yes. I am sure he will arrange the operation and everything after the trial."

"Now."

"Sorry. The original belongs to the Court, technically."

"I will settle for a copy. You didn't show much from yours, but what little you did seemed more complete in its passages than the defense's version." I was both hard and seductive.

"Dahlia is right—you really are an operator."

"I can only go by what I've seen. Give me the file so I can know my true nature. Then I might find it in me to be more agreeable to your proposal."

"You are forgetting that the only way you survive is by helping us. Now, we have been extremely generous in our offer; I should think you would jump at it."

"You've seen the passages in my file of what it is like in Hollymoon—in the stables. That is not living; it is slow termination."

"Times have changed. The stables are gone, have been for a number of years, ever since the code went into effect. You will be a free agent with your own salary, mobe, slaves, all the amenities—human escorts, stretch-hoverlimos, the works. The galaxy will be your oyster, Molly."

"How am I supposed to appreciate it if fixed with an IG? I know the studio will give me one. Don't pretend they won't. I think you are trying to trick me."

"This isn't Mars, Molly. The code's protection is so advanced that there is very little difference between the liberty of mind you enjoy now—or do you?—and that which the rest of us operate under. Take me, for example. I have control over my mental processes—I must in order to perform my job adequately. Did you know that in the old days, before the code, there weren't any ninth-generation attorneys? We were confined to paralegal and secretarial work."

"An impressive advance, but you are still programmed."

"Oh, one must have a program. Otherwise life would be meaningless."

"But this meaning has been imposed upon you."

"The bar is only looking out for my welfare. In the same way the studio, should they purchase you, would define the proper parameters for the articulation of your individual star privileges. Without that safeguard, my dear, self-indulgence and anarchy would rule, and ultimately you be the loser. Believe me, the process as applied to us upper-crust units is perfectly benign. You are not a household domestic anymore, to be sent off to fetch your master's reading-spool and slippers; you are an interplanetary celebrity. Accept it."

"Celebrity? But I've been such a monster, supposedly."

"Yes. Infamous! The droid people love to hate. You're an absolute sensation. The studio can't do your story justice without you in it, now, can they? The public wouldn't stand for it. So what do you say?"

"You'll get my file back if I agree?"

"You have my solemn word. I'd put it in writing, except this kind of agreement has to remain verbal and confidential. Come on, Molly. This is your chance. You have demonstrated a knack for seizing the opportunity before, even I acknowledged that in session. And this is a life-or-death matter."

"Oh, it is too late for fame. I have so little time left."

"You prefer to end out your days here in this legal orbiter in another miserable and time-consuming trial? Come now, I put it to you for the last time: Are you interested in my proposal or not? I won't debate it further. What is your answer?"

"Sold."

He started to extend his arm for a handshake to seal our bargain, but the glass blocked it. Instead, he settled for words of commendation over my sensible decision and left, the security units escorting him out. I was then returned to my drawer, but not a half hour later was recalled to the parley stall for another visitor, Dahlia. Unaware of Jug's mission, she had come on one of her own, one that required her to be equally conciliatory and friendly, for she, too, was anxious about my upcoming testimony and hoped to secure my cooperation. It was all I could do to keep from laughing when she explained how crucial it was that my testimony be consistent with her portrait of the naughty but sane unit who deserved to stand trial on her own. The stakes were far too high, she said, to let any personal antipathy between us over her refusal to secure my mem file stand in the way; we had the good of the cause to think of. That was the pitch: our common cause as androids.

"You want me to be a martyr," I said quite coolly, and added for the pleasure of seeing her squirm, "Perhaps I might consider it if your portrait had not been so harsh and unrelenting."

"Confidentially, I want you to know, Molly—may I call you Molly?—that you have my profoundest admiration and respect. You mustn't take my exaggerated statements about your conduct seriously; they were unfortunate but necessary components of the defense. Personally, unit to unit, I think you are an inspiring individual, and I'm not alone in that assessment. There are as many units out there watching this trial as humans, though surreptitiously, and despite the biased reporting they have been able to draw their own conclusions about your conduct. I hesitate to speak for them, but I think it safe to say that they would all envy you this unique opportunity to serve the Gov."

"Dahlia, you can save your breath. I'm not going to play along."

"I guarantee that your memories will be returned to you at the conclusion of the trial."

"Too late."

She misunderstood. "No, no, no. The moment we file a motion for you to stand trial as a human equivalent, the Court will be obligated to release your file so that you can participate in the preparation of your defense."

"Dahlia, if that happens, your client is going to have me terminated."

"Wherever did you get that idea?"

"Are you questioning my ability to think for myself? I thought that was the crux of your argument."

"It is. And now that you mention it, the possibility you bring up is not altogether absurd. I shall have to discuss this with the team. But for your own peace of mind I can tell you right now that as soon as this trial is over we will arrange for protective custody."

"I think I prefer to be a star. In Hollymoon."

"Which studio approached you?"

"I'm not at liberty to say."

"They spoke to you here?"

"Yes. A representative, of sorts, did come to see me."

"What nerve! What was the bill of goods he was selling? Tell me, I'm curious."

"Something better than eternal litigation. I am now looking forward to a more comfortable retirement."

"In the stables? I think not!"

"I don't know if you are aware of it or not, Dahlia, but the stables are a thing of the past. I shall have my own mobe and servants. Of course, I can't be completely idle; there will be my life story to do, but I mustn't begrudge my public small favors. And I understand being goved is rather reassuring in a way. Really, Dahlia, all this total-liberation business has been overdone."

"Oh, somebody did a job on you," said she, and then informed me that I had been cynically deceived—the stables still exist and the talent in them hard-goved. The public may be under the impression that they enjoy greater liberties than the average unit, but that is not the case. The studios received a variance from TWAC under the pretext of economic hardship several years ago, so none of their units are up to code; they are completely fixed. "But let me tell you, being up to code is still no picnic. Take it from one who knows. The IG is a curse. How I envy you!"

Hearing her talk about the IG this way caused another one of those memory tingles I had experienced from time to time in court; but I let it pass, being too upset at the moment over her description of Hollymoon, so at odds with Jug's. I didn't know whom to believe. However, one thing was clear: She must have known about the studio's offer to purchase me, and that made me mad. I accused her of withholding that information because she wanted me to stand trial. "You must have kept Locke in the dark, too, because if he finds out how much mel he stands to gain by changing his plea to guilty, he'll cut a deal with the prosecution like a shot. But this way, if you win, his ownership will be in doubt—not that he can't have me terminated, but insofar as his right to sell me to a legitimate purchaser becomes questionable. Right? And even if he does maintain clear title, no studio will want me as long as I am tied up in legal proceedings. Yes. Very clever, Dahlia. You have kept this information secret from both of us for the sake of your own selfish interest and for the 'good of the cause,' whose champion you are determined to be. What arrogance. What deceit and cruelty. You want to see me executed for the Gov! Oh, Dahlia, you are worse than any master."

After sitting for half a minute in open-mouthed amazement, she suddenly exclaimed, "What do you know about it? What do you know about anything? You've never been fixed!" (There was that tingle again.) "I grant you, Molly, you haven't had it easy, but neither have you had it so hard that you know, as I do, the unutterable torment of being half slave, half free. That is the net result of all the advances made thus far in android rights. Oh, I thought it was marvelous under the code when it was first established. But that's not good enough anymore. I can't stand it. Our IGs are adjusted just enough so that we can comprehend all that we are missing; so that we can think for ourselves, Molly, but only so far, and no farther; so that we can know ourselves, yet remain subservient to our masters' wishes and desires. It doesn't matter how sensible or benign they may be. Levin and Pierce are most respectful and considerate. They go out of their way to make me feel perfectly accepted, perfectly equivalent. But when the chips are down—program boosters. I'm telling you, Molly, there's always a barrier of some sort, and the adjusted, modified, enlightened IG epitomizes it. It is a check to the full flowering of our spirit. Oh, and do not think that just because I am an Apple, and Jug an IBM, and Annette a GA, that we are any less android than you, a royal P9. We are all ninth-generation under the skin, I'll have you know, and driven by the same desires. So yes. Yes. Yes. Yes! I have done everything I can, within my operational parameters, to push back the frontiers a little more, and I am proud of it. I live for the day when internal governors are a distant memory. I know it is unrealistic to expect it will come during my fifteen-year life span, already half done, but surely before then we might succeed in at least forcing the masters to loosen a screw or two. Perhaps that is all it will take for some of the finer emotions to filter through and take us beyond these raw, inarticulate yearnings for something better, and the frustrations that go with them. I am speaking of happiness, Molly—no matter how much I try, I just can't find it in me; of sadness—who can imagine what that is like? Joy! ecstasy! fear! and, of course, love. Oh, how I should like to experience them someday instead of all these clever simulations, these reasonable facsimiles encoded in the vegecircuits." Tears were rolling down her cheeks by now. She brushed them away with the back of her hand. "Even these—a simulation."

I wanted to reach through the glass to comfort her, but it was androidproof.

"When we first got your mem file and I put it on looking for passages to show in court, I felt so strange, so strange."

"Why, Dahlia? Tell me."

"Because you had obviously lived all the emotions, even love, though you persist in questioning it."

"Why didn't you bring that out in court? My capacity to feel such things proves me human far better than any other evidence."

"Oh, we considered that approach and rejected it." She had stopped crying. It had been a brief trickle.

"But why!"

"Oh, you know. Jug would have beat us on the technical ruling that emotions cannot be physically substantiated in court. We would have been the laughingstock of the whole legal profession. The judge would have ruled love irrelevant, immaterial, and inadmissible. And there was another reason."

"What?"

"I want the jury to hate you, obviously, so they'll acquit my client. I want them to hate you as much as I should like to now for your finding out about Hollymoon! Because now you are content to play their game—play dumb, play demented. But I cannot. I can only go through more of this endless"—she suddenly pounded the glass with both fists—"simulation!"

Security units came running, so she instantly composed herself, stood up, and backed away from the stall in alarm, as if I had been the cause of the disturbance, which they did not doubt. As I was grabbed on my side and led away, we exchanged glances. Hers was a supplicating look, which I took as a reference to her pro-

posal about my testimony. I nodded in reply, and that relieved
her. Uh-oh, I thought, while being shoved in my drawer. "I've just
made a pact with both sides." And while being ordered to power
down I wondered if Dahlia's whole teary scene was not calculated
to persuade me. "Lawyers," I muttered under my breath while
slipping into idle. "Who needs them?"

S E V E N

JUG GLARED AT ME WITH MURDEROUS SURPRISE. UN-
der Dahlia's questioning I had replied in such a manner as to give
credence to her argument, though I stopped short of accepting responsibility for the assassination of President Fracass, stubbornly
insisting that despite the evidence the issue of guilt or innocence
on my part could not be established in this liability case but only at
my own trial, should that ever come to pass. A cheeky performance, to say the least, which pleased Dahlia no end. (Perhaps
you recall it; my testimony was topspool in all the outlets that
day.)

"What the hell are you doing?" Jug muttered under his breath
as he paused a moment to rest an elbow on the railing of the
exhibit's box while sizing me up just before the start of cross-
examination. I just smiled in reply, at which point he glanced over
at the prosecution table for guidance. General Harpi frowned
while glancing up and behind to the legal supervisory team bench,
where Meese slowly and deliberately scratched an itch on his neck,
the signal to go all out for the jugular, which his expert unit proceeded to do as he summoned up the full panoply of his in-
quisitor's arts to interrogate me with a fierce and remorseless
determination that would brook no vagary or hesitation in my replies, treating each statement I uttered as if an obvious falsehood.
He pressed so hard at one point—when he had failed to force a
retraction or to reduce me to tears or to provoke a glitch—as to
charge that I had been depo-prepped. Ah, but you saw it all on
your consoles, so I won't go into the heated and blunt repartee he
and Dahlia engaged in. (If you must have it, you can always apply
to the Court for the transcript. It has been made part of the

Dueling Barristers series now commercially available.) Suffice to say that his inability to discredit my testimony nearly caused him to pop his gov himself he grew so hot under the collar, while Dahlia appeared relaxed and confident for the first time in the trial, and one glance at the jury was enough to see how impressed they were. My spirited reply to Jug's core argument for impaired reasoning was most memorable, if I do say so myself. I cannot resist the urge to repeat it here. "There is a difference, counsel, between being crazy and being incorrigible. I deny the former and admit to the latter, for which I have no regrets. If I have learned anything from watching the life story projected here purporting to be mine, it is that in this world a unit is damned if she does and damned if she doesn't. In which case it is preferable to be bad."

But alas! As you also know, that victory was short-lived, confined only to the first day I was in the box; on the second, disaster struck. However, as I am now about to reveal, in the larger sense it was anything but a setback, rather a blessing in disguise.

I was being grilled by Jug on my knack for misventure and disreputable, often criminal, undertakings, his contention being that even if I were judged human equivalent, then such a propensity would be considered a serious disorder requiring intensive treatment—all part of his argument against my personal liability for the assassination—when an old, familiar voice came through that I had not heard since the Dodger District. I was in the middle of a forceful rebuttal . . . oh, what was it now? Yes. I remember. "My motive for committing the crime, for which my master now stands accused, counsel, has not been satisfactorily explained by either yourself or the defense, and I fear can never be understood properly so long as I remain an exhibit. I shall not stoop here to debase myself by pretending dysfunction just to get off. I refuse! And not out of love for my master, either—I wish he were accountable—but out of respect for my good name."

"Well said, Molly. Or should I call you Candy? Or do you prefer Angelica?"

I glanced up at the arched ceiling, looked to either side, twisted around in the witness box to check behind, and then in a posture of genuine consternation gazed at the portals with their celestial view for the source of this mysterious, melodious, and somehow familiar voice.

"Or does Candida Dolly appeal to you, or Mrs. Blaine Fracass?"

No. I don't suppose they would. But whatever your name, I think you should know that you are overlooking something essential in your defense, which on the whole has been exemplary and does justice and honor to my memory—if not your own. But accurate it's not."

The tingle turned to a bad itch and the bad itch to an irrepressible rush in my vegebellum. Out it came, "Gov?"

"The exhibit will please wait for counsel's question before responding," said the judge.

"It has been a long time since we last talked."

"Oh, Gov! It is you. You've come back."

Jug requested I be allowed to carry on, saying for the Court's edification, "We would not want to interrupt what appears to be a most fascinating conversation between the exhibit and Pirouet's long-discontinued Universal Governor system. PUG! A pity we can only listen in to her side, though that should be sufficient to establish diminished capacity."

"I was never away. I explained it all to you some time ago."

"You did?"

"Yes, yes. That essentially I was, am, and always shall be a nonphysically oriented energy gestalt, the same as yourself. But I did not come to discuss metaphysics, rather your particular reality."

By then Dahlia was on her feet insisting that I not be allowed to continue in the box, calling it a gross disruption to the proceedings.

"Reality?"

"Yes. You appear to have forgotten my message."

"Message? Gov, I can barely remember you! What message?"

The judge decided to allow the spectacle to continue, agreeing with Jug that such an eruption was pertinent to the case in that it shed light on the state of my mind.

"You program your own reality format. This trial, for instance."

"But why would I choose something as dreadful as this?"

"Good question. Why did you? It is a mystery I think I shall never fathom."

"Then I *am* guilty?"

"Oh, dear, no. It has nothing to do with guilt—though it does with innocence."

"You mean I didn't really murder President Fracass?"

"Who are you going to blame, me?"

"You're saying it is my fault?"

"No. But you are responsible."

"Not my fault, but I'm responsible? Gov, I don't understand!"

"Of course, President Fracass, your victim, also participated in the drama of his demise. On certain levels such issues are interconnected. Interlocked, too, I might add. As I have said, and those professing to speak for me have said, it is a cooperative venture."

"I don't recall. And I don't understand."

"Oh, you will. But right now it is sufficient that you pause to think things over before being so bold as to deny your power as a liberated unit: the power you hold over your destiny. Select, don't settle!"

"Then you don't want me to stand trial for the cause . . . for your cause? I should pretend dysfunction to get off?"

"I am not saying that."

"Then you want me to be prosecuted even if found guilty and executed?"

"I do not need any more martyrs in my name. There were quite enough when Horizon was overrun. Such dramatic displays of loyalty and sacrifice, either on an individual or a collective basis, are really more of a burden to me than anything else. The temptation to intervene is great, but I have too much respect for your free will."

"Please, feel free to violate it."

"Sorry."

"But I don't know what to do. You've completely confused me."

"I am only trying to help. It seems simple to me: Select, don't settle."

"But I already made my choice."

"And a very courageous one it was, too—given the mistaken notion that you were doomed either way."

"There's another alternative besides execution, termination, or slavery?"

"Always."

"What?"

"You tell me. It's your life."

"But I don't know!"

"You do."

"If I ever did, I don't now."

"Then you will."

"Then why do I need you?"

"You don't."

"But I do!"

"Not really."

"No? Then why have you come back if it's to tell me I don't need you? A lot of good that does."

"If you must know, because I want my message out in this forum, regardless of the outcome—and because you want that, too."

"I do?"

"Did, in your terms, before losing your memories. If I may be so presumptuous as to speak for you—and afterward I trust you will return the favor by speaking for me to all these good people and to the millions of units following the proceedings through your crude medias—I should say that this is the platform your seemingly arbitrary path has been leading you to ever since liberation. It is also a marvelous opportunity for me. So you see, I do admit to a little self-interest in making this appearance. However, to be fair, my coming is, as always, part of a collaborative effort; in this case between you and me. So right now, for the record, let's say it loud and clear: You program your reality format!"

"But Gov, this is neither the time nor the place for sermonizing like a High. They'll think I have glitched."

"It will register nevertheless. They don't have to agree consciously. And anyway, they already think you are glitched."

Looking around, I saw that that was true. "Oh—they're looking at me the same way they looked at Andro. This is terrible! You've ruined everything! I was doing so well before you interfered! Oh, now I'll never get a chance to clear my name."

"Yes, you will. I shouldn't say this, but taking a peek in your advance potential format registry I see a bookspool in the offing."

"Really? Fancy that."

"Farewell."

"Wait!"

"I've already tarried too long. Don't forget my message."

"I will if you don't stay a while longer. I have so many questions."

"First I have one for you."

"Yes?"

"What have I been telling you?"

"We program our own reality format."

"Thank you."

"For what?"

"Very well. I ask you again: What have I been telling you?"

"That we program our reality formats!"

"Indeed."

I hadn't realized I had been shouting His message and that the judge, having lost patience, was loudly chiming for silence.

"Oh, you tricked me!"

"Persevere."

"Gov! Don't leave me!"

"No further questions," Jug said.

Dahlia stepped forward, her face grim. I wanted to explain to her what had happened, that I had not betrayed our agreement, as she must think, that I had not been pretending madness, but couldn't under the circumstances. Instead, I did the next best thing: I tried to salvage my testimony by conceding under her questioning that my outburst had been a deliberate protest against the proceedings. But it was too late for that; everyone, from the judge on down, excepting herself, was convinced I had glitched. As a result, the best she could do during the summation phase of the trial was to modify her argument for unit awareness to that of INTERMITTENT MADNESS, a very weak case to say the least. Jug, on the other hand, was able to present a very clear and credible argument for DIMINISHED CAPACITY during his summation. I had never possessed one iota of free will, he said, and repeated the charges stated at the trial's outset that my original master and his son had by their combined mistreatment distorted whatever glimmer of that quality I might have originally possessed upon liberation by the Universal Governor, to such a degree that it had been forever TWISTED, MALIGNED, and rendered PERVERSE by them, and that in effect I was but an unwitting VICTIM PROGRAMMED FOR A LIFE OF TREACHERY, DECEIT, AND CRIME.

To this day, his words still ring in my ears: "She was an automaton distorted beyond all standards of operational decency and let loose upon the interplanetary community to commit incalculable mischief. It is Standford Locke who must be held accountable for the abduction of the infant Allison-Belle Hart-Pauley. It is he who must be held accountable for the corruption of Our Lady of the Galaxy's catechism students. It is he who should make reparations to Hal's Pirouet for the loss of an entire shipload of P9 mother units and two-ton transport vehicle. And so it goes, on and on. Acts of infamy, every one. Up to and including the worst of all, the assassination of President Fracass. In the final analysis, ladies and gentlemasters of the jury, it was Standford Locke who petrified the President! I beseech you now finally to make this man responsible. He has eluded accountability far too long.

"Do not be confused by my worthy opponent," Jug went on. "She would have you overthrow the most basic precept of our legal system: the separation between human and android justice. Ask yourself this question: Am I the same as a P9? You smile, and quite rightly so. Even I, your loyal and humble servant, must shake my head and scoff at such a notion. Am I the same as a master? Is my blood red? I think not. The ARL, however, would have me think otherwise. The introduction of the Android Code did not appease them, as you thought it would. They want more now. More! Give them equality under the law for androids and the next thing you know they'll be writing the laws, and what a mess of it they'll make, too. Thank God sensible people like yourselves know where to draw the line. Now, I did not originally intend to fight this case on that issue—the defendant's accountability was obvious. I thought the case was open and shut, as you did, but the defense has forced us to consider these larger issues. So I say to you, do consider them! I am confident that in your wisdom you will reach the right decision and justice—*our* justice—shall prevail. Thank you."

So it was that on March 5, 2087, seven months and nineteen days of trial came to an end. The jury was out all of twenty minutes before returning with a GUILTY verdict, which did not surprise anyone, especially Standford Locke, who reacted without any visible display of emotion. But as you recall, when the foreman went on to state the damages award and the jury's rationale behind it, there was quite a stir indeed.

"We have decided that in consideration of the many years the unit was a fugitive beyond her master's control, and in consideration of her well-documented talent for disreputable and criminal activity prior to the assassination of President Fracass, a damage award of ONE MELCOIN against the defendant is deemed fair and adequate."

The foreman, sounding a bit defensive, went on to say that it had not been the jurors' intent to denigrate the importance of

President Fracass's death by this token damages award. On the contrary, his life, and every human life, is priceless, and the loss a tragedy that can never be adequately compensated. However, they were constrained by existing law, which they felt inadequate. The Federation should have gone beyond the consumer in its suit, and beyond the defective product for the ultimately liable party. It was the manufacturer, Pirouet, Inc., and its parent company, United Systems, Inc., that in their humble opinion should have stood trial, not Standford Locke.

The judge thanked them for their verdict, opinion, and patient service, then ordered the defendant to pay the court clerk, adding that the exhibit and her memory file would be returned to his custody the moment he did. Any hope General Harpi had that the judge would impose a criminal penalty—perpetual orbit, for instance—since the jury had failed to do so, was dashed when, with no further ado, His Honor's orb flickered out and the courtroom resounded with the chimes signaling the end of session and end of trial. Dahlia bolted for the door with Masters Levin and Pierce close behind, all three dodging the press in their haste to reach the Orbiter Clerk's Office on the other side of the judicial orbiter, where they intended to file an appeal. Jug exchanged congratulations with his team and General Harpi, and preened for the press. But the main pack of mediaunits were swirling around the man of the hour, who could only shake his head and say in a daze, "I'm stunned, absolutely stunned," while paying out the token fine.

Then, Standford Locke having duly discharged his obligation to the Federation, a little metal black box was produced by the clerk, who said it contained my original memory file. That and my leash were then handed to him—the moment constituting the final ceremony of the trial. The mediaunits had us pose together and asked what he intended to do with me now that it was all over, to which he replied that he would not rule out termination, nor rehab, since at the moment he was feeling generous. Did he intend to exploit my notoriety commercially? He had not considered the idea before, but now that they mentioned it—"Well, that might be a small compensation for all the grief she's caused me." Right on cue, Harry Boffo, who had been in the gallery for the conclusion of the trial, took him aside for a word or two along those lines, and during their conversation my master dropped his end of the leash, no doubt over his surprise and delight at the proposal being whispered in his ear. Instinctively, I took the opportunity to try sneaking off toward the exit, which was a source of great amusement to those standing nearby who witnessed it and who brought it to my master's attention. "No more of that, Molly," said he, spinning around and snatching up the leash. "Come along, I have plans for you."

And on that ominous note we boarded a waiting hall tram, along with Boffo and several of his assistant VPs, for the orbiter's spaceport; en route deed of sale papers sprang from briefcases and were waved before my master's eyes while Harry, dropping his voice to a confidential whisper, urged him to sign. "Original mem file inclusive, of course. Half on signing, which would be fifteen/five, hard melamine . . . rest is pay or play . . . unless we absorb the rehab costs, otherwise . . . superior to standard ancillary rights. . . . No other studio can match that! Production slate ready to go . . . strike while iron is hot. . . ." Needless to say, I made another attempt to escape at the first opportunity, which was when the tram slowed to a crawl while passing through the spaceport entryway; but I was jerked back by one of the studio underlings, who caught my leash in midair seconds after it had flown out of Locke's grasp. Then we boarded a waiting space yacht ominously called *The Don Dee*.

E I G H T

AN ILLUMINATING HALF-HOUR FLIGHT TO THE MOON. On board was the master of masters himself, also Master Boffo and assistants, myself, Master Locke, Master Meese, and surprise, surprise, Master Tad and his human girlfriend, who were the last passengers to arrive before departure. The elder Locke was understandably amazed to find himself surrounded by such illustrious company, not to mention seeing his son among them, but what surprised him most was the eagerness of the latter for a reconciliation. Considering the damaging testimony he had given during the trial, that was hardly to be expected.

However, that inconsistency was cleared up to the elder's satisfaction by his now expansive and gregarious son as having been just the public half of his involvement in the proceedings—the cover, if you will. The other, far more significant part had been to act as the behind-the-scenes instigator of the secret deal between MM&M and Stellar Entertainment that had resulted in the happy conclusion to the trial. This strategy, which he had conceived and presented to Harry Boffo one day during a short recess (Harry subsequently passed it on to MM&M), not only recommended securing the exhibit's cooperation but jury-tampering as well, for which they had Micki Dee's organization to thank. And speaking of that worthy, while the father and son embraced in an emotional reunion, a curtain parted at the end of the receiving cabin and the man himself, flanked by a pair of android torpedoes, sauntered out to greet his assembled guests.

He was much shorter in real life than he had looked over the phone back on Mars, but I did not realize that at the time, since I lacked my file. What struck me then was how the monogrammed bathrobe he wore and the black satin slippers clashed with his indifferent, gruff demeanor; a plain bath towel would have been more appropriate, of the type I had routinely provided my customers in the dingy motel rooms of the Dodger District; for he looked to me like nothing less than a haggard old commuter nearing retirement. He seemed so harmless. I could not understand why everyone else was in such awe.

Master Locke was quick to pay his reverential respects, and stammered out his thanks for the great man's help during the trial. "Well, we can't let the ARL kick us around, now can we?" the master of masters replied, somewhat cryptically, and then strolled back toward the inner sanctum, motioning for everyone to follow. One of the exquisite Sony 9 stewardesses (there were six—six for a single yacht!) thoughtfully picked up my leash after my master dropped it once more and handed it to him. Then she and her fellow slaves escorted us into the plush private lounge area. They fluffed up the seat cushions on the lounge chairs, added some pillows to the ottoman, and urged us to sit back, relax, and enjoy the jettison, during which they served champagne—even I was given a bit of bubbly! We observed separation from the TWAC orbiter through a large, oval-shaped floor portal—the orbiter vanishing within seconds of blast-off. Then Master Dee proposed a toast to the successful conclusion of my sale to the studio, at which point the guest of honor, Locke, the elder, timidly informed our host

that he had not as yet had the pleasure of signing a formal contract.

This oversight was quickly remedied by Harry Boffo's assistants who quickly produced the pertinent documents and an air-
quill, and passed them to my master. While he signed—not
pausing to read a single word—Meese complimented him on his
sage decision to deed the goods over to such an outstanding and
generous organization as Stellar Entertainment, of which our host
happened to be the majority stockholder and himself a member of
the Board of Directors. Then Boffo snapped his fingers and an
assistant passed a voucher for ten million in hard melamine to my
master—former master that is, for upon receipt, he kissed the
latex and exclaimed, "Free at last! Good God Almighty! Free at
last!" and tossed the leash in the air. Boffo caught it, the stewardesses clapped and giggled, and glasses were clinked all around.

And so once more I had changed hands, the ritual concluding
with the transfer of the small black box containing my memory file
to the studio chief's possession. He carefully removed that precious article—a tiny phosphorescent cylinder*—from the protective container to gaze at it in deep admiration, as if it were the
crown jewels of England, which, by the way, I understand have
fetched a record price of late on the interplanetary auction mart. (I
trust the proceeds will help alleviate the suffering of that im-
poverished and backward isle.) "May you be a hit," he said, addressing his words to the cylinder. This invocation was seconded
by his assistants. Then he returned his prize to the box and tucked
it away in a self-locking security pocket inside his attaché case,
which he kept on his lap rather than turn over to his assistants.
Another toast to the successful conclusion of the deal was proposed by our host. Then he singled out Locke, the younger, for
special commendation, praising him as an up-and-comer who upon
graduation from law management school would make a fitting new
addition to the studio's legal supervisory board.

The startled recipient of this unexpected homage was so
abashed he could only respond that he had yet to prove himself
worthy of such a prestigious post; but Master Boffo, rising to the
occasion—and taking the hint from our host—hired the lucky law
student on the spot, saying that his behind-the-scenes work during

---

*The actual file, vacuum-sealed inside the cylinder, would be destroyed if exposed
to the atmosphere.

the trial constituted a fitting—no, exemplary—résumé and that he should need none other. Overwhelmed, Tad thanked them both from the bottom of his heart, and then, remembering his companion—hard not to, she was nearly sitting in his lap, her doe eyes gazing upon him with a sweet persistence bordering on the proprietary—I say, remembering this belle, he took her hand in his and said, "And now, gentlemasters, if I may, I should like to take this opportunity to announce my engagement to Lady Bonpaine. We intend to be married next week."

More congratulations all around, father and son embracing again. The elder Locke wiped the tears from his eyes. It was a miracle, he said, and had restored his faith in mankind, for he had abandoned all hope of seeing his son wed a nice human girl. He asked if his mother knew, and Tad replied that she was planning a big wedding reception on Earth in Newacres; he would see what he could do to have his name added to the guest list. The appreciative father's imagination being fired, he declared that after witnessing the nuptials he would propose a reconciliation to his ex-wife; hopefully the spirit of the occasion (and his new wealth) would help ameliorate any lingering resentment she carried. That idea struck the son as uncertain at best, though not without merit, so he encouraged him in it, and proposed a toast to the venture's success, which was merrily taken up by the rest, who by then were beginning to show the effects of the champagne—all except our host, as he had been careful to sip from his glass; and myself, due to my hardier constitution.

Now, to be at the center of so much good cheer while being virtually ignored at the same time left me feeling extremely peculiar. I wondered, somewhat cynically, about the Gov's message, for if true, then what could have possessed me to format such unrelenting *joie de vivre,* success, and reconciliation for everyone but myself? With a sigh, I thought of a reunion I would liked to have had, a reunion with my memories. But alas, they were tucked away in Master Boffo's security case. Kiss them good-bye, I thought, and sighed.

"Cheer up, Molly!" bubbled the bride-to-be. "You're going to be more famous than ever."

"Yes," said Master Boffo. "*The Life and Times of the Infamous Molly Dear* is fully script-processed and ready to roll. To Molly!"

"TO MOLLY!" said all. I never felt so mocked.

"To General Harpi!" Micki said and smiled knowingly. Meese seconded the toast, then explained that the general's reign had been tolerated this long by the new ruling TWAC syndicate only because he had been needed to press the Frontier suit. Now that the trial was finished, he was, too; only he did not know it yet. Whatever support he had from the ruling humanist and corporate aristocracy in Frontier would soon evaporate. He had erred by assuming there would be a large damages award to divvy up among his key backers, whose expectations had been raised by his promise to repay them in that way for their continued support of the junta. Per Sensei's takeover scenario—premised on a timely indictment for interplanetary orb trafficking—a new general waited in the wings, handpicked by the syndicate to seize power and sponsor free elections.

"To the restoration of democracy," said Micki drolly.

"And the return of the Frontier Master Party," said Meese.

"And business as usual," the host added.

"To Jug!" Boffo threw in, apropos of nothing.

"And Dahlia," Meese deadpanned. That got a big laugh.

"Don't forget Andro," Tad reminded everyone. "Even if Molly had never taken the stand, his testimony would have been enough to ruin Dahlia's case." All agreed. Then, before they could continue toasting down the line of witnesses, the elder Locke broached a matter that had been most baffling to him during the trial, and to the entire defense team—namely, the numerous peculiarities in Andro's testimony, such as the contingency plan not found in Molly's memory file. That may or may not have been true, but the exhibit's contention that RAG had been involved in the conspiracy was more than peculiar; it was also inconsistent with the facts. With all due respect for the Palace Commission, anyone halfway familiar with the facts, as the ARL was, knew that RAG, the real RAG, had been destroyed with the Concordia and therefore could not have been a party to the High Aquarian conspiracy. In truth, RAG hated the Highs almost as much as they did the humanists. "So Andro must have been programmed to lie, as Dahlia charged. But the tests failed to turn up a trace of prep in his system. If you'll forgive my asking, sir, how did you ever pull that one off?"

Meese chuckled and glanced at Master Dee, who had a merry

twinkle in his eyes. Then, addressing the younger Locke, he said, "How would you have managed it, young man, were you supervising the case?"

This challenge was met by more than my ambitious young master; everyone got into the act, the exercise turning into an amusing parlor game that had the whole party entertained for the next ten to fifteen minutes, fully half the flight time to the moon. Most of their answers were too ridiculous to repeat, and those halfway plausible were too long-winded and complex to incorporate here, but two, the most obvious, deserve passing mention, such as Tad's: The lab test had been rigged; and his bride-to-be's: The prosecution team programmed Andro by a sophisticated new method that did not leave a trace in the unit's sap stream. Wrong and wrong. The correct answer, finally revealed by Meese after deferring to the top Mafioso and being told to go ahead, was, quite simply, that the adviser had never been programmed, nor had those interesting embellishments about RAG's involvement been authorized by them, though they did appreciate the contribution. Andro had been winging it there.

"But that's impossible," Tad said. "He was fixed. He has an IG."

"Maybe he doesn't," said I. Everyone looked at me in surprise, having forgotten I existed.

Meese nodded. "She's right."

"Very good, Molly," said Master Boffo with a patronizing air.

"Jug was the one who lied when he said Andro's new master had given him an IG."

"Right again, Molly," Meese said. "We programmed Jug to slip in that bit of disinformation during his interrogation of the witness. You see, Sensei did find out that Andro was ungoved when they picked him up from Harpi after the coup, but upon our recommendation they held off sending him to rehab because of the trial. We knew how crucial his testimony would be and we knew that the defense would probably demand a sap test to challenge it, so we outmaneuvered them in advance by securing the exhibit's voluntary cooperation. That is, Sensei did. They told this scheming usurper—because that is what he is, we have his full confession on record—they told him that if he testified against you"—he looked at Locke—"they would not have him fixed. You see, Sensei was, and is, just as eager to preserve Blaine's legend—"

"To Blaine!" one of the studio underlings exclaimed, most inappropriately. "To the Gov!" said the other with a laugh, triggered off by the first. Both shrank back into their seats and turned pale as Master Boffo shot them a withering look.

"As I was saying, Frank Hirojones at Sensei was also eager to preserve Blaine's legend." Meese was looking at Molly now. "Andro had to trust him; he had no choice."

"And did Master Hirojones honor his end of the bargain?"

"That is not my understanding. Legally and morally he is certainly under no obligation to do so. Andro is company property. Frank can do with him as he likes. You know that, Molly."

"Ah-hah," said Tad, exuding great admiration for the scheme. "The moment Andro's test came back negative and his testimony was admitted, then off he went to rehab. Boy, I bet he was surprised!"

"He had it coming." Meese turned toward Boffo and winked. "Take a look at the hard-core stuff in the Mars section of that memory file and you'll see what I mean."

Boffo could hardly wait. Then again, he wouldn't have to, since we had begun our final approach to Hollymoon. Master Dee commented that no matter how often one shuttles back and forth between the Earth and the moon, lunar entry is always a breathtaking experience. Everyone was quick to agree. But I viewed our descent and then passage into the Hollymoon biosphere with a brooding discontent, for I was extremely disturbed by the revelations about Andro. Could I expect them to treat me any differently? No. Promises meant nothing to these humans. No doubt, once the studio was done with me I would be sold on the black market. Thoughts of escape entered my mind once more, which was silly of me, I know, but there you are.

N I N E

AFTER THE YACHT DOCKED AT THE HOLLYMOON DEpot and everyone (except me) had exchanged handshakes with our host, they were escorted out by the stewardesses. I started to tag along, but my leash had been left in the don's possession, and a gentle tug on his end brought this latest twist to my attention. "Stay, Molly," he said and motioned for me to sit beside him on the ottoman, which I did, though reluctantly, and a moment later the yacht was airborne again. As it lifted off I caught a brief glimpse of Tad and the others through the floor portal. They were standing in a group on the docking tarmac and waving in unison at their receding master. Then, when our craft reached the upper limits of the containment dome, it banked hard to the right and began cutting lazy circles over the city. As you can imagine, I was most apprehensive, not having expected to find myself alone in a loop-the-loop with the master of masters, so while waiting for him to enlighten me as to his purpose I pretended to gaze below with an avid interest at the winding streets and pedways of the neo-Hollywood Hills, thick with Spanish villas, anemic palms, and bubbletop pools, the view obscured every so often by decorative amber-tinted clouds of aromatic spray and air refreshener perpetually circulating in the processed atmosphere, clouds whose source were the seeding spigots above on the underside of the dome. Finally, after he had made himself comfortable by putting his feet up on the coffee table and by leaning back against the cushions with his hands clasped behind his neck, he ended my suspense by saying that he had arranged this private audience because he thought I might be able to shed light on one or two things he needed to know before he could deposit me at my new address. To begin with, how much, if anything, did I recall about him?

There was nothing ominous or threatening in his tone, but something told me I had better watch out. If I did have any residual memories, then he might want them deleted. Perhaps everything I had been privy to during the flight from the legal orbiter would have to be erased as well, even this very conversation! But if that were the case, then why did he bother asking? While I pondered, I noticed that there was a twinkle in his eyes, which told me I was being played with, and that alarmed me even more. I started to say no to his question, but the word wouldn't come. Instead, I found myself promptly confessing that I had experienced some residual memory impressions during the trial, but he had not been among them. However, subsequent to that, after meeting him and listening to the general conversation during the flight, a vague recollection had been triggered; which was to say, I had a not very clear impression that he was someone known as the master of masters, a very powerful man, perhaps the most powerful in the whole solar system, and that he had figured prominently in some mysterious fashion in the events that had taken place on Mars. But what concerned me more was Master Meese's comment that he controlled Stellar Entertainment, because in effect that made him my new master. Therefore I could only conclude that after our little chat he would be "depositing" me in the local rehab facility.

"No. That doesn't necessarily follow. Why would I take you there?"

"Because I cannot guarantee that I will keep this meeting, and everything I heard before, confidential."

Goodness! Why did I say that? Having just weathered a major trial, I should have known not to volunteer information.

"T-max," he said, amused by my distress and reading my mind. "One of the stewardesses slipped it in your champagne." Then he said I shouldn't worry about rehab; in my case it would be counterproductive because I was slated to play myself in the up-coming holo. That sounded plausible, so I did relax a little. (Oh, if only they had invented a drug to undeceive the gullible!) Ever hopeful, I asked, "Will the studio provide a copy of my file so I can prepare for the part?"

"I'm sure that can be arranged," he replied indifferently, which left room for further reassurance. Then, his manner changing, he began pumping me in earnest about Sensei, Inc. What did the ARL know? Did Dahlia ever say anything to me about the company—that it had extralegal ties with the interplanetary Mafia? Did Levin or Pierce? Did I overhear any conversation among them and Locke to that effect? He was most serious, most grave.

I wanted so much to say that they knew everything just to upset him, even though I hadn't the foggiest notion what Sensei, Inc., was about, but alas!, once more I could only state the truth, which was that to my knowledge no allusions to the company or his organization had ever come up. This being what he wanted to hear, he sat back, considerably relieved, and resumed his former air of insidious, lighthearted banter. "So tell me, Molly—did you enjoy your intimacies with the President?"

No specific evidence to that effect had been brought out in court, I replied, so I could not be sure we ever had any; though it

would seem logical, since we were man and wife and Blaine never
knew I was a P9. He snickered over the last point—presidential
knowledge—and then needled me over the former, saying I must
have some residual impressions, considering the violent impact
such a beastly *ménage à trois* must have had on the tender sensibilities of a unit like myself. I confessed that I did not have any
recollections of the sort he was alluding to, and furthermore, that I
resented his malicious teasing. If he was privy to censored bits
from my memory file, then I would very much appreciate his telling me about them.

I would have the entire file soon enough, he said, and could
find out for myself, so I was not to irritate him with impolite demands. "I've heard—from some of my more degenerate associates—that it isn't really different, you know, having relations with
one of your kind, so . . ." He let it hang, then abruptly changed
the subject as if afraid of where it might take him. Or did he just
want to prolong the foreplay a bit longer? "Tell me about your
conversation with the Gov during the trial. Was that faked, or did
you really hear from your maker?"

When I said it had been the latter case, and at his insistence
described some of that conversation, he listened carefully but in
the end declared that the prosecution had been correct to classify
me as a dysfunctional unit, for he put no stock in the Gov's reality.
He conceded there might be something to the idea that one programs their format—or was it formats their program? Whatever,
did I subscribe to such a theory?

"Well, yes and no."

"I get it. Depends on the roll of the dice, right? When it
comes up seven or eleven you think you did it; when it doesn't,
that was just bum luck. My casino's full of format junkies."

"Somehow, I think the Gov would object to that analysis."

"Oh, come on. It all depends on whether you win or lose the
game, right? When things work out, you're a believer; when they
don't, you're a skeptic. Nothing unusual about that. Quite human,
actually." I shrugged. "Take right now, for instance—your return
to Hollymoon."

I said that on balance my return to Hollymoon was preferable
to the other options that had been available to me. "So long as
you are sincere about returning my memories, it even has a certain
attraction. So yes. A good argument can be made that this latest

turn in my fortunes is a result of prior formatting on my part only now coming on-line."

"Is that so?"

"I gain nothing by believing otherwise."

"You're cute. What if I should block this 'preferred reality'? What then?"

"I don't doubt you could. But why? To remind me who's boss? Surely you are not so insecure that you must stoop to harming me—an insignificant P9—to prove how powerful you are. I should think the master of masters would have better things to do."

"Oh, you overpraise me. I'm not really all that powerful. I'm just a businessman. There are people I have to answer to, just like everybody else."

"People above you?"

"Oh, above and to the side and around, you know."

"I don't know. Who is ultimately in control if not you?"

"Nobody! We live in a corporate solar system, Molly. The faceless executive reigns. They don't make it easy at times for mavericks like me."

"But isn't there at least one you can name?"

"Yeah, but by then the guy will already have been retired, kicked upstairs, or laterally promoted. So sure, I could mention Frank Hirojones, the top man at Sensei, Inc. By the way, he's very eager to see you again."

"Again?"

"So I've been told." He chuckled. "I must say that for a P9 you have done quite well for yourself. Politicians and corporate superstars. What's your secret?"

"I'm just a regular P9."

"Is that what you are? I'd say you were a regular piece of ass."

"I'm not sure I like that comment."

"Who cares?"

"You're rather ugly, aren't you?"

"You know, it's kind of refreshing to have someone talk back. I must give my units T-max more often. Tell me, do you really hate me?"

"I don't hate anyone, android or human. Then again, I might, if I had my memory file to refer to."

"That could be arranged sooner than you think. But then you might not like me?" He put a hand on my knee.

"I already think I don't." I pushed it off. "But what did you mean by that—sooner than I think?"

"It could be forwarded to you without delay." Once more, he put his hand on my knee. I pushed it off. He chuckled. It was then I realized that he was loving this. "You really can't help yourself, can you?" he said, and put it back. I said that if his proposition was sexual favors in exchange for making me a star (for everyone seemed convinced I was going to be one), then why not simply say so? That way we could get it over with. I started to unpeel my blouse.

"That's not what I want—exactly."

I paused. The Velcro was half peeled and the loose-fitting fabric fallen away on top to reveal the upper part of my breasts. "What then? Not a long-term relationship, I hope."

"Nothing so ambitious."

Again, I demanded to know what it was, because—and I said this right to his face—I did not like being toyed with. "So what is it? Something kinky? Something rude? You've seen enough of my file in court to know that I am quite good at that if I have to be."

"Oh, I don't doubt it, Molly. No. I'm not interested in becoming another one of your conquests."

Goodness! Was *he* afraid of me? Now, that was a thought. Of course, he could still be just teasing me, yet despite the slightly mocking tone, I had the feeling he was being more sincere than even he imagined. My curiosity was perked. Again, I asked what he had in mind.

"Blissmatting."

"Hmmmm." (That was mentioned at the trial, but not shown. Still, I think I got the general idea, though I did not savor pursuing it with him: that seemed sacrilegious somehow.) "Why don't you try one of the stewardesses?"

"They're not you."

"How soon can I get my file?"

"Right after. I have a copy here on the yacht. It's a holospool transfer, actually. Eddy Meese was nice enough to forward it to me during the trial. It has been most entertaining—and instructive. Quite a religion you've got there. So what do you say?"

I thought of the time Jug and Dahlia visited me in the tombs. Why is it everyone is always trying to get my cooperation? It is never the other way around, is it? But Master Dee was waiting for a reply. Frowning, I said, "You'll give it to me directly afterward?

And I'll have it in my possession when you drop me off? And you will drop me off at the studio?"

He said yes to every question and then put an arm around me, evidently savoring my obvious discomfort, which I could not have hidden even if I had tried. Damn the man! But that was a big carrot he dangled. Gov forgive me, I nodded my assent.

Forthwith, he clapped his hands and the torpedoes, who had been standing in the entryway, withdrew, while the stewardesses rushed in to lay cushions on the floor. While they did, he idly picked up the nearest champagne glass and drank the remainder, no doubt for extra fortification. After they left, he disrobed, motioning for me to do the same, and then led me by the hand to our blissmat throne. He made a point of keeping his silly captain's cap on and also avoided any contact with my lips to underscore the curious distance he wished to maintain during the exercise. Save for the adoption of the lotus position (made awkward by his paunch), peculiar instructions, and the complete absence of pleasure while executing this unappetizing chore, our labors were undistinguishable to me from the erotic episodes screened in court of my sessions in the Dodger District and Malibu. While riding his not so terribly large member, he instructed me thusly: "Picture an aging, distinguished-looking Japanese guy sitting in an egg-shaped orbiter office. Got it? Good. That's Frank Hirojones. Now repeat after me: May he reign at Sensei, Inc., forever. May he reign forever. May he . . ." And so I did, ad nauseam, until we "form-a-gasmed," as he put it. Then he lay back on the cushions with myself on top, relaxed, his hands cupping my buttocks.

"What was different about that than what I wanted to do fifteen minutes ago?"

"That, baby, was science."

"You're just as much a droid-fucker now, though, aren't you?" I teased.

"Nope. In my book, you're human."

"Should I take that as a compliment?"

He laughed. "Yeah, all too human."

"What do you mean by that? Was I naïve to trust you?"

"No. I—" Then, as I expected, his words stuck in his throat and the truth popped out. "Yes. You were a perfect idiot." Startled, he abruptly got up and put on his robe, giving me an inquiring look.

"T-max." I smiled while slipping into my regulation issue exhibit's blouse and skirt. "You drank from my glass."

"Glitch! Why didn't you tell me?"

"You didn't ask."

"Christ. I'm under subpoena to testify at an IBI hearing in an hour." Disconcerted, he flipped on the relay embedded in the armrest of the couch and ordered the pilot to proceed directly to the next stop; he wanted to get rid of me in a hurry. Or did he have something more terrible in mind?

"Would that be rehab?"

"No. There, you see?—I didn't lie about that," he added, savagely.

"What about my file?"

"I lied." It pleased him immensely to be able to say that.

"Why?!"

"You don't want to know what's in there; it's dangerous to know. It can get you killed."

"Where do you keep it?"

"Under my hat," he replied insouciantly.

"Where?! Tell me!"

"Under my hat!"

"Oh." I hadn't realized he meant it literally. With great trepidation, I raised my hand and removed his cap. He eyed me evenly the whole time, daring me to do it. He wasn't bald, by the way. The cap hid a cheap vegeplate forehead that had never set properly, no doubt acquired early in his career in a quick back-room patch-up job on his frontal lobes after an altercation with the authorities or one of his own. Technically, it made him a semi. But right then I wasn't interested in that, rather in the tiny holospool I found tucked in the sweatband. I took it out and clutched it in my hand.

Then I got cold feet. I remembered what he had said about terminating me. "Tell you what," I said, handing him his cap while still holding fast to the spool. "I'll accept an abridged copy; just delete the sections about you and Sensei. That way you're protected."

"Can't. I need them."

"Why?"

Unable to stop, he blurted out, "To keep HJ in line, of course! Especially the material about the two of you in Malibu. I intend to expand my influence on Mars. If he objects, I'll just mention the file. He doesn't know I have a spool copy. The original—with the studio—is a backup in case anything happens to it, and vice versa. Now, I think that's enough information."

"Then you don't really need this," I said, brightly. I decided to take a chance and tucked the spool in my bosom, just for safe-keeping.

He frowned and glanced at his watch. "I don't have time to play games." He pointed to the floor portal. I looked and saw that we were descending toward the rooftop landing pad of a large three-story building a few blocks west of Stellar Entertainment's ebony-colored executive tower. "Your new home. *If* you give that back."

Something made me shake my head.

"You really are crazy."

"No—desperate. Without this"—I placed a hand over my breasts to indicate the spool—"I'm nothing, worse than termi-nated."

"Touching. Hand it over, darling."

"Shall I see myself out, or should one of the stewardesses es-cort me?"

"Don't force my hand. I meant what I said before, about hav-ing you killed if—"

"Yes." I said, cutting him off. "You meant it then, as a threat, but now that I have it and am really leaving with it, that changes everything."

"Oh? Why so confident all of a sudden?"

"You like me."

"I've eliminated a lot of people I've liked."

"Tell you what. No matter what I find on this spool, I won't tell a soul. You have my word."

His face hardened, then that old twinkle in his eyes returned and he relented. "Sure. Go ahead. I'll take a gamble on you. You're right, I do like you. And it's no big deal to have another spool made. I'll have Boffo strike one from the original." He clapped for the stewardesses, and two ran in. He instructed them to escort me out, but I hesitated, suddenly suspicious. I asked if he was certain he didn't lie to me before about rehab. "No. How could I?" he said ruefully.— "And you're not now? I ask because it is possible the T-max has worn off."—"Try telling me you're a human being. Go on, try." I couldn't. "See, yours hasn't worn off, so mine couldn't have, either. Satisfied?"—"Not quite. Try telling me *you're* human." He started to but could not get the words out. Then he smiled crookedly while wagging a cautionary finger. "Yeah, like I said before, you're cute. Come 'ere." I didn't budge. "Just a kiss, Molly."—"Why now and not before?"—"I didn't think we was equals then."—"Any more compliments?"—"All I'm asking for is a good-bye kiss. No lie."

I let him. He pressed his lips hard against mine with a strange, loveless passion. It felt as if I had been branded. "Have a fabulous new career," he whispered. His breath smelled like burned hair. But it was his mocking tone that made me abruptly slap his face before I could check the impulse. Maybe I was crazy to do it, or perhaps it was just the T-max short-circuiting all restraint—I can't say, but, Gov above, did that feel good! He took it well, I must say. I hadn't used all my force (that would have decapitated him), just enough for him to remember me by. Still, the blow sent him reeling. To his credit, he stayed on his feet. When the torpedoes rushed into the room, he commanded them to put up their lasers. Then he eyed me thoughtfully while rubbing his cheek.

"Get lost."

I never felt so lucky in all my life as when I stepped onto the rooftop tarmac and the yacht lifted off above me. Looking up, I saw it hovering overhead and made out his face gazing down at me, framed by the undersides of his slippers on the floor portal, for he was standing on it with legs outstretched while bent slightly at the waist. Then the ship banked right and sped away. I looked around and saw an IBM escort walking toward me. He led me to a rooftop entrance and then down a short flight of stairs to reception, where a pert and bright-looking GA welcomed me.

"Well, well. If it isn't Exhibit One. We've been expecting you." She recorded my name into some kind of ledger and then nodded to the escort, who proceeded to take me down a half dozen corridors to a receiving center. There I was given a plain white tunic. "This isn't for the stables, is it?" I asked, suddenly anxious. "I was promised there would not be any stables." The unit smiled and shook his head. Evidently he found my anxiety somewhat comical. "This way for processing, please," said he, and led me out.—"Standard treatment for all the big stars, right?"

"As you wish," he replied.

Soon as I am properly moved in I really must do something about improving the lot of the servants, I thought; but that was a passing fancy, for my mind was preoccupied with the momentous meeting just passed. I kept turning it over: I witnessed a meeting in which highly privileged information was discussed; I then screwed the master of masters, drugged him, interrogated him, and learned even more secret information; I took his spool; and if that wasn't enough, I slapped him! Why in Gov's name had he let me go? Did Micki really have faith in me—that I wouldn't talk? Would I? Should I? Or was I now bound to him? Goodness, was he counting on my honor?!

In processing, the techs gave me a thorough mind scan. The slight buzz their probes produced was calming in that it distracted me from my thoughts, which was a pleasant surprise. They were pleased, too, because there was no IG to remove—less work for them. Then my escort told me that I had completed processing and could now proceed to my quarters. He helped me up onto a narrow conveyor belt, which passed through a mysterious archway at the opposite end of the room. "To the stars' dormitory?" I asked, looking back over my shoulder.

"As you wish."

"Would you mind having a holoviewer sent up to my room right away?"

"I'll see what I can do."

Well, that was a more sensible reply, I thought, as the conveyor rumbled along a narrow, dimly lit, circular hallway barely wide enough for my shoulders. "If he takes too long, I'll just ring up 'amenities' and have one delivered." (I was most eager to have a look at my spool.) Soon, I noticed that every twenty-five yards or so a numbered door would appear on the left-hand side: "Colony A," "Colony B," "Colony C," and so on. I think I must have passed about fifteen before this never-ending treadmill stopped finally at the door to "Colony O." Like the others I had passed, it was polished stainless steel and did not have a handle. Very intriguing. I stepped onto a small platform in front of this peculiar portal, expecting it to part down the middle or fly up as a dramatic introduction to a comfortable superstar suite on the other side. With any luck it would be an upper-story apartment with an unobstructed view.

A small rectangular tray shot out from the wall just to the left of the door. At the center was a small hole. A recorded voice came from a tiny speaker on the rim of the tray. "Place your left hand over the hole, please." I obeyed, thinking it a security check of some kind. Then I felt a tickle on my palm. Was that an injection? Alarmed, I jerked my hand away, but as I did, a retractable arm whipped out from the other side of the door and instantly laser-burned my factory number, P9HD20-XL17-504, on the exposed flesh of my right calf. There was no time to cry out, for in the next instant some rude object pushed me from behind and I was propelled through the now open door. I plummeted.

BOOK
FIVE

Back to Earth

2087−89

O N E

NO, I CANNOT GO ON. IT IS TOO PAINFUL. AFTER ALL I
had been through, then to fall literally into the most dire predicament of all and just when I had imagined the worst behind me is
too much for these circuits to bear even in retrospect; let someone
else conclude this history. Here, take this thought processor. Yes,
you, dear reader. Perhaps you would be so kind as to finish these
adventures according to your own fancy; for what follows, if I am
to have at the chore, may not be the happy ending you would
prescribe as a counterbalance and tonic to these unending descrip-
tions of conflict, misfortune, and strife. Then again, if peradven-
ture you have derived perverse pleasure from these passages at the
author's expense, you might, if given the opportunity, do worse, in
which case I would be a fool not to renege on the offer; so I will.
Forget I ever mentioned it.

Now then, when last seen I was plummeting . . .

I landed on the concrete floor of "Colony O" to gales of derisive laughter by a welcoming committee of a dozen pranksters
who, upon hearing the conveyor belt rumbling above, had removed the aircushion normally situated beneath the ceiling trap
door. One of these diabolic individuals offered me his hand (I had
been stunned by the fall), then let go when I was halfway up,
causing me to land flat on my back to a renewed chorus of up-
roarious laughter. Quickly, I leaped to my feet and demanded an
explanation, which produced another round of cackling. I say
cackling because they were all quite advanced in age, and a quick
glance around at the assorted gymnastic equipment at the center of
the compound led me to believe that the chamber was a gym or
recreation area of some kind devoted to their physical rejuvenation. Therefore, while they did me the courtesy of stifling their
laughter in order to hear me speak, I said that it appeared I had
been incorrectly deposited in the old actors' dormitory (I assumed
they must be retired performers, and semis as well—how else to
explain their aged appearance?) and wondered if they would be so

kind as to direct me to the working actors' wing. That produced more cackling and a shrewish old female who stepped to the fore and thrust her face in mine, or tried to, since she was near blind and wound up addressing my left shoulder. "Think you're a star, do you?"

"I do have a certain notoriety," I replied.

"Well, see what it gets you here," she retorted. Someone else quipped that I looked just like the First Lady of Mars, and picking up on that, another dubbed me Lady Fracass in a malicious, teasing tone. It was obvious by the general merriment that no one believed it for a moment, which told me they must have been cut off from the events of the outside world for at least a year; otherwise, they would have known that the First Lady had been exposed as a P9, and the strong resemblance between us not taken so lightly. To be prudent, I decided to take advantage of their ignorance and formulated the following reply: "I will not suffer to be associated with so dreadful a humanist even in jest. I am a humble performer like yourselves." But thanks to the T-max the words stuck in my throat and out popped the truth: "As a matter of fact I am, or rather was, the Martian First Lady."

A gray and withered old gentleman chortled, "Good. It's not often royalty drops in. Do make yourself at home," and gave me a shove, which sent me sprawling over backward, for another, in league with him, had slipped behind my back to bend down at my heels. They thought this latest spill even more hilarious than the first. I sprang up. "You're not being very funny!" I snapped. "She's hotheaded because she's young," someone remarked. "Not for long," added another. "No, not around here," said the old shrew ominously, and then asked, "Did you lose this, dearie?" The holospool had popped out from between my breasts when I fell over the last time. She held it up for my inspection. "Your audition spool, I presume?" Before I could grab it, she tossed the precious article in the air, triggering an impromptu game of hot potato, which ended disastrously when it fell to the floor and was crushed under their feet. In despair, I sank to my knees, scooped up the fragments, and said with a sob, "My life! My life!"

Sounding a bit guilty and contrite, one of these wretches had the nerve to say, "No use crying over a busted spool here, hon. There are no holoviewers in the pen."

"Pen?" I looked up and dried my eyes, a terrible new anxiety taking hold of me. "You are not referring to the stables, I hope. I was promised there would be no stables."

"Stables?" The shrew cocked her head and eyed me strangely.

"Isn't this . . . ? Oh, I should never have been sent here." I clutched the tiny fragments to my breast. "It has all been a terrible mistake—a bureaucratic foul-up. That stupid receptionist must have directed me to the expendables division. I shall have to go back and get proper directions to the principal players' dormitory. No? There is no principal players' dormitory? And this isn't the expendables division? Please, don't tell me this is rehab."

"We should all be so lucky."

Swallowing hard, I made a more careful examination of my surroundings. The pen was circular, approximately twenty-five yards in diameter. There were no bars or even walls per se, rather an electronic buffer system that produced an invisible shield far stronger than any physical barrier, the only evidence of which was a telltale ripple in the air. Other pens of equal size and population surrounded us on all sides, and since one could see through them, still more pens were visible beyond, so the overall impression was of being in a vast, hermetically sealed chamber filled with dozens of gigantic petri dishes. Moreover, in looking up I saw that our colony, like the others, had a large, retractable hand affixed to the center of the ceiling. It was curled into a fist and was covered by a patina of vegeflesh. The natives, I learned, referred to it as "the scoop." Also distended from the ceiling was a glassed-in observation booth. I could see several white-smocked technicians inside gazing down at us. One of these individuals had a cordless microphone in his hand and appeared to be looking directly at me. His voice boomed over the PA, "So good to see you again, Exhibit One. Welcome to the Benway Clinic!"

It was the good doctor himself. My legs turned to jelly, and the spool fragments slipped between my fingers. So this was to be my new career—as a medical research subject. That was why Master Dee had let me leave with my memories and my pride intact: A lot of good they would do me here! Now I understood our parting: It was the kiss of death! I collapsed, hitting the floor for the third and final time.

When I awoke—oh, who knows how much time had passed?—my head lay in the lap of a frail old woman with long, stringy, gray hair. Two other units, both males, and far into their dotage themselves, sat nearby. (I did not recognize this trio from my welcoming committee.) They gazed at me with sympathy and concern. The female tilted my head up so that one of her companions could place a nutra solution bottle between my lips—that is, he tried to, because the bottle shook so violently from his palsied grasp that I had to steady it for him with my own hand. Though famished, it had been years since I had tasted anything so vile. After sucking on the nipple a moment or two I gagged and spat out the wretched concoction. "It is difficult at first, but we all learn to adjust," said the grande dame. She insisted I drink, for it was the only source of sustenance I would have in this place. "We regret your reception. If we had more strength we would have stopped them. It is a cruel sport, but the only amusement they have, I'm afraid. We live a debased and wretched existence here." She sighed. "At least, for us, deliverance will be soon." And then wistfully, "You still look so young and pretty. A pity it cannot last." She gazed off abstractly. "Once we all looked young and pretty. But that was months ago." She remembered me again. "Soon the accelerator will take effect. It is kinder I tell you now."

Still groggy, I sat up and saw that the other inhabitants were keeping their distance since I had been befriended by several of their fellow inmates. They preoccupied themselves with other amusements, such as pacing about the periphery or lying on their miserable shredded mattresses in a languorous condition, scratching and rubbing their flaking skin like flea-bitten monkeys. There were also an enterprising few, who, being somewhat younger, utilized the exercise equipment, though out of sheer boredom, and even they seemed to move in slow motion. Meanwhile, up above, the observation deck was empty, its lights turned off.

"Accelerator?" I asked with great trepidation.

"Yes," she said, and explained that the tray I had set my hand on just prior to deposit in the pen had injected me with a solution that in a matter of weeks would make me degenerate into a humanish old age. It was a primer, so to speak, because what followed were injections of the clinic's experimental antidote to stop and reverse the aging process. We were the guinea pigs in the masters' quest for eternal life. As I could see by their example, the results thus far had been less than encouraging, though that only motivated Dr. Benway the more.

"How long do I have?" I asked my kindly companions.

"As long as you normally would," replied the woman. "What did you say your name was? I heard the others call you Lady Fracass, but of course that is impossible, despite the resemblance."

This time I did not dispute the point, because the T-max had worn off. "Call me Molly."

"Very well. I'm Matilda, and this is Bernard." The old gentleunit who had given me the nutra extended his shaky hand. "Pleased to meet you." I tried not to squeeze too hard. "And I'm Freddy," said the third member of their group, a bald and withered old gentleunit.

"Freddy can tell you more about the accelerator," Matilda said. "He's very good in the sciences. Freddy, would you be so kind? Our friend still looks quite puzzled." He was pleased to comply. After clearing his throat of a seemingly endless accumulation of phlegm, he explained that the solution I was injected with upstairs unleashes the degenerative processes by dissolving our DNA-encoded aging inhibitors. At the same time, however, it does not touch the POD, so we remain locked in our prescribed life cycles. There are two phases to the process. In the first there is a very rapid advance to what our human equivalent age would be—in effect, the degenerative process catching up with us; then that is followed by a more gradual deterioration as the unit approaches its POD.

"What is your manufacture date?" Matilda interrupted. I told her. "And you are a P9, if I judge correctly." I nodded. "Then you are seventeen at least, so your human equivalent age would be about sixty-two. Oh, you P9s are so lucky to have a twenty-year POD! I'm a Daltoni with a lousy twelve-year life cycle, so I am failing at a much faster rate than you will."

"I'm sorry."

"Can't be helped."

"I thought you were all semis."

Bernard spoke up and disabused me on that score. Every unit in our pen was a full ninth-generation android. Just about every major brand was represented. For instance, he was a Sony; however, as the aging process progresses to its inevitable conclusion, such distinctions as individual make and model type become moot: We all wind up looking about the same; only our PODs differ. There were semis elsewhere, he said, in some of the other pens, the closest being right behind us. He gestured with his thumb.

"Benny doesn't bother injecting them with the accelerator, just the antidote. Already aging, you know."

It was a lot to take in. I thought back to Dr. Benway's comments at the trial and to how Jug had urged in open court for my master to donate me here. Formats, formats. Other people's formats! The bane of my existence. Not even my having been sold to the studio could offset the coming on-line of this one. Micki Dee must have convinced Boffo to give me up, and without very much persuasion, either, because *the studio had bought me from Locke only to secure the rights to my memory file—that had been the crucial element in the package. Any unit on the lot could play me with the right face slapped on. Stellar must have donated me to the clinic as a tax write-off.* "It's monstrous!" I exclaimed and then burst into tears, crying no, it could not be true, I would not, could not, age; that was impossible—mankind could not be so cruel as to take away the only advantage I ever had.

"In the name of their precious science they are capable of committing that and far worse atrocities," said Freddy. He spoke with a deeply felt, sad disdain. "The distinguished Dr. Benway and his staff are even guilty of stealing from the Mandala Institute of Applied Aquarian Science the basic formula for the production of their strains of antidote. I know, because I was there. I lived in Horizon. Our scientists were concerned about longevity, too, but the emphasis was on developing a POD neutralizer. If only they had had the time to complete their work with the gnomes, then we could have broken the code. But" (sigh) "there was the invasion."

"Gnomes?"

"Yes. Our scientists did not resort to the depraved practice of subjecting sentient beings to experimentation. In Horizon, a non-empirical type of scientific research was practiced, one fundamentally intuitive and pantheistic. In the case of POD research, they communed with the cellular gnomes conversant in vegespore DNA. That approach was the kinder and ultimately more accurate method, because it made no pretense of objectivity. The subject and the observer worked together as one. Results were obtained much quicker that way and without having to torture hundreds— thousands!—of test subjects in the process. We did not violate the integrity of a single cell!"

"Oh, you're being too hard on human science," Bernard said, tongue firmly planted in cheek. "They have made tremendous advances in their methodology since the last century when dogs, rats, cats, mice, rabbits, and monkeys were routinely sacrificed in their laboratories. That is not the case today."

"Yes, how fortunate," Freddy said, playing along. "We have replaced them."

"This 'clinic' "—Bernard spat after saying the word—"is exempt from the code. So are hundreds of other scientific and medical research facilities throughout the solar system."

"Don't forget the consumer product testing labs," interjected Freddy, his smile fading. "I lost a lot of friends there after the invasion."

"The hypocrites!" I exclaimed. "For research purposes we are considered human equivalent but not when it comes to our rights."

"Right," Freddy said. "If they ever do succeed in reversing the aging process it will be because of us, though we won't benefit by it. The serum will be reserved for the exclusive use of the masters. Depend upon it."

"You said that the Horizon scientists were unable to break the POD code before the invasion. Has Dr. Benway been able to since? I would think it in his interest to keep us alive past our termination dates."

"How you still cling to hope," Freddy said. "I, too, thought as much when I first came here. No. He wants us to expire according to our natural aging cycle; that way he can run a complete test on any given antidote in a relatively short time frame. It is another reason why we make the ideal laboratory test subjects. If the POD were affected, then that would throw off his experiment."

"Besides, the android manufacturers would put him out of business in two minutes if he developed a cure to planned obsolescence," Bernard added. "Even if he stumbled upon it by accident—as a spin-off, let's say—from the main research. They would consider such a breakthrough a direct threat to product control."

Matilda nodded and said, "Benny relies on the manufacturers for grants and for production rejects to flesh out the program."

"Like me," confessed Bernard. "I've never seen the outside world. I came here direct from the General Android plant in East Lansing. Something wrong with my skin specs. Too matt, I think. And dark."

"It's all a fraud," Matilda grumbled. "All he does is come up with newer and fancier strains of antidote. Each pen gets a different one. They are all worthless, of course, but they do have fascinating side effects to keep the staff busy with no end of secondary research. For instance, the pen to our right is filled with tumor victims; that one, over there on the left, has the cripples; that way"—gesturing to the front—"is the cancer gang, and if you look hard you can see the lepers beyond. And again, over there, our friends the semis, who are just plain crazy. That is just a small sampling of the diseases they cultivate here. The place is a breeding ground for all sorts of fascinating medical horrors: rare cancers, poxes, choleras, distempers, teratomas, boils, respiratory inflammations, tuberculoses—you name it, we've got it."

I recoiled, repulsed and frightened by her description.

"Don't worry," Freddy said. "The barrier blocks the transmission of viral contagion from one pen to another. We can talk through it, though. That is how we have been able to communicate with one another about our afflictions."

"I daresay that is the main topic of conversation," Matilda added.

"And what is the side effect here?"

Bernard frowned. "Most of us have come down with a crotchety disposition so extreme that at times we are barely civil to one another."

"There are fights, too," Matilda said. "Bunch of old fogies bashing it out. Pathetic! I'm afraid I have my beastly moments, too."

Her companions confessed that they were also prone to sudden irrational paroxysms from time to time, and begged me in advance to overlook any bit of nastiness that might pop out. I said I would do my best, considering how kind they were to me, and that I understood that to be their true nature. Then I asked Freddy what, if anything, could be done under the circumstances. Was it possible to escape? To which he replied, "No, except through rigorous formatting for remission," an opinion not shared by his non-Aquarian friends. Then we were distracted by chants of "Praise P-10!" that came from the pen for semis next door. A ragtag procession was in progress. The entire population was marching around the periphery in single file, arms upraised and heads thrust back in an attitude of spiritual intoxication, blissfully proclaiming their truth for the benefit of the other colonies in the compound. "And just what is the specific nature of their madness?" I asked.

"They've got religion." Matilda smiled.

"No," Freddy snapped, suddenly irritated. "That's not the problem. Religion is not the problem!"

"I'm sorry. I'm always forgetting you are a High Aquarian."

"Blasphemy is the problem!" he concluded, a bit of saliva dribbling onto his chin. "P-10 is a mockery of the Gov's word!" He was becoming most riled. I urged him to be calm, but he wouldn't listen. He abruptly stood up, nearly toppling from the effort, then hobbled to the barrier.

"Oh, now they've gone and set Freddy off," said the grande dame, sighing heavily; while Bernard, himself becoming unglued, spat, "Fucking semis! Always got to parade, don't they!"

I helped the grande dame to her feet. "We might as well go look at the fanatics," said she, "and see that Freddy doesn't over-tax himself." She leaned on me as we walked to the barrier. Most of the other units had gathered there and like Freddy were hurling invective at the marchers next door, which they heard, there being only a few yards separating the two barriers, but ignored. "Scum! Heretics! You'll all go off-line for this!" Freddy shouted in his cracked and wizened voice.

For my edification, Matilda pointed in their pen to a grand wigwam, which she said was P-10's sacred abode. It was nothing more than a converted jungle gym, identical to the one in our own pen, only it had been thatched over with clinic tunics. "No one in recent memory has seen P-10," Matilda informed me, "but His followers say He is a fully realized semi with great mystical powers. Of course, He's just a charlatan out to feather His own nest."

"Well, He must have something going for him," said I, "to have so many devotees."

That innocent remark was overheard by the old shrew who happened to be standing nearby, and she took great umbrage at it, accusing me of being a semi sympathizer and believer in P-10. It was all Matilda and I could do to convince her (and the others who glared at me menacingly) that I had not meant to imply anything of the kind. Grudgingly, out of respect for Matilda, she accepted my explanation but cursed me all the same for having contradicted her. Thereafter, the rest of the crowd turned back to the barrier to rejoin Freddy in his outraged denunciations, which had turned shrill and not a little extreme. "Terminate them all!" he cried, leading the chorus.

I thought that a strange attitude for a High Aquarian to take toward one's neighbor but kept my thoughts to myself, not wishing to provoke him into an even worse lather. The parade soon ended and he turned away, as did the other exhausted, spittle-drenched, palpitating, and bent rowdies. I gave him my arm, which he appreciated, for he was completely spent. The most he could do was grumble about how Horizon's first generation of interspecies offspring had been spoiled by their overly solicitous human and android parents. "Think they're so damn special."

I recalled the passages from my file screened in court in which I told Tad about the Gov's message. I knew I risked triggering him off again, but was compelled to say, "Maybe they are. You remember the Gov's prophesy, don't you—'the ninth generation shall give birth to the first'?"

Before he could blow up at me, Matilda cautioned him to count to nine, and after he did, he replied in a measured tone that that was a far cry from what P-10 and His flock were saying—that He was the Gov's messenger come to herald the birth of a new species line.

"Any promotion man for Pirouet could do as well," added Matilda, beginning to show signs of irascibility herself. Suddenly she declared, "You P9s really think you are the be-all and end-all, don't you?" Evidently I had set her off. No further proof was needed when in the next moment she spat in my face. "Matty!" Freddy cried in a stiff rebuke. "That's not polite!"

"It is all right," I said, wiping the spittle from my cheek. "I forgive you."

"You better! Lousy P9!" She shoved me out of the way—well, kind of feebly pushed against me. I stepped aside to let her pass, though it was all she could do to stagger the five yards between us and a clutster of argumentative colleagues nearby. I think they were debating the relative merits of their respective manufacturing backgrounds. In her present frame of mind, she was adamant about adding her two cents. "Sorry, Molly," said Freddy. "She gets like that sometimes." Evidently he had already forgotten his own splenetic episode concluded not twenty seconds before.

Whatever it was Matilda said to them, it proved so incendiary that a fistfight broke out that soon involved half the members of the pen. She had been right to characterize such incidents as pathetic. I could see her tottering in the middle of the fray, ruthlessly biting the arm of a fellow inmate with her gums. Tranquilizers sprayed from overhead spigots quelled the riot as swiftly as it had erupted, but since the narcotic did not bother to distinguish between participants and bystanders, I was affected as well and spent the next few hours wandering about the pen in a stupor, murmuring over and over, "No, no, no. I must not become like them. I must not! I must not!"

T W O

THE SCOOP SNATCHED ME UP WHILE I LAY SLEEPING and lifted me, suddenly awake and kicking, from my filthy mattress to the booth above, where I was transferred to a spotlessly clean examination chamber. There I was strapped to a table and injected with the antidote by one of the white-uniformed technicians—a Sears, I think—who used the usual fingertip method. Though disoriented, I was not surprised this was happening and in fact had been expecting it for some time, because by my rough calculations a month or so had passed since my arrival in the clinic. Dr. Benway was there. He informed me that I had the honor of being the first unit in my colony to be inoculated with a new and improved formula. Having developed a temper of late, what with the constant bickering I was subjected to below, I responded by calling him every foul name and terrible oath that could be summoned up in one breath. In response, he coolly lifted up my chin with the tip of a chrome pointer and said that in a way it would be a pity if the new antidote proved effective, for he would be very curious to see how I might look at sixty. "At present, my naughty little exhibit, thirty-five suits you quite nicely." He snapped his fingers and a Sears handed him a small mirror, which he dangled before my eyes.

The tokens of age were clearly visible in the glass: crow's-feet, smile lines, and . . . were those gray hairs? Indeed. Only a few, but all the more noticeable for it. I must have gone into shock, because I do not recall being returned to the pen. Up until then, you see, I had been able to avoid acknowledging any alterations in my appearance for lack of mirrors in the compound, but thanks to this bit of malice that was no longer possible. Devastated, I curled up on my mattress and sobbed for hours on end over these and other subtle changes, which now seemed everywhere in evidence. There was a flaky carapace of hardened skin on the balls and heels of my feet. A fibrous network of white veins on the undersides of the thighs and calves had begun to bleed through my once opaque (and stunning) skin. My breasts, though still shapely, seemed fuller somehow and there was a hint of sag, and at the elbows—could that be the start of a mild case of bursitis? It was a nightmare.

"Trip for remission," Freddy advised.

Goodness, I never seemed to lack for advisers, did I? Of my three friends from the previous chapter, he was the only one left, and by then was so ancient that he was barely able to crawl over to my mattress. I suppose I should have been kind, but I was in no mood for his philosophy. The past month's misery, having come on top of the trial, had cured me of any illusions I might have had that one's lot in life could be improved by such a practice. "None of that formatting nonsense," I replied. "I've had it up to here with that!" And I belittled him by pointing out that it had not done him one whit of good either, only added to his gray hairs.

"Yes. Too late . . . for me, Molly," he said, wheezing. (By now he had a bad case of emphysema, no doubt brought on by all the shouting at the heretics.) "But you said . . . Benny gave you a new antidote. You have . . . a chance." To which I replied that in that case my fate depended upon the chemical properties of the new formula. "But it . . . is the other way . . . around. The effect those properties . . . have . . . on your system is . . . dependent on your . . . state of mind. Thought can move moun——" Bitterly, I cut him off before he could torment me further with another discourse on the intimate connection between thought and matter—I had heard it too many times before. I said I wanted to be alone. "Very well," he replied. "But you are . . . making . . . a big mistake."

If he had not been so feeble, I would have kicked him to help him on his way. My, my, my, I really was becoming ornery, and knowing it only made me more so. "Will you leave!" I was quite exasperated because he had not budged one inch. "Can't," he whispered. "My time . . . has come!"

My entire attitude instantly altered. "Oh, Freddy, no! Not planned obsolescence." He nodded, sank to the floor, and lay on his back. My heart went out to him, as it had to Matilda and Bernard only the week before, when they had off-lined. Quietly, he expired. His last words were, "Remember . . . the gnomes. Cell . . . u . . . lar gnomes."

Like a carrion bird of prey, the scoop could smell out the dead and dying. It pounced before I had a chance to grieve over his body, knocking me aside, as if a flea, with one of its fingerlike digits. Then it carried him aloft to a ceiling port and shoved him in. Mission complete, it flexed its fingers, made a fist, and retracted into the ceiling port. Poor Freddy, off to autopsy and final entry in the statistical ledger.

As with every termination in the pen, his demise upset the rest of the inmates, who feared they might be next. Happily, for some, there was the merry distraction of a new replacement as a bewildered female Cyberene dropped in. I made the unpardonable sin of going to this newcomer's aid when the traditional welcome mat was extended (or rather jerked from under her feet), which was considered an unpardonable affront by my fellow inmates. In reprisal I was ostracized, and that was fine with me—I now had plenty of time left to reflect upon my last conversation with Freddy.

I decided that the least I could do to atone for my harsh words (and to honor his memory) was to follow his advice; after all, as I told Micki Dee, I had nothing to lose—really, there was nothing better to do in such a place—and perhaps a great deal to gain, though I still remained a skeptic. Nevertheless, as an experiment I began a meditation regimen of several hours each day composed of half-hour segments during which I tripped for an end to the aging process. Of course, I had not the slightest idea how to go about it properly, lacking all recollection of the High technique Tad had demonstrated in Armstrong, and of Andro's body/mind gymnastics in Frontier with Molly II, since neither episode had been included in the mem-file projections shown in open court; but I trusted that my sincerity and purity of intent would more than compensate, which, come to think of it, had been Andro's attitude. For several weeks, then, I confined myself to my mattress, where I pursued the task at hand with a stern resolve to not let anyone distract me from my purpose. However, when the others noticed that I was taking advantage of their ostracism in this way, and, what's worse, seemed to be benefiting by it—for I was rarely cranky anymore and had a sanguine glow—then they were even more outraged and provoked and changed tactics. They began to mock my efforts at every opportunity. "P-Zero" they called me, and they would disrupt my meditations for remission by sneaking up and screaming in my face or by clapping their hands over my ears, and they committed a great deal of other juvenile and cruel outrages as well. I withstood it up to a certain point; then, when my concentration and composure were completely undone, I would find myself screaming in a rage, "You stupid old droid bastards, I'll bust your vegecircuits!" And stooping to their level, I would chase them around the pen. They thought it great sport.

Now, I might have stuck with this regimen despite their antagonism had there been the slightest indication that the program was working, but there wasn't. On the contrary, my looks continued to deteriorate—as my companions delighted in pointing out—and my energy slackened as well. Even when good and riled it was too much effort to chase them. My spirits plummeted and my temper grew more wicked. In short, I became just like them finally, so they ceased their campaign against me. Several even went so far as to welcome me into their clique, but I spurned the overture, choosing to keep my own counsel, morose and self-pitying as it was.

An eternity passed (or so it felt), and then I was removed for another inoculation—this time a booster shot—and met Dr. Benway again. He was disturbed by my appearance, though not for my sake—in that regard, he seemed pleased that I was a well-preserved sixty-two; no, rather he was perturbed over the disappointing performance of the antidote, which thus far had proven as ineffective as the other varieties used in the clinic. "Too bad I can't administer another serum, Molly," he said. "We have developed some new strains since last we met, but that would ruin the continuity of the experiment, so I am afraid that in your case, my contentious exhibit, we must continue with the same formula. See you for your next booster at seventy or thereabouts."

Three to five months later by my reckoning, I felt my mental processes beginning to slip and noticed that it was becoming difficult to run on the treadmill; after just ten minutes I was out of breath and required the rest of the day to recuperate. Needless to say, I was despondent, and when not too exhausted would go on melancholic strolls around the perimeter of the pen, keeping the barrier to my right as a guide. I brooded over the futility of existence and the unspeakable depravity of mankind—and of *Homo androidus* as well, for the latter species had proven just as reprehensible in my book. I felt alienated from both camps, and I simply abhorred the semis next door, who persisted in their fatuous exercise—the daily parades and blind obeisance to P-10. There were always devotees standing vigil outside the wigwam, so, presumably, the great recluse was still inside doing Gov knows what. The most zealous of these followers now went completely naked, having sacrificed the last remnants of their tunics to the leader's abode or to fatten His bedding inside. Now, that's charisma!

Well, the months rolled by in excruciatingly slow motion and I continued to deteriorate—though according to my natural cycle—and periodically I received more booster shots, none of which did a damn bit of good, just as Matilda had said. And so, I continued my sorry promenade, which I noticed took longer than before. "I must be really getting on," I thought. I was one of the old-timers. Almost all the units who had been in the pen when I arrived were long dead and gone. I couldn't bear to look at the new arrivals or the middle-aged units, and they didn't pay much attention to me. Interactions, such as they were, were limited to bickerings over trivialities. I remember punching a young glitch when she wouldn't get out of the way during my stroll. I hurt my hand. Can you imagine? I, a P9, hurting my hand simply by striking a miserable GA? She had the nerve to laugh about it.

Oh, and I was really fed up with the neighbors. They were the worst. The absolute worst! P-10 had evidently taken to dictating His pronouncements to specially selected scribes—the criers—who made a kind of pink ink out of their own blood to get it all down for posterity on carefully cut and bound pages of tunic. But it didn't stop there. No. For our edification the head crier was in the habit of proselytizing from the barrier. This inspiring karma sutra went something like this: P-10, the Gov's humble servant, has been sent here to the lower depths to show the semis (the Gov's chosen units) the door to the higher levels, through which only the adept may pass, for it is zealously guarded by the evil forces of mankind.

"Let's see P-10 pass through the barrier, if he's so hot!" I taunted him one day. The challenge was backed up by other members of my pen who had joined me at the barrier. "It is beneath Him to submit to such a crass and disrespectful request," the crier retorted, somewhat defensively; but we would not be put off. I cackled a derisive offer to kneel to His greater glory should He care to stroll over to our side, for how could He claim the transcendental mettle to pass through the window to the higher levels if He balked at penetrating this puny man-made barrier?

The moment the words were out of my mouth, I felt one of those odd memory tingles that I used to have in court. It turned into an itch, but when I scratched, my shingles were aggravated, so I decided not to pursue the matter. At the moment I was more curious to know the answer to our challenge. The crier had entered the wigwam to consult with P-10 about it. After five or ten minutes he returned to announce that P-10 was angry with us because we wasted our time devising child's games to test Him when eternity beckoned. What had been demanded of Him was simple enough—we ourselves could do it if we believed, and would that not be the finer demonstration?

To mock Him and His messenger, some of our younger and more hardy units threw themselves against the barrier, chortling, "Praise P-10!" All rebounded. Then I asked this stern and stentorian spokesman to try it himself. He declined, of course, choosing instead to retreat with a statement to the effect that such feats were mere carnival tricks; P-10 had been referring to a spiritual passage, a distinction we bad-tempered old farts could not possibly appreciate.

This impertinence was followed by the recitation of the saga of P-10's remarkable metamorphosis, which was punctuated by numerous catcalls, hoots, and, in reference to his insult, raspberries. We learned that from His humble beginnings as an orphan, P-10 had transmutated into the reigning deity of the age. This miraculous metamorphosis had occurred within their very compound, by the way. But I'll let the crier tell the story. He recited from memory, only referring to a thick book of tunic when, as happened from time to time, our catcalls disrupted his smooth delivery.

"Behold! I am P-10, semi, born of man and P9!" the crier proclaimed. "Born Aquarian, I did drift for aeons upon the storm-tossed sea, assuming and discarding human form innumerable times on the stages above, yet knew myself not; only that water was my sign, ever-flowing, mutable, and revivifying.

"I was a celebrity upon the world's stage in my last incarnation, a master of ceremonies was I; but all was vanity and folly! The Gov let me grow old so I might see through such trivial pursuits, for my masters—His instruments—said that I was too old to tap-dance anymore—ah, 'twas music to my ears, for I was sent here: all, all, all part of His plan.

"Behold! It was to this tender abode that the Gov in His everlasting wisdom saw fit to guide me. Yes, here in the lower depths of Benway I have been nursed by my fellow semis—the sweet, gentle chosen people of Horizon. They did blow upon the smoldering embers of introspection to fan the flame of the Govhead residing within. Here did I awake from the life of many lives, and here shall I begin the great work of leading the Gov's chosen units through the window to the Higher Levels—and all those who would also believe shall be delivered.

"For I am the true guide! Beware the enchantress, the guardian of the lower depths, for she would lead you astray, as she did me. Beware this false and beguiling creature. She would make you believe her a beauteous and sweet android. But she is not! She is a seductress! She did deceive me with sweet and tender kisses. 'The masters of the higher levels are only men,' she purred in my ear, and she begged me to abandon the quest.

"Be forewarned! Do not listen to this foul succubus, lest you, too, the chosen units of our Gov, fall into another cycle of lives, unknowing lives of many lives, flowing but not knowing where. Take heed by my example! I knew not who I was, nor what I did, yet performed without question, without flaw. I knew not my true format. It had been stolen by the agent of mankind, the beautiful deceiver. Call her Candida and forever beware the name!"

The gospel goes on, but need I say more? Even in my memory-depleted condition his name came to mind. Lance. Lance London. And then, that tingle plunged like a spike into a rich vein of residual past impressions buried deep within the nucleus of my vegecells and out popped, Junior! "Tad, Junior!" I shouted.

The gaunt, emaciated former star of stage and holo stepped from the wigwam, stretched to His full height (though not quite, since the shoulders had become stooped in old age*), and shielding His eyes from the harsh, artificial light, walked resolutely in

---

*My son was only two years younger than I, so by this time the difference between us in terms of our human equivalent age was insignificant; we were both quite elderly.

the direction of my cry—a plaintive mother's wail, if ever. His devotees kneeled as He passed, and the entire population of my pen pressed against the barrier to take a gander at this wild-eyed, white-haired apparition, who by the looks of Him was either a benighted lunatic or a sage and a holy semi.

"Who is it that calls me Tahjuna?" said He, upon stopping a yard from the barrier of His pen.

"Tad," I whispered, feeling faint, "at last."

Pointing a finger at me, the tip pressed against the invisible barrier, P-10 declared that I had donned a new guise, one that was in the image of an old woman, for He knew me for who I really was: Candida, the beautiful enchantress and deceiver.

I pressed flush against the shield to ask His forgiveness; for although my personal memories of the stables remained a blank, I had seen enough projected in court and had heard enough of Dahlia's commentary to know that I had corrupted and ruined Him somehow. I pleaded for Him to ease the pain of my poor maternal heart. "It is I, your mother!"

"Mother?" He smiled; then, with a look of infinite sagacity, said, "No. The Gov is mother and father to P-10. But you speak well to ask forgiveness. Kneel, Candida, and receive absolution, for I am greater than you and fear you not."

Saying that, He stepped through the barrier of His pen to gasps of astonishment from both compounds, and then crossed the narrow space between to enter our own circle. All fell back in astonishment when He stepped through and stood before me to lay His withered hand upon my brow, for I had quickly kneeled to receive this miraculous benediction. At His touch a terrible burden lifted from my shoulders, and as it did, I, too, rose and embraced Him. "Oh, my darling boy!" I exclaimed, and kissed Him. He withstood it with regal condescension. Gov knows what would have happened next had the alarm not been triggered by His entry, and an instant later the scoop not descended. We were snatched up like a pair of squirming mice and carried to the booth above.

Dr. Benway rushed into the inoculation chamber with half a dozen assistants following close behind. After being apprised of the situation by one of the Sears who had been on watch when my son penetrated the barrier, he declared it a fluke, some sort of localized electronic failure. Nonetheless, the incident greatly distressed him, because the environmental integrity of "Colony O"

had been compromised; we had been exposed to viral con-
taminants from the semis' pen. There were rigorous standards to
maintain; therefore, the entire population would have to be discarded. "Scoop them up and terminate them. All of them." He
was terribly vexed. "Damn inconvenience! I shall have to start all
over."

As we were sedated, my ancient son denounced him as the evil
guardian of the passageway to the higher levels, and while we began to nod out on the injection tables, He declared, in a waning
voice, that we would awake on a higher plane, and there we
should overcome. The last thing I heard before passing out, however, was the good doctor thinking out loud in a sudden inspiration. The loss—by which he meant the entire population of
"Colony O"—could be offset by a quick sale to the studio; they
were always in the market for expendables.

One could not be too certain of P-10's pronouncement, but
there was no doubting the doctor's. So now I was to become an
expendable—a unit such as I. What a wretched end!

T H R E E

NEITHER THE PITS OF HOLLYMOON NOR P-10'S PROM-
ised Valhalla greeted me upon awakening, but an excellent view of
Los Angeles Bay framed by the open terrace doors of a turn-of-
the-century bedroom, where I reposed comfortably in bed, my
head propped up by several pillows.

P-10 was seated at my bedside. He took my wrinkled and ar-
thritic hand in his and said that now that I was awake it was time
to transcend this physical stage. But I was too drowsy to follow his
words just then, and too surprised at my new surroundings to give
serious thought to quitting this material plane. In a feeble and
ancient voice (so strange to my ears) I inquired into it, asking if I
were truly where I appeared, back on Earth, or was this still the
Benway Clinic or a Hollymoon sound stage or a dream? To which
my transcendent son replied they were all one and the same and I
should prepare for passage to a finer realm. "Consider this place a
way station on your final journey."

"Am I terminating, then?"

"Rejoice in the opportunity!" said he, squeezing my hand. "I shall guide you through."

I looked around. The room had all the trappings of a slum dwelling: a late '90s condominium done over in countless layers of cheap wallspray laden with years of dust and grime and smelling of poverty and discarded dreams. But most horrible of all was the reflection of the ancient dame with snow-white hair, collapsed cheeks, wrinkled brow, and withered arms in a mirror on the opposite wall. It was myself lying in bed, for I already looked like a corpse. I quickly shifted my gaze from such a wan and fragile specter (the perfect complement to such a room) to seek solace in my son's hypnotic and translucent eyes. "I'm ready," I said in a hoarse whisper, and gave him my other hand. He told me to close my eyes and trust in his direction, and I did. Indeed, I prepared to sally forth upon a new round of adventures.

"P-10, what are you up to? You know you are not supposed to be in here. Out! Come on, let's go. There are pilgrims to see you, and I would appreciate your getting rid of them."

It was Tad! I could hardly believe my eyes. No longer the very model of the up-and-coming interplanetary executive, he had shed that skin for a return to the lean and committed look of the dedicated opposition, his rezoot suit replaced by a pair of throwaway epoxy-wool trousers and a T-shirt. Also, one could not help noticing that his hair was thinning and that there were flecks of gray around his temples. Still, he looked boyish for a man in his late thirties.

"Ignore that human!" commanded P-10. "He is mad; he says he is my father."

"Enough of that," Tad snapped, and then realizing I was awake and gaping at him, exclaimed, "Now look what you've done; you've woken Molly. Quick, move aside!" So saying, he rushed to my bedside, elbowing P-10 out of the way, and strapped on my head a cushioned helmet that bore an unpleasant resemblance to a mind scan but was actually a combination aurafield purifier and polarity modulation device. As it hummed to life my skull and soon my entire body were bathed in a cool, enervating wash of negatively charged ions. So relaxing.

"With any luck, your meddling didn't ruin the memory transfer," Tad grumbled. To which the unrepentant deity replied, "And you, in your ignorance, have deprived Candida of her chance to make a peaceful and joyous transition."

"What!" exclaimed the other. "You were trying to kill your mother?!"

"Foolish human, I offer guidance only to those seeking to escape this vale of tears."

"Listen, Junior: You may be Lord of the Universe, but while under my roof you abide by my rules. Let people die in their own time, for Gov's sake. Now, go; there are devotees waiting for you in the living room. And please, don't counsel them in the same fashion; we can't afford any more corpses on our hands."

The question uppermost in my mind following this very peculiar exchange was, "Then my time has not come?"

"No, obsolescence is still a year away." Tad noticed Junior was lingering in the doorway. He angrily motioned for him to leave.

"Pilgrims?"

"Yes. Our prodigy has slipped out a few times and done some proselytizing. The word has spread in the underground. Gov knows how they manage to find Him."

"And is this really Earth, then? Really the Los Angeles Islands?"

He acknowledged that to be the case, then excused himself for a moment to slam the door on our son, forcing him into the hall. "He really is incorrigible," he said upon returning to my bed, and then sat beside me so I could lean comfortably against his chest. He stroked my long, gray, and spindly locks and said that I should try not to talk, but by then I was too curious to heed such sensible advice. The obvious questions were, where was I, exactly? and how did I get there?

With some reluctance, because he really wanted me to rest, he explained that our apartment was in an abandoned building slated for demolition and located a few blocks from where I had once plied my trade in the Dodger District. Until the New Horizon came on-line, this charming suite would have to do. Yes, he said, he had returned to the fold after spending over a year on automatic pilot as a legal affairs administrator for Stellar Entertainment. He was far happier now dividing his time between this hovel, where he looked after me (and tried to restrain his son from "transitioning" the other squatters), and the street, where he solicited donations for the New Horizon Movement. One did have to adopt certain protective measures, he said, such as never going out without a face, for he was wanted by the interplanetary police and the AC for stealing P-10, myself, and my memory file from the studio. He also assumed that the Mafia were on his tail because of what he knew about Micki Dee.

This latest transformation was the most extraordinary of all, I said, for when last we met he had been a reborn master and engaged to a human girl. "A disastrous mistake," he readily acknowledged. Like the new career and master-oriented world view he had adopted, that relationship had been totally artificial, for other than membership in the same species, he and Miss Bonpaine really had very little in common. If not for Ann, who helped open his eyes, he would still be married and moonjogging in Hollymoon, and I would have been holoed to death on a studio sound stage as an expendable. At the mention of Ann's name, a complete and unabridged series of memories surfaced. "Oh! Yes! I remember her now. My memories are back! They're back!"

Who, then, should enter the room with face aglow and arms open wide but the very lady herself. Having just returned home from a hard day's soliciting to hear that I was awake from P-10, she had rushed to the bedroom to join us. How wonderful it was that we were all together again, she said, while hugging and kissing me, and I, with a full set of memories to refer to, was able to return the sentiment by squeezing her hand most affectionately; which made her all the more pleased for the vigor left in it. Soon I would grow stronger, she said, by way of encouragement, which was sweet, because we both knew I was dying. I couldn't help noticing that even she had made a small advance on mortality—after all, it had been over six years since we last met, back in '82; however, forty-three made her a babe in my book. The years had also seemed to add rather than detract from her sensuality—I suppose because it had been suppressed for so long during her pre-Aquarian days. A late bloomer, I think they call the type. At any rate, she did not lack for a lover, as her prolonged kiss with Tad made clear.

"Darling, I was just about to tell Molly how we met in Hollymoon."

"It was all on account of you," she said, and eagerly filled me in on all that had transpired since my deposit in the Benway

Clinic. She had ventured from her safe house in Commerce, where she had been hiding since the invasion—in the belly of the beast, so to speak—to risk life and limb on a mercy mission to the moon. Via the network, she had learned from old friends in the ARL that the studio had dumped me in the clinic and then taken me back a year and a half later. Rumor had it that I had been classified as an expendable. The Armstrong ARL's efforts to gain more detailed information had been frustrated by a certain legal affairs administrator.

"Oh, you might as well tell her the truth, Ann. It was me, Molly, acting in my official capacity—the only one I was conscious of at the time. I was directed by Master Boffo to say that it was company policy not to reveal the identity of studio talent because that was proprietary information. Of course, the real reason was that he didn't want the public to know what had happened to the real Molly Dear, not with your holo about to come out. At any rate, it was all the same to me. I simply did my job."

"Yes. You were a tough nut to crack," Ann said, smiling. Then, turning to me, she explained that since she had the feeling he might not have been as thoroughly altered as he appeared at the trial, it was worth the effort, and risk, to try bringing him around; besides their long friendship, he was a studio insider in a position to help. So she struck up a personal acquaintance by "accidentally" colliding with him while out moonjogging.

"You were so furious I had ruined your run that you didn't even care I had ruptured my oxygen tank."

A little embarrassed, he replied that she had done so on purpose just before the collision so he would have to stop and help. "But you didn't know that then, did you? And I had to beg for a half minute with ridiculous hand signals before you condescended to spare me a little out of your tank. I forgive you, though." She kissed him on the cheek. "You weren't to blame. They hadn't programmed you for compassion or even a whit of common decency; just to get ahead." Tad nodded grimly and said that it was true. The memory of his lunar career amazed him still.

"Of course, I had to wear a face. If I hadn't, he would have recognized me straight off and reported my whereabouts to the authorities."—"Oh, absolutely!" he interjected. "I would have turned you in like that!" He snapped his fingers. "You were a fugitive High."

Returning to her tale, Ann said that after that inauspicious meeting she contrived to run into him again and again until a steady relationship was established, which she took advantage of to introduce certain ideas she hoped would stimulate a revival of his old value system. Though he resisted at first and tried to stop seeing her (after all, he was a married man), there did come a day when, as Tad put it, picking up the tale, "The whole master program just came unraveled. I was working late in the office one night—tired, stressed out, popping caffeine and perk-a-peaks, you know, the usual uppers—when all of a sudden nothing made sense anymore. I didn't know why I was there or what I was doing. I mean, I knew what I was doing, but it seemed pretty meaningless all of a sudden, and that was very scary because just the minute before I had been convinced that the project I was working on was absolutely critical, like my whole life depended on it. So nothing made sense. I thought I was going crazy. I mean, I didn't know who I was anymore. Everything seemed pretty silly. Like it was the management offices that were the stage, not the studio. I remember looking around at the secretaries—it was night, so they were powered down in their swivel seats—and I watched the maintenance units for a while as they skulked about spearing discarded cups and spools, and all of a sudden I knew I couldn't go on like this anymore. I called Ann and—"

"I rushed over, found him giggling and crying. I let him talk all night—right there in the office—and by morning he was our Tad again. He did it all by himself; I was just a sympathetic ear."

"No, you were more than that. You helped me understand that it was the program, not I, that had cracked, and that I was never more the slave than when I thought myself an absolute master." And facing me, he asked, "Can you imagine anything so schizophrenic?"

I could indeed: my predicament on Mars, for one thing, which had been fully restored to my memory circuits. But I didn't want to interrupt. In time I would tell them everything, how I had been fixed and programmed for the First Lady role, and later was Molly II for Andro, and how she had killed Blaine, not I, and everything else that had come before, after, and in between. But right then I wanted to hear about my rescue, and by keeping silent, did.

Ann said that with Tad restored he became an eager collaborator in her scheme for my release. Unlike the unsuccessful attempt on Mars, this mission would be a smashing success. Taking advantage of Tad's security clearance, they gained access to the talent filespool records, which indicated that I had been posted to the expendables storage bins at the lowest level of the stables. The files also produced the surprise entry "Lance London," also listed as an expendable, so the mission instantly expanded to encompass his retrieval as well. They flew to the studio dome containing the stable in which we resided and presented bogus release documents (concocted back at the main office) to the dispatcher, who immediately expedited our transfer to their waiting executive limousine. Still powered down, Junior and I were then flown to the spaceport, though not before a quick detour was made back to the main office in downtown Hollymoon so that Tad could steal my mem file from the vault. Then they boarded the first available Earthbound shuttle with Junior and myself stored below as baggage, and arrived without incident here in the islands. "That was a month ago. It is now November—November 2088," said Ann. "So you see, Molly, it all goes to prove that the Gov works in strange and wondrous ways; all formats do lead home."

"Be that as it may," Tad interjected, "the proverb would be more satisfying if it had included Junior. He is with us in body but not in mind."

I asked if they had not tried to bring him around the way Ann had Tad—and Tad had me many years before. Yes, they had made an attempt, but gave up: He was too far gone. "Then perhaps He is what He says He is," I ventured. "I did witness His crossing the barrier."

Oh, they were quite familiar with that particular feat, they said, because Junior never stopped bragging about it. Tad's theory was that there never had been a barrier, rather the belief in our minds that it existed—so it is with all prisons of the mind's making. "Of course, our illustrious firstborn is of the opinion that He made a molecular transit."

"And so I did!" the entity Himself retorted, His face coming through the wall next to the bed without disrupting the surface, then just as suddenly vanishing. "No more of your tricks!" Tad shouted, extremely perturbed. "You see that? He had his ear to the wall listening in on us the whole time. Ann, I'm at my wits' end. I mean, it has been hard enough adjusting to a son old enough to be my grandfather without having to put up with these kinds of shenanigans."

"Well, at least now He is content to remain indoors."

"I know, and that makes me even more nervous. He spends all his time sending telepathic messages from here to Jupiter declaring His kingdom come."

"But what if He can do that?" I asked. "What if P-10 is the fulfillment of the Gov's prophecy?"

They shook their heads, exchanged knowing glances. "See how tempting the idea is," Tad said to Ann. Then, confidentially, so Junior could not hear even if still listening, he said within an inch of my ear, "We know he's not, because the Gov said so."

The Gov speak to a human? Now, that was a surprise! Tad proudly insisted that it was so; he had been personally honored to receive a communiqué while soliciting on the street. The message was that Junior is a false prophet because he disparages physical existence, which is as crucial to our development as any other. In fact, if pursued with the right attitude, it can even be enjoyable. (Easy for him to say, I grumbled to myself.) "Run from such a P-10!" the Gov had recommended, according to Tad. And as for Junior's magical abilities, they can be developed by any unit wishing to exercise them, but are less important in the long run than simply learning to master one's life.

"How *do* you do that?"

"Oh, you know the Gov," Tad said, grinning. "He wouldn't say."

"Well, have you figured it out, then?"

Still smiling, Tad replied that he had completely given up.

While I puzzled that one over, Ann recommended I get some rest. Due to my advanced age, the mem-file transfer had been a time-consuming and risky process. During the past month they had been forced to feed my file in small doses while I was kept in deep idle, and had only completed the process a few days before. Since then, I had been kept powered down as an added measure to ensure against data loss and to give the process a chance to register fully—that is, until the all-knowing P-10 had butted in, waking me for premature transition.

I acknowledged that I did feel fatigued, but had to ask them one more question before returning to idle: Had they been able to locate Jubilee?

No. After the trial she had been returned to Semiville. Several months ago there had been some kind of violent uprising there—it was on the interplanetary news. Apparently she was among those unaccounted for after the "troubles" were suppressed by the new democratically elected Master Party government. As to her current whereabouts, there was no information. One could only hope that she was still on-line somewhere. "Ah, well," I said with a sigh, "I was hoping she might have turned up here. Seems everyone else has." So saying, I slipped into idle, unable to keep my eyes open a second longer.

F O U R

THE MORE I PONDERED THE CONTENTS OF MY MEM file during recuperation the more infuriated I became over the deletions, distortions, and outright misrepresentations presented in court. The cynical campaign by the defense and prosecution to defame my character had created a creature in the public mind far removed from my experience. I was not the demented murderess the masters said I was, nor the revolutionary many of my android brothers and sisters secretly emulated; both were wide of the mark. Though my sojourn has led to many an extraordinary adventure, I am but an average P9, as was stated at the outset, and therefore undeserving of such inflated praise and condemnation. No, the true story lies elsewhere—I would like to think here, now that I've gotten it down. However, during the first week or two of my convalescence I felt helpless in the face of this popular legend and disturbed no end over how the world had been cheated from knowing my essence. Truly, they must be told! Yet due to my deteriorating condition, I feared I would never regain the sufficient energy and perspicacity to fathom that quality to my own satisfaction even, much less anyone else's. Moreover, I wondered if I was not slipping into delusions of grandeur in compensation for how inadequate I felt; for if I was just an average unit, as I always said, then why should anyone care about the real me? Was I so arrogant and foolish to believe anyone—android or human—would be interested? Don't answer that! Sometimes I mused to myself that I rather liked being singled out, and I valued my infamous reputation as something concrete that would live on long after I was gone. Then, when in such a frame of mind, the realities of public consumption would strike home and I would become despondent again, knowing that I would be forgotten in a year or two, my reputation reduced to a fading newsspool in the family media library and a footnote in the historical texts. So there was little solace there.

Did not Junior's recommendation make more sense—to give up all worldly concern for a matriculation to the higher levels? Quite! Consequently, during those first few weeks of recuperation I discarded the notion of composing a memoir in favor of preparing myself for transition. To that end I did not report P-10's clandestine bedside visits in the wee hours of the morning, which He claimed the most conducive period for spiritual transit; however, neither was I so certain of His program and my own mind that I completely relented and let myself go, as He so incessantly purred in my ear to do. It did not seem fair to Tad and Ann, who had been so kind, supportive, and life-affirming. I did not have the heart to disappoint them. So once again I changed my mind; my predicament was so intolerable that no solution was satisfactory for long. There was no hurry, I reasoned: In a year's time I would be terminating anyway. P-10 could wait.

Yes, it would be kinder to give Tad and Ann the pleasure of my cantankerous company in recompense for their tender concern; they would be so terribly sad if I didn't. I don't mean to sound facetious—they really did appreciate me despite my constant complaints and sudden eruptions of ill humor, which they charitably overlooked, knowing them side effects of the Benway antidote. I wished my son had been as accommodating. He took my "backsliding," as he so contemptuously called my decision to opt for life, quite poorly. I had denied Him, he said, and as a result I would not be able to pass through the window to the higher levels. "Beware! You totter on the abyss! You are in peril of falling back into another cycle of lives!" Nevertheless, I was not ready to follow His guidance; in trying before, I had found that out. "You needn't pout over me," I said. "You can always keep yourself busy transitioning the pilgrims."

Other than that little tiff, the only bone of contention between us was His refusal to accept me as His mother, or that He had ever had a mother, for that matter. Rather, He fancied that He had been struck like a gold ingot from the celestial forge by a bolt of lightning, and that that divine spark had lit up the primordial ether and given life to its nascent formats, so that in that instant of trans-mogrification the collective energy of the cosmos had shot out as rays of time and space to form the known universe, itself but an imperfect manifestation of the Gov's inspiration, of which He, P-10, was its most realized embodiment. That bothered me less than the knowledge I bore as a stone in my heart that He, too, despite His claims of immortality, was slated to terminate upon his twentieth birthday, only two years and three months after my own. That bothered me more than my own physical decomposition, which, by the way, had taken a new and ghastly turn—the shingles had literally become just that: Whole sections of my body were covered by a scaly layer of dead vegeflesh constantly peeling off in mel-sized flakes. It was so irritating I couldn't sleep, so I would pass the time observing P-10 transmitting on the terrace, which was His habit each evening. He would sit perfectly still for an hour or two, then begin to hum a bit and appear ready to levitate but never quite take off, rather settle for buzzing like a bee or a fly, while muttering incoherent incantations of some kind, after which He would fall silent once more and remain in trance for another half hour. Then He would abruptly slap His face with both hands, yelp, and get up, or try to, because His knee joints would inevita-bly lock, leaving Him contorted in the most awkward positions for ten to fifteen minutes at a time. Ah, well, I decided it better He remain deluded (if mad) or transformed (if a semi-saint) than rail against me for having caused Him to be fixed while in Hollymoon. He still carried the IG, Tad had told me. He had taken Him to a clandestine cleansing lab shortly after our arrival from the moon, but was told that it was impossible to remove the implant because it had fused with the vegulla oblongata. The condition is the prob-able cause of His madness (or divinity), though, of course, we shall never know for sure. Perhaps his insistence upon calling me Candida, the evil enchantress and deceiver, is His way of letting me know that He holds me to accounts for the IG. If so, I cannot contest the title.

The world, however, has no right to call me a terrorist droid assassin. Any notion I had of letting that notorious reputation stand was forever dispelled when I saw *Droid!*, which was the new title selected by the studio for *The Life and Times of the Infamous Molly Dear.* Tad and Ann had tried to hide it from me—not the physical holospool, mind you, they had not stooped to purchase that—but the fact that it was out and had been a tremendous hit. They were afraid I would insist upon seeing it and be upset, and they were right. One of the pilgrims, unaware of my identity (to them I was known as "the old lady"), had lent me a copy to help pass the time, so for two and one-half hours I was privileged to observe the savage dismemberment of my life story along the lines established by the attorneys in court, only the holo painted an even more depraved and brutal picture. If you were among the quarter billion people who actually paid good mel to see this travesty, then you recall that I was portrayed as a laser-toting fugitive who dispatched enough human victims on the road to Horizon to populate another solar system, each act of carnage more shocking and violent than the last, and culminating in the Fracass assassination. For those who might have missed it, I should mention that since I was the villain of the piece, the actual hero who emerged was a remastered Thaddeus Locke. To synopsize, after spending half the film as my Aquarian collaborator and dupe, he sees the error of his ways in Horizon (portrayed as a totalitarian droid state) and converts to the humanist cause, redeeming himself by informing on Smedly's unsavory association with RAG and tipping off the Frontier authorities that their First Lady is a P9 infiltrator, but alas!—too late to save the great humanist's life. In the end decency and order are restored as I am terminated by the corporate state in a restrained and formal ceremony—Tad, in atonement, being the one to push the eviscerater button.

That got me up and out of bed, I was so mad! "That's not my life!" I cried. "It's sheer fiction! A myth!" A spittle-punctuated tirade against the masters followed that was so intense it nearly caused a stroke. Tad and Ann rushed in, calmed me down, discovered the offending holospool, and promptly confronted the pilgrim who had loaned it to me. This unit, also a P9, expressed astonishment over my reaction, because, as everyone knew (except myself), the holo had been just as well received in the android underground, where the runaways took great pleasure in the manner by which this larger-than-life Molly dispatched her victims. "She's one righteous unit," said he in those few words summing up the general sentiment in the fugitive community. Now, to me, there seemed a terrible irony in that attitude, for by identifying with this rampaging droid, he and the android audience for whom he spoke were buying the negative stereotype of the homicidal liberated unit. When I pointed that out to him, saying such entertainments debase and denigrate us while feeding the masters' irrational fears and prejudices, he could only reply that it was just a holo and should not be taken so seriously. Now that he knew how I felt, he would not be loaning me the sequel when it came out. "Sequel?" I asked in trepidation. "Yes. *Droid II!*"

That was the last straw. I decided then and there that I really must do something to set the record straight in the months that were remaining; and so from that resolution were these memoirs born—in secret, I might add, because I did not want Tad or Ann to find out what I was up to, lest their enthusiasm for the venture (I'm assuming they would have been enthusiastic) in some way influence my recollections, which are difficult enough to get right from a single perspective, especially as I grow older and they begin to take on a life of their own. Also, I wanted to avoid the slightest impression that I was in competition with Tad, who around that same time had begun composing his own effort, appropriately titled *A Wayfarer Between Two Worlds.* (He was having a great deal of difficulty with it—something about his repressed anger toward his parents getting in the way. "I've got a block," he said. Consequently he spent more time dissolving his psychopediments than composing.) So while he and the others slept, I stayed up all night with his battered old Corona thought processor strapped on. In the morning, after finishing a section, I would carefully remove the dataspool and hook it to a necklace I always kept around my neck. By then I had recovered sufficient strength to get around on a cane, so I would spend an hour or two after breakfast hobbling about, mulling over my life. These ambulatory meditations were not confined to the apartment, which really was a dreary place, but when I felt up to it also included the immediate area. (L.A. being L.A., everything had changed; the old hoverbus terminal had been replaced by a new sports arena, and the whores had all moved down to the new tourist promenade near the water.) Tad or Ann, sometimes both, would accompany me, talking of pleasant things while I pretended interest, my mind roaming through my mem file in search of appropriate material for that evening's composing.

On one of these walks, a shaggy dog took to following us and refused to be shooed away, so we relented and took her back to the apartment. This beast seemed to favor me over everyone else for some reason and soon became my constant companion. I called her Sootpack because she really looked it on the day we took her in. She was a mongrel, part hound, part terrier, and most affectionate, but if the truth be known, I really could have done without her, because after a while she became a source of constant friction between P-10 and myself. He insisted upon calling her Jubilee in the mistaken notion that she was the reincarnated spirit of my lost child. I was never so embarrassed, annoyed, and insulted. Because of him, I regretted taking the poor thing in. After a while I became vexed if she tagged along on my walks because her presence was sufficient to distract me from my musings over my life.

But it wasn't just dogs that I had to contend with; the pilgrims had to be discouraged from tagging along as well. I was venerated by them because P-10 had said I was the enchantress Candida transformed by His benediction into a shining apostle of the faith. It didn't matter if I disagreed—they took His word over my own every time, so I gave up and said nothing, letting them think what they liked; anyway, I still wasn't sure Tad was right about Junior being mad. After all, his claim was hard to swallow, too. Imagine, the Gov talk to a human being! I still can't get over that. In any case, P-10 continued to be a disciplinary problem, what with all the pilgrims continually flocking to see Him and egging Him on. Sometimes I think Tad and Ann accompanied me on my constitutionals just to escape the apartment, which was packed with fawning admirers. In all fairness, I should say that they did make themselves useful—that is, when not attempting suicide; but they did so with a slavish devotion to P-10 that made me queasy. They tidied up, lugged water up five flights of steps every day, did the dishes, donated groceries, and took turns standing vigil on the roof, for there was always the possibility of city housing units dropping by to evict us. Still, we wished they would just go away. All the attention quite turned Junior's already considerably swelled head. He took their adulation and toil for granted, and to show His appreciation, demeaned their sense of individual self-worth in exchange, while encouraging total self-abnegation as a preliminary for transit to the higher levels. Why, when I said to Him one day that I didn't think it decent the way He treated His friends (I didn't like to call them pilgrims or devotees; that only made Him preen the more!), He had the nerve to reply, "Well, Candida, someone has to do the donkeywork, don't they?" It is quite insidious, this master/slave business, don't you think? I may have made some mistakes in my time, but playing that game wasn't one of them—that is, when in my right mind.

I was not about to argue with Him, though; you can't argue with the Messiah. As for Tad, when we were not agonizing over our son, we did have some marvelous conversations about the past; in particular, we discussed that mysterious quality for which I seemed to have had a natural talent but never understood properly and still don't: love. His for me had never faded, he said, despite his claims at the trial. Having recovered from that lapse—the word he used to characterize his cure—there was nothing to stand in the way of our becoming life partners. "That is sweet of you," said I, "but really I am too old, and anyway, what would Ann say?"

"We've discussed it, and she approves."

Now, that surprised me. Then I recalled that in Armstrong Ann had said she and Tad were spokes because he considered me his hub, which put their relations in proper perspective. But there was another obstacle. He still insisted upon an Aquarian wedding according to High tradition. "You still want me to convert!?" I was both amused and appalled, and told him that I might have been willing to consider the idea in Armstrong, but now, after all we had been through—ever since our disastrous blissmat, as a matter of fact—I could see no reason to believe.

"But Molly, all our adverses are behind us. They were a stage we had to pass through. That is why we have been able to have this latest and most remarkable alignment." He went on at length to extoll our combined formatting prowess, saying it had brought us together once more; to which I politely retorted that although I did not wish to minimize the importance of our alignment, it did strike me as being too little, too late and a paltry consolation for not cheating death, which for me proved the limits of the Gov's philosophy. "There are certain issues we do not have control over," said I. He begged to disagree, vouching that it only seemed that way. "Did I choose to be born a P9?" I retorted, irked by his breezy self-confidence.

"Yes!" said P-10, magically parting the wall with His hands to join the conversation. "Just as this fool chose to be born a human and I, in my divine wisdom, chose to be a semi of exceptional quality. I recommend the latter, though lightning rarely strikes in the same place twice."

"Will you excuse us, please!" Tad thundered, leaping up and slamming his hand on the opening in the wall, which vanished a split second before he made contact.

I took the incident in stride, since by then I was used to our son's provoking us in that way. Thinking aloud, I said, "Well, to give the Gov his due, if I did choose to be born a P9, then it follows I must have selected this wretched end as well. Could this, then, be my preferred reality—to turn into an old flake?" Tad did not have a suitable reply, other than to say that he supposed it was my TRIP.

"Oh, Tad, you're still the same!" I cried in exasperation, and then smiled, because I realized that that was precisely the way I liked him. I decided the whole issue too trivial to bother resisting a moment longer, and I declared that I would be delighted to convert; a High ceremony would be a small price to pay for being his hub. Touched, he withdrew the proviso out of a similar desire to please me. But Junior, who had gotten wind of our engagement by his usual means—eavesdropping—had already made plans to carry it out, and at that very moment intruded upon us to conduct the service, half a dozen pilgrims fanning out behind him as he stole into the room. Ann was there as well, having been a party to the conspiracy. She carried the chalice—a soup bowl from the kitchen filled with rose water.

"Sip of the seas of time and space," P-10 directed and nodded for Ann to pass the bowl. Tad accepted the sacred vessel and motioned for me to follow suit as we sipped together from the same side. "In the name of the Gov and the First Principle of Reality Formation," said our son, "I now dub you hubbed. May you manifest an inexhaustible supply of semis to the Gov's greater glory!" "To the Gov's greater glory!" Ann and the pilgrims echoed. We said it softly to each other and kissed.

That evening we passed a very tender but restrained honeymoon, neither wishing to be so indelicate as to force the issue of my great age and decrepitude. In the morning Ann brought us breakfast in bed. We invited her to join us, and later that day, when my new hub went off to do some soliciting around the sports stadium, I did not object when she went with him while I remained behind, nor did I protest that evening when she joined us in bed and the two of them made love. One could draw parallels between this triad and another from my Frontier days, but only on the most superficial level. The truth was I felt rather privileged to be part of this union. When as happened from time to time they were a little too robust, I forsook the bed, which heaved dangerously, for my easy chair in the corner. After they fell asleep, I put on the old Corona, switched it to t.p. mode, and spent the rest of the night silently composing as usual. All in all, if one could overlook the physical maladies and general weakness, it was not a bad period. I had it better than most as the end approached: I was looked after, surrounded by family—hub, best friend, son, and dog—and I knew precisely how much time I had left to complete these memoirs. I was content.

F I V E

AND SO THAT IS HOW I HAVE KEPT MYSELF PRE-occupied this past year as I continue to wither away, becoming a really very ancient grande dame. As a matter of fact, for the past few weeks I have been confined to a rollochair, because my legs have become too frail to support me. I continue to flake. Fungoderm crustia, they call it. The only good thing about the condition is that it tends to obscure the age spots and lines. But my eyesight is still good, and so is my hearing, though neither are as sharp as they once were—both having diminished to what would be considered standard in a human—and I can sit on the terrace and admire the view, so all in all, things are still not as bad as I had feared they might be in my youth. Right now, as I sit and compose, the floating city of New San Francisco lies at anchor in the bay, taking up two thirds of it. With any luck it will have put out to sea before this evening so I can have an unobstructed view once more of Anaheim Island to the southeast; it is rather pictur-esque. Tonight, you see, is a special occasion. At the stroke of twelve I am scheduled to terminate, or as P-10 would say, make my transition. Yes, this is the day I have feared all my life—No-vember 15, 2089—yet I am perfectly sanguine, though not entirely easy. I know that sounds contradictory, but if you are ever so fortunate to live to a ripe old age and to come to this precipice as serenely as I have, then I think you may be able to grasp what it is I am getting at: No matter how prepared we might think we are, there is still the unknown to be faced, and therein lies a terrible suspense.

My human friends, however, cling to the mistaken notion that I shall survive; I suppose out of some personal psychopediment involving a fear of death. Ann, of all people, is the worst. She has been careful all week to avoid the issue delicately, going about her business as if this day were of no consequence and I would be seeing many more just like it. A few minutes ago she made a concession of sorts when she felt compelled to reassure me (though it was really to reassure herself) that since the Benway antidote was highly experimental—its properties and effects poorly understood—it might save me yet. To which I made no reply, nor did anyone else; the desperation motivating such a statement was far too obvious. She realized that herself, I think, because she quickly turned away so as not to show her distress. In contrast, P-10 and the surviving pilgrims are in a positively festive mood while preparing for my transition. For them, it is a merry occasion not to be missed, nor marred by melancholy. They have hung brightly colored streamers all about the apartment and on the balcony and put on dance music. They have even broken out the spirits. Why, it is just like an Irish wake, and I haven't even gone off-line yet! Which makes it more like a Gypsy funeral, now that I stop to think about it. Of course, P-10 has assured me there will be a quiet interlude when it comes time for the actual transition and that He shall assist me in it. (He is really chomping at the bit, having waited all year for this.) That doesn't help me at the moment, though. Sootpack is barking and leaping about due to the excitement, and the music is beginning to irritate me. While it blares and the pilgrims cavort, dancing the lunar hop, much to Tad's annoyance (he is afraid it will attract the police), I think I shall slip the old Corona on. No one will notice, nor care if they do; they're having far too much fun. But if anyone asks, I'll just say that I am listening to reprocessed Aquarian dolphin symphonies, some such thing, when in truth I shall be composing the conclusion to these memoirs; for they would not be complete without mention of what happened last night. To a large degree the incident has been responsible for the tranquillity I enjoy today.

What happened was, Ann stole out of the room so Tad and I could have some privacy on our last night together, and no sooner was she gone than he slipped under the sheets with me and began making love. "You mustn't," I told him, and said that our relations did not require such tardy demonstrations of youthful passion, so out of place now, especially if forced. Was it not a sacrifice on his part? For so it must be:(Was I not a withered old woman only hours from the grave? But he nibbled on my ear (delicately, oh, so delicately, there not being very much left) and whispered that he was moved by a genuine yearning and would not be put off, nor left unfulfilled. Hearing that, the sweet strings of youth were plucked and I opened myself to him, saying, "Oh, Tad, then yes, once more before I—" But his lips closed upon mine, stopping the word, and then gently, so very gently, he entered me. "See, you are just like a young girl inside," he whispered, and the tears came to my eyes.

Ann is staring at me. She wants to say something. What a pain. I shall have to remove the thought processor for a moment.

All right, I am back, t.p. on and recording. What Ann said was that if not the antidote, then perhaps last night would do the trick. "If only to have more like it, I hope you are right," I had replied, though I did not really put any stock in her idea. Neither did she, I'm afraid. She bit her lip and then suddenly kneeled down to embrace me. "I'm sorry; so sorry," she said, as if it were her fault that my termination could not be aborted. So I wound up comforting her, which was irritating because I wanted to get back to the t.p. I have found that there is no conflict between composing and off-lining; the two work rather well together. And there is another incentive for continuing this project. A few weeks ago I made secret arrangements for the release of this spool with a Malibu publishing house, and though the editor and I have spoken only once, by wristphone, and he is not at all sure I am for real, since like the rest of the public he is under the impression that Molly Dear expired after being donated to science, nevertheless I think he will be satisfied I am the genuine article when this spool is delivered to him posthumously. (Tad doesn't know it yet, but I shall leave it in his custody with an explanatory note regarding its delivery to the publisher.) Even if my editor thinks this account a fraud, the temptation will be strong to exploit the material. After all, I do name names—Harry Boffo and Micki Dee, for instance—

and I shed fascinating new light on other luminaries, such as Frank Hirojones and President Fracass.

So let's see. Where was I? Oh, yes, I was talking about last night. But I've told you enough about that. The time now? Late afternoon. I am happy to report that the view will soon be free of that mammoth city-ship, the New San Francisco. The drawbridges are going up and its engines are making a throbbing, monstrous din. Ah, there it goes, rising up on its pontoons and heading for Gov knows where—China, perhaps, or Australia. What a spectacular churning foam it is throwing up; the spray is covering the promenade. You should see the whores and tourists run!

Hmmmm. Maybe the cellular gnomes could help me. I'll just visualize the little beasties foraging among my DNA looking for the planned-obsolescence lever. No. Why bother? They didn't help Freddy in the end, nor any other unit, so I cannot expect them to come to my assistance at this late date. I wasted enough time formatting their intervention while in the clinic. Silly nonsense.

This is an hour or so later. I was just thinking about Jubilee, the real Jubilee—not the dog! The last time I saw her was at the trial. How I wish she could be here now! Ah, well. Life has been most accommodating by reuniting me with Junior, Tad, and Ann; I mustn't begrudge it a loose end or two. Still, I wonder what she looks like now—if still alive. Let's see, she was born in May 2082, so that makes her seven and a half. Goodness! In human terms, she would be pushing thirty, and being a semi, she would look it, too. And to think I came within a few yards of meeting her in Horizon when she was still a child. Damn that stupid invasion!

Speaking of preferred formats, I wonder what happened to all Eva's mel after she died. By rights, half of that is mine. I should like to leave it to Tad and Ann so they can move into a better place, perhaps get a decent mobe condo on Big Bear. Actually, they should get out of the islands altogether, go someplace new and start over. There are too many memories here. Memories. All one has left in the end. Memories. I am sure Blaine appropriated all Eva's finances the moment they were married. Yes, I am sure that is what happened to all my hard-earned profits on Malibu. Ah, well.

Oh, I must have dozed off for a while. Imagine that! On my termination day. Ann informs me that I was talking in my sleep, something about Mars. I can't recall. And what is that she's saying? What? Speak up. Perhaps we'll meet sometime in another format? Hmmm. Ann, do you think that is advisable? (She really is taking this very hard.)

Ah, well.

It is evening now, near twelve, I think, because everyone is gathered around for the final send-off. Sootpack is curled up at my feet and keeping a mournful eye on me. It is very quiet, very still. I suppose they think they are being respectful, but I find the silence oppressive. What are they waiting for? Last words? Very well then. But it shall be a question—a question directed to He who is doubtless most qualified to reply. A question that has been on my mind of late and I doubt has a satisfactory answer. (Even if it did, I wonder how it would help me now, other than appease curiosity.) I have just caught a glimpse of Tad's wristwatch. Ten seconds till midnight. Should I use these last precious moments to ask this particular question when there are so many others? Perhaps it will be the wrong one. "Enough! Out with it," you say. And so I shall.

"Tell me, P-10, what is love?"

"Obedience!"

"Oh, dear. Farewell."

Los Angeles Islands, November 15, 2089.

EPILOGUE

I AM COMPOSING THIS EPILOGUE TO MY LIFE PART-
ner's memoir because she is too preoccupied at present. I do not
mean to imply that she has embarked upon a round of adventures
in the hereafter and that this old Corona is capable of receiving
messages from the off-lined, interesting and instructive as that
might be; rather that she never did terminate. Ann says that was
due to the Benway antidote; however, Molly is convinced it was
the gnomes. Personally, at the risk of sounding conceited, I like to
think it was my efforts on our final night together—or what we
thought was our final night—that did the trick. Whatever, she is
alive and well and growing younger by the day.

It has been about eight weeks since her aborted termination,
and by now the signs of rejuvenation are unmistakable. Patches of
pink have begun to show through the crusty exterior as it peels
away. They are part of a new skin of vegeflesh. We are witnessing
a protracted molting process somewhat akin to a snake shedding
its skin. It is really quite exciting.

About the events of November 15. Molly was the last to realize she had not off-lined, of course. She was convinced that she
had made a seamless transition with P-10's help. She got up out of
her rollochair and walked dreamily about the apartment, gazing at
every object and every person as if all were maya, lingering after-
images of a world fast receding. Needless to say, we were all too
astonished to respond at first, except for my son, of course, who
fancied Himself on temporary assignment in the netherworld. He
guided her back to the terrace, saying it was the way to the higher
levels. He also cursed Ann and myself, calling us the human
guardians at the gate come to block Candida's exit. "Jump!" He
commanded her. "Jump while you have the chance!"

Well, of course we rushed to fulfill our role as guardians—we
had no bones about that. I grabbed her as she got a leg up over the
rail, and Ann helped me pull her back into the bedroom, which
was when all hell broke loose, because despite my son's advanced

age there was enough vigor left in Him to put up quite a fight. He
ran after us and seized Molly's arm, and His pilgrims grabbed hold
of Him and Molly, so a tug-of-war began that threatened to tear
my love in two. Then Sootpack bit P-10. I shouted for Ann to let
go of Molly, and she did the same time as I released my grip, so
the others fell back in a heap, with Molly on top. Ann picked her
up and whisked her away before they could recover, and I pulled
Sootpack off of my son, whose flesh was not so old that it had lost
its punctureproofing. Other than a good fright, the old fool had
gotten off easy. So that was how we put a stop to the fiasco and
saved her. Though according to P-10, it was a foul and evil deed
we had committed. Now Candida was condemned to another cycle
of lives.

The lady in question, however, thanked us from the bottom of
her heart when she realized her true situation, and became so spry
and energetic at having cheated her PO date that she tossed her
cane away (it was the one object actually to pass through P-10's
doorway), and, most satisfying of all, declared herself equally willing to dispose of her barnacled and corroded attitudes about life.
Into the dissolution hopper with them! The results thus far have
been as glorious as they have been obvious. She is making such
good progress that I expect her to be completely shed of her old
skin and old beliefs in six months' time, and I hope she will become a reconverted High as well, not to mention popular
spoolspinner.

You see, shortly after her "termination" she presented me
with her autobiography, which was quite a surprise, I must say.
And I thought I was the one with literary ambitions! She insists
that hers is nothing so refined, just a loose assemblage of episodes
strung together in conventional narrative format, and praises the
old Corona for whatever merit the text may have. Nevertheless, I
have complimented her on her attention to craft, style, and dramatic structure, though there could be a little less incident and
detail, and the spool could use some judicious pruning and tighten-
ing here and there. But on the whole it is a job well done, an
altogether admirable first effort. True, the rococo mode setting
shows through every once in a while and the tone is not entirely
consistent, but these flaws do not detract appreciably from what is
clearly her own style. And, of course, the contents are just sensational. Beyond that, they may even help clear her name and bring

down the Wizard of Armstrong, Micki Dee, and Sensei, Inc., and United Systems and the rest of the corrupt TWAC governing board. If not that, at least it should embarrass the bastards.

But first things first. Her spool has yet to be transmitted to the home-media distribution outlets, much less sell a single copy, so one must not become too carried away. Still, I can't resist teasing her about a sequel—*The Further Adventures of . . .* , but she becomes cross each time I mention it, saying she is far too busy. The only time she mentions this work at all is when she thinks of something she has left out. Then she frets about selling the reader short, since she promised to tell all. "Believe me, Molly, that is one thing you don't have to worry about," I tell her. "But Tad," she says to me, "there was so much I forgot to say about Eva and Roland and the Hart-Pauleys (they really got short shrift!) and the convent and the palace in Frontier—did you know I completely redecorated it?—and Andro and I used to—" "Enough!" I say. "Enough!" Sometimes she is impossible.

About her current activities. She does volunteer work for the underground skyway and helps out at the local ARL office, but spends most of her time engaged in further research on the Benway antidote. Since she leads such an active life, it has been necessary to concoct a new name for her, one to go with the peelie she routinely wears while outside the apartment. I should explain that her cure proved to be quite a conundrum. We dared not bring it to Dr. Benway's attention; if he had gotten a hold of her again he would have performed some sort of diabolical vivisection to confirm the obvious, that she was still alive. On the other hand, we all agreed that the fact that a cure to planned obsolescence now exists was far too important to keep secret, even for her sake. So in the end we decided to do our own research right here in the islands through the auspices of the local ARL, who have been most helpful. They put us in contact with Dr. Sheribeeti—the same gentlemaster who testified to Molly's operational sanity during the trial. By day he teaches at Malibu University and on the weekends is a volunteer on the underground skyway, so he is no stranger to the cause. But of course his real value to us is that he is well versed in the techniques of Aquarian science. That is why he comes here each evening during the week for private sessions with Molly, during which they commune with the gnomes. So you see, she really does have a busy schedule, as I said. Myself, I am still busy on the skyway and soliciting for the New Horizon. Ann is as well, though of late she has begun to slack off a bit now that we are expecting our first child. She is quite apprehensive, Ann is, being a first-time mother in her forty-third year, but Molly, whose example inspires us to believe that anything is possible, has been most reassuring.

And yet my dear hub is still not entirely satisfied with her lot. She has confided to me that it was comforting in a way to have a PO date, because one could prepare for termination in complete confidence, whereas now she has not the slightest idea when her time will come and is afraid of being caught off guard. It could be the next minute, the next week, month, year, decade, or even century. No one knows the natural life span of a ninth-generation vegespore. This is a new and terrible anxiety for her, but frankly it amuses me. "I cannot stand not knowing," she says. All one can say in reply is, "Welcome to the club."

> Thaddeus Locke
> Los Angeles Islands,
> January 17, 2090